S0-BRW-521

THE DANCE OF TIME

**For a complete list of Baen Books
by David Drake and Eric Flint,
please go to www.baen.com**

THE DANCE OF TIME

ERIC FLINT
DAVID DRAKE

THE DANCE OF TIME

This is a work of fiction. All the characters and events portrayed in this book are fictional, and any resemblance to real people or incidents is purely coincidental.

Copyright © 2006 by Eric Flint & David Drake

All rights reserved, including the right to reproduce this book or portions thereof in any form.

A Baen Books Original

Baen Publishing Enterprises
P.O. Box 1403
Riverdale, NY 10471
www.baen.com

ISBN-13: 978-1-4165-0931-8
ISBN-10: 1-4165-0931-3

Cover art by Alan Pollock
Maps by Randy Asplund

First printing, February 2006

Library of Congress Cataloging-in-Publication Data

Flint, Eric.
    The dance of time / Eric Flint, David Drake.
        p. cm.
    "A Baen Books original"—T.p. verso.
    ISBN 1-4165-0931-3 (hc)
    1. Belisarius, 505 (ca.)-565—Fiction. 2. Supercomputers—Fiction. I. Drake, David. II. Title.
    PS3556.L548D36 2006
    813'.6—dc22

                                          2005034212

Distributed by Simon & Schuster
1230 Avenue of the Americas
New York, NY 10020

Production & book design by Windhaven Press, Auburn, NH (www.windhaven.com)
Printed in the United States of America

10 9 8 7 6 5 4 3 2 1

To Lucy

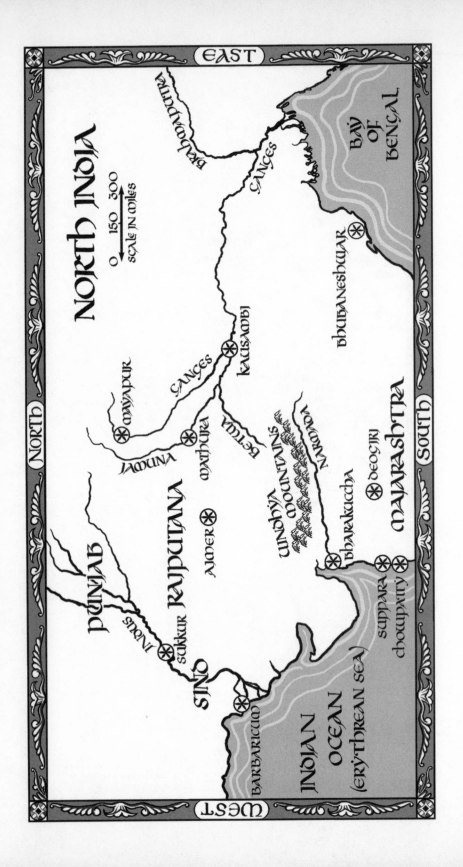

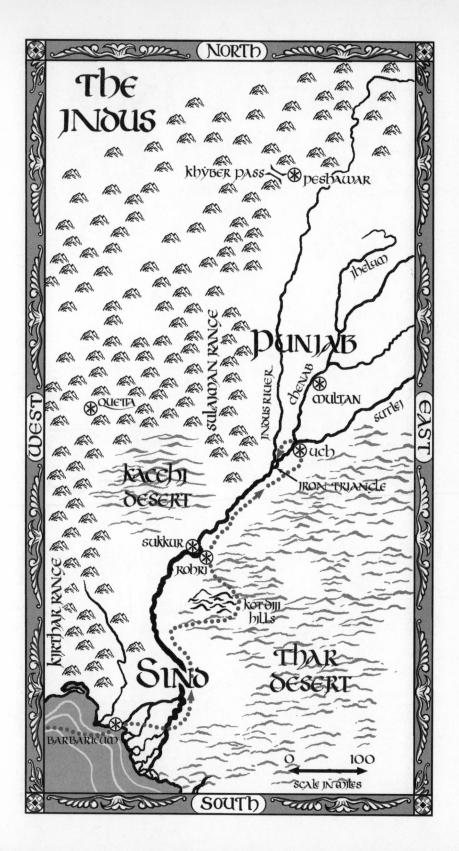

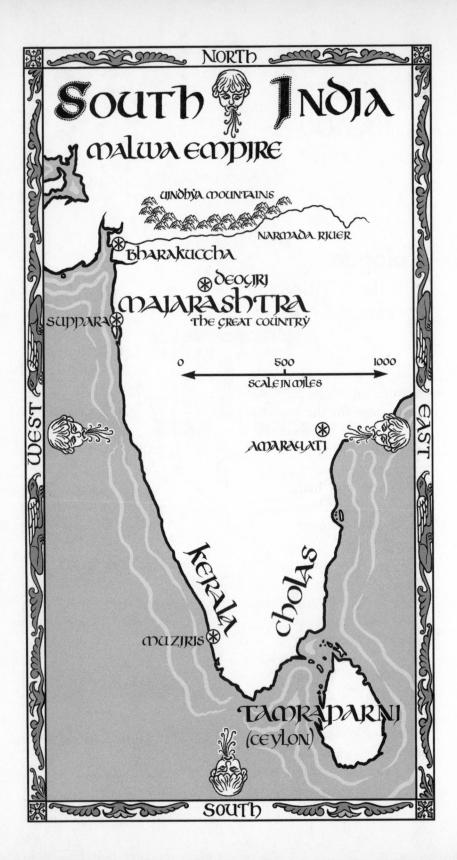

NORTH

SOUTH INDIA

MALWA EMPIRE

VINDHYA MOUNTAINS

NARMADA RIVER

⊛ BHARAKUCCHA

⊛ DEOGIRI

MAHARASHTRA
THE GREAT COUNTRY

SUPPARA ⊛

0   500   1000

SCALE IN MILES

⊛ AMARAVATI

KERALA

CHOLAS

MUZIRIS ⊛

TAMRAPARNI
(CEYLON)

WEST

EAST

SOUTH

Prologue
THE IRON TRIANGLE
Autumn, 533 AD

Belisarius watched Eusebius and his crew as they carefully slipped the mine off the deck of the *Victrix*, using a ramp they'd set up in the stern for the purpose. Because of its design, it had been relatively easy to adapt the fireship to the task of becoming a mine-layer. Doing so with the *Justinian* would have required a major reconstruction of the armored gunship.

The sun still hadn't come up, but there was enough light from the approaching dawn for Belisarius to see. Quietly, almost soundlessly, the mine slid below the surface of the water. Eusebius measured off the depth of the mine's placement using the prepared lines, squinting at the marks nearsightedly.

A trio of ducks flew past swiftly, just above the level of the reeds. Their quacking sounded like the slap of bamboo canes.

You are fortunate to see them, said Aide, the crystalline being that rested in Belisarius' neck pouch. **Those are pink-headed ducks, very rare here in the Indus Basin. Indeed, they're not common even in Brahmaputra.**

When we've defeated the Malwa, Belisarius replied silently to the voice in his mind, *perhaps I'll retire to a monastery and write a treatise on natural history based on my travels. Of course, first we have to defeat the Malwa.*

We will, said Aide firmly; and *that* was not a joke.

Aide had come—been sent—to Belisarius from the far future;

1

from one of two alternate futures, more precisely. Aide's purpose was to prevent the Malwa Empire from conquering the world as it had already conquered most of the Indian subcontinent.

The real horror of a Malwa victory would come tens of tens of thousands of years in the future, when the Earth was ruled by the so-called "new gods" that had evolved from men. In human terms, though, what a Malwa victory meant in this 533rd Year of Christ was bad enough.

Laying the mine took some time, because the crew had to lower it slowly and carefully. There wasn't really much danger of the charge going off simply due to a rough landing on the river bottom, especially as muddy as the Indus was. But, understandably, no one wanted to take any chances.

Eventually, the lines grew slack. The heavy stone weight that had dragged the mine below the surface had reached the bottom.

"About where we want it," Eusebius proclaimed, checking the marks on the lines. "She'll be sitting just the right depth to cave in any ironclads the Malwa send at us."

By now, his crew had placed so many mines in the rivers that formed two sides of the Iron Triangle that the rest was routine. The lines were hauled up, after the ends were released so they could slip easily through the mine's handles. Very easily, since the shell of the mine was nothing more than an amphora sealed to contain the charge and the air that kept it floating above the weight that anchored it to the river bottom.

All that was left was the very thin wire that would transmit the detonation signal when given. Like all the mines the Romans had placed in the Indus and the Chenab, the mines were designed to be exploded on command. It would have been possible to design contact fuses, but the things were tricky and Belisarius saw no need for them.

In fact, mines with contact fuses could conceivably become a handicap. Belisarius wasn't expecting to use the rivers for a rapid assault, but war was unpredictable. If he did find himself doing so, he didn't want to be delayed by the dangerous and finicky work of removing the mines. With command detonation mines, if need be, he could clear the rivers in less than a minute. Just blow up all the mines.

Eusebius leaned over the rail of the *Victrix* and handed the end of the signal wire to a soldier in a rowboat. Moments later, while the soldier holding the wire kept a good grip on it, the other soldiers in the boat rowed it ashore. The wire would join others in one of the many little mine bunkers that lined the banks of both rivers in the Triangle. A spotter in the bunker would already have noted the location of the mine.

Eusebius straightened. "And that's pretty much all there is to the business, General. The old emperor had the right of it."

Grinning, then: "Much as he still pisses and moans about how much he'd like to build a submarine. But the fact is that for the purpose of fending off those ironclads the Malwa are building upriver, these mines will do the trick just fine. And it's a lot less risky than spar torpedoes."

"Not to mention a submarine," Belisarius chuckled. "All right. I just wanted to get a sense of how it was going."

Had the Malwa been simply an Indian dynasty, they would not have posed a threat to the present world, let alone that of the far future. Aide had showed Belisarius visions of both past and future. Indian nations had often been rich and powerful and influential, and would be again; but never in the timeline that led to Aide and those who created him had the men and women who ruled India looked beyond their own subcontinent. Missionaries and traders from India would turn most of Southeast Asia into a cultural extension of Hindu India; and, through Buddhism, India would have a major impact on the societies of the Far East. Still, no Indian ruler in that timeline ever attempted to conquer the world in the manner that the Malwa Empire was doing—using methods of conquest that were even more savage than Genghis Khan's, with an end goal that had none of the Mongols' tolerance as actual rulers.

But the ruler of the Malwa Empire was not a man or woman, to begin with. The real ruler of the empire was not the official emperor, Skandagupta. It was Link, a machine, a *monster*, which the "new gods" had sent to change the past and bring their bleak future into existence. If the Malwa armies defeated Belisarius and his outnumbered forces here in the angle of the Indus and Chenab Rivers, the losers would not only be the citizens of the Roman Empire but also all other humans in all times.

Belisarius glanced to the side, where the *Justinian* was slowly steaming. The gunship was keeping a distance from the mine-laying activity, but it was still close enough to come to the *Victrix's* support in the unlikely event that the Malwa tried to launch an attack on the fireship.

The very unlikely event. The *Victrix* herself had already proven to the Malwa, several times, that she could destroy any wooden riverboats sent against her. And the one time the Malwa had sent down a partially armored boat, the *Justinian* had blown it into wreckage in less than a minute. For the past several weeks, there had been no Malwa incursions on the river at all. From the reports of spies, the enemy had apparently decided to wait until their new heavy ironclads were finished.

Furthermore, if Justinian and Eusebius were right, even those wouldn't do them any good. The Malwa had no way to build completely iron ships; none, at least, that would have a shallow enough draft for these rivers. Their ironclads were just that: *clad* in iron. The underlying boats were still wooden—and even these small mines would be enough to break such hulls in half.

"To tell you the truth, General," Eusebius commented, "I don't even understand why the Malwa have kept building those ironclads. There's no way to lay these mines secretly, even working at night the way we've been doing. By now, they must know we've got both rivers saturated with them."

Belisarius had wondered about that himself. Link had just as much knowledge of future warfare as Aide did. The effectiveness of mines against warships in any constricted area of water was so well established in that future that he couldn't imagine Link having any real hope his ironclads could bull their way through a large and well-laid mine field.

Your theory's the right one, I think, Aide said. **Link is shifting to the defensive.**

Yes. I hadn't thought it would, not this quickly. I'd expected the monster to try a massive assault to drive us out of the Punjab, before we could get really settled in. But . . . it's not. And if it waits much longer, it'll be too late.

Too late, indeed. The Romans and their Persian allies were slowly but surely gaining control of the Indus and both of its banks all the way from the Sukkur gorge to the Iron Triangle, after already having conquered the Sind south of the gorge. So the spearhead that Belisarius had driven into the Punjab during the course of his campaign the previous year would soon be well supplied. The fortifications across the northern side of the

Triangle were already strong enough to break any army Link could send against them within a year or two. Not even the Malwa Empire had an inexhaustible supply of men and munitions, ready to hand.

Especially men. Their morale must be close to the breaking point, I think. Link's army needs a rest, and it knows it. That's why it didn't order the assault. It can afford a stalemate, even for long period, where it can't afford another string of defeats.

The sun was coming up.

Softly, proudly: **You really hammered them, these past few years.**

Chapter 1
BUKKUR ISLAND, ON THE INDUS RIVER

He dreamed mostly of islands, oddly enough.

He was sailing, now, in one of his father's pleasure crafts. Not the luxurious barge-in-all-but-name-and-glitter which his father himself preferred for the family's outings into the Golden Horn, but in the phaselos which was suited for sailing in the open sea. Unlike his father, for whom sailing expeditions were merely excuses for political or commercial transactions, Calopodius had always loved sailing for its own sake.

Besides, it gave him and his new wife something to do besides sit together in stiff silence.

Calopodius' half-sleeping reverie was interrupted. Wakefulness came with the sound of his aide-de-camp Luke moving through the tent. The heaviness with which Luke clumped about was deliberate, designed to allow his master to recognize who had entered his domicile. Luke was quite capable of moving easily and lightly, as he had proved many times in the course of the savage fighting on Bukkur Island. But the man, in this as so many things, had proven to be far more subtle than his rough and muscular appearance might suggest.

"It's morning, young Calopodius," Luke announced. "Time to clean your wounds. And you're not eating enough."

Calopodius sighed. The process of tending the wounds would be painful, despite all of Luke's care. As for the other—

"Have new provisions arrived?"

There was a moment's silence. Then, reluctantly: "No."

Calopodius let the silence lengthen. After a few seconds, he heard Luke's own heavy sigh. "We're getting very low, truth to tell. Ashot hasn't much himself, until the supply ships arrive."

Calopodius levered himself up on his elbows. "Then I will eat my share, no more." He chuckled, perhaps a bit harshly. "And don't try to cheat, Luke. I have other sources of information, you know."

"As if my hardest job of the day won't be to keep half the army from parading through this tent," snorted Luke. Calopodius felt the weight of Luke's knees pressing into the pallet next to him, and, a moment later, winced as the bandages over his head began to be removed. "You're quite the soldiers' favorite, lad," added Luke softly. "Don't think otherwise."

In the painful time that followed, as Luke scoured and cleaned and rebandaged the sockets that had once been eyes, Calopodius tried to take refuge in that knowledge.

It helped. Some.

"Are there any signs of another Malwa attack coming?" he asked, some time later. Calopodius was now perched in one of the bastions his men had rebuilt after an enemy assault had overrun it—before, eventually, the Malwa had been driven off the island altogether. That had required bitter and ferocious fighting, however, which had inflicted many casualties upon the Roman defenders. His eyes had been among those casualties, ripped out by shrapnel from a mortar shell.

"After the bloody beating we gave 'em the last time?" chortled one of the soldiers who shared the bastion. "Not likely, sir!"

Calopodius tried to match the voice to a remembered face. As usual, the effort failed of its purpose. But he took the time to engage in small talk with the soldier, so as to fix the voice itself in his memory. Not for the first time, Calopodius reflected wryly on the way in which possession of vision seemed to dull all other human faculties. Since his blinding, he had found his memory growing more acute along with his hearing. A simple instinct for self-preservation, he imagined. A blind man *had* to remember better than a seeing man, since he no longer had vision to constantly jog his lazy memory.

After his chat with the soldier had gone on for a few minutes, the man cleared his throat and said diffidently: "You'd best leave here, sir, if you'll pardon me for saying so. The Malwa'll likely be starting another barrage soon." For a moment, fierce good cheer filled the man's voice: "They seem to have a particular grudge against this part of our line, seeing's how their own blood and guts make up a good part of it."

The remark produced a ripple of harsh chuckling from the other soldiers crouched in the fortifications. That bastion had been one of the most hotly contested areas when the Malwa launched their major attack the week before. Calopodius didn't doubt for a moment that when his soldiers repaired the damage to the earthen walls they had not been too fastidious about removing all the traces of the carnage.

He sniffed tentatively, detecting those traces. His olfactory sense, like his hearing, had grown more acute also.

"Must have stunk, right afterward," he commented.

The same soldier issued another harsh chuckle. "That it did, sir, that it did. Why God invented flies, the way I look at it."

Calopodius felt Luke's heavy hand on his shoulder. "Time to go, sir. There'll be a barrage coming, sure enough."

In times past, Calopodius would have resisted. But he no longer felt any need to prove his courage, and a part of him—a still wondering, eighteen-year-old part—understood that his safety had become something his own men cared about. Alive, somewhere in the rear but still on the island, Calopodius would be a source of strength for his soldiers in the event of another Malwa onslaught. Spiritual strength, if not physical; a symbol, if nothing else. But men—fighting men, perhaps, more than any others—live by such symbols.

So he allowed Luke to guide him out of the bastion and down the rough staircase which led to the trenches below. On the way, Calopodius gauged the steps with his feet.

"One of those logs is too big," he said, speaking firmly, but trying to keep any critical edge out of the words. "It's a waste, there. Better to use it for another fake cannon."

He heard Luke suppress a sigh. *And will you stop fussing like a hen?* was the content of that small sound. Calopodius suppressed a laugh. Luke, in truth, made a poor "servant."

"We've got enough," replied Luke curtly. "Twenty-odd. Do any more and the Malwa will get suspicious. We've only got three real ones left to keep up the pretense."

As they moved slowly through the trench, Calopodius considered the problem and decided that Luke was right. The pretense was probably threadbare by now, anyway. When the Malwa finally launched a full-scale amphibious assault on the island that was the centerpiece of Calopodius' diversion, they had overrun half of it before being beaten back. When the survivors returned to the main Malwa army besieging the city of Sukkur across the Indus, they would have reported to their own top commanders that several of the "cannons" with which the Romans had apparently festooned their fortified island were nothing but painted logs.

But how many? That question would still be unclear in the minds of the enemy.

Not all of them, for a certainty. When Belisarius took his main force to outflank the Malwa in the Punjab, leaving behind Calopodius and fewer than two thousand men to serve as a diversion, he had also left some of the field guns and mortars. Those pieces had savaged the Malwa attackers, when they finally grew suspicious enough to test the real strength of Calopodius' position.

"The truth is," said Luke gruffly, "it doesn't really matter anyway." Again, the heavy hand settled on Calopodius' slender shoulder, this time giving it a little squeeze of approval. "You've already done what the general asked you to, lad. Kept the Malwa confused, thinking Belisarius was still here, while he marched in secret to the northeast. Did it as well as he could have possibly hoped."

They had reached one of the covered portions of the trench, Calopodius sensed. He couldn't see the earth-covered logs which gave some protection from enemy fire, of course. But the quality of sound was a bit different within a shelter than in an open trench. That was just one of the many little auditory subtleties which Calopodius had begun noticing lately.

He had not noticed it in times past, before he lost his eyes. In the first days after Belisarius and the main army left Sukkur on their secret, forced march to outflank the Malwa in the Punjab, Calopodius had noticed very little, in truth. He had had neither the time nor the inclination to ponder the subtleties of sense perception. He had been far too excited by his new and unexpected command and by the challenge it posed.

Martial glory. The blind young man in the covered trench stopped for a moment, staring through sightless eyes at a wall of earth and timber bracing. Remembering, and wondering.

The martial glory Calopodius had sought, when he left a new wife in Constantinople, had certainly come to him. Of that, he had no doubt at all. His own soldiers thought so, and said so often enough—those who had survived—and Calopodius was quite certain that his praises would soon be spoken in the Senate.

Precious few of the Roman Empire's most illustrious families had achieved any notable feats of arms in the great war against the Malwa. Beginning with the top commander Belisarius himself, born into the lower Thracian nobility, it had been largely a war fought by men from low stations in life. Commoners, in the main. Agathius—the now-famous hero of Anatha and the Dam—had been born into a baker's family, about as menial a position as any short of outright slavery.

Other than Sittas, who was now leading Belisarius' cataphracts in the Punjab, almost no Greek noblemen had fought in the Malwa war. And even Sittas, before the Indus campaign, had spent the war commanding the garrison in Constantinople that overawed the hostile aristocracy and kept the dynasty on the throne.

Had it been worth it?

Reaching up and touching gently the emptiness which had once been his eyes, Calopodius was still not sure. Like many other young members of the nobility, he had been swept up with enthusiasm after the news came that Belisarius had shattered the Malwa in Mesopotamia. Let the adult members of the aristocracy whine and complain in their salons. The youth were burning to serve.

And serve they had . . . but only as couriers, in the beginning. It hadn't taken Calopodius long to realize that Belisarius intended to use him and his high-born fellows mainly for liaison with the haughty Persians, who were even more obsessed with nobility of bloodline than Greeks. The posts carried prestige—the couriers rode just behind Belisarius himself in formation—but little in the way of actual responsibility.

Standing in the bunker, the blind young man chuckled harshly. "He used us, you know. As cold-blooded as a reptile."

Silence, for a moment. Then, Calopodius heard Luke take a deep breath.

"Aye, lad. He did. The general will use anyone, if he feels it necessary."

Calopodius nodded. He felt no anger at the thought. He simply wanted it acknowledged.

He reached out his hand and felt the rough wall of the bunker with fingertips grown sensitive with blindness. Texture of soil, which he would never have noticed before, came like a flood of dark light. He wondered, for a moment, how his wife's breasts would feel to him, or her belly, or her thighs. Now.

He didn't imagine he would ever know, and dropped the hand. Calopodius did not expect to survive the war, now that he was blind. Not unless he used the blindness as a reason to return to Constantinople, and spent the rest of his life resting on his laurels.

The thought was unbearable. *I am only eighteen! My life should still be ahead of me!*

That thought brought a final decision. Given that his life was now forfeit, Calopodius intended to give it the full measure while it lasted.

"Menander should be arriving soon, with the supply ships."

"Yes," said Luke.

"When he arrives, I wish to speak with him."

"Yes," said Luke. The "servant" hesitated. Then: "What about?"

Again, Calopodius chuckled harshly. "Another forlorn hope." He began moving slowly through the bunker to the tunnel which led back to his headquarters. "Having lost my eyes on this island, it seems only right I should lose my life on another. Belisarius' island, this time—not the one he left behind to fool the enemy. The *real* island, not the false one."

"There was nothing *false* about this island, young man," growled Luke. "Never say it. Malwa was broken here, as surely as it was on any battlefield of Belisarius. There is the blood of Roman soldiers to prove it—along with your own eyes. Most of all—"

By some means he could not specify, Calopodius understood

that Luke was gesturing angrily to the north. "Most of all, by the fact that we kept an entire Malwa army pinned here for two weeks—by your cunning and our sweat and blood—while Belisarius slipped unseen to the north. *Two weeks.* The time he needed to slide a lance into Malwa's unprotected flank—we gave him that time. *We did. You did.*"

He heard Luke's almost shuddering intake of breath. "So never speak of a 'false' island again, boy. Is a shield 'false,' and only a sword 'true'? Stupid. The general did what he needed to do—and so did you. Take pride in it, for there was nothing false in that doing."

Calopodius could not help lowering his head. "No," he whispered.

But was it worth the doing?

THE INDUS RIVER IN THE PUNJAB
BELISARIUS' HEADQUARTERS
THE IRON TRIANGLE

"I know I shouldn't have come, General, but—"

Calopodius groped for words to explain. He could not find any. It was impossible to explain to someone else the urgency he felt, since it would only sound . . . suicidal. Which, in truth, it almost was, at least in part.

But . . .

"May—maybe I could help you with supplies or—or something."

"No matter," stated Belisarius firmly, giving Calopodius' shoulder a squeeze. The general's large hand was very powerful. Calopodius was a little surprised by that. His admiration for Belisarius bordered on idolization, but he had never really given any thought to the general's physical characteristics. He had just been dazzled, first, by the man's reputation; then, after finally meeting him in Mesopotamia, by the relaxed humor and confidence with which he ran his staff meetings.

The large hand on his shoulder began gently leading Calopodius off the dock where Menander's ship had tied up.

"I can still count, even if—"

"Forget that," growled Belisarius. "I've got enough clerks." With a chuckle: "The quartermasters don't have that much to count, anyway. We're on very short rations here."

Again, the hand squeezed his shoulder; not with sympathy, this time, so much as assurance. "The truth is, lad, I'm delighted to see you. We're relying on telegraph up here, in this new little fortified half-island we've created, to concentrate our forces quickly enough when the Malwa launch another attack. But the telegraph's a new thing for everyone, and keeping the communications straight and orderly has turned into a mess. My command bunker is full of people shouting at cross-purposes. I need a good officer who can take charge and *organize* the damn thing."

Cheerfully: "That's you, lad! Being blind won't be a handicap at all for that work. Probably be a blessing."

Calopodius wasn't certain if the general's cheer was real, or simply assumed for the purpose of improving the morale of a badly maimed subordinate. Even as young as he was, Calopodius knew that the commander he admired was quite capable of being as calculating as he was cordial.

But . . .

Almost despite himself, he began feeling more cheerful.

"Well, there's this much," he said, trying to match the general's enthusiasm. "My tutors thought highly of my grammar and rhetoric, as I believe I mentioned once. If nothing else, I'm sure I can improve the quality of the messages."

The general laughed. The gaiety of the sound cheered up Calopodius even more than the general's earlier words. It was harder to feign laughter than words. Calopodius was not guessing about that. A blind man aged quickly, in some ways, and Calopodius had become an expert on the subject of false laughter, in the weeks since he lost his eyes.

This was real. This was—

Something he could *do*.

A future which had seemed empty began to fill with color again. Only the colors of his own imagination, of course. But Calopodius, remembering discussions on philosophy with learned scholars in far away and long ago Constantinople, wondered if reality was anything *but* images in the mind. If so, perhaps blindness was simply a matter of custom.

"Yes," he said, with reborn confidence. "I can do that."

✧　　✧　　✧

For the first two days, the command bunker was a madhouse for Calopodius. But by the end of that time, he had managed to bring some semblance of order and procedure to the way in which telegraph messages were received and transmitted. Within a week, he had the system functioning smoothly and efficiently.

The general praised him for his work. So, too, in subtle little ways, did the twelve men under his command. Calopodius found the latter more reassuring than the former. He was still a bit uncertain whether Belisarius' approval was due, at least in part, to the general's obvious feeling of guilt that he was responsible for the young officer's blindness. Whereas the men who worked for him, veterans all, had seen enough mutilation in their lives not to care about yet another cripple. Had the young nobleman not been a blessing to them but rather a curse, they would not have let sympathy stand in the way of criticism. And the general, Calopodius was well aware, kept an ear open to the sentiments of his soldiers.

Throughout that first week, Calopodius paid little attention to the ferocious battle which was raging beyond the heavily timbered and fortified command bunker. He traveled nowhere, beyond the short distance between that bunker and the small one—not much more than a covered hole in the ground—where he and Luke had set up what passed for "living quarters." Even that route was sheltered by soil-covered timber, so the continual sound of cannon fire was muffled.

The only time Calopodius emerged into the open was for the needs of the toilet. As always in a Belisarius camp, the sanitation arrangements were strict and rigorous. The latrines were located some distance from the areas where the troops slept and ate, and no exceptions were made even for the blind and crippled. A man who could not reach the latrines under his own power would either be taken there, or, if too badly injured, would have his bedpan emptied for him.

For the first three days, Luke guided him to the latrines. Thereafter, he could make the journey himself. Slowly, true, but he used the time to ponder and crystallize his new ambition. It was the only time his mind was not preoccupied with the immediate demands of the command bunker.

Being blind, he had come to realize, did not mean the end

of life. Although it did transform his dreams of fame and glory into much softer and more muted colors. But finding dreams in the course of dealing with the crude realities of a latrine, he decided, was perhaps appropriate. Life was a crude thing, after all. A project begun in confusion, fumbling with unfamiliar tools, the end never really certain until it came—and then, far more often than not, coming as awkwardly as a blind man attends to his toilet.

Shit is also manure, he came to understand. A man does what he can. If he was blind . . . he was also educated, and rich, and had every other advantage. The rough soldiers who helped him on his way had their own dreams, did they not? And their own glory, come to it. If he could not share in that glory directly, he could save it for the world.

When he explained it to the general—awkwardly, of course, and not at a time of his own choosing—Belisarius gave the project his blessing. That day, Calopodius began his history of the war against the Malwa. The next day, almost as an afterthought, he wrote the first of the *Dispatches to the Army* which would, centuries after his death, make him as famous as Livy or Polybius.

Chapter 2
AXUM
CAPITAL CITY OF THE ETHIOPIAN EMPIRE

Across the Erythrean Sea, Belisarius' wife Antonina woke to the rising sun, coming through the window in her chamber in the Ta'akha Maryam. By now, more than a year and a half since Malwa agents had blown up the royal palace of the Ethiopian kingdom of Axum, the Ta'akha Maryam's reconstruction was virtually complete.

Stubbornly, as was their way in such things, the Axumites had insisted on rebuilding the palace exactly as it had been. If the heavy stonework was still susceptible to well-placed demolitions, they would prevent such by the spears of their regiments, not the cleverness of their architects.

In the mornings, at least, Antonina was glad of it. At night, in the gloom of candlelight, she sometimes found the Ta'akha Maryam oppressively massive. But, in the daytime—especially at daybreak, with her east-facing chamber—the Ethiopian penchant for placing many windows even in outer walls was very pleasant.

The windows were massive too, admittedly, with their Christian crosses in every one to serve as supports for the heavy stone as well as reminders of the new Ethiopian faith. Still, the sunlight flooding through bathed her sleeping chamber in a golden glory that matched her mood.

Which it did, she suddenly realized. Sitting up in her bed, holding the coverings tight to ward off the chill, she pondered the fact.

Why?

It wasn't the morning. Yes, the sunlight was splendid. On the other hand—this late in autumn, in the mile-high altitude of the Ethiopian highlands—it was also damnably cold.

She shivered a little. But that was solely a matter of the body. Her spirits remained higher than they'd been in . . .

Months. Since Eon died, leading the Axumites in their seizure of the Indian port of Chowpatty. Not only had Antonina lost one of her closest friends in that battle, but the unexpected death of the young ruler of Ethiopia—the *negusa nagast,* or "King of Kings"—had plunged the kingdom of Axum into a succession crisis. A crisis which Eon himself, as he lay dying, had appointed Antonina to solve.

She'd dreaded that task almost as much as she'd grieved Eon's death. Yet now, this morning, she felt light-hearted again.

Why?

It was not an idle question. By now, a lot closer to the age of forty than thirty, Antonina had come to know herself very well. Her mind did not work the same way as her husband's. Belisarius was a calculator; a man who considered all the angles of a problem before deciding how he would handle it. Antonina, on the other hand, reached her conclusions through more mysterious, instinctive ways.

This was not the first time in her life she'd awakened in the morning, flush with the satisfaction of having come to a decision during her sleep. And if Belisarius sometimes shook his head wryly over the matter, Antonina remained serene in the knowledge that her way of handling such difficult business was *so* much easier than her husband's.

A servant entered, after politely coughing to announce her arrival. The woman didn't knock, for the simple reason that the Ta'akha Maryam had very few doors—and knocking on the thick walls of the entrance would be akin to rapping on a granite cliff.

"The *aqabe tsentsen* wishes an audience."

Antonina grinned. She really *was* in a good mood.

"I'll bet he didn't put it that way."

The servant rolled her eyes. "So rude, he is! No, Lady, he did not. He—ah . . ."

Antonina slid from under the thick coverings and scampered

toward her wardrobe against the far wall. Her haste was not caused by any concern for keeping Ousanas waiting, it was simply due to the cold.

"He told you to roll the lazy Roman slut out of bed." Still grinning, Antonina removed her night clothes and began dressing for the day.

"Well. He didn't call you a slut. Lazy Roman, yes."

Ousanas was waiting impatiently in the salon of her suite.

"About time," he grumbled. He gave her figure a quick look, up and down. "How does it take so long to put on such simple garments? By now—almost mid-morning—I expected to see you bedecked in jewels and feathers."

Antonina turned her head and looked out a window. The sun had just barely cleared the rim of Mai Qoho, the great hill to the east of Ethiopia's capital.

"If this is 'mid-morning,' I'd love to see your definition of 'dawn.'" She moved to a nearby settee and sat down. "Oh, leave off, Ousanas. Whatever brought you here at this unfit hour, it can't be *that* urgent."

She pointed to a nearby chair. "Sit, will you?"

Ousanas sneered at the chair. Then, folded himself onto the carpet in a lotus position. Ever since he'd traveled to India with Belisarius, he claimed that awkward-looking posture was a great aid to thought—even if he'd have no truck with the ridiculous Indian notions concerning philosophy.

"That depends on how you define 'urgent.' Antonina, we *must* resolve the succession problem. Soon. Garmat's agents are telling him that the Arabs in the Hijaz are getting restive, especially in Mecca. And, especially, of course, the Quraysh tribe."

Antonina pursed her lips. "What about the Ethiopians themselves? Not to be crude about it, Ousanas, but so long as it's only the Arabs who are 'restive,' there's really not much they can do about it. Militarily speaking, at least."

"To be sure. The regiments of Axum can suppress any combination of Arabs, even with much of the army in India. But neither I nor Garmat is worried about an actual rebellion. What we *are* concerned with is the erosion of trade. Things had been going very well, in that regard, until the news of Eon's death arrived. Now . . ."

He shrugged. "All the Arab merchants and traders had thought the situation secure for them, with Eon married to a princess of the Quraysh and the succession running through his half-Arab son. But with a babe for a prince and a young girl for a widowed regent queen, they are fretting more and more that the dynasty will be overthrown by *Ethiopians*. Who will impose a new dynasty that will return the Arabs to their earlier servitude."

Antonina grimaced. "In other words, the Axumites are reasonably content with the situation but the Arabs don't believe it, and because they don't believe it there'll be more and more trouble, which will start making the Axumites angry."

The aqabe tsentsen nodded curtly. "Yes. We really can't postpone this matter, Antonina. The longer we wait, the worse it will get. We need to assure everyone that the dynasty is stable."

"More than 'stable,'" Antonina mused. "Those Arab merchants—the Axumites, too, for that matter—won't simply be worrying about attempts at rebellion. There's also a more insidious, long-term danger."

She rose and moved slowly toward another window. The glorious mood she'd awakened with was growing stronger by the minute. She was on the verge of making her decision; she could sense it. She thought the sight of the southern mountains would help. So majestic, they were. Serene, in their distance and their unmoving steadiness.

The problem was figuring out what the decision was in the first place. At was often the case, she'd made her decision while asleep—and now couldn't remember what it had been.

She smiled, thinking of how Belisarius had reacted so many times in the past to her habits. Peevish, the way men usually got when the workings of the world upset their childish notions.

How in the world can you make a decision without knowing what it is in the first place?

Antonina was moving slowly enough that she was able to finish her thought before reaching the window.

"There are really only two options, it would seem—neither of which will please anyone. The first option, and the simplest, would be for Rukaiya to remain unmarried. If not for the rest of her life, at least until the infant negusa nagast is old enough to take the throne and rule himself."

"Unmarried *and* chaste," Ousanas grunted. "We can't afford any royal bastards, either. Not produced by a widowed queen."

His tone skeptical, he added: "And I don't see much chance of that, being honest. Wahsi is only a few months old, and Rukaiya . . ."

"Has the normal urges of a young woman. Yes, I know."

She did know, in fact—and in considerable detail. She was not guessing based on generalities. In the time after their wedding, Rukaiya had confided in Antonina the great physical pleasure she took from being married to Eon.

"She's only eighteen. Expecting her to abstain from sex until she is in her late thirties is . . . not a gamble anyone will be pleased with. Rukaiya least of all, once her grief for Eon finally fades away. As it happens, I think she'd do it, if she agreed. She's a very strong-willed and self-disciplined person. But she wouldn't like it—and even if she restrained herself, the gossip would be endless."

"Endless—and savage," Ousanas agreed. "That would be true for any young widowed queen, even an ugly one. For one as beautiful as Rukaiya? Not a chance, Antonina. Long before Wahsi could reach an age to assume the throne, the ugly rumors would be believed by half the populace—and a much bigger portion of the kingdom's elite."

Antonina had reached the window, by now, but didn't look out of it yet. Instead, she turned to face Ousanas.

"Yes. That leaves the second option, which is no better. If she marries anyone prestigious enough to be an acceptable match, everyone will start worrying that her children by her second husband will become too powerful. A second and informal dynasty, as it were, growing up within the formal one. A recipe for civil war, a generation from now."

Ousanas nodded. "The Axumites would not accept an Arab husband, and the Arabs—though they'd have no choice, given the military realities—wouldn't like an Axumite one any better. For that matter, the *Axumites* wouldn't like it—except those who were part of the husband's clan."

He scowled at the floor's covering. "Ugly carpet. Ethiopians may know stone and iron work, but their weaving is wretched. You should get a Persian one."

His eyes widened, slightly, and he looked up. "Persian . . . You know, Antonina, that may be the solution. Find her a foreign husband of suitable rank. A Persian grandee or a Roman senator."

Antonina shook her head. "That won't work, either. A Persian husband is impossible, from Rukaiya's standpoint. Now that she's had the experience of being Eon's wife, just how well do you think she'd take to a Persian husband? With *their* attitudes?"

Ousanas went back to scowling at the carpet. "She'd have him poisoned, within a year. Or simply stab him herself. But a Roman . . ."

"No. I could probably find her a suitable Roman husband— suitable from *her* standpoint—but that wouldn't solve the political problem. Rome is now simply too strong, Ousanas. A Roman husband during Rukaiya's regency would make everyone fear—Arabs and Ethiopians alike—that Axum was becoming a Roman satrapy. In reality, if not in name."

"True." He gave her a sly little look. "Perhaps you should poison *your* husband, Antonina. It's his fault, you know. If Belisarius hadn't spent the past five years proving to everyone that Roman military power is supreme . . . even against the Malwa empire, the world's greatest . . ."

Antonina smiled back, sweetly. "Can't, I'm afraid. I'm here and he's in the Punjab. Damnation. One of the reasons I'd like to settle the succession problem is so that I can get back to him—at which point, I assure you, poisoning the fellow will be the last thought on my mind. I'm finding that my own urges haven't subsided any, even at my advanced and decrepit age."

Finally, she turned and looked out the window. "So. We need an impressive husband. Impressive to Rukaiya as much as her subjects, so she isn't tempted to stray and no one thinks otherwise. But—*but!*—one who has no preexisting ties that will make anyone worry about undue influences. And whose loyalties to Axum are unquestioned."

Far to the south, the snow-capped peaks of the Simien Mountains shone brightly, but the flanks were still dark. The sun hadn't risen high enough yet to bathe them in light.

Dark, massive, majestic beneath their crowns—and quite indifferent to any of those words. What did mountains care about attempts to depict them—much less the petty political frets and worries of humans? They simply *were*. And, being so, dwarfed any dynasty.

She understood her decision, then. It came to her, all at once, and in all its splendor.

"It's so *obvious*," she said happily. "I can't believe it took me this long to figure it out."

"Perhaps you will be so kind as to make clear this 'obvious' decision to me, at some point?" Ousanas said grumpily.

Antonina bestowed the sweet smile on the mountains. "Oh, yes. You can be sure of it, when the time comes."

PESHAWAR, IN THE HINDU KUSH

Kungas launched the final assault just before dawn. By sunrise, his Kushan soldiers had demonstrated to the Pathan clansmen that they were just as adept at fighting in the rocks as the rebels—and far more disciplined.

Not to mention numerous. Kungas had calculated—correctly, it was now clear—that the Malwa were too preoccupied with Belisarius in the southern Punjab at the moment to launch any serious attack on the new Kushan kingdom he was forging in the mountains to the northwest. So, he'd left a skeleton force guarding the passes while he took most of his army to suppress this first attempt by any Pathan tribesmen to rebel against his rule.

First—and hopefully last. For all his ruthlessness, when need be, Kungas took no pleasure in killing.

"Suppress" was a euphemism.

By late morning, the clansmen were routed and the Kushans had broken into their walled town nestled in the rocks of the mountains. Then, they began the massacre Kungas had ordered. No member of that Pathan clan would be allowed to survive. Not women, not children, not oldsters. All animals in the town were to be slaughtered also. Then, the town itself would be completely destroyed. Not simply gutted by fire, but blown up. Razed from existence. Kungas had enough gunpowder to afford that, now that the supply lines through Persia had been stabilized.

While his Kushans finished that business, Pathans from other clans allied to Kungas chased down and butchered the Pathan warriors who tried to flee into the shelter of the mountains.

There weren't many of those. Pathans could be as stupid as any humans alive, but they never lacked courage. All but a handful of the defeated clansmen died in the town, desperately trying to defend their kinfolk.

By mid-afternoon, it was done. The entire clan had ceased to exist.

Throughout, Kungas remained at his position high on a nearby mountain—a spur of the same range, really—watching.

Throughout, there was no expression on his face. None at all. To the Pathan chieftains who stood there with him, the leaders of the allied clans, it did not even seem like a face at all. Just an unmoving, iron mask.

Those old men had been told that, in his palace in Peshawar, the new king of the mountains was known to show an expression, now and then. Not often, and usually only in the presence of his Greek wife.

That was possible, they thought, although they had their doubts. It was hard to imagine that inhuman mask of a face ever showing an emotion.

Still . . .

Maybe. The woman was known to be a sorceress, after all.

What the clan chieftains *knew*, however, was that with a king like this and his witch of a queen, rebellion was insane.

Any form of open resistance. The destroyed clan hadn't even rebelled. They'd simply thought to use the old and well-tested method of intimidating a new would-be ruler of the mountains by assassinating one of his officials.

The official had, indeed, been assassinated.

In return, Kungas had now proved that he was, indeed, the king of the mountains. The arithmetic of the equation was clear even to those illiterate clan leaders.

Clans assassinated officials.

Kings—real ones—assassinated clans.

So be it. The old men, no strangers to brutality themselves, chose to look on the bright side. The new king did not meddle with them much, after all, as long as they obeyed him. And trade was picking up a lot. Even the clans in the far mountains were getting richer.

When Kungas returned to Peshawar, he was in a very foul mood.

"That was a filthy business," he told his wife Irene. Scowling openly, now, in the privacy of their quarters in the palace. "It's your fault. If you hadn't stirred up those idiot clansmen letting their young women claim to be Sarmatians and join your idiot so-called 'queen's guard,' it wouldn't have happened."

The accusation was grossly unfair, and on many counts, but Irene kept silent. Until Kungas' mood lightened, there was no point arguing with him.

Yes, it was true that Irene's subtle undermining of Pathan patriarchalism irritated the clan chiefs. So what? *Everything* irritated those barbaric old men. They were to "conservative thinking" what an ocean was to "wet and salty." They practically defined the term.

And, again, so what? Irene and Kungas—with Belisarius, in times past, while they'd still been with him in Persia—had discussed the matter thoroughly. No one had ever ruled these mountains, in the sense that "ruled" meant in the civilized lowlands. Just as no one had ever "ruled" the great steppes to the north into which she and Kungas planned to expand their kingdom.

But if a king couldn't rule the mountains and the steppes, he could *dominate* them. Dominate them as thoroughly and as completely as, in a future era in another universe, the Mongol khans would dominate them.

There was one key difference, though, and Kungas understood it as well as she did. The new Kushan realm in central Asia would use the same methods as the Mongols, true enough. Methods which, in the end, amounted to the simple principle: *oppose us and we will slaughter all of you, down to the babes and dogs.*

But it did not have the same goal. In the future of that different universe, Genghis Khan and his successors had had no other purpose than simply to enjoy the largesse of their rule which came with the annual tribute. Kungas and Irene, on the other hand, intended to forge a real nation here in central Asia, over time. And that could not be done simply by dominating the ancient clans. The domination was itself but a means to an end—and the end was to undermine them completely, in the only way the human race had ever found it possible to do so.

"Civilization," in a word. Create a center of attraction in the new cities and towns, with their expanding wealth and trade and education and culture and opportunities for individuals from anywhere. And then just let the old clan chiefs rot away, while their clans slowly dissolved around them. Irene's "Sarmatian women's guard" that Kungas had just denounced was only one of a hundred methods that she and Kungas were using for that purpose.

It was not even the one that irritated the clan chiefs the most. That honor probably belonged to the new Buddhist monasteries that Kungas was starting to set up all over. In the end, for all their savage attitudes toward women, the old clan chiefs didn't really care what women did—as long as they did it outside their tightly controlled villages.

Why should they? From their viewpoint, beyond the sexual pleasure they provided, women were simply domestic animals and beasts of burden. No different, really, from their other livestock. As long as they had enough women to keep breeding clansmen, who cared what wild women did somewhere else?

Boys, on the other hand, *mattered*. And now—curse him!—the new king was seducing boys away from their proper and traditional allegiances to babble mystical nonsense in monasteries. Even teaching them to read, as if any Pathan tribesman ever needed such an effeminate skill.

The process would take decades, of course, even generations. But it would work, as surely as the sunrise—provided that Kungas established from the beginning that however much the clan chiefs hated him they did not dare to oppose him openly. Or try any violent tactic against him, whatsoever.

Which he had just done. More efficiently, ruthlessly, pitilessly, and savagely than any of the clan chiefs had ever imagined he would. Just as, in a different universe, the Mongols had obliterated the cult of the Hashasin which had given the world the term "assassin" to begin with—by demonstrating that they were perfectly willing to transform the definition of the word by an order of magnitude.

Yet . . .

Irene knew her husband very well, by now. Kungas enjoyed

her intelligence and her sense of humor, but this was no time for rational argument, much less jests.

She fell back on an emotional appeal that was even more powerful than horror and disgust and anger.

"There's this, if it helps. The dynasty is secured."

She looked down, stroking the silk raiment covering her belly. She was still, to all appearances, as slender as ever. "Well. Most likely. I might have a miscarriage."

His eyes were drawn to her waist, and she could sense Kungas' mood shifting. So, smiling gently, she ventured a little joke.

"Of course, you'll make that good, soon enough."

For a moment, Kungas tried to maintain his ferocious mood. "Typical! Salacious Greek women. Seductresses, every one of you. If you weren't so beautiful . . ."

In point of fact, Irene wasn't beautiful at all. Attractive, perhaps, but no more than that. Her thick and luxurious chestnut hair was not even much of an asset, any longer, tied back as she now had it in a pony tail. And she'd found, to her disgruntlement, that becoming a queen hadn't made her big nose any smaller or made her narrow, close-eyed face any fuller. Even with the ponytail, she still looked like exactly what she was—an intellectual, not a courtesan.

Happily, none of that mattered to Kungas. Her little joke wasn't really even that. By the end of the evening, most likely—tomorrow night, at the latest—Kungas would demonstrate that there wasn't any danger that the new dynasty would die out from lack of vigor.

Kungas sighed. "It really was a hateful business, Irene. Damn those old men! I would have preferred . . ."

He let the thought trail away. Then, gave her something in the way of an apologetic shrug.

In point of fact, it had been Irene who suggested that he restrict himself to simply executing all of the clan chiefs—and Kungas who had declined the suggestion.

"No," he'd said. "That won't be enough. However stupid and vicious, no clan chief is a coward. They'll accept their own deaths, readily enough, as stubborn as they are. The only thing that will really terrify them is the extinction of their entire clan. So I have no choice but to demonstrate that I'm quite willing to do so. Maybe if I do it once, right now, I'll never have to do it again."

He'd been right, and Irene had known it. She'd only advanced her suggestion because she knew how much Kungas detested the alternative. As hard a man as he was, and as hard a life as he'd led, not even Kungas could butcher babies to punish octogenarians without shrieking somewhere in his iron-masked soul.

Finally, she could sense the mood breaking. The surest sign came when Kungas made his own jest.

"And who's the father, by the way?"

Irene's eyes narrowed. "Don't be stupid. As often as you mount me, when would I have the time to cuckold you? Even assuming I wasn't too exhausted, you insensate brute."

Kungas was still scowling. In his own way, he could teach stubbornness to clan chiefs.

"Not that," he said curtly, waving the notion aside with an economical little gesture. "I don't doubt my cock's the only one that gets into you. But it's just a conduit. Spiritually speaking. Who's the *real* father? Have we moved up to gods, yet? Will I discover as an old man that the children I thought mine were actually sired by Zeus and who knows how many randy members of the Hindu pantheon?"

"What a heathen notion!" Irene exclaimed. "You should be ashamed of yourself!"

"I'm not a Christian," he pointed out.

"You're not really a Buddhist, either, even if you insist on the trappings. So what? It's still a barbarous notion."

She drew herself up with as much dignity as she could manage. That was . . . hard, given that she was almost laughing.

"And it's all nonsense, anyway. Of course, you're the *father.* The ancestry gets interesting, though."

His first smile came, finally. "More interesting than Alexander the Great? Whom—to my immense surprise—you have explained was one of my forefathers. Odd, really, given that he passed through this area long before we Kushans got here."

"My scholars assure me it is true, nonetheless. But now, they tell me, it seems that in addition—"

"Please! Don't tell me I'm descended from Ashoka also!"

Irene *had* considered Ashoka, in fact, and quite seriously. But, in the end, she'd decided that claiming India's most famous and revered emperor as one of her husband's forefathers would probably cause too many political problems. India's ever-suspicious rulers would assume that meant the Kushans had designs on India also.

Which, they didn't. To meddle in India's affairs—even the Punjab, much less the great and populous Gangetic plain—would be pure folly. As long as she and Kungas controlled the Khyber Pass and the Hindu Kush, they could expand to the north without stirring up animosities with either the Indians or the Persians. Animosities, at least, that would be severe enough to lead to war. Soon enough, of course, Persians and Indians—and Romans and Chinese too, for that matter—would be complaining bitterly about Kushan control of the trade routes through central Asia.

But those quarrels could be negotiated. Irene was an excellent negotiator—even without the advantage of having a husband who could terrify Pathan clan chiefs.

"Nonsense," she said firmly. "You're no relation to Ashoka at all, so far as my scholars can determine. Just as well, really, since we have no ambitions toward India. However—what a happy coincidence, given the centrality of Buddhism to our plans—would you believe that—"

Kungas choked. Irene pressed on.

"It's true!" she insisted. "Not the Buddha *himself*, of course. After he became the Buddha, that is. He was quite the ascetic sage, you know. But *before* that—when he was still just plain Siddhartha Gautama and was married to Yashodhara. It turns out that their son Rahula—"

Kungas burst into laughter, and Irene knew that she'd saved his soul again. That was always her greatest fear, that a soul which had shelled itself in iron for so long would eventually become iron itself.

The mask, the world could afford. Even needed. But if the soul beneath the mask ever became iron, in fact, she dreaded the consequences. If so, in the new universe they were helping to shape, the name "Kungas" would someday become a term like "Tamerlane" had been in another. A name that signified nothing but savagery.

No fear of that, so long as she could make Kungas laugh that way. No fear at all.

THE IRON TRIANGLE

As always, the sound of Luke's footsteps awakened Calopodius. This time, though, as he emerged from sleep, he sensed that other men were shuffling their feet in the background.

He was puzzled, a bit. Few visitors came to the bunker where he and Luke had set up their quarters. Calopodius suspected that was because men felt uncomfortable in the presence of a blind man, especially one as young as himself. It was certainly not due to lack of space. The general had provided him with a very roomy bunker, connected by a short tunnel to the great command bunker buried near the small city that had emerged over the past months toward the southern tip of the Iron Triangle. The Roman army called that city "the Anvil," taking the name from the Punjabi civilians who made up most of its inhabitants.

"Who's there, Luke?" he asked.

His aide-de-camp barked a laugh. "A bunch of boys seeking fame and glory, lad. The general sent them."

The shuffling feet came nearer. "Begging your pardon, sir, but we were wondering—as he says, the general sent us to talk to you—" The man, whoever he was, lapsed into an awkward silence.

Calopodius sat up on his pallet. "Speak up, then. And who are you?"

The man cleared his throat. "Name's Abelard, sir. Abelard of Antioch. I'm the hecatontarch in charge of the westernmost bastion at the fortress of—"

"You had hot fighting yesterday," interrupted Calopodius. "I heard about it. The general told me the Malwa probe was much fiercer than usual."

"Came at us like demons, sir," said another voice. Proudly: "But we bloodied 'em good."

Calopodius understood at once. The hecatontarch cleared his throat, but Calopodius spoke before the man was forced into embarrassment.

"I'll want to hear all the details!" he exclaimed. "Just give me a moment to get dressed and summon my scribe. We can do it all right here, at the table there. I'll make sure it goes into the next dispatch."

"Thank you, sir," said Abelard. His voice took on a slightly aggrieved tone. "T'isn't true, what Luke says. It's neither the fame nor the glory of it. It's just . . . your *Dispatches* get read to the Senate, sir. Each and every one, by the Emperor himself. And then the Emperor—by express command—has them printed and posted all over the Empire."

Calopodius was moving around, feeling for his clothing. "True enough," he said cheerfully. "Ever since the old Emperor set up the new printing press in the Great Palace, everybody—every village, anyway—can get a copy of something."

"It's our families, sir," said the other voice. "They'll see our names and know we're all right. Except for those who died in the fighting. But at least . . ."

Calopodius understood. "Their names will exist somewhere, on something other than a tombstone."

Chapter 3
THE EUPHRATES
Autumn, 533 AD

They had approached Elafonisos from the south, because Calopodius had thought Anna might enjoy the sight of the great ridge which overlooked the harbor, with its tower perched atop it like a hawk. And she had seemed to enjoy it well enough, although, as he was coming to recognize, she took most of her pleasure from the sea itself. As did he, for that matter.

She even smiled, once or twice.

The trip across to the island, however, was the high point of the expedition. Their overnight stay in the small tavern in the port had been . . . almost unpleasant. Anna had not objected to the dinginess of the provincial tavern, nor had she complained about the poor fare offered for their evening meal. But she had retreated into an even more distant silence—almost sullen and hostile—as soon as they set foot on land.

That night, as always since the night of their wedding, she performed her duties without resistance. But also with as much energy and enthusiasm as she might have given to reading a particularly dull piece of hagiography. Calopodius found it all quite frustrating, the more so since his wife's naked body was something which aroused him greatly. As he had suspected in the days before the marriage, his wife was quite lovely once she could be seen. And felt.

So he performed his own duty in a perfunctory manner. Afterward, in another time, he might have spent the occasion idly

31

considering the qualities he would look for in a courtesan—now that he had a wife against whose tedium he could measure the problem. But he had already decided to join Belisarius' expedition to the Indus. So, before falling asleep, his thoughts were entirely given over to matters of martial glory. And, of course, the fears and uncertainties which any man his age would feel on the eve of plunging into the maelstrom of war.

When trouble finally arrived, it was Anna's husband who saved her. The knowledge only increased her fury.

Stupid, really, and some part of her mind understood it perfectly well. But she still couldn't stop hating him.

Stupid. The men on the barge who were clambering eagerly onto the small pier where her own little river craft was tied up were making no attempt to hide their leers. Eight of them there were, their half-clad bodies sweaty from the toil of working their clumsy vessel up the Euphrates.

A little desperately, Anna looked about. She saw nothing beyond the Euphrates itself; reed marshes on the other bank, and a desert on her own. There was not a town or a village in sight. She had stopped at this little pier simply because the two sailors she had hired to carry her down to Charax had insisted they needed to take on fresh water. There was a well here, which was the only reason for the pier's existence. After taking a taste of the muddy water of the Euphrates, Anna couldn't find herself in disagreement.

She wished, now, that she'd insisted on continuing. Not that her insistence would have probably done much good. The sailors had been civil enough, since she'd employed them at a small town in the headwaters of the Euphrates. But they were obviously not overawed by a nineteen-year-old girl, even if she did come from the famous family of the Melisseni.

She glanced appealingly at the sailors, still working the well. They avoided her gaze, acting as if they hadn't even noticed the men climbing out of the barge. Both sailors were rather elderly, and it was clear enough they had no intention of getting into a fracas with eight rivermen much younger than themselves—all of whom were carrying knives, to boot.

The men from the barge were close to her, and beginning to spread out. One of them was fingering the knife in a scabbard attached to his waist. All of them were smiling in a manner which even a sheltered young noblewoman understood was predatory.

Now in sheer desperation, her eyes moved to the only other men on the pier. Three soldiers, judging from their weapons and gear. They had already been on the pier when Anna's boat drew up, and their presence had almost been enough to cause the sailors to pass by entirely. A rather vicious-looking trio, they were. Two Isaurians and a third one whom Anna thought was probably an Arab. Isaurians were not much better than barbarians; Arabs might or might not be, depending on where they came from. Anna suspected this one was an outright bedouin.

The soldiers were lounging in the shade of a small pavilion they had erected. For a moment, as she had when she first caught sight of them, Anna found herself wondering how they had gotten there in the first place. They had no boat, nor any horses or camels—yet they possessed too much in the way of goods in sacks to have lugged them on their own shoulders. Not through this arid country, with their armor and weapons. She decided they had probably traveled with a caravan, and then parted company for some reason.

But this was no time for idle speculation. The rivermen were very close now. The soldiers returned Anna's beseeching eyes with nothing more than indifference. It was clear enough they had no more intention of intervening than her own sailors.

Still—they *could*, in a way that two elderly sailors couldn't.

Pay them.

Moving as quickly as she could in her elaborate clothing—and cursing herself silently, again, for having been so stupid as to make this insane journey without giving a thought to her apparel—Anna walked over to them. She could only hope they understood Greek. She knew no other language.

"I need help," she hissed.

The soldier in the center of the little group, one of the Isaurians, glanced at the eight rivermen and chuckled.

"I'd say so. You'll be lucky if they don't kill you after they rob and rape you."

His Greek was fluent, if heavily accented. As he proceeded to demonstrate further. "Stupid noblewoman. Brains like a chicken. Are you some kind of idiot, traveling alone down this part of Mesopotamia? The difference between a riverman here and a pirate—"

He turned his head and spit casually over the leg of the other Isaurian. His brother, judging from the close resemblance.

"I'll pay you," she said.

The two brothers exchanged glances. The one on the side, who seemed to be the younger one, shrugged. "We can use her boat to take us out of Mesopotamia. Beats walking, and the chance of another caravan . . . But nothing fancy," he muttered. "We're almost home."

His older brother grunted agreement and turned his head to look at the Arab. The Arab's shrug expressed the same tepid enthusiasm. "Nothing fancy," he echoed. "It's too hot."

The Isaurian in the middle lazed to his feet. He wasn't much taller than Anna, but his stocky and muscular build made him seem to loom over her.

"All right. Here's the way it is. You give us half your money and whatever other valuables you've got." He tapped the jeweled necklace around her throat. "The rivermen can take the rest of it. They'll settle for that, just to avoid a brawl."

She almost wailed. Not quite. "I *can't.* I need the money to get to—"

The soldier scowled. "Idiot! We'll keep them from taking your boat, we'll leave you enough—just enough—to get back to your family, and we'll escort you into Anatolia."

He glanced again at the rivermen. They were standing some few yards away, hesitant now. "You've no business here, girl," he growled quietly. "Just be thankful you'll get out of this with your life."

His brother had gotten to his feet also. He snorted sarcastically. "Not to mention keeping your precious hymen intact. That ought to be worth a lot, once you get back to your family."

The fury which had filled Anna for months boiled to the surface. "I don't *have* a hymen," she snarled. "My husband did for that, the bastard, before he went off to war."

Now the Arab was on his feet. Hearing her words, he laughed aloud. "God save us! An abandoned little wife, no less."

The rivermen were beginning to get surly, judging from the scowls which had replaced the previous leers. One of them barked something in a language which Anna didn't recognize. One of the Aramaic dialects, probably. The Isaurian who seemed to be the leader of the three soldiers gave them another glance and an idle little wave of his hand. The gesture more or less indicated: *relax, relax—you'll get a cut.*

That done, his eyes came back to Anna. "Idiot," he repeated. The word was spoken with no heat, just lazy derision. "Think you're the first woman got abandoned by a husband looking to make his fortune in war?"

"He already *has* a fortune," hissed Anna. "He went looking for fame. Found it too, damn him."

The Arab laughed again. "Fame, is it? Maybe in your circles! And what is the name of this paragon of martial virtue? Anthony the Illustrious Courier?"

The other three soldiers shared in the little laugh. For a moment, Anna was distracted by the oddity of such flowery phrases coming out of the mouth of a common soldier. She remembered, vaguely, that her husband had once told her of the poetic prowess of Arabs. But she had paid little attention, at the time, and the memory simply heightened her anger.

"He *is* famous," Anna insisted. A certain innate honesty forced her to add: "At least in Constantinople, after Belisarius' letter was read to the Senate. And his own dispatches."

The name *Belisarius* brought a sudden little stillness to the group of soldiers. The Isaurian leader's eyes narrowed.

"Belisarius? What's the general got to do with your husband?"

"And what's his name?" added the Arab.

Anna tightened her jaws. "Calopodius. Calopodius Saronites."

The stillness turned into frozen rigidity. All three soldiers' eyes were now almost slits.

The Isaurian leader drew a deep breath. "Are you trying to tell us that you are the wife of *Calopodius the Blind*?"

For a moment, a spike of anguish drove through the anger. She didn't really understand where it came from. Calopodius had always seemed blind to her, in his own way. But . . .

Her own deep breath was a shaky thing. "They say he is blind now, yes. Belisarius' letter to the Senate said so. *He* says it himself, in fact, in his letters. I—I guess it's true. I haven't seen him in many months. When he left . . ."

One of the rivermen began to say something, in a surly tone of voice. The gaze which the Isaurian now turned on him was nothing casual. It was a flat, flat gaze. As cold as a snake's and just as deadly. Even a girl as sheltered as Anna had been all her life understood the sheer physical menace in it. The rivermen all seemed to shuffle back a step or two.

He turned his eyes back to Anna. The same cold and flat gleam was in them. "If you are lying . . ."

"Why would I lie?" she demanded angrily. "And how do you expect me to prove it, anyway?"

Belatedly, a thought came to her. "Unless . . ." She glanced at the little sailing craft which had brought her here, still piled high with her belongings. "If you can *read* Greek, I have several of his letters to me."

The Arab sighed softly. "As you say, why would you lie?" His dark eyes examined her face carefully. "God help us. You really don't even understand, do you?"

She shook her head, confused. "Understand what? Do you know him yourself?"

The Isaurian leader's sigh was a more heartfelt thing. "No, lass, we didn't. We were so rich, after Charax, that we left the general's service. We—" he gestured at his brother "—I'm Illus, by the way, and he's Cottomenes—had more than enough to buy us a big farm back home. And Abdul decided to go in with us."

"I'm sick of the desert," muttered the Arab. "Sick of camels, too. Never did like the damn beasts."

The Arab was of the same height as the two Isaurian brothers—about average—but much less stocky in his frame. Still, in his light half-armor and with a spatha scabbarded to his waist, he seemed no less deadly.

"Come to think of it," he added, almost idly, "I'm sick of thieves, too."

The violence that erupted shocked Anna more than anything in her life. She collapsed in a squat, gripping her knees with shaking hands, almost moaning with fear.

There had been no sign; nothing, at least, that she had seen. The Isaurian leader simply drew his spatha—so quick, so quick!—took three peculiar little half steps and cleaved the skull of one of the rivermen before the man even had time to do more than widen his eyes. A second or two later, the same spatha tore open another's throat. In the same amount of time, his brother and the Arab gutted two other rivermen.

Then—

She closed her eyes. The four surviving rivermen were desperately trying to reach their barge. From the sounds—clear enough, even to a young woman who had never seen a man killed before—they weren't going to make it. Not even close. The sounds, wetly horrid, were those of a pack of wolves in a sheep pen.

Some time later, she heard the Isaurian's voice. "Open your eyes, girl. It's over."

She opened her eyes. Catching sight of the pool of blood soaking into the planks of the pier, she averted her gaze. Her eyes fell on the two sailors, cowering behind the well. She almost giggled, the sight was so ridiculous.

The Isaurian must have followed her gaze, because he began chuckling himself. "Silly looking, aren't they? As if they could hide behind that little well."

He raised his voice. "Don't be stupid! If nothing else, we need you to sail the boat. Besides—" He gestured at the barge. "You'll want to loot it, if there's anything in that tub worth looting. We'll burn whatever's left."

He reached down a hand. Anna took it and came shakily to her feet.

Bodies everywhere. She started to close her eyes again.

"Get used to it, girl," the Isaurian said harshly. "You'll see plenty more of that where you're going. Especially if you make it to the island."

Her head felt muzzy. "Island? What island?"

"*The* island, idiot. 'The Iron Triangle,' they call it. Where your husband is, along with the general. Right in the mouth of the Malwa."

"I didn't know it was an island," she said softly. Again, honesty surfaced. "I'm not really even sure where it is, except somewhere in India."

The Arab had come up in time to hear her last words. He was wiping his blade clean with a piece of cloth. "God save us." He half-chuckled. "It's not really an island. Not exactly. But it'll do, seeing as how the general's facing about a hundred thousand Malwa."

He studied her for a moment, while he finished wiping the blood off the sword. Then, sighed again. "Let's hope you learn *something*, by the time we get to Charax. After that, you'll be on your own again. At least—"

He gave the Isaurian an odd little look. The Isaurian shrugged. "We were just telling ourselves yesterday how stupid we'd been, missing out on the loot of Malwa itself. What the hell, we may as well take her the whole way."

His brother was now there. "Hell, yes!" he boomed. He bestowed on Anna a very cheerful grin. "I assume you'll recommend us to the general? Not that we deserted or anything, but I'd *really* prefer a better assignment this time than being on the front lines. A bit dicey, that, when the general's running the show. Not that he isn't the shrewdest bastard in the world, mind you, but he *does* insist on fighting."

The other two soldiers seemed to share in the humor. Anna didn't really understand it, but for the first time since she'd heard the name of Calopodius—spoken by her father, when he announced to her an unwanted and unforeseen marriage—she didn't find it hateful.

Rather the opposite, in fact. She didn't know much about the military—nothing, really—but she suspected . . .

"I imagine my husband needs a bodyguard," she said hesitantly. "A bigger one than whatever he has," she added hastily. "And he's certainly rich enough to pay for it."

"Done," said the Isaurian leader instantly. "Done!"

Not long afterward, as their ship sailed down the river, Anna looked back. The barge was burning fiercely now. By the time the fire burned out, there would be nothing left but a hulk carrying what was left of a not-very-valuable cargo and eight charred skeletons.

The Isaurian leader—Illus—misunderstood her frown. "Don't worry about it, girl. In this part of Mesopotamia, no one will care what happened to the bastards."

She shook her head. "I'm not worrying about *that*. It's just—"

She fell silent. There was no way to explain, and one glance at Illus' face was enough to tell her that he'd never understand.

Calopodius hadn't, after all.

"So why the frown?"

She shrugged. "Never mind. I'm not used to violence, I guess."

That seemed to satisfy him, to Anna's relief. Under the circumstances, she could hardly explain to her rescuers how much she hated her husband. Much less why, since she didn't really understand it that well herself.

Still, she wondered. Something important had happened on that pier, something unforeseen, and she was not too consumed by her own anger not to understand that much. For the first time in her life, a husband had done something other than crush her like an insect.

She studied the surrounding countryside. So bleak and dangerous, compared to the luxurious surroundings in which she had spent her entire life. She found herself wondering what Calopodius had thought when he first saw it. Wondered what he had thought, and felt, the first time he saw blood spreading like a pool. Wondered if he had been terrified, when he first went into a battle.

Wondered what he thought now, and felt, with his face a mangled ruin.

Another odd pang of anguish came to her, then. Calopodius had been a handsome boy, even if she had taken no pleasure in the fact.

The Isaurian's voice came again, interrupting her musings. "Weird world, it is. What a woman will go through to find her husband."

She felt another flare of anger. But there was no way to explain; in truth, she could not have found the words herself. So all she said was: "Yes."

The next day, as they sailed back to the mainland, he informed Anna of his decision. And for the first time since he met the girl, she came to life. All distance and ennui vanished, replaced by a cold and spiteful fury which completely astonished him. She did not say much, but what she said was as venomous as a serpent's bite.

Why? he wondered. *He would have thought, coming from a family whose fame derived from ancient exploits more than modern wealth, she would have been pleased.*

He tried to discover the source of her anger. But after her initial spate of hostile words, Anna fell silent and refused to answer any of his questions. Soon enough, he gave up the attempt. It was not as if, after all, he had ever really expected any intimacy in his marriage. For that, if he survived the war, he would find a courtesan.

Chapter 4
THE IRON TRIANGLE, IN THE PUNJAB
Winter, 533 AD

"You can describe it better than that," rasped Justinian. The former Emperor of the Roman Empire was now its Grand Justiciar, since his blinding at the hands of traitors and Malwa agents had made him ineligible for the throne under Roman law. But he'd lost very little of his peremptory habits.

No reason he should, really. Although Belisarius' son Photius was officially the new Emperor, Justinian's wife Theodora was the Empress Regent and the real power in Constantinople. Still, it was exasperating for the premier general of the Roman empire to be addressed like an errant schoolboy. Tightening his jaws a bit, Belisarius brought the telescope back to his eye.

"At an estimate—best I can do, since they haven't finished it yet—the tower will be at least three hundred feet tall. From the looks of the—"

"Never mind, never mind," interrupted Justinian. "It doesn't really matter. With a tower that tall, they're obviously planning for general AM broadcasting."

The former emperor's badly scarred eye sockets were riveted on the distant Malwa tower, as if he could still see. Or glare.

"In God's name, *why*?" he demanded. "For military purposes, directional broadcasting would make a lot more sense and require a lot less massive construction. That's what we're doing."

Justinian waved a hand toward the south, where the Roman

army was erecting its own "antenna farm" almost at the very tip of the triangle of land formed by the junction of the Indus and Chenab rivers.

Only the tips of the antennas could be seen from the fortifications on the north side of the Iron Triangle. The Roman radios were designed to be directional, not broadcast, so there was no need for an enormous tower. The key for directional radio was mostly the length of the antennas, not their height.

Folding up the telescope, Belisarius shrugged. "Maybe for the same reason we're having Antonina and Ousanas build exactly such a tower in Axum. It'll give us general relaying capability we wouldn't have otherwise."

"That's nonsense," Justinian grumbled. "I could understand them building a tower like that in their capital city of Kausambi. But why build one *here*, on the front lines? We're not, after all."

Belisarius said nothing.

After an uncomfortable moment, Justinian chuckled harshly. "Fine, fine. Presumably they don't have quite our motivation. At least, I think it's safe to assume that monster from the future doesn't have a peevish wife like I do."

Belisarius smiled crookedly. Although they had never discussed it quite openly, both he and Justinian knew perfectly well—and knew each other knew—that one of the main reasons they'd tacitly agreed not to build a general AM tower in the Iron Triangle was so that the Empress Regent could not easily bombard them with instructions.

More easily bombard them, it might be better to say. As it was, just using the telegraph, Theodora averaged at least two messages a day to the Iron Triangle.

One of which, almost every day, was either a peremptory demand that Justinian stop playing soldier and get back to a position of safety far to the south in Barbaricum, or a pleading request for the same, or a threat of dire consequences if he didn't—or, often enough, all three rolled into one.

"Is there something we're overlooking?" Justinian demanded.

The question wasn't aimed at Belisarius so much as it was at the "jewel" that hung in a pouch suspended from the Roman general's muscular neck. Inside that pouch rested Aide, the crystalline being from the future who had come back into the human past to thwart—hopefully—the intervention of the so-called "new gods" of the future.

Aide's response came only into Belisarius' mind. **No,** the crystal being said, rather curtly. **We're not overlooking anything. Tell that nasty old man to stop being so paranoid. And tell him to stop being so nasty, while you're at it.**

Since Justinian couldn't see the expression, Belisarius grinned openly. Outside of himself, Justinian was the only human being who regularly communicated with Aide via direct contact with the jewel. Most people found direct contact with Aide rather unsettling. The jewel's means of communication typically involved a flood of images—many of them quite disturbing—not simply words, which could be easily sanitized in the mind of the recipient.

Justinian probably found it unsettling also. Belisarius certainly did, often enough. But if the former emperor was "nasty" and "paranoid"—terms which Belisarius would allow were fair enough, even if "old" was a bit off the mark—he was also just about as tough-minded as any human being who'd ever lived. So he seemed to tolerate the problem well enough—and, on the other hand, got the benefit of the direct contact with Aide that had enabled Justinian, in a very short time, to become the Roman Empire's master artisan.

Or designer for artisans, it might be better to say. Blind as he was, it was difficult for Justinian to do the work himself.

Although Aide tolerated that extensive contact for the sake of their mutual project, he didn't like it at all. He didn't like Justinian.

And why should he, really? Most people didn't like Justinian.

His peeve apparently satisfied by the remarks, Aide added uncertainly: **I don't really know why they're doing it. But I'm sure it's not some clever trick we're missing.**

Belisarius gave Aide the mental equivalent of a nod. Then, said to Justinian: "Aide doesn't think so, although he doesn't know why they're doing it. What I think is that—"

"Oh, it's obvious enough," interrupted Justinian, as if he hadn't been the one to demand an answer in the first place. "Morale, that's all."

Again, he waved toward the south. "That mass of wires we've got stuck all over down there is just something that annoys the soldiers. We've even had to position guards to keep the silly bastards from stumbling over them in the dark. Especially when they're drunk on the local beer. As many defeats as the Malwa have suffered these past few years, that monster Link has got to be worried about morale. A great big impressive-looking radio tower will help boost its soldiers' spirits, even if it isn't really that useful. Especially *those* soldiers. Ignorant and illiterate peasants, most of them."

Again, Belisarius grinned. "Ignorant and illiterate peasants" was a fair description of most of the Malwa army, true enough. On the other hand, it could be applied to most Roman soldiers also. Over time, the changes Aide had brought to the world would produce a rapid increase in the general level of literacy—was already doing so, in fact, among many of the Empire's young-sters. The ones living in big cities, at least. But, even five years after Aide's arrival, very little of that had penetrated the Roman soldiery. It was still true that, below the rank of hecatontarch, not more than one in ten of them could read and write. For that matter, a hefty percentage of the empire's officer corps was illiterate also, beyond—in most cases—being able to painfully write out their own name.

So be it. Wars were fought with the armies available. Whatever weaknesses and limitations the Roman army possessed, Belisarius knew it was far superior to that of the enemy. Man for man, certainly, on average. The Roman Empire, whatever its many flaws and failures, was still a society in which a determined and capable man could rise based on his own merits. The Malwa, on the other hand, with their rigid adherence to a caste system, had to rely primarily on the sheer mass of the army that northern India's teeming population could produce.

That had been, from the very beginning of the war, the basic equation Belisarius had had to deal with: using quality against quantity, in such a way as to eventually defeat the Malwa with-out ever giving them the chance to use their immense strength against him in a way that was effective.

It had worked, so far—but it took time. Time, and patience.

Alas, patience was not a virtue often associated with Justin-ian, as he proved an hour later, once they entered the sunken bunker behind the front lines that served Belisarius for his headquarters.

"So how much longer are you going to dilly-dally?" he asked, after taking a chair.

Belisarius decided to try the tactic of misunderstanding. "About the submarine?" He harrumphed very sternly, almost majestically. "*Forever*, Justinian—so you can just forget about trying to cajole me—"

He didn't think the tactic would work. Sure enough:

"Stop playing the fool. I don't even disagree with you about the submarine—as you know perfectly well. I just think it'd be an interesting experiment, that's all. I'm talking about the offensive against the Malwa that you keep postponing and postponing. I'm beginning to think you've converted to that heathen Hindu way of looking at things. All time is cyclical and moves in great yugas, so why bother doing anything for the next billion years or so? Or is it that you think the way your soldiers are copulating with the local natives, you'll have a huge population of your own within a generation or two?"

The former emperor sneered. "Idiot. The population density here is already horrible. You'll be facing starvation soon enough, you watch."

Belisarius tried to keep from scowling, but . . . couldn't, quite. Given that the Romans controlled the Indus south of the Iron Triangle and their Persian allies were rapidly bringing agricultural production in the Sind back up to normal, he wasn't really worried about running out of food. Still, rations were tight, and . . .

He sighed, audibly. There wasn't much point trying to keep anything from Justinian, as smart as he was. "It's a problem, I admit. Not the food, just the endless headaches. I'm beginning to think—"

"Forget it! I'm the Grand Justiciar of the *Roman* Empire. There's no way I'll let you wheedle me into adjudicating the endless squabbles you're having with the damn natives here. Bunch of heathens, anyway."

"Actually, they're not," said Belisarius mildly. "A good portion of them, at least. You'd be surprised how many are converting to Christianity."

Justinian's eye sockets were too badly scarred for him to manage the feat of widening them with surprise. Perhaps thankfully, since they were horrible-enough looking as it was. Justinian, naturally, refused to cover them with anything.

Calopodius did the same, but in his case that was simply a young man's determination to accept adversity squarely. In Justinian's, it was the ingrained, arrogant habit of an emperor. What did he care if people flinched from his appearance? They'd done so often enough when he'd still been sighted. More often, probably. Justinian had never been famous for his forbearance.

"It's true," Belisarius insisted. "Converting in droves. By now, the priests tell me, at least a fourth of the Punjabis in the Triangle have adopted our faith."

Justinian's head swiveled toward the bunker's entry, as if he could look out at the terrain beyond. Out and up, actually, since the bunker was buried well beneath the soil.

"Why, do you think?"

"It might be better to say, why not?" Belisarius nodded toward the entrance. "Those are all peasants out there, Justinian. Low caste and non-Malwa. It's not as if the Malwa Empire's mahaveda brand of Hinduism ever gave them anything."

Justinian was almost scowling. He didn't like being puzzled. "Yes, yes, I can see that. But I'd still think they'd be afraid . . ."

His voice trailed off.

Belisarius chuckled harshly. "Be afraid of what? That the Malwa will slaughter them if they overrun the Triangle? They will *anyway*, just as an object lesson—and those Punjabi peasants know it perfectly well. So they're apparently deciding to adhere to Rome as closely as possible."

Still looking at the heavily timbered entrance to the bunker, Belisarius added: "It's going to be a bit of a political problem, in fact, assuming we win the war."

He didn't need to elaborate. Emperor he might no longer be, but Justinian still thought like one—and he'd been perhaps the most intelligent emperor in Rome's long history.

"Ha!" he barked. "Yes, I can see that. If a fourth have already converted, then by the time"—his scowl returned briefly—"you finally launch your long-delayed offensive and we hammer the Malwa bastards—"

"I'm glad *you're* so confident of the matter."

"Don't be stupid!" Justinian snapped impatiently. "Of course you will. And when you do—as I was saying before I was interrupted—probably two-thirds of them will be Christians. So what does that leave for Khusrau, except a headache? Don't forget that you *did* promise him the lower Punjab as Persian territory."

Belisarius shrugged. "I didn't 'promise' the Emperor of Iran anything. I admit, I did indicate I'd be favorable to the idea—mostly to keep him from getting too ambitious and wanting to gobble all of the Punjab. That would just lead to an endless three-way conflict between the Persians, the Kushans and the Rajputs."

"You'd get that anyway. You want my advice?"

Naturally, Justinian didn't wait for an answer before giving it. "*Keep* the Iron Triangle. Make it a Roman enclave. It'd be a good idea, anyway, because we could serve as a buffer between the Persians, the Kushans and the Rajputs—and now we could justify it on religious grounds."

He made an attempt to infuse the last phrase with some heartfelt piety. A very slight attempt—and even that failed.

Belisarius scratched his chin. "I'd been thinking about it," he admitted. "Kungas won't care."

"*Care?* He'd be delighted! I never would have thought those barbarous Kushans would be as smart as they are. But, they are that smart. At least, they're smart enough to listen to Irene Macrembolitissa, and *she's* that smart."

In point of fact, while Belisarius knew that the king of the Kushans listened carefully to the advice of his Greek wife, Kungas made his own decisions. He was quite smart enough on his own to figure out that getting his new Kushan kingdom embroiled in endless conflicts with Persians and Rajputs over who controlled the Punjab would just weaken him. A Roman buffer state planted in the middle of the Punjab would tend to keep conflicts down—or, at least, keep the Kushans out of it.

"The Rajputs . . ."

"Who cares what they think?" demanded Justinian. "All of this is a moot point, I remind you, until and unless you finally get your much-delayed offensive underway—at which time the Rajputs will be a beaten people, and beaten people take what they can get."

That was Justinian's old thinking at work. Shrewd enough, within its limits. But if nothing else, the years Belisarius had spent with Aide's immense knowledge of human history in his mind had made him highly skeptical of imperialism. He'd been able to scan enormous vistas of human experience, not only into the future of this planet but on a multitude of other planets as well. Out of that, when it came to the subject of empires, Belisarius had distilled two simple pieces of wisdom:

First, every empire that ever existed or would exist always thought it was the end-all and be-all.

Second, none of them were. Few of them lasted more than two hundred years, and even the ones that did never went more than a couple of centuries without a civil war or other major internal conflict. The human race just naturally seemed to do better if it avoided too much in the way of political self-aggrandizement. The notion that history could be "guided"—even by someone like Belisarius, with Aide to serve as his adviser—was pure nonsense. Better to just set up something workable, that contained as few conflicts as possible, and let human potential continue to unfold within it. If the underlying society was healthy, the political structure tended to sort itself out well enough to fit whatever the circumstances were.

In short, not to his surprise, Belisarius had come to conclude that the ambitions and schemes of his great enemy Link and the "new gods" who had created the monster were simply the same old imperial folly writ large. Belisarius didn't really know exactly what *he* believed in. But he knew what he didn't—and that was good enough.

"Agreed, then," he said abruptly. "We'll plan on keeping the Triangle. Who knows? Khusrau might even be smart enough to see that it's in his benefit, too."

"Might be," grunted Justinian skeptically. "I doubt it, though. Don't forget he's an emperor. Wearing the purple automatically makes a man stupider."

The scarred, savaged face grinned. "Take my word for it. I *know*."

Their conversation was interrupted by a particularly loud ripple in the never-ceasing exchange of barrages between the Romans and the Malwa. Some of the enemy shells even landed close enough to make the bunker tremble.

Not much. But enough to bring Justinian's scowl back.

"I'm getting tired of that. When in the name of all that's holy are you going to stop lolling about and start the offensive?"

Belisarius didn't bother to answer.

When the time is right, came Aide's voice. Then, a bit plaintively: **Which is when, by the way? I'd like to know myself.**

Et tu, Aide? The answer is that I don't know. When it feels right. Which it doesn't yet. Things have to keep brewing for a while, in the Hindu Kush—and most of all, in Majarashtra.

You don't have any way to get in touch with Rao by radio, Aide pointed out. **Or Kungas, for that matter.**

Teach your grandfather to suck eggs! I know I don't. What's worse still, is that even if I did have radio contact with India, I couldn't talk to the three men who matter the most.

There was silence for a moment, as Aide tried to follow Belisarius' train of thought. For all his immense intellect, Aide had little of the Roman general's intuitive sense of strategy.

Oh, he said finally. **Narses the eunuch.**

Yes. And Rana Sanga. And, most of all, Lord Damodara.

There was a moment's silence, again. Then Aide added, somewhat timidly: **You probably better not mention to Justinian—certainly not Theodora!—that you're stalling the offensive because you're counting on a Roman traitor and the two best generals on the enemy side.**

Teach your grandfather to suck eggs!

Chapter 5
BHARAKUCCHA, ON INDIA'S WEST COAST

"It must be unnerving," Ajatasutra said chuckling.

"*What* must be unnerving?" asked Narses irritably. "And why do you keep thinking such pointless chatter will help you win?" The old eunuch moved his bishop, taking the assassin's knight. "Check. It distracts you more than it does me. That's partly why you lose, nine games out of ten. The other part is because I'm smarter than you."

Ajatasutra didn't even glance at the chess board. His thin smile was still directed at Narses. "It must be unnerving to have Rana Sanga watching you the way he does, whenever you're in sight. Reminds me of a tiger, trying to decide if you're prey."

Narses' lips tightened, slightly. "He doesn't *know* anything. He only suspects."

"Just as I said. Trying to decide whether you're prey."

That was enough to make Narses scowl, although he still didn't look up from the board. "Why? Until he's sure he knows the truth, he won't do anything. He'd be too afraid to. And once he does discover the truth, why would he . . ."

His voice trailed off. Even Narses couldn't help but wince a little.

Ajatasutra chuckled again. "I will say you love playing with danger, old man. I'd never gamble at the odds you do. Yes, there's the chance that the fiercest warrior of Rajputana—not to mention its greatest king—might forgive you once he finds out that his

50

wife and children, whom he thought murdered by bandits, are alive and well. Then again—"

Ajatasutra cleared his throat. "He might be a bit peeved at the man who had them kidnapped in the first place and faked the murders."

Narses pointed to the chessboard. "*Check,* I said."

Smiling, Ajatasutra moved up a pawn to block the bishop. "Granted, you had them hidden in a safe place afterward. Even in a comfortable place. Granted, also, that the Malwa had ordered you to have them *actually* murdered, so looking at it from one angle you saved their lives. But, then again, that brings up the next problem. What will Lord Damodara—Malwa's best general and a blood relative of the emperor—"

"*Distant* relative," Narses growled.

"Not distant at all," the assassin pointed out mildly, "if your scheme works. And stop trying to change the subject. What will Damodara think when he discovers you corralled *his* wife into the kidnapping? And thereby put *his* children in mortal danger?"

Narses took the pawn with the bishop. "Mate in four moves. I didn't *corral* the woman into providing Sanga's family with a hideaway. That was Lady Damodara's idea in the first place."

"So? When all the rocks are turned over and your machinations exposed to the light of day, the fact remains that Damodara and Rana Sanga will discover that you manipulated and cajoled their wives into the riskiest conspiracy imaginable—and, unfortunately for you, both men dote on those wives."

Casually, Ajatasutra reached out and toppled his king. "I concede. So when the wives bat their eyelashes at their husbands and look demure—like only Indian women can do!—and insist that they were pawns in your hands, which way you do you think the lightning will strike?"

Finally, Narses looked up. His eyes were half-slits; which, as wrinkled as his face was anyway, made the eunuch look more like a reptile than usual. "And why are *you* so amused? I remind you that—every step of the way—it was *you* who did the actual work."

"True. Another game?" The assassin began setting up the pieces again. "But I'm in prime physical condition, and I made sure I've got the fastest horse in Bharakuccha. You aren't, and you didn't. That mule you favor probably couldn't outrun an ox, much less Rajput cavalry."

"I like mules." The board now set up—Narses playing the white pieces, this time—the eunuch advanced his queen's pawn. "And I've got no intention of running anyway, no matter how the lightning strikes."

The assassin cocked his head. "No? Why not?"

Narses looked aside, staring at a blank wall in the chambers he shared with Ajatasutra. All the walls in the palace suite were blank, except for those in the assassin's bedroom. The old eunuch liked it that way. He claimed that useless decorations impeded careful thought.

"Hard to explain. Call it my debt to Theodora, if you will."

Ajatasutra's eyebrows lifted. Although his gaze never left the wall, Narses sensed his puzzlement. "I betrayed her, you know, for the sake of gaining an empire."

"Yes, I was there. And?"

"And so now that I'm doing it again—"

"You're not betraying *her.*"

Narses waved his hand impatiently. "I'm not betraying my current employers, either. But I'm still gambling everything on the same game. The greatest game there is. The game of thrones."

The assassin waited. Sooner or later, the explanation would come. For all the eunuch's acerbic ways, Ajatasutra had become something of a son to him.

It took perhaps three minutes, during which time Narses' eyes never left the blank wall.

"You can't cheat forever," he said finally. "I'll win or I'll lose, but I won't run again. I owe that much to Theodora."

Ajatasutra looked at the same wall. There still wasn't anything there.

"I've been with you too long. That actually almost makes sense."

Narses smiled. "Don't forget to keep feeding your horse."

KAUSAMBI, THE MALWA CAPITAL
AT THE CONFLUENCE OF THE GANGES
AND YAMUNA RIVERS

Less than a week after his thirteenth birthday, Rajiv knew the worst despair and the two greatest epiphanies of his short life. One coming right after the other.

Gasping for breath, he lowered himself onto a stool in one of the cellars beneath Lady Damodara's palace. He could barely keep the wooden sword in his hand, his grip was so weak.

"I'll never match my father," he whispered, despairingly.

"Don't be an idiot," came the harsh voice of his trainer, the man he called the Mongoose. "Of course, you won't. A man as powerful as Rana Sanga doesn't come to a nation or tribe more than once a century."

"*Listen* to him, Rajiv," said his mother. She had watched this training session, as she had watched all of them, from her stool in a corner. With, as always, the stool surrounded by baskets into which she placed the prepared onions. Cutting onions relaxed the woman, for reasons no one else had ever been able to determine.

The epiphany came, then.

"*You* couldn't match him, either."

The narrow, weasel face of the Mongoose twisted with humor. "Of course I couldn't! Never thought to try—except, like a damn fool, at the very end."

Casually—not a trace of weakness in *that* grip—the Mongoose leaned his own imitation sword against a wall of the cellar. Then, with the same lean right hand, reached up and parted his coarse black hair. The scar beneath was quite visible. "Got that for trying."

Rajiv was as disturbed as he was exhilarated by his new-found wisdom. "I should stop . . ."

Almost angrily, his mother snapped: "Yes! Stop trying to imitate your father!" She pointed to the Mongoose with the short knife she used to cut onions. "Learn from *him*."

She went back to cutting onions. "You're not big enough. Never will be. Not so tall, not so strong. Maybe as fast, maybe not." The onion seemed to fly apart in her hand. "So what?"

Again, the knife, pointing like a finger. "Neither is he. But the Mongoose is still a legend."

The man so named chuckled. Harshly, as he did most things. "My name is Valentinian, and I'm just a soldier of Rome. I leave legends to those who believe in them. What I *know*, boy, is this. Learn from me instead of resisting me, and you'll soon enough gain your own fame. You're very good, actually. Especially for one so young."

Valentinian took the wooden sword back in his hand. "And now, you've rested enough. Back at it. And remember, this time—*small* strokes. Stop trying to fight as if you were a king of Rajputana. Fight like a miser hoarding his coins. Fight like me."

It was difficult. But Rajiv thought he made some progress, by the end of the session. He was finally beginning to understand— really understand—what made the Mongoose so dangerous. No wasted effort, no flamboyance, nothing beyond the bare minimum needed. But *that*—done perfectly.

The session finally over, the second epiphany came.

Rajiv stared at his mother. She was almost the opposite of his father. Where Rana Sanga was tall and mighty, she was short and plump. Where the father was still black-haired and handsome—had been, at least, until the Mongoose scarred his face in their famous duel—the mother was gray-haired and plain.

But he saw her. For the first time, really. As always, the baskets were now full—those to her right, of the prepared onions; those to her left, of the discarded peelings.

"This is how you cut onions."

"My boy too," she said calmly. "Yes. This is how I cut onions. And men are easier to cut than onions. If you don't think like a fool."

"Listen to your mother," said the Mongoose.

Later, in the evening, in the chamber they all used as a central salon, Valentinian complained with the same words. "Listen to your mother, you little brat!"

Baji gaped up at him cheerfully, in the manner of infants the world over. He said something more-or-less like: "Goo." Whatever the word meant, it was clearly not an indication that the infant

intended to obey his mother's instructions to stop pestering the
Roman soldier. In fact, Baji was tugging even more insistently
on his sleeve.

"What does he want, anyway?" Valentinian demanded.

"*Goo*," Baji explained.

Dhruva laughed. "You spoil him, Valentinian! That's why he
won't pay attention to me." She rose from her stool and came
over to pluck her infant son out of Valentinian's lap.

Baji started wailing instantly.

"Spoil him, I say."

Perched on his own stool in the chamber, and looking much
like a rhinoceros on the small item of furniture, Anastasius
started laughing. The sound came out of his huge chest like so
many rumbles.

Valentinian glared at his fellow Roman cataphract. "What's so
damn funny?"

"Do you really need to ask?"

Lady Damodara came into the room. After taking in the scene,
she smiled.

Valentinian transferred his glare to her. "You realize we're
almost certainly doomed? All of us." He pointed a stiff finger at
Baji, who was still wailing. "If we're lucky, they'll cut the brat's
throat first."

"Valentinian!" Dhruva exclaimed. "You'll scare him!"

"No such luck," the Roman cataphract muttered. "Might shut
him up. But the brat doesn't understand a word I'm saying."

He glared at Lady Damodara again. "Doomed," he repeated.

She shrugged. "There's a good chance, yes. But it's still a better chance than my husband would have had—and me and the
children—if we'd done nothing. Either you Romans would have
killed him because he wasn't a good enough general, or the
Emperor of Malwa would have killed him because he was. This
way there's at least a chance. A pretty good one, I think."

Valentinian wasn't mollified. "Narses and his damned schemes.
If I survive this, remind me to cut his throat." As piously as he
could, he added: "He's under a death sentence in Rome, you
know. The rotten traitor. Just be doing my duty."

Anastasius had never quite stopped rumbling little laughs.
Now, the rumbles picked up their pace. "Should have thought
of that sooner!"

There was no answer to that, of course. So Valentinian went back to glaring at the infant.

"And besides," Lady Damodara said, still smiling, "this way we have some entertainment. Dhruva, let your child go."

As pleasantly as the words were said, Lady Damodara was one of the great noblewomen of the Malwa empire. More closely related to the emperor, in fact, than her husband. So, whatever her misgivings, Dhruva obeyed.

Set back on the floor, Baji immediately began crawling toward Valentinian.

"Goo!" he said happily.

Still later, in the chamber they shared as a bedroom, Anastasius started rumbling again.

Not laughs, though. Worse. Philosophical musings.

"You know, Valentinian, if you'd stop being annoyed by these minor problems—"

"I kind of like the brat, actually," Valentinian admitted. He was lying on his bed, his hands clasped behind his head, staring at the ceiling.

"It'd be better to say you dote on the little creature." Anastasius chuckled. "But that's not even a minor problem. I was talking about the other things. You know—the danger of being discovered—hiding out the way we are here in their own capital city—swarmed by hordes of Ye-tai barbarians and other Malwa soldiers, flayed and impaled and God knows what else by maha-mimamsa torturers. Those problems."

Valentinian lifted his head. "You call those *minor* problems?"

"Philosophically speaking, yes."

"I *don't* want to hear—"

"Oh, stop whining." Anastasius sat up on his bed across the chamber and spread his huge hands. "If you refuse to consider the ontology of the situation, at least consider the practical aspect."

"What in God's name are you talking about?"

"It's obvious. One of two things happens. We fall prey to a minor problem, in which case we're flayed and impaled and gutted and God knows what else—but, for sure, we're dead. Follow me so far?"

Valentinian lowered his head, grunting. "An idiot can follow you so far. What's the point?"

"Or we *don't* fall prey to a minor problem. In which case, we survive the war. And *then* what? That's the real problem—the major problem—because that's the one that takes real thinking and years to solve."

Valentinian grunted again. "We retire on a pension, what else? If the general's still alive, he'll give us a good bonus, too. Enough for each of us to set up on a farm somewhere in . . ."

"In *Thrace?*" Anastasius rumbled another laugh. "Not even you, Valentinian! Much less me, half-Greek like I am and given to higher thoughts. Do you really want to spend the rest of your life raising pigs?"

Silence came from the other bed.

"What's so fascinating about that ceiling, anyway?" One of the huge hands waved about the chamber. "Look at the *rest* of it. We're in the servant quarters—the *old* servant quarters, in the rear of the palace—and it's still fancier than the house of the richest peasant in Thrace."

"So?"

"So why settle for a hut when we can retire to something like this?"

Anastasius watched Valentinian carefully, now. Saw how the eyes never left the ceiling, and the whipcord chest rose and fell with each breath.

"All right," Valentinian said finally. "All right. I've thought about it. But . . ."

"Why not? Who better than us? You know how these Hindus will look at it. The ones from a suitable class, anyway. The girls were rescued from a brothel. Nobody knows who the toddler's father is. Hopelessly polluted, both of them. The kid, too."

Valentinian scowled, at the last sentence.

More cheerfully still, seeing that scowl, Anastasius continued. "But we're just Thracian soldiers. What do we care about that crap? And—more to the point—who better for a father-in-law than the peshwa of Andhra?"

Valentinian's scowl only seemed to deepen. "What makes you think *he'd* be willing? The way they look at things, we're about as polluted as the girls."

"Exactly! That's what I meant, when I said you had to consider the ontological aspects of the matter. More to the point, consider this: who's going to insult the girls—or the kid—with him for a father and us for the husbands?"

Anastasius waited, serenely. It didn't take more than a minute or so before Valentinian's scowl faded away and, in its place, came the smile that had terrified so many men over the years. That lean, utterly murderous, weasel grin.

"Not too many. And they'll be dead. Right quick."

"You see?"

As easily and quickly as he could when he wanted to, Valentinian was sitting up straight. "All right. We'll do it."

Anastasius cocked his head a little. "Any problems with the philosophy of the matter?"

"What the hell does that—"

"The kid's a bastard and the girl's a former whore with a face scarred by a pimp. If any of that's a problem for you, I'll take her and you can have the other sister, Lata."

Valentinian hissed. "You stay the hell away from Dhruva."

"Guess not," said Anastasius placidly. "We have a deal. See how easy it is, when you apply philosophical reasoning?"

Chapter 6
THE NARMADA RIVER,
IN THE NORTHERN DECCAN

Lord Damodara reined in his horse and sat a little straighter in the saddle. Then, casually, swiveled his head back and forth as if he were working out the kinks in his neck. The gesture would seem natural enough, to anyone watching. They'd been riding along the Narmada river for hours, watching carefully for any sign of a Maratha ambush.

In fact, his neck *was* stiff, and the movement was pleasant. But the real reason Damodara did it was to make sure that no one else was within hearing range.

They weren't. Not even the twenty Rajputs serving as his immediate bodyguard, who were now halting their mounts also, and certainly not the thousand or so cavalrymen who followed them. More to the point, the three Mahaveda priests whom Nanda Lal had instructed to accompany Damodara today were at least a hundred yards back. When the patrol started, the priests had ridden just behind Damodara and Sanga. But the long ride—it was now early afternoon—had wearied them. They were not Rajput cavalrymen, accustomed to spending days in the saddle.

"Tell me, Rana Sanga," he said quietly.

The Rajput king sitting on a horse next to him frowned. "Tell you what, Lord? If you refer to the possibility of a Maratha ambush, there is none. I predicted as much before we even left Bharakuccha. Rao is playing a waiting game. As I would, in his position."

The Malwa general rubbed his neck. "I'm not talking about that, and you know it. I told you this morning that I knew perfectly well this patrol was a waste of time and effort. I ordered it—as you know perfectly well—to keep Nanda Lal from pestering me. Again."

Sanga smiled, thinly. "Nice to be away from him, isn't it?" He reached down and stroked his mount. As long as his arm was, that was an easy gesture. "I admit I prefer the company of horses to spymasters, myself."

Damodara would have chuckled, except the sight of that long and very powerful arm stroking a Rajput horse brought home certain realities. About Rajputs, and their horses—and the Malwa dynasty, and its spymasters.

"It is *time*, Sanga," he said, quietly but forcefully. "Tell me."

The Rajput kept stroking the horse, frowning again. "Lord, I don't . . ."

"You know what I'm talking about. I've raised it before, several times." Damodara sighed. "Perhaps a bit too subtly, I admit."

That brought a flicker of a smile to the Rajput's stern face. After a moment, Sanga sighed himself.

"You want to know why I have not seemed to be grieving much, these past months." The flickering smile came and went again. "And my references to philosophical consolations no longer satisfy you."

"Meaning no offense, King of Rajputana, but you are about as philosophically inclined as a tiger." Damodara snorted. "It might be better to say, have a tiger's philosophy. And you are *not* acting like a tiger. Certainly not an enraged one."

Sanga said nothing. Still stroking the horse, his eyes ranged across the Vindhya mountains that paralleled the river on its northern side. As if he were looking for any signs of ambush.

"Luckily," Damodara continued, "I don't think Nanda Lal suspects anything. He doesn't know you well enough. But I do—and I need to know. I . . . cannot wait, much longer. It is becoming too dangerous for me. I can sense it."

The Rajput king's face still had no expression beyond that thoughtful frown, but Damodara was quite certain he understood. Sanga kept as great a distance as possible from the inner workings of the Malwa empire, beyond its military affairs. But he was no fool; and, a king himself, he knew the realities of political maneuver. He was also one of the very few people, outside of the Malwa dynasty, who had communed directly with Malwa's hidden master. Or mistress, if one took the outer shell for what it was.

"I do not think my family is dead," Sanga said finally, speaking very softly. "I am not certain, but . . ."

Damodara closed his eyes. "As I suspected."

He almost added: *as I feared*. But did not, because Rana Sanga had become as close to him as Damodara had ever let a man become, and he would not wish that terrible grief on the Rajput.

Even if, most likely, that absence of grief meant that Damodara would soon enough be grieving the loss of his own family.

"Narses," he murmured, almost hissing the word. He opened his eyes. "Yes?"

Sanga nodded. "I am not certain, you understand. But . . . yes, Lord. I think Narses spirited them away. Then faked the evidence of the massacre."

Damodara scowled. "Faked *some* of the evidence, you mean. There were plenty of dead Ye-tai on the scene."

Sanga shrugged. "How else would Narses fake something? He is as dangerous as a cobra. A very old and wise cobra."

"So he is," agreed Damodara. "I've often thought that employing him was as perilous a business as using a cobra for a guard in my own chambers."

Again, he rubbed his neck. "On the other hand, I need such a guard. I think."

"Oh, yes. You do." Sanga left off his pointless scrutiny of the Vindhyas and twisted his head to the west, looking toward Bharakuccha. "You're far more likely to be ambushed back there, by Nanda Lal, than you are here by Raghunath Rao."

Since Damodara had long ago come to that same conclusion, he said nothing. No need to, really. There were no longer many secrets between him and Rana Sanga. They had campaigned together across central Asia and into Mesopotamia, winning every battle along the way, even against Belisarius. And had still lost the campaign, not through any fault of theirs but because Malwa had failed them.

In the upside-down world of the Malwa empire, his accomplishments placed him in greater peril than defeat would have done. Malwa feared excellent generals, in many ways, more than it did bad ones.

"We will return to Bharakuccha," Damodara announced. "This patrol is pointless, and I'd just as soon reach the city before nightfall."

Sanga nodded. He started to rein his horse around, but paused. "Lord. Remember. I swore an oath."

After Sanga was gone, Damodara stared sourly at the river. *Rajputs and their damned sacred oaths.*

But the thought came more from habit, than anything else. Damodara knew how to circumvent the oath that the Rajputs had given to the emperor of Malwa, swearing their eternal fealty. He'd figured it out long ago—and hadn't need any of Narses' hints to do so.

The thing was quite obvious, really, if a man was prepared to gamble everything on a single daring maneuver. The problem was that, military tactics aside, Damodara was by nature a cautious and conservative man.

Damn Narses!

That thought, too, after a moment, Damodara dismissed as simply old habit. True enough, the Roman eunuch was maneuvering Damodara, and doing so ruthlessly—and entirely for Narses' own purposes. The fact remained that he was probably wiser in doing so, than Damodara had been in hesitating. Could you curse a man who manipulated you in your own best interests?

Of course, you could—and Damodara did it again. *Damn Narses!*

But . . . Malwa remained. Malwa and its secret ruler. The greatest, the most powerful—and certainly the most venomous—cobra in the world. Next to which, even Narses was a small menace.

So, finally, on a dirt road next to the Narmada river, Malwa's greatest general made the decision that had been long years in the making.

Many things went into that decision.

First, that he knew himself to be caught in a trap, if he did nothing. If Malwa won the war, it was Damodara's assessment that he himself would be eliminated as too dangerously capable. Most likely, however—another assessment, and one that he was growing ever more sure about—the war would *not* be won. In which case, Damodara would join in the general destruction of the dynasty.

Second, his fears for his family. Either of those two outcomes—certainly the first—would result in their destruction also. In the event of a Roman victory, Damodara did not think that the victors would target his family. But that meant nothing. In the chaos of a collapsing Malwa empire, rebellions were sure to erupt all over India—and all of them would be murderous toward anyone associated with the Malwa dynasty. The likelihood that Damodara's wife and children would survive that carnage was almost nil.

Third, and finally—and in some ways, most of all—Damodara was sick and tired of Malwa's secret overlord. Looking back over the years of his life, he could see now that the superhuman intelligence from the future was . . .

An idiot. A beast and a monster, too. But most of all, just an arrogant, blithering, drooling idiot.

Damodara remembered the one conversation he'd had with Belisarius, and the Roman general's musings on the folly of seeking perfection. He'd thought, at the time, that he agreed with the Roman. Now, he was certain of it.

So, he came to his decision.

Damn all new gods and their schemes.

He might have added: *Damn Malwa.* But, given his future prospects—if he had any—that would be quite absurd. From this moment forward, Damodara and his family would only survive insofar as he *was* Malwa.

He spent the rest of the ride back to the city convincing himself of that notion. It was not easy. The inner core of Damodara that had kept him sane since he was a boy was laughing at himself all the way.

Once the patrol returned to Bharakuccha, just after sunset, Damodara went immediately to Narses' chambers. The Malwa general made no attempt to hide his movements. Nanda Lal would surely have spies watching him, but so what? Damodara regularly consulted with Narses, and always did so openly. To have begun creeping about would raise suspicions.

"Yes, Lord?" Narses asked, after politely ushering Damodara into the inner chamber where they always discussed their affairs. In that chamber—for a certainty—Nanda Lal's spies could overhear nothing. "Some wine? Food?"

The old eunuch indicated a nearby chair, the most luxurious in the chamber. "Please, be seated."

Damodara ignored him. He was carefully studying the third man in the room, the hawk-faced assassin named Ajatasutra who had been Narses' chief associate since the failure of the Nika revolt in Constantinople.

"Do I want to ask him to leave, Narses?" Damodara asked abruptly.

The question brought a sudden stillness to the room. Along with a tightness to Narses' expression, and—perhaps oddly—a little smile to the face of the assassin.

Damodara waited. And waited.

Finally, Narses replied. "No, Lord, I think not. Ajatasutra can answer all your questions. Better than I can, actually, because..."

"He's been there. Yes." Damodara's eyes had never left the assassin. "My next question. Do I *need* to ask him to leave?"

For the first time since he entered the room, he glanced at Narses. "Or would it be wiser for me to summon Rana Sanga? For my protection."

Seeing Narses' little wince, Damodara issued a curt little laugh. "Not looking forward to that, are you? I thought not." He turned his gaze back to the assassin. "Well, then. Perhaps three other Rajputs."

Ajatasutra's thin smile widened. "Unless one of them is Jaimal or Udai, I'd recommend four. Five would be wiser. However..."

Gracefully, Ajatasutra slid off his chair. Then, to the Malwa general's surprise, went down on one knee. From nowhere, a dagger appeared. Flipped easily and now held by the tip, Ajatasutra laid the blade across his extended left forearm, offering the weapon's hilt to Damodara.

"There is no need for Rajputs, Lord of Malwa." There was not a trace of humor in the assassin's tone of voice, and the smile was gone. "This blade is at your service. I have served Malwa faithfully since I was a boy. Never more so than now."

Damodara studied the man, for a moment. A quick decision was needed here.

He made it. Then, reached out and barely touched the dagger hilt with the tip of his fingers.

"Keep the weapon. And now, Ajatasutra, tell me of my family. And Rana Sanga's."

Narses was fidgeting a bit. Smiling as thinly as the assassin had done, Damodara murmured to him: "I shall stand, I think. But perhaps you should be seated. Have some food. Some wine. Now that the assassin's blade is sworn to me, it may be your last meal."

Ajatasutra barked a laugh. "Ha! Like cutting an old crocodile's neck. Take me an hour, afterward, to sharpen the edge properly."

Narses scowled at him. But he took a seat—and some wine. No food. Perhaps his appetite was missing.

By the time the assassin had finished his report, and answered all of Damodara's questions, the Malwa general was seated on the luxurious chair. Seated on it, his neck perched against the backrest, and staring at the ceiling.

"Guarded by the Mongoose, no less," he murmured. "The arms trainer for a Rajput prince, no less. Narses, were this a fable told to me by a story-teller, I should have him discharged for incompetence."

Wisely, Narses said nothing.

Damodara rubbed his face with a hand. Once, both the hand and the face had been pudgy. Two years of campaigning had removed most of the general's fat. Along with much else.

"The moment I move, my family—Sanga's too, once they're discovered—are as good as dead. May I presume that among all these other incredibly intricate schemes, you have given *some* thought to that problem?"

There was little visible sign of it, but Damodara could sense Narses relaxing. As well he might. That last question made clear that he'd survive this night.

"Quite a bit more than 'some.' First—meaning no offense, Lord—it is not true that 'the moment you move' anything will happen. Kausambi is hundreds of miles and a mountain range away from here. Great Lady Sati and the main Malwa army are in the Punjab, still farther than that."

"Telegraph," Damodara stated. "And, now, the new radio."

"Seven of the nine telegraph operators in Bharakuccha are mine. In the event the eighth or ninth are on duty, I have men ready to cut the wires. I'd rather not, of course. That would itself be a signal that something is amiss. They wouldn't assume rebellion, simply Maratha marauders. But a patrol would be sent out to investigate."

Damodara waved his hand impatiently. "I have Rajputs to deal with patrols. But I, also, would rather not have the little problem."

Narses glanced at Ajatasutra.

"All I need is to know the day," the assassin said calmly. "Not even that. A three-day stretch will do. Nanda Lal will be suspicious regarding the unfortunate deaths, of course, but won't have time to do anything about it."

Damodara nodded. "I can manage the three days. That still leaves the radio."

Narses smiled. "The radio station is guarded by Ye-tai. A special detachment—chosen by Toramana and under his direct authority."

Damodara brought his gaze down from the ceiling. "Toramana..." he mused. "Despite his upcoming marriage to Rana Sanga's half-sister Indira, can we really trust him?"

"Trust him?" Narses shrugged. "No, of course not. Toramana's only real loyalty is to his own ambition. But we can trust *that.*"

Damodara frowned. "Why are you so certain his ambition will lead him to us? Nanda Lal is just as aware of the implications of Toramana's marriage to a Rajput princess as we are. Yet he seems completely confident in Toramana's loyalty. Even to the point of insisting that I place Toramana in charge of the city's security, whenever I leave Bharakuccha."

"Lord..." Narses hesitated. "Forgive me, but you are still too much the Malwa."

"Meaning?"

"Meaning that you are still a bit infected—pardon me for the term—with that unthinking Malwa arrogance. Your dynasty has been in power too long, too easily, and with..."

The eunuch let the sentence trail off. For an instant, his eyes seemed to move, as if he had started to glance at Ajatasutra and stopped himself.

Damodara understood the significance of that little twitch of the eyes. Narses, other than Rana Sanga and Belisarius, was the only human being not a member of the Malwa dynastic family who had had direct contact with Link, the cybernetic organism who was the Malwa empire's secret overlord and provided the dynasty with its ultimate source of power.

And—yes, its ultimate source of arrogance.

Damodara pondered Narses' words, for a moment. Then, decided the eunuch was probably right. It would be fittingly ironic if a dynasty raised and kept in power by a superhuman intelligence should fall, in the end, because that same power made the dynasty itself stupid.

Not stupid, perhaps, so much as unseeing. Nanda Lal, for instance, was extremely intelligent. But he had been so powerful, and so feared, and for so long, that he had grown blind to the fact that there was other power—and that not all men feared him.

"What are Toramana's terms?" he asked abruptly. "And do not irritate me by pretending you haven't already discussed it with him. Your life is still hanging by a thread, Narses."

"Nothing complicated. A high position for himself, of course. Acceptance of his ties to the Rajputs through his upcoming marriage. Beyond that, while he does not expect the Ye-tai to continue to enjoy the same special privileges, he wants some guarantees that they will not be savaged."

Damodara cocked his head. "I shouldn't think he'd care about that, if he's solely driven by his own ambitions."

Narses looked uncomfortable, for a moment. "Lord, I doubt if there is any man who is *solely* driven by ambition." His lips grew twisted. "Not even me."

Ajatasutra spoke. "Toramana still has his clan ties, Lord. They wear lightly on him, true, but they exist. Beyond that . . ."

The assassin lifted his shoulders, in a movement too slight to be really considered a shrug. "If the Ye-tai are singled out for destruction, how long could a single Ye-tai general remain in favor? No matter what his formal post."

"True." Damodara thought about the problem, for a time. The chamber was silent while he did so.

"All right," he said finally. "It would be ridiculous to say that I'm happy with your plan. But . . . it seems as good as any. That leaves Rao, and his Marathas."

Now that the discussion had returned to the matter of war, a subject on which Damodara was an expert, the Malwa general sat up straight.

"Three things are needed. First, I need to extract the army from Bharakuccha. It's one thing for me to begin the rebellion—"

"Please, Lord!" Narses interrupted, raising his hand. "The restoration of the rightful emperor to his proper place." He waved the hand negligently. "I assure you that I have all the needed documentation—not here, of course—to satisfy any scholar on the matter."

Damodara stared at him. The eunuch's face was serene, sure, certain. To all appearances, Narses thought he was speaking nothing but the solemn truth.

The general barked a laugh. "So! Fine. As I was saying, it's one thing for me to begin the—ah—*restoration* with the army in the field. The men in their ranks, the officers at their head. Quite another to try to launch it here, with the men scattered all over the city in billets."

Narses nodded. So did Ajatasutra.

"Second—leading directly from that—I need to draw out Rao."

Narses grimaced. "Lord, even if you could get Rao out of Deogiri . . . the casualties . . . you really need your army intact—"

"Oh, be silent, you old schemer. Leave matters of war to me. I said '*draw* him out.' I said nothing of fighting a battle. First, because I need that excuse to pull the entire army out of Bharakuccha. Second, because I will need to make a quick settlement with the Marathas. I can't start a new war without ending *this* one."

Hearing a little cough from Ajatasutra, Damodara looked at him.

The assassin waggled his hand. "A single combat. Rao against Rana Sanga. All of India has been waiting for years to see that match again."

Narses frowned. "Why in the name of—"

"Quiet, Narses." Damodara pondered the notion, for a moment.

"Yes . . . That might very well work." He eyed Ajatasutra intently. "With the right envoy, of course."

Despite the command, Narses could no longer restrain himself. "Why in the name of God would Rao be so stupid as to accept such an idiotic proposal as—"

The eunuch's jaws almost literally snapped shut. "Oh," he concluded.

Ajatasutra's thin smile came. "No one has ever suggested that Raghunath Rao was stupid. Which is precisely the point."

He gave Damodara a little nod. "I will take the message."

"You understand—"

"Yes, Lord. Nothing may be said directly. Rao will do as he will."

Damodara nodded. "Good enough. If it doesn't work, so be it. Then, the third thing I need. We will have to secure Bharakuccha instantly, when the time comes. I can't afford a siege, either. Once the rebellion—ah, restoration—begins, I'll have to cross the Vindhyas and march on Kausambi immediately. If I can't reach and take the capital before Sati and whatever forces she brings arrives from the Punjab, there's no chance. Even for me, much less my family."

Narses frowned. "Lord, I am sure I can get your family out of Kausambi before Emperor Skandagupta—ah, the false emperor—realizes they're gone. Why take the risk of a hasty assault on the city? Kausambi's defenses are the greatest in the world."

"Do not teach me warfare, spymaster," Damodara stated flatly. "Do *not*. You think I should launch a rebellion—let's call things by their right name, shall we?—in one of the provinces. And then what? Years of civil war that shreds the empire, while the Romans and the Persians wait to pick up the pieces. Of which there won't be many."

Damodara rubbed his face. "No. I have never been able to forget Ranapur. There are times I wake up in the middle of the night, shaking. I will not visit twenty Ranapurs upon India."

"But . . . Lord . . ."

"Enough!" Damodara rose to his feet. "Understand this, Narses. What a general can do, an emperor cannot. I will succeed or I will fail, but I will do so as an emperor. There will be no further discussion on the matter."

"Be quiet, old man," Ajatasutra murmured coldly.

He rose to his feet and gave Damodara a very deep bow. "Lord of Malwa. Let us do the thing like an assassin, not a torturer."

Chapter 7
CHARAX, ON THE PERSIAN GULF

"I *can't*," said Dryopus firmly. Anna glared at him, but the Roman official in charge of the great port city of Charax was quite impervious to her anger. His next words were spoken in the patient tone of one addressing an unruly child.

"Lady Saronites, if I allowed you to continue on this—" He paused, obviously groping for a term less impolite than *insane*. "—headstrong project of yours, it'd be worth my career."

He picked up a letter lying on the great desk in his headquarters. "This is from your father, demanding that you be returned to Constantinople under guard."

"My father has no authority over me!"

"No, he doesn't." Dryopus shook his head. "But your husband Calopodius *does*. Without his authorization, I simply can't allow you to continue. I certainly can't detail a ship to take you to Barbaricum."

Anna clenched her jaws. Her eyes went to the nearby window. She couldn't see the harbor from here, but she could visualize it easily enough. The Roman soldiers who had all-but-formally arrested her when she and her small party arrived in the great port city of Charax on the Persian Gulf had marched her past it on their way to Dryopus' palace.

For a moment, wildly, she thought of appealing to the Persians who were now in official control of Charax. But the notion died as soon as it came. The Aryans were even more strict than Romans when it came to the independence of women. Besides—

Dryopus seemed to read her thoughts. "I should note that *all* shipping in Charax is under Roman military law. So there's no point in your trying to go around me. No ship captain will take your money, anyway. Not without a permit issued by my office."

He dropped her father's letter back onto the desk. "I'm sorry, but there's nothing else for it. If you wish to continue, you will have to get your husband's permission."

"He's all the way up the Indus," she said angrily. "And there's no telegraph communication between here and there."

Dryopus shrugged. "No, there isn't—and it'll be some time before the new radio system starts working. But there is a telegraph line between Barbaricum and the Iron Triangle. And by now the new line connecting Barbaricum and the harbor at Chabahari may be completed. You'll still have to wait until I can get a ship there—and another to bring back the answer. Which won't be quickly, now that the winter monsoon has started. I'll have to use a galley, whenever the first one leaves—and I'm *not* sending a galley just for this purpose."

Anna's mind raced through the problem. On their way down the Euphrates, Illus had explained to her the logic of travel between Mesopotamia and India. He'd had plenty of time to do so. The river voyage through Mesopotamia down to the port at Charax had taken much longer than Anna had expected, mainly because of the endless delays caused by Persian officials. She'd expected to be in Charax by late October. Instead, they were now halfway into December.

During the winter monsoon season, which began in November, it was impossible for sailing craft to make it to Barbaricum. Taking advantage of the relatively sheltered waters of the Gulf, on the other hand, they could make it as far as Chabahari—which was the reason the Roman forces in India had been working so hard to get a telegraph line connecting Chabahari and the Indus.

So if she could get as far as Chabahari . . . She'd still have to wait, but if Calopodius' permission came she wouldn't be wasting weeks here in Mesopotamia.

"Allow me to go as far as Chabahari then," she insisted.

Dryopus started to frown. Anna had to fight to keep from screaming in frustration.

"Put me under guard, if you will!"

Dryopus sighed, lowered his head, and ran his fingers through thinning hair. "He's not likely to agree, you know," he said softly.

"He's my husband, not yours," pointed out Anna. "You don't know how he thinks." She didn't see any reason to add: *no more than I do.*

His head still lowered, Dryopus chuckled. "True enough. With that young man, it's always hard to tell."

He raised his head and studied her carefully. "Are you *that* besotted with him? That you insist on going into the jaws of the greatest war in history?"

"He's my *husband*," she replied, not knowing what else to say.

Again, he chuckled. "You remind me of Antonina, a bit. Or Irene."

Anna was confused for a moment, until she realized he was referring to Belisarius' wife and the Roman Empire's former head of espionage, Irene Macrembolitissa. Famous women, now, the both of them. One of them had even become a queen herself.

"I don't know either one," she said quietly. Which was true enough, even though she'd read everything ever written by Macrembolitissa. "So I couldn't say."

Dryopus studied her a bit longer. Then his eyes moved to her bodyguards, who had been standing as far back in a corner as possible.

"You heard?"

Illus nodded.

"Can I trust you?" he asked.

Illus' shoulders heaved a bit, as if he were suppressing a laugh. "No offense, sir—but if it's worth *your* career, just imagine the price *we'd* pay." His tone grew serious: "We'll see to it that she doesn't, ah, escape on her own."

Dryopus nodded and looked back at Anna. "All right, then. As far as Chabahari."

On their way to the inn where Anna had secured lodgings, Illus shook his head. "If Calopodius says 'no,' you realize you'll have wasted a lot of time and money."

"He's my *husband*," replied Anna firmly. Not knowing what else to say.

THE IRON TRIANGLE

After the general finished reading Anna's message, and the accompanying one from Dryopus, he invited Calopodius to sit down at the table in the command bunker.

"I knew you were married," said Belisarius, "but I know none of the personal details. So tell me."

Calopodius hesitated. He was deeply reluctant to involve the general in the petty minutiae of his own life. In the little silence that fell over them, within the bunker, Calopodius could hear the artillery barrages. As was true day and night, and had been for many weeks, the Malwa besiegers of the Iron Triangle were shelling the Roman fortifications—and the Roman gunners were responding with counter-battery fire. The fate of the world would be decided here in the Punjab, Calopodius thought, some time over the next year or so. That, and the whole future of the human race. It seemed absurd—grotesque, even—to waste the Roman commander's time . . .

"Tell me," repeated Belisarius. For all their softness, Calopodius could easily detect the tone of command in the words.

Still, he hesitated.

Belisarius chuckled. "Be at ease, young man. I can spare the time for this. In truth—" Calopodius could sense, if not see, the little gesture by which the general expressed a certain ironic weariness. "I would enjoy it, Calopodius. War is a means, not an end. It would do my soul good to talk about ends, for a change."

That was enough to break Calopodius' resistance.

"I really don't know her very well, sir. We'd only been married for a short time before I left to join your army. It was—"

He fumbled for the words. Belisarius provided them.

"A marriage of convenience. Your wife's from the Melisseni family."

Calopodius nodded. With his acute hearing, he could detect

the slight sound of the general scratching his chin, as he was prone to do when thinking.

"An illustrious family," stated Belisarius. "One of the handful of senatorial families which can actually claim an ancient pedigree without paying scribes to fiddle with the historical records. But a family which has fallen on hard times financially."

"My father said they wouldn't even have a pot to piss in if their creditors ever really descended on them." Calopodius sighed. "Yes, General. An illustrious family, but now short of means. Whereas my family, as you know . . ."

"The Saronites. Immensely wealthy, but with a pedigree that needs a *lot* of fiddling."

Calopodius grinned. "Go back not more than three generations, and you're looking at nothing but commoners. Not in the official records, of course. My father can afford a *lot* of scribes."

"That explains your incredible education," mused Belisarius. "I had wondered, a bit. Not many young noblemen have your command of language and the arts."

Calopodius heard the scrape of a chair as the general stood up. Then, heard him begin to pace about. That was another of Belisarius' habits when he was deep in thought. Calopodius had heard him do it many times, over the past weeks. But he was a bit astonished that the general was giving the same attention to this problem as he would to a matter of strategy or tactics.

"Makes sense, though," continued Belisarius. "For all the surface glitter—and don't think the Persians don't make plenty of sarcastic remarks about it—the Roman aristocracy will overlook a low pedigree as long as the 'nobleman' is wealthy *and* well educated. Especially—as you are—in grammar and rhetoric."

"I can drop three Homeric and biblical allusions into any sentence," Calopodius said, chuckling.

"I've noticed!" The general laughed. "That official history you're writing of my campaigns would serve as a Homeric and biblical commentary as well." He paused a moment. "Yet I notice that you don't do it in your *Dispatches to the Army.*"

"It'd be a waste," said Calopodius, shrugging. "Worse than that, really. I write those for the morale of the soldiers, most of whom would just find the allusions confusing. Besides, those are really *your* dispatches, not mine. And you don't talk that way, certainly not to your soldiers."

"They're *not* my dispatches, young man. They're yours. I approve them, true, but you write them. And when they're read aloud by my son to the Senate, Photius presents them as *Calopodius'* dispatches, not mine."

Calopodius was startled into silence.

"You didn't know? My son is eleven years old, and quite literate. And since he *is* the Emperor of Rome, even if Theodora still wields the actual power, he insists on reading them to the Senate. He's very fond of your dispatches. Told me in his most recent letter that they're the only things he reads which don't bore him to tears. His tutors, of course, don't approve."

Calopodius was still speechless. Again, Belisarius laughed. "You're quite famous, lad." Then, more softly, almost sadly: "I can't give you back your eyes, Calopodius. But I *can* give you the fame you wanted when you came to me. I promised you I would."

The sound of his pacing resumed. "In fact, unless I miss my guess, those *Dispatches* of yours will someday—centuries from now—be more highly regarded than your official history of the war." Calopodius heard a very faint noise, and guessed the general was stroking his chest, where the jewel from the future named Aide lay nestled in his pouch. "I have it on good authority that historians of the future will prefer straight narrative to flowery rhetoric. And—in my opinion, at least—you write straightforward narrative even better than you toss off classical allusions."

The chair scraped as the general resumed his seat. "But let's get back to the problem at hand. In essence, your marriage was arranged to lever your family into greater respectability, and to provide the Melisseni—discreetly, of course—a financial rescue. How did you handle the dowry, by the way?"

Calopodius shrugged. "I'm not certain. My family's so wealthy that a dowry's not important. For the sake of appearances, the Melisseni provided a large one. But I suspect my father *loaned* them the dowry—and then made arrangements to improve the Melisseni's economic situation by linking their own fortunes to those of our family." He cleared his throat. "All very discreetly, of course."

Belisarius chuckled dryly. "Very discreetly. And how did the Melisseni react to it all?"

Calopodius shifted uncomfortably in his chair. "Not well, as you'd expect. I met Anna for the first time three days after my father informed me of the prospective marriage. It was one of those carefully rehearsed 'casual visits.' She and her mother arrived at my family's villa near Nicodemia."

"Accompanied by a small army of servants and retainers, I've no doubt."

Calopodius smiled. "Not such a small army. A veritable host, it was." He cleared his throat. "They stayed for three days, that first time. It was very awkward for me. Anna's mother—her name's Athenais—barely even tried to disguise her contempt for me and my family. I think she was deeply bitter that their economic misfortunes were forcing them to seek a husband for their oldest daughter among less illustrious but much wealthier layers of the nobility."

"And Anna herself?"

"Who knows? During those three days, Anna said little. In the course of the various promenades which we took through the grounds of the Saronites estate—God, talk about chaperones!—she seemed distracted to the point of being almost rude. I couldn't really get much of a sense of her, General. She seemed distressed by something. Whether that was her pending marriage to me, or something else, I couldn't say."

"And you didn't much care. Be honest."

"True. I'd known for years that any marriage I entered would be purely one of convenience." He shrugged. "At least my bride-to-be was neither unmannerly nor uncomely. In fact, from what I could determine at the time—which wasn't much, given the heavy scaramangium and headdress and the elaborate cosmetics under which Anna labored—she seemed quite attractive."

He shrugged again. "So be it. I was seventeen, General." For a moment, he hesitated, realizing how silly that sounded. He was only a year older than that now, after all, even if . . .

"You were a boy then; a man, now," filled in Belisarius. "The world looks very different after a year spent in the carnage. I know. But then—"

Calopodius heard the general's soft sigh. "Seventeen years old. With the war against Malwa looming ever larger in the life of the Roman Empire, the thoughts of a vigorous boy like yourself were fixed on feats of martial prowess, not domestic bliss."

"Yes. I'd already made up my mind. As soon as the wedding was done—well, and the marriage consummated—I'd be joining your army. I didn't even see any reason to wait to make sure that I'd provided an heir. I've got three younger brothers, after all, every one of them in good health."

Again, silence filled the bunker and Calopodius could hear the muffled sounds of the artillery exchange. "Do you think that's why she was so angry at me when I told her I was leaving? I didn't really think she'd care."

"Actually, no. I think . . ." Calopodius heard another faint noise, as if the general were picking up the letters lying on the table. "There's this to consider. A wife outraged by abandonment—or glad to see an unwanted husband's back—would hardly be taking these risks to find him again."

"Then why is she doing it?"

"I doubt if she knows. Which is really what this is all about, I suspect." He paused; then: "She's only a year older than you, I believe."

Calopodius nodded. The general continued. "Did you ever wonder what an eighteen-year-old girl wants from life? Assuming she's high-spirited, of course—but judging from the evidence, your Anna is certainly that. Timid girls, after all, don't race off on their own to find a husband in the middle of a war zone."

Calopodius said nothing. After a moment, Belisarius chuckled. "Never gave it a moment's thought, did you? Well, young man, I suggest the time has come to do so. And not just for your own sake."

The chair scraped again as the general rose. "When I said I knew nothing about the details of your marriage, I was fudging a bit. I didn't know anything about what you might call the 'inside' of the thing. But I knew quite a bit about the 'outside' of it. This marriage is important to the Empire, Calopodius."

"Why?"

The general clucked his tongue reprovingly. "There's more to winning a war than tactics on the battlefield, lad. You've also got to keep an eye—always—on what a future day will call the 'home front.'" Calopodius heard him resume his pacing. "You can't be *that* naïve. You must know that the Roman aristocracy is not very fond of the dynasty."

"*My* family is," protested Calopodius.

"Yes. Yours—and most of the newer rich families. That's because their wealth comes mainly from trade and commerce. The war—all the new technology Aide's given us—has been a blessing to you. But it looks very different from the standpoint of the old landed families. You know as well as I do—you *must* know—that it was those families who supported the Nika insurrection a few years ago. Fortunately, most of them had enough sense to do it at a distance."

Calopodius couldn't help wincing. And what he wasn't willing to say, the general was. Chuckling, oddly enough.

"The Melisseni came *that* close to being arrested, Calopodius. Arrested—the whole family—and all their property seized. If Anna's father Nicephorus had been even slightly less discreet . . . The truth? His head would have been on a spike on the wall of the Hippodrome, right next to that of John of Cappadocia's. The only thing that saved him was that he *was* discreet enough—barely—and the Melisseni are one of the half-dozen most illustrious families of the Empire."

"I didn't know they were that closely tied . . ."

Calopodius sensed Belisarius' shrug. "We were able to keep it quiet. And since then, the Melisseni seem to have retreated from any open opposition. But we were delighted—I'm speaking of Theodora and Justinian and myself, and Antonina for that matter—when we heard about your marriage. Being tied closely to the Saronites will inevitably pull the Melisseni into the orbit of the dynasty. Especially since—as canny as your father is—they'll start getting rich themselves from the new trade and manufacture."

"Don't tell them that!" barked Calopodius. "Such work is for plebeians."

"They'll change their tune, soon enough. And the Melisseni are very influential among the older layers of the aristocracy."

"I understand your point, General." Calopodius gestured toward the unseen table, and the letters atop it. "So what do you want me to do? Tell Anna to come to the Iron Triangle?"

Calopodius was startled by the sound of Belisarius' hand slapping the table. "Damn fool! It's time you put that splendid mind of yours to work on *this*, Calopodius. A marriage—if it's to work—needs grammar and rhetoric also."

"I don't understand," said Calopodius timidly.

"I know you don't. So will you follow my advice?"

"Always, General."

Belisarius chuckled. "You're more confident than I am! But . . ."
After a moment's pause: "Don't *tell* her to do anything, Calopodius. Send Dryopus a letter explaining that your wife has your permission to make her own decision. And send Anna a letter saying the same thing. I'd suggest . . ."

Another pause. Then: "Never mind. That's for you to decide."

In the silence that followed, the sound of artillery came to fill the bunker again. It seemed louder, perhaps. "And that's enough for the moment, young man. I'd better get in touch with Maurice. From the sound of things, I'd say the Malwa are getting ready for another probe."

Calopodius wrote the letters immediately thereafter, dictating them to his scribe. The letter to Dryopus took no time at all. Neither did the one to Anna, at first. But Calopodius, for reasons he could not determine, found it difficult to find the right words to conclude. Grammar and rhetoric seemed of no use at all.

In the end, moved by an impulse which confused him, he simply wrote:

Do as you will, Anna. For myself, I would like to see you again.

Chapter 8
BHARAKUCCHA

The day after his meeting with Narses, Damodara went to the chambers occupied by Nanda Lal, in a different wing of the great palace. Politely, he waited outside for permission to enter. Politely, because Damodara was now officially the Goptri of the Deccan; and thus, in a certain sense, the entire palace might be said to be his personal property.

But there was no point in being rude. Soon enough, the chief spymaster of the Malwa empire emerged from his private chambers.

"Yes, Damodara?" he asked. Not bothering, as usual, to preface the curt remark with the general's honorifics.

Nanda Lal seemed to treasure such little snubs. It was the only sign of outright stupidity Damodara had ever seen him exhibit.

"I have decided to take the field against Rao and his rebels," Damodara announced. "Within a month, I think."

"At last! I am glad to hear it. But why move now, after . . . ?" He left the rest unstated. *After you have resisted my advice to do so for so long?*

"The army is ready, well enough. I see no reason to wait until we are well into *garam* season. As it is, we'll be campaigning through the heat anyway. But I'd like to end the business, if possible, before the southwest monsoon comes."

Above the lumpy, broken nose that Belisarius had given him,

years ago, Nanda Lal's dark eyes were fixed on Damodara. The gaze was not quite suspicious, but very close.

"You still lack the heavy siege guns—that *you* have insisted for months are essential to reducing Deogiri."

Damodara shrugged again. "I don't intend to besiege Deogiri. It is my belief that Rao will come forth from the city to meet me on the field of battle. I sense that he has grown arrogant."

Nanda Lal turned his head, peering at Damodara from the side of his eyes. The suspicion had come to the surface now. "You 'sense'? Why? I have gotten no such indications from my spies."

Damodara decided it was time to put an end to courtesy. He returned the spymaster's sideways look with a flat, cold stare of his own. "Neither you nor your spies are warriors. I am. So it is my sense—not yours—which will guide me in this matter."

He looked away, as if indifferent. "And I am also the Goptri of the Deccan. Not you, and certainly not your spies. The decision is made, Nanda Lal." Casually, he added: "I presume you will wish to accompany the expedition."

Tightly, Nanda Lal replied: "You presume incorrectly. I shall remain here in Bharakuccha. And I will insist that you leave Toramana and his Ye-tais here with me." After a brief pause, in a slightly more conciliatory tone, he added, "To maintain the city's security."

Damodara's eyes continued to rove casually about the corridors of the palace, as if he were looking for security threats—and finding none.

"You may have half the Ye-tai force," he said at length, dismissively. "That's more than enough to maintain security. But I will leave you Toramana in command, even though I could certainly use him myself."

That night, as soon as it was dark, Ajatasutra slipped out of the city. He had no great difficulty with the task, as many times as he'd done it. Would have had no difficulty at all, except that he was also smuggling out the fastest horse in Bharakuccha.

The horse was too good to risk breaking one of its legs riding on rough Deccan roads with only a sliver of a crescent moon to see by. So, once far enough from the city, Ajatasutra made camp for the night.

It was a comfortable camp. As it should have been, since

he'd long used the site for the purpose and had a cache already supplied.

He slept well, too. Woke very early, and was on his way south to Deogiri before the sun rose.

By mid-morning, he was in excellent spirits. There still remained the not-so-minor problem of avoiding a Maratha ambush, of course. But Ajatasutra was sanguine with regard to that matter, for the good and simple reason that he had no intention of attempting that difficult feat in the first place.

All he had to do was not get killed when the Maratha caught him by surprise. Which, they probably would. With the possible— no, probable—exception of Raghunath Rao, Ajatasutra thought he was the best assassin in India. But the skills of an assassin, though manifold, do not automatically include expertise at laying or avoiding ambushes in broken country like Majarashtra.

No matter. He thought it unlikely that the Marathas would kill a single man outright. It was much more likely they would try to capture him—a task which they would find supremely easy since he intended to put up no resistance at all.

Thereafter, the letter he carried should do the rest.

Well . . . It would certainly get him an audience with the Empress of Andhra and her consort. It was also possible, of course, that the audience would be followed by his execution.

Ajatasutra was not unduly concerned over that matter either, however. A man who manages to become the second best assassin in India is not, in the nature of things, given to fretfulness.

The ambush came later than he expected, a full three days after he left Bharakuccha and long after he'd penetrated into the highlands of the Great Country. On the other hand, it did indeed come as a complete surprise.

"That was very well done," he complimented his ambushers, seeing a dozen of them popping up around him. "I wouldn't have thought a lizard could have hidden in those rocks."

He complimented them again after four of them seized him and hauled him off the horse, albeit a bit more acerbically. The lads went about the task with excessive enthusiasm.

"No need for all that, I assure you!"

He's got a dagger, Captain!

"Three, actually. There's another in my right boot and a small one tucked between my shoulder blades. If you'll permit to rise just a bit—no?—then you'll have to roll me over to get it."

He's got three daggers, Captain! One of them's a throwing knife! He's an assassin!

A flurry of harsh questions followed.

"Well, yes, of course I'm an assassin. Who else would be idiotic enough to ride alone and openly through Maratha territory? But you may rest assured that I was not on my way to make an attempt on Rao's life. I have a letter for him. For the empress, actually."

A flurry of harsher accusations followed.

"Oh, that's nonsense. If I wanted to assassinate the empress, I'd hardly use a blade for the purpose. With Rao himself to guard her? No, no, poison's the thing. I've studied Shakuntala's habits, from many spy reports, and her great weakness is that she refuses to use a food-taster."

A flurry of still harsher proposals followed. They began with impalement and worked their way down from there.

Fortunately, by the time they got to the prospect of flaying the assassin alive, the captain of the Maratha squad had finally taken Ajatasutra's advice to look in his *left* boot.

"See? I told you I was carrying a letter for the empress."

There came, then, the only awkward moment of the day.

None of them could read.

"And here I took the time and effort to provide a Marathi translation, along with the Hindi," sighed Ajatasutra. "I'm an idiot. Too much time spent in palaces. Ah . . . I don't suppose you'd just take my word for it?"

A very long flurry of very harsh ridicule followed. But, in the end, the Maratha hillmen agreed that they'd accept the letter as good coin—provided that Ajatasutra read it aloud to them so they could be sure it said what he claimed it did.

PESHAWAR
CAPITAL CITY OF THE KUSHAN KINGDOM

Kungas, also, found that the first Malwa assassination attempt came later than he'd expected.

He was not, however, caught by surprise. In fact, he wasn't caught at all.

Kungas was certainly not one of the best assassins in India. Not even close. He was, however, most likely the best assassin-*catcher.* For years, the Malwa had used him as a security specialist. After he broke from them to join Shakuntala's rebellion, she'd made him the commander of her imperial bodyguard.

"They're in that building," Kujulo murmured, pointing with his chin out of the window. He was too far away from the window to be seen from the outside, but he was also too experienced to run the risk that a large gesture like a pointing finger might be spotted. The human eye can detect motion easier than it can detect a still figure. "One of the two you predicted they'd use."

"It was fairly obvious," said Kungas. "They're the only two buildings fronting the square that have both a good angle for a shot and a good rear exit to make an escape from."

Next to him, also carefully standing back from the window so as not to be spotted, Vima chuckled softly. "It helps, of course, that we prepared the sites well. Like bait for rats."

Kungas nodded. The gesture, like Kujulo's chin-pointing, was minimal. Something that couldn't possibly be spotted even fifty feet away, much less across an entire city square.

Bait, indeed. The king of the Kushans—his queen, rather, acting on his instructions—had bought the two buildings outright. Then, placed her own agents in the position of "landlords," with clear and explicit instructions to rent any of the rooms to anyone, no questions asked—and make sure that their reputation for doing so became well known in Peshawar.

Inevitably, of course, that quickly made both buildings havens for prostitution and gambling. All the better, as far as Kungas was concerned. Within a week, all of the prostitutes were cheerfully supplementing their income as informers for the queen.

Irene had known the Malwa assassins were there within half an hour of their arrival.

Piss-poor assassins, in Kungas' opinion, when she told him. They'd started by annoying the whores with a brusque refusal of their services.

"All right," he said. "I see no reason to waste time."

"How do you want to do it?" asked Kujulo. "You don't want to use the charges, I assume."

In the unlikely event he might need it a last resort, Kungas had had all the rooms in the buildings that would be suitable for assassination attempts fitted with demolitions. Shaped charges, basically, that would spray the interior with shrapnel without—hopefully—collapsing the walls.

Still, with the ubiquitous mudbrick construction in Peshawar, Kungas saw no reason to take the risk. There was always the chance the building might collapse, killing dozens of people. Even if that didn't happen, the expense of repairing the damage would be considerable, and the work itself disruptive. Such an extreme measure might aggravate the residents of Peshawar.

Irene's spies had reported that Kungas was now very popular in the city, even among the non-Kushan inhabitants, and he saw no reason to undermine that happy state of affairs.

The new king's popularity was not surprising, of course. Kungas had maintained at least as much stability as the Malwa had. More, really, since the Pathan hillmen had completely ceased their periodic harassment of the city-dwellers. He'd also lowered the taxes and levies, eliminated the most egregious of the Malwa regulations, and, most of all, abolished all of the harsh Malwa laws regarding religion. The enforced Malwa cult of mahaveda Hinduism had never sat well in the mountains. The moment Kungas issued his decrees, the region's underlying Buddhist faith had surged back to the surface.

No, there was no reason to risk undermining all that by blowing up parts of the city. Especially such visible parts, fronting on the main square.

"I've got my men ready," Kujulo added.

"What are they armed with? The assassins, I mean. Guns?"

"No. Bows. Probably be using poisoned arrowheads."

Kungas shook his head. "In that case, no. Keep your men ready, but let's try the Sarmatian girls."

Kujulo looked skeptical. Vima looked downright appalled.

"Kungas—ah, Sire—there isn't a one of them—"

"Enough," Kungas said. "I know they have no experience. Neither did you or I, once. How else do you get it?"

He shook his head again. "If the Malwa were armed with guns, it might be different. But bows will be awkward in the confines of those rooms. The girls will have a good chance. Some of them will die. But . . . That's what they wanted. To be real warriors. Dying comes with it."

The crack of a smile reappeared. "Besides, it's only fair—since we're using one of them as the decoy."

A few minutes later, the business began. The Sarmatian girl posing as Irene came into the square on horseback, surrounded by her usual little entourage of female guards.

Watching from the same window, Kungas was amused. Irene often complained that the custom in the area of insisting that women had to be veiled in public was a damned nuisance, personally speaking—but a blessing, from the standpoint of duplicity.

Was that Irene down there? Who could say, really? Her face couldn't be seen, because of the veil. But the woman was the right height and build, had the same color and length of hair in that distinctive ponytail, wore the proper regalia and the apparel, and had the accustomed escort.

Of course, it was the queen. Who else would it be?

Kungas knew that the assassins across the square wouldn't even be wondering about it. True, Irene was almost certainly not their target and the assassins would make no attempt here. They'd wait for Kungas to show himself. Still, the appearance of the queen in the square so soon after their arrival would be a good sign to them. They'd want to study her movements carefully. All their attention would be fixed on the figure moving within range of the bows in the windows.

He waited for the explosions that would signal the attack. For all that Kungas was prepared to see Irene's girl warriors suffer casualties, he'd seen no reason to make them excessive. He didn't want to risk destroying the walls with the implanted shaped charges, true—but there was no reason not to use the much smaller charges it would take to simply blow open the doors.

Blow them open—and spray splinters all through the room. That should be enough to give the inexperienced girls the edge they'd need.

A bigger edge than he'd expected, in the event. A moment later, the explosions came—and one of the Malwa assassins was blown right out the window. From the way he toppled to the ground twenty feet below, Kungas knew he was already uncon- scious. A big chunk of one of the doors must have hit him on the back of the head.

He landed like a sack of meal. From the distance, Kungas couldn't hear the impact, but it was obvious that the assassin hadn't survived it. Most of the street square was dirt, but it was very hard-packed. Almost like stone.

"Ruptured neck, for sure," Vima grunted. "Probably half his brains spilling out, too."

Another assassin appeared in the same window. His back, to be precise. The man was obviously fighting someone.

A few seconds later, he too toppled out of the window. Still clutching the spear that had been driven into his chest, he made a landing that was no better than his predecessor's.

Worse, probably. This assassin had the bad luck of landing on the flagstones in front of the building's entrance.

The shouts and screams and other sounds of fighting could be heard across the square for a bit longer. Perhaps ten seconds.

Then, silence.

Kungas glanced down into the center of the square, to assure himself that the decoy was unharmed. He had no particular concern for the girl in question—in fact, he didn't even know who it was—but he didn't want to face Irene's recriminations if she'd been hurt.

Self-recriminations, really. But Irene was not exempt from the normal human tendency to shed blame on others as a way of handling guilt.

That left the question of how many of the Sarmatian squad that launched the attack had been killed or injured. But that was a different sort of matter. Getting killed in a fight with weapons in hand didn't cause the same gut-wrenching sensation as getting killed serving as a helpless decoy.

"Odd, really," Kungas murmured to himself. "But that's the way it is. Someday I'll have to ask Dadaji if he can explain the philosophy of it to me."

He turned and headed for the door. "Come. Let's find out."

It was better than he'd thought. Certainly better than he'd feared.

"See?" he demanded of Vima. "Only one girl dead. One badly injured, but she'll probably survive."

"She'll never walk right, again," Vima said sourly. "Might lose that leg completely, at least from the knee down."

Kujulo chuckled. "Will you listen to him? Bad as a doddering old Pathan clan chief!"

For a moment, he hunched his shoulders and twisted his face into a caricature of a prune-faced, disapproving, ancient clansman. Even Vima laughed.

"Not bad," Kujulo stated firmly, after straightening. "Against five assassins? Not bad."

Irene was upset, of course. The dead and injured girls were names and faces to her. People that she'd known, even known well.

But there were no recriminations. No self-recriminations, even. Her Sarmatian guards themselves were ecstatic at their success, despite the casualties.

It probably wasn't necessary, but Kungas put it into words anyway.

"Make Alexander the Great and the Buddha's son the forefathers of a dynasty—this is what comes with it, Irene."

"Yes, love, I know."

"They were all volunteers."

"Yes, love, I know. Now please shut up. And go away for a few hours."

AXUM, IN THE ETHIOPIAN HIGHLANDS

Ousanas glowered at the construction crew working in the great field just on the outskirts of the city of Axum. Most of the field was covered with the stone ruins of ancient royal tombs.

"I ought to have the lot of them executed," he pronounced, "seeing as how I can't very well execute you. Under the circumstances."

Antonina smiled. "Approximately how much more of your Cassandra imitation will I be forced to endure?"

"Cassandra, is it? You watch, woman. Your folly—that of your husband's, rather—will surely cause the spiritual ruin of the great kingdom of Axum." He pointed an accusing finger at the radio tower. "For two centuries this ridiculous field given over to the grotesque monuments of ancient pagan kings has been left to decay. As it should. Now, thanks to you and your idiot husband, we'll be resurrecting that heathen taste in idolatry."

Antonina couldn't help but laugh. "It's a *radio* tower, Ousanas!"

The aqabe tsentsen of Ethiopia was not mollified. "A Trojan horse, what it is. You watch. Soon enough—in the dark, when my eagle eye is not watching—they'll start carving inscriptions on the damned thing."

Gloomily, his eyes ranged up and down the huge stone tower that was nearing completion. "Plenty of room for it, too."

Antonina glanced back at the Greek artisan who was overseeing the project. "Tell me, Timothy. If I understand this right, once the tower is in operation anyone who tries to climb onto it in order—"

The artisan winced. "They'll be fried." Warily, he eyed the tall and very muscular figure of the man who was, in effect if not in theory, the current ruler of Ethiopia. "Ah, Your Excel—"

"See?" demanded Ousanas, transferring his glare to the hapless artisan. "It's already starting! I am not an 'excellency,' damnation, and certainly not *yours*. A humble keeper of the royal fly whisks, that's all I am."

Timothy sidled back a step. He was fluent in Ge'ez, the language of the Axumites, so he knew that the title *aqabe tsentsen* meant "the keeper of the fly whisks." He also knew that the modesty of the title was meaningless.

Antonina came to the rescue. "Oh, stop bullying the poor man. Timothy, please continue."

"Well . . . it's hard to explain without getting too technical. But the gist of it is that a big radio tower like this needs a big transmitter powered by"—here he pointed his finger at a huge stone building—"the steam engine in there. In turn, that—"

The next few sentences were full of mysterious terms like "interrupter" and "capacitor bank" that meant absolutely nothing to Antonina or Ousanas. But Timothy's concluding words seemed clear enough:

"—every time the transmitter key is depressed, you'd have something like two thousand watts of power shorting across your body. 'Fry' is about the right word for what'd happen, if you got onto the tower itself. But you'd never make it that far, anyway. Once you got past the perimeter fence you'd start coupling to the radials implanted around the base of the tower. Your body would start twitching uncontrollably and the closer you got, the worse it'd get. Your hair might even catch on fire."

Ousanas grimaced, but he was still not mollified. "Splendid. So now we will have to post guards to protect idolators from idolatry."

Antonina laughed again. "Even for you, Ousanas, this display is absurd! What's really bothering you? It's the fact that you still haven't figured out what I'm going to decree tomorrow regarding the succession. Isn't it?"

Ousanas didn't look at her, still glowering at the radio tower. After a moment, he growled, "It's not so much me, Antonina. It's Rukaiya. She's been pestering me for days, trying to get an answer. Even more, asking for my opinion on what she should do, in the event of this or that alternative. She has no more idea than I do—and you might consider the fact that whatever you decide, *she* will be the one most affected."

Antonia struggled—mightily—to keep her satisfaction from showing. She had, in fact, deliberately delayed making the announcement after telling everyone she'd reached a decision, in the specific hope that Rukaiya would turn to Ousanas for advice.

"I'd have thought she'd mostly pester Garmat," she said, as if idly.

Ousanas finally stopped glowering and managed a bit of a grin. "Well, she has, of course. But I have a better sense of humor than the old bandit. She needs that, right now."

So, she does. So, she does.

"Well!" Antonina said briskly. "It'll all be settled tomorrow, at the council session. In the meantime—"

She turned to Timothy. "Please continue the work. Ignore this grumbler. The sooner you can get that finished, the sooner I can talk to my husband again."

"And that's another thing!" Ousanas grumbled, as they headed toward the Ta'akha Maryam. "It's just a waste. You can't say anything either secret or personal—not with that sort of broadcast radio—and it won't work anyway, once the monsoon comes with its thunderstorms. So I've been told, at least."

Antonina glanced at the sun, now at its midday altitude, as if gauging the season. "We're still some months from the southwest monsoon, you know. Plenty of time."

Chapter 9
CONSTANTINOPLE

"You'd be putty in your father's hands," Theodora sneered.

"Which one? Belisarius or Justinian?"

"Either—no, *both*, since they're obviously conspiring with each other."

The dark eyes of the Empress Regent moved away from Photius and Tahmina to glare at a guard standing nearby. So far as Photius could determine, the poor man's only offense was that he happened to be in her line of sight.

Perhaps he also bore a vague resemblance to Belisarius. He was tall, at least, and had brown eyes.

Angrily, Theodora slapped the heavily decorated armrest of her throne. "Bad enough that he's exposing my husband to danger! But he's also giving away half my empire!"

She shifted the glare back to Photius. "Excuse me. *Your* empire."

The correction was, quite obviously, a formality. The apology was not even that, given the tone in which she'd spoken the words.

"You hate to travel," Photius pointed out, reasonably. "And since you're actually running my empire"—here he bestowed a cherubic smile on his official adoptive mother—"you can't afford to leave the capital anyway."

"I detest that smile," Theodora hissed. "Insincere as a crocodile's. How did you get to be so devious, already? You're only eleven years old."

Photius was tempted to reply: *from studying you, Mother.* Wisely, he refrained.

If she were in a better mood, actually, Theodora would take it as a compliment. But, she wasn't. She was in as foul a mood as she ever got, short of summoning the executioners.

Photius and his wife Tahmina had once, giggling, developed their own method for categorizing Theodora's temper. First, they divided it into four seasons:

Placid. The most pleasant season, albeit usually brief.

Sour. A very long season. More or less the normal climate.

Sullen. Not as long as sour season. Not quite.

Fury. Fortunately, the shortest season of all. Very exciting while it lasted, though.

Then, they ranked each season in terms of its degree of intensity, from alpha to epsilon.

Photius gauged this one as a Sullen Epsilon.

Well . . . Not quite. Call it a Sullen Delta.

In short, caution was called for here. On the other hand, there was still some room for further prodding and pushing. Done gingerly.

"I like to travel myself," he piped cheerfully. "So I'm the logical one to send on a grand tour to visit our allies in the war. And it's not as if you really need me here."

He did not add: *or want me here, either.* That would be unwise. True, Theodora had all the maternal instincts of a brick. But she liked to pretend otherwise, for reasons Photius had never been able to fathom.

Tahmina said it was because, if she didn't, it would give rise to rumors that she'd been spawned by Satan. That might be true, although Photius was skeptical. After all, plenty of people *already* thought the Empress Regent had been sired by the devil.

Photius didn't, himself. Maybe one of Hell's underlings, but not Satan himself.

Theodora was back to glaring at the guard. No, a different one. His offense . . .

Hard to say. He resembled neither Belisarius nor Justinian. Except for being a man, which, in Theodora's current humor, was probably enough.

"Fine!" she snapped. "You can go. If nothing else, it'll keep Antonina from nattering at me every day once the radio starts working. By now, months since she left, she'll be wallowing in guilt and whining and whimpering about how much she misses her boy. God knows why. Devious little wretch."

She swiveled the dark-eyed glare onto Tahmina, sitting next to Photius. "You too. Or else once the cunning little bastard gets to Ethiopia he'll start nattering at me over the radio about how much he misses his wife. God knows why. It's not as if he's old enough yet to have a proper use for a wife."

Yet a third guard received the favor of her glare. "You can celebrate your sixteenth birthday in Axum. I'll send the gifts along with you."

Tahmina smiled sweetly and bowed her head. "Thank you, Mother."

"I'm not your mother. You don't fool me. You're as bad as he is. No child of mine would be so sneaky. Now go."

Once they reached the corridor outside Theodora's audience chamber, Photius whispered to Tahmina: "Sullen Delta. Close to Epsilon."

"Oh, don't be silly," his wife whispered back, smiling down at him. To Photius' disgruntlement, even though he'd grown a lot over the past year, Tahmina was still taller than he was. "That wasn't any worse than Sullen Gamma. She agreed, didn't she?"

"Well. True."

The announcement was made publicly the next day. Photius wasn't surprised. It was usually hard to wheedle Theodora into anything. But the nice thing was that, if you could, she'd move quickly and decisively thereafter.

The Emperor of Rome will visit our allies in the war with Malwa. All the way to India itself! The Empress will accompany him, sharing the hardships of the journey.
All hail the valiant Photius!
All hail the virtuous Tahmina!

After reading the broadsheet, the captain of the Malwa assassination team tossed it onto the table in the apartments they'd rented. It was all he could do not to crumple it in disgust.

"Three months. Wasted."

His lieutenant, standing at the window, stared out over the Golden Horn. He didn't bother, as he had innumerable times since they'd arrived in Constantinople, shifting his gaze to study the imperial palace complex.

No point in that, now.

The three other members of the team were sitting at the table in the kitchen. The center of the table was taken up by one of the small bombards that Malwa assassination teams generally carried with them. The weapons were basically just simple, very big, one-round shotguns. Small enough that they could be hidden in trunks, even if that made carrying the luggage a back-breaking chore.

All three of them were glowering at it. The captain would insist that they bring the bombard with them, wherever they went. And, naturally, being the plebeians of the team, they'd be the ones who had to tote the wretched thing.

One of the three assassins spoke up. "Perhaps . . . if we stayed here . . . Theodora . . ."

The captain almost snarled at him. "Don't be stupid. Impossible, the precautions she takes. Not even Nanda Lal expects us to have a chance at *her.*"

"She hasn't left the complex once, since we arrived," the lieutenant chimed in, turning away from the window. "Not once, in three months. Even Emperor Skandagupta travels more often than that."

He pulled out a chair and sat down at the table. A moment later, the captain did the same.

"We had a good chance with the boy," the lieutenant added. "High-spirited as he is. He and his wife both. Now . . ."

He looked at his superior. "Follow them?"

"Yes. Only thing we can do."

"Not one of us speaks Ge'ez, sir," pointed out one of the assassins. "And none of us are black."

Gloomily, the captain shook his head. "Don't belabor the obvious. We'll have to move fast and reach Egypt before they do. Try and do it there, if we can. All of us can pass as Persians among Arabs—or the reverse, if we must."

"We may well have to," cautioned his lieutenant. "The security in Egypt is reportedly ferocious. Organized by Romans, too. It'll be easier in Persia—easier still, in Persian-occupied Sind. The

Iranians insist on placing grandees in charge of security, and grandees tend to be sloppy about these things."

"True." The captain stared down at the broadsheet. Then he did crumple it.

THE IRON TRIANGLE

"They're not even going to try to run the mines, I don't think," Menander said. He lowered the telescope and offered it to Belisarius.

The general shook his head. "Your eyes are as good as mine. At that distance, for sure. What are you seeing?"

Before answering, Menander came down from the low platform he'd been standing on to observe the distant Malwa naval base. Then, stooped slightly so that his head would be well below the parapet. That brought his face on a level with the general's, since Belisarius was standing in a slight crouch also.

That was something of a new habit, but one that had become well ingrained. Beginning a few weeks earlier, the Malwa had demonstrated that they, too, could produce rifles good enough for long-range sniping.

"Both ironclads just came out of the bunker. But they steamed north. They're headed away from us."

Belisarius closed his eyes, thinking. "You're probably right. I'd already pretty much come to the conclusion that the Malwa were assuming a defensive posture. From that standpoint, building the ironclads actually makes sense—where it would be a pure waste of resources to build them to attack us here in the Triangle. They'd never get through the mine fields."

Menander frowned, trying to follow the general's logic. "But I still don't see . . . oh."

"Yes. 'Oh.' You've gotten a better look at those ironclads than anyone—certainly a longer one. Could you defeat them—either one—with the *Justinian*? Or the *Victrix*?"

"The *Victrix* would just be suicide. They've got a couple of big guns in the bows. Eighteen-pounders, I think. They'd blow the *Victrix* to pieces long before it could get close enough to use the fire cannon."

He paused, for a moment. "As for the *Justinian* ... Maybe. Against one of them, not both. It would depend on a lot of things, including plenty of luck. I'd do better in a night battle, I think."

Belisarius waited, patiently. Excellent young officers like Menander always started off their assessments too optimistically. He preferred to give them time for self-correction, rather than doing it himself.

With Menander, it only took half a minute. He was well accustomed to Belisarius' habits, by now.

"All right, all right," he said, smiling slightly. "The truth? I *might* win—against one of them. But it would depend on some blind luck working in our favor. Even with luck, I'm not sure I could do it in the daytime."

Belisarius nodded, almost placidly. "That's how they *designed* them, Menander. Those ironclads weren't designed to break into the Triangle. They were designed to keep *you* from breaking out."

He stretched, while still being careful to keep his head out of sight of any snipers. "Look at this way. The Malwa now figure, with those ironclads finished and in service, that they've got the same control over the rivers north of the Triangle that we have of them to the south. That means *they're* in position to do to us the same thing we did to them last year—cut our supply lines if we attempt any major prolonged offensive. There's no way to supply that kind of massive campaign without using water transport. It just can't be done. Not, at least, with more than fifteen or—at most—twenty thousand men. By the standards of this war, that isn't a powerful enough force to win a pitched battle. Not here in the Punjab, anyway."

He glanced at the wall of the fortifications, as if he could see through it to the Malwa trenches beyond. "I estimate they've got upwards of a hundred thousand men out there. 'Out there' meaning in this immediate vicinity, facing us here in the Triangle. They've probably got another twenty thousand—maybe thirty—facing Kungas at the Khyber Pass, and thirty or forty thousand more held as a reserve in Multan."

"And we've got ..."

"By now? Forty thousand in the Triangle itself, with another twenty thousand or so on their way here from the Empire, in a steady trickle. The Persians have about forty thousand troops actively engaged on this front. But most of them are still in the Sind, and even in the best of circumstances Khusrau would have to leave a third of them there to administer the province."

The young officer made a sour face. Belisarius smiled.

"He's an emperor, Menander. Emperors think like emperors; it's just the nature of the beast. And Khusrau has the additional problem that he's bound and determined to keep his new province of Sind under direct imperial control, rather than letting his noblemen run the show. But that means he has to use a lot of soldiers as administrators. Whether he likes it or not—much less whether *we* like it or not."

Menander's sour expression shaded into a simple scowl. "In short, we're outnumbered at least two-to-one, and that's not going to change."

"Not for the better, that's for sure. The only way it'll change will be for the worse. If the Malwa succeed in crushing Shakuntala's rebellion in the Deccan, that would free up Damodara and his army. Another forty thousand men, and, in terms of quality, undoubtedly the best army in the Malwa empire."

He let that sink in for a few seconds. Then: "It'd be worse than that, actually. The Maratha revolt inspired and triggered off smaller revolts and rebellions all over India. I estimate the Malwa are forced to keep one-half to two-thirds of their army in India proper, just to maintain control of the empire. The truth is this, Menander. So far, we've been able to fight a Malwa empire that could only use one hand against us, instead of two. And the weaker hand, at that, since Damodara's in the Deccan. If they break Shakuntala and Rao and the Marathas, all those smaller rebellions will start fading away quickly. Within a year, we'd be facing another hundred thousand men here in the Punjab—and Damodara could get his forty thousand here within two months. Three, at the outside."

The general shrugged. "Of course, by then we'd be so well-fortified here that I doubt very much if even a Malwa army twice this size could drive us out. But there's no way we could go on the offensive ourselves, either—certainly not with those ironclads controlling the rivers. They'll build a few more, I suspect. Enough to place two ironclads on the Indus and at least one on each of its four main tributaries."

"A war of attrition, in other words." Menander sucked his teeth. "That . . . stinks."

"Yes, it does. The casualties will become horrendous, once you let enough time pass—and the social and political strain on the kingdoms and empires involved will be just as bad. That's what that monster over there is counting on now, Menander. It thinks, with its iron control over the Malwa Empire, that it can outlast a coalition of allies."

Menander eyed the general. "And what do you think, sir?"

"I think that superhuman genius over there is just a grandiose version of a village idiot."

The young officer's eyes widened, a little. "Village idiot? That seems . . ."

"Too self-confident on my part?" Belisarius smiled. "You watch, young man. What you're seeing here is what Ousanas would call the fallacy of confusing the shadow for the true thing—the pale, sickly, real world version of the ideal type."

"Huh?"

The general chuckled. "Let me put it this way. Emperors—or superhuman imitations thereof—think in terms like 'iron control,' as if it really meant something. But iron is a metal, not a people. Any good blacksmith can control iron. No emperor who ever lived can really control people. That's because iron, as refractory a substance as it may be, doesn't dispute the matter with the blacksmith."

He looked now, to the southeast. "So, we'll see. Link thinks it can win this waiting game. I think it's the village idiot."

DEOGIRI
THE NEW CAPITAL OF THE REBORN ANDHRA EMPIRE IN MAJARASHTRA—THE "GREAT COUNTRY"

"It's *ridiculous*," Shakuntala hissed. "Ridiculous!"

Even as young as she was, the black-eyed glare of the Empress of Andhra was hot enough to have sizzled lizards in the desert.

Alas, the assassin squatting before her in a comfortable lotus seemed completely unaffected. So, she turned to other means.

"Summon my executioners!" she snapped. "At once!"

The glare was now turned upon her husband, sitting on a throne next to hers. A slight movement of Rao's forefinger had been enough to stay the courtiers before one of them could do her bidding.

"A moment," he said softly. He turned to face her glare, his expression every bit as calm and composed as the assassin's.

"You are, of course, the ruler of Andhra. And I, merely your consort. But since this matter touches upon my personal honor, I am afraid you will have to defer to my wishes. Either that, or use the executioners on me."

Shakuntala tried to maintain the glare. Hard, that, in the face of her worst fear since reading the letter brought by the assassin.

After five seconds or so, inevitably, she broke. "Rao—*please*. This is insane. The crudest ruse, on the part of the Malwa."

Rao transferred the calm gaze to the figure squatting on the carpet in the center of the audience chamber. For a moment, India's two best assassins contemplated each other.

"Oh, I think not," Rao murmured, even more softly. "Whatever else, not that."

He rose abruptly to his feet. "Take him to one of the guest chambers. Give him food, drink, whatever he wishes within reason."

Normally, Rao was punctilious about maintaining imperial protocol. Husband or not, wiser and older head or not, Rao was officially the consort and Shakuntala the reigning monarch. But, on occasion, when he felt it necessary, he would exert the informal authority that made him—in reality, if not in theory—the co-ruler of Andhra.

Shakuntala did not attempt to argue the matter. She was bracing herself for the much more substantial issue they would be arguing over as soon as they were in private.

"Clear the room," she commanded. "Dadaji, you stay."

Her eyes quickly scanned the room. Her trusted peshwa was a given. Who else?

The two top military commanders, of course. "Shahji, Kondev, you also."

She was tempted to omit Maloji, on the grounds that he was not one of the generals of the army. Formally speaking, at least. But . . . he was Rao's closest friend, in addition to being the commander of the Maratha irregulars.

Passing him over would be unwise. Besides, who was to say? Sometimes, Maloji was the voice of caution. He was, in some ways, even more Maratha than Rao—and the Marathas, as a people, were not given to excessive flamboyance on matters of so-called "honor." Quite unlike those mindless Rajputs.

"Maloji."

That was enough, she thought. Rao would not be able to claim she had unbalanced the private council in her favor.

But, to her surprise, he added a name. "I should like Bindusara to remain behind also."

Shakuntala was surprised—and much pleased. She'd considered the Hindu religious leader herself, but had passed him over because she'd thought Rao would resent her bringing spiritual pressure to bear. The sadhu was not a pacifist after the manner of the Jains, but neither was he given to much patience for silly kshatriya notions regarding "honor."

It took a minute or so for the room to clear. As they waited, Shakuntala leaned over and whispered: "I wouldn't have thought you'd want Bindusara."

Rao smiled thinly. "You are the treasure of my soul. But you are also sometimes still very young. You are over your head here, girl. I wanted the sadhu because he is *also* a philosopher."

Shakuntala hissed, like an angry snake. She had a disquieting feeling, though, that she sounded like an angry *young* snake.

Certainly, the sound didn't seem to have any effect on Rao's smile. "You never pay enough attention to *those* lessons. Still! After all my pleading." The smile widened, considerably. The last courtier was passing through the door and there was no one left to see but the inner council.

"Philosophy has form as well as substance, girl. No one can be as good at it as Bindusara unless he is also a master of *logic*."

Shakuntala began the debate. Her arguments took not much time, since they were simplicity itself.

We have been winning the war by patience. Why should we accept this challenge to a clash of great armies on the open field, where we would be over-matched?

Because one old man challenges another to a duel? Because both of the fools still think they're young?

Nonsense!

❖   ❖   ❖

When it came his turn, Rao's smile was back in place. Very wide, now, that smile.

"Not so old as all *that,* I think," he protested mildly. "Neither I nor Rana Sanga. Still, my beloved wife has penetrated to the heart of the thing. It *is* ridiculous for two men, now well past the age of forty—"

"Almost fifty!" Shakuntala snapped.

"—and, perhaps more to the point, both of them now very experienced commanders of armies, not young warriors seeking fame and glory, to suddenly be gripped by a desire to fight a personal duel."

To Shakuntala's dismay, the faces of the three generals had that horrid *look* on them. That half-dreamy, half-stern expression that men got when their brains oozed out of their skulls and they started babbling like boys again.

"Be a match of legend," murmured Kondev.

The empress almost screamed from sheer frustration. The day-long single combat that Rao and Rana Sanga had fought once, long ago, was famous all across India. Every mindless warrior in India would drool over the notion of a rematch.

"You were twenty years old, then!"

Rao nodded. "Indeed, we were. But you are not asking the right question, Shakuntala. Have you—ever once—heard me so much as mention any desire for another duel with Sanga? Even in my sleep."

"No," she said, tight-jawed.

"I think not. I can assure you—everyone here—that the thought has not once crossed my mind for at least . . . oh, fifteen years. More likely, twenty."

He leaned forward a bit, gripping the armrests of the throne in his powerful, out-sized hands. "So why does anyone think that Rana Sanga would think of it, either? Have I aged, and he, not? True, he is a Rajput. But, even for Rajputs, there is a difference between a husband and a father of children and a man still twenty and unattached. A difference not simply in the number of lines on their faces, but in how they think."

Shahji cleared his throat. "He has lost his family, Rao. Perhaps that has driven him to fury."

"But *has* he lost them?" Rao looked to Dadaji Holkar. Not

to his surprise, the empire's peshwa still had one of the letters brought by the Malwa assassin held in his hand. Almost clutched, in fact.

"What do you make of it, Dadaji?"

Holkar's face bore an odd expression. An unlikely combination of deep worry and even deeper exultation. "Oh, it's from my daughters. There are little signs—a couple of things mentioned no one else could have known—"

"Torture," suggested Kondev.

"—that make me certain of it." He glanced at Kondev and shook his head. "Torture seems unlikely. For one thing, although the handwriting is poor—my daughters' education was limited, of course, in the short time I had before they were taken from me—it is not shaky at all. I recognized it quite easily. I can even tell you which portion was written by Dhruva, and which by Lata, from that alone. Could I do so, were the hands holding the pen trembling with pain and fear as well as inexperience? Besides . . ."

He looked at the door through which the courtiers had left—and, a bit earlier, an assassin. "I do not think that man is a torturer."

"Neither do I," said Rao firmly. "And I believe, at my advanced age"—here, a sly little smile at Shakuntala—"I can tell the difference."

Shakuntala scowled, but said nothing. Rao gestured at Holkar. "Continue, please."

"The letter tells me nothing, naturally, of the girls' location. But it does depict, in far more detail than I would have expected, the comfort of their lives now. And there are so many references to the mysterious 'ladies' to whom they have—this is blindingly obvious—grown very attached."

"You conclude from this?"

Dadaji studied the letter in his hand, for a moment. "I conclude from this that someone—not my daughters, someone else—is sending me a message here. Us, rather, a message."

Rao leaned back in his throne. "So I think, also. You will all remember the message sent to us last year from Dadaji's daughters, with the coin?"

Several heads nodded, Shakuntala's among them.

"And how Irene Macrembolitissa convinced us it was not a trap, but the first step in a complex maneuver by Narses?"

All heads nodded.

Rao pointed to the letter. "I think that is the second step. Inviting us to take a third—or, rather, allow someone else to do so."

That statement was met by frowns of puzzlement on most faces. But, from the corner of her eye, Shakuntala saw Bindusara nodding.

She could sense that she was losing the argument. For a moment, she had to struggle desperately not to collapse into sheer girlish pleading—which would end, inevitably, with her blurting out before the council news she had not yet even given to Rao. Of the new child that was coming.

Suddenly, Rao's large hand reached over and gave her little one a squeeze. "Oh, be still, girl. I can assure you that I have no intention whatsoever of fighting Rana Sanga again."

His smile was simply cheerful now. "Ever again, in fact. And that is precisely why I will accept the challenge."

In the few seconds those two sentences required, Shakuntala swung from despair to elation and back. "You don't need to do this!"

"Of course, I don't. But Rana Sanga *does*."

Chapter 10
AXUM

"What, no elephants?" Antonina asked sarcastically.

Ousanas shook his head. "They won't fit in the corridors, not even in the Ta'akha Maryam. We tried. Too bad, though. It would have made a nice flourish. Instead—"

He gestured before them, down the long hallway leading to the throne room. "—we must walk."

Antonina tried to picture war elephants inside the Ta'akha Maryam, her mind boggling a little. Even if the huge beasts could have been inserted into the halls . . .

She looked down the long rows of guards and officials, flanking both sides. "They'd have crushed everybody," she muttered.

"Oh, not the soldiers. Most of them would have scampered aside in time, and the ones who didn't had no business being sarwen anyway. In fact, Ezana thought it would be a useful test."

Ezana was the senior commander of the three royal regiments. Antonina thought he was probably cold-blooded enough to have said that. There was something downright scary about Ezana. Fortunately, he was not hot-tempered, nor impulsive. Even more fortunately, his devotion to the dynasty was unquestioned by anyone, including Antonina.

Ezana had been one of Eon's two bodyguards while he'd still been a prince. That was a very prestigious position for the soldiers who made up Ethiopia's regiments—the "sarwen," as they called themselves. When Eon had assumed the throne, Ezana had become the commander of the royal regiments—and the other bodyguard, Wahsi, had been appointed the military commander of the Ethiopian naval expedition that Antonina had used to rescue Belisarius and his army from the siege of Charax.

Wahsi had died in battle in the course of that expedition. Eon's son, the new Axumite King of Kings, had been named after him.

So, Antonina had no doubt at all of Ezana's loyalty to the infant *negusa nagast*, sired by the prince he'd guarded and named after his best friend. Still, he was . . . scary.

"The slaughter among the officials, of course, would have been immense," Ousanas continued cheerfully, "seeing how half of them are as fat as elephants, and eight out of ten have brains that move more ponderously. But it was my assessment that the loss of one-third would be a blessing for the kingdom. Ezana was hoping that half would be crushed."

Antonina thought the *aqabe tsentsen* was joking, but she wasn't sure. There were ways in which Ousanas was even scarier than Ezana. But since they were nearing the entrance to the throne room, she decided she'd simply pretend she hadn't heard.

One-third of Ethiopia's officials, slain in a few minutes! Half, according to Ezana!

Bloodthirsty African maniacs. Antonina would have been quite satisfied with a simple, unostentatious Roman decimation.

"All be silent!"

As if his booming commander's voice wasn't enough, Ezana slammed the iron-capped ferrule of his spear onto the stone floor. *"Be silent!"*

The throne room had become perfectly quiet even before the ferrule hit the floor. Leaving aside the fact that no one in their right mind was going to disobey Ezana under these circumstances, the crowd packed into the huge chamber was waiting to hear Antonina's decrees. Eagerly, in some cases; anxiously, in others; fearfully, in some. But not one person there was indifferent, or inclined to keep chattering.

Actually, there hadn't been much chatter anyway. Antonina had noticed the unusual quiet the moment she entered the room. Ethiopians had informal habits, when it came to royalty, certainly compared to Roman or Persian custom. As a rule, even during an official session, the royal audience chamber had a constant little hubbub of conversation in the background. Nothing boisterous or intrusive, to be sure. But neither Ethiopian soldier-seamen nor Arab merchants saw any reason not to conduct quiet business in the back of the chamber while the negusa nagast and his officials made their various judgments and rulings around the throne.

Not today. The chamber had been subdued when Antonina entered, and now it was utterly silent.

Well . . . not quite. Softly and contentedly, the baby ruler of the kingdom was suckling his mother's breast, as she sat on the throne.

That was being done on Antonina's instructions. Normally, for such a session, Rukaiya would have used a wet nurse just as readily as any Roman empress. But Antonina had thought the sight of the baby feeding would help remind everyone of the cold and hard facts that surrounded that softest of realities.

On one side, the cold and hard facts that this *was* the son of Eon the Great, this was his successor—and this *was* the woman Eon had chosen to be his queen. On the other, the colder and harder facts that the successor was a babe, and the queen a teenager. The same cold and hard facts that had existed when Alexander the Great died—and, within a few short years, had led to civil war, the eventual division of the empire between the Diadochi, and the murder of Alexander's widow and child.

Ezana waited until Antonina had climbed the steps that led up to the royal dais. The steps were wide, but shallow. Wide enough to give the guards positioned just behind the throne time to intercept any would-be assassin. Shallow enough, that the ruler was not so elevated above his subjects that a normal conversation couldn't be held with those seeking an audience.

There was a chair waiting for her there, to the right of the queen's. A throne, really, though not as large or elaborate as the one in which Rukaiya sat with the infant negusa nagast. But Antonina had already decided she'd make her decrees while standing. She'd learned that trick from watching her friend Theodora rule Rome.

Sit, when you're judging and negotiating—but always stand, when you're really laying down the law.

As soon as Antonina had reached her position and given him a little nod—she'd already told Ezana she wouldn't be using the chair for this—the regimental commander's voice boomed out again.

"As decreed by Eon the Great on his deathbed, the Roman woman Antonina will rule on the measures to be taken to ensure the royal succession. Eon gave her complete authority for the task. I was there, I heard, I bear witness. Her decrees are final. Her decrees are absolute. They will not be questioned."

That was . . . not entirely true. No decrees laid down by any-one other than God could cover all the details and complexities. Antonina knew full well that, starting on the morrow, she'd be sitting in that chair and dickering over the fine points. Still, for the moment—

In case anyone had any lingering doubts, Ezana slammed the spear butt on the stones again. "Not by anyone!"

Before she began, she glanced around the room. All the prin-cipals were there. Ousanas was standing on the lowest step of the dais, to her right, as was customary for the aqabe tsentsen. Ezana occupied the equivalent position to the left, as befit the commander of the royal regiments. Just to his left, on the stone floor, were the rest of the commanders of the regiments stationed in Axum.

Directly front of the dais were assembled the kingdom's officials, with old Garmat at the center. Officially, he was the viceroy of the Axum-controlled portions of Arabia. In reality, he also served as one of the ruler's closest advisers. Garmat had served Eon's father Kaleb in the same posts that Ousanas had later served Eon himself—first, as the dawazz for the prince; then, as the aqabe tsentsen for the king. The half-Arab one-time bandit was cunning and shrewd, and much respected by everyone in the kingdom.

Spread out to either side of the officials, and ranging beyond throughout the throne room, was the elite of the realm. The majority were Ethiopians, but perhaps a third were Arabs. All of the latter were either tribal or clan chiefs, or experienced and wealthy merchants and traders—or, more often than not, both together.

There was one Arab standing next to Garmat, in the small group of officials at the center. That was Rukaiya's father, who was one of the wealthiest of the Quraysh merchants in Mecca—and had been appointed by Eon himself as the viceroy for Arabia's west coast. The Hijaz, as it was called, the area north of Yemen that was dominated by the Quraysh tribe.

"You all understand the problem we face," Antonina began. She saw no reason to bore everyone with a recitation of the obvious. Everyone there had had months to consider the situation, and by now everyone understood it perfectly well.

"The future for Axum is splendid, provided the kingdom can pass through the next twenty years without strife and turmoil. To do so, in my judgment, the throne needs an additional bulwark."

Since Axumites were expert sailors as well as stone masons, she added another image. "An outrigger, if you will, to keep the craft from overturning in heavy seas."

She had to fight down a smile, seeing Ousanas and Garmat wince slightly. Both men were fond of poetry—Garmat more than Ousanas—and she knew she'd be hearing wisecracks later concerning her pedestrian use of simile and metaphor.

Ezana's expression, on the other hand, was simply intent. And it was ultimately Ezana who mattered here. Not simply because he commanded the spears of the regiment, but because he—unlike Ousanas and Garmat, each outsiders in their different ways—was Ethiopian through and through. If Ezana accepted her ruling, with no hesitations or doubts, she was confident the rest would follow.

"So, I have decided to create a new post for the kingdom. The name of this official will be the *angabo*."

She paused, knowing that the little murmur which swept the room was both inevitable and worked to her advantage.

The term "angabo" was well known to those people, especially the Ethiopians. The kingdom of Axum had several legends concerning its origins. The predominant one, contained in the *Book of Aksum,* held that the founder of the city of Axum was Aksumawi, son of Ethiopis and grandson of the Noah of the Bible. A related legend had it that the kings of Axum were descendants of Solomon and Makeda, the queen of Sheba. Those were the officially favored legends, of course, since they gave the now-Christian kingdom an impeccably Biblical lineage for their rulers.

But Axum had only converted to Christianity two centuries earlier, and there still existed a third and older legend. This legend had no formal sanction, but it was well-respected by the populace—and neither the kings of Ethiopia nor its Christian bishops had ever made any attempt to suppress it. Axumites were not much given to doctrinal asperity, certainly by the standards of Rome's contentious bishops and patriarchs. All the more so since the legend, however pagan it might be, was hardly derisive toward the monarchy.

According to that older legend, Ethiopia had once been ruled by a great and evil serpent named Arwe or Waynaba. Once a year, the serpent-king demanded the tribute of a young girl. This continued until a stranger named Angabo arrived, slew the serpent, saved the girl, and was then elected king by the people. His descendant, it was said, was the Makeda who was the queen of Sheba of the Solomon story—although still another version of the legend claimed Makeda was the girl he rescued.

Antonina glanced down at Garmat. The old adviser was managing to keep a straight face—which must have been hard, since he was the one person with whom Antonina had discussed her plans. And he, unlike her, was standing where he could see Ousanas directly.

Such a pity, really. By now, the quick mind of Ousanas would have realized where she was going with this—and Antonina would have paid a princely sum to have been able to watch the expression on his face.

She tried, surreptitiously, out of the corner of her eye. But, alas, the aqabe tsentsen was just that little bit too far to the side for her to see his face as anything other than a dark blur.

"The *angabo* will command all the regiments of Axum except the three royal regiments. Those will, as now, remain under the authority of the senior commander. Ezana, as he is today."

The regimental commanders wouldn't much like that provision. Traditionally, they'd been equals who met as a council, with no superior other than the negusa nagast himself. But Antonina didn't expect any serious problems from that quarter. Ethiopia had now grown from a kingdom to an empire, and the sarwen were hard-headed enough to recognize that their old egalitarian traditions would have to adapt, at least to a degree. Over half of the regiments were now in India, after all—so how could the council of commanders meet in the first place?

In essence, Antonina had just re-created the old Roman division between the regular army and the Praetorian Guard. That hadn't worked out too well for Rome, in the long run. But Antonina didn't think Axum would face the same problem that the Roman Empire had faced, of being so huge and far-flung that the Praetorian Guard wound up being the tail in the capital that wagged the dog in the far-off provinces.

Even with the expansion into the African continent to the south that Eon and Ousanas had planned, Axum would still remain a relatively compact realm. The three royal regiments would not have the ability of the Praetorian Guard to override the army, seeing as how most of the regular regiments under the control of the angabo would be stationed no farther away than southern and western Arabia—just across the Red Sea. They'd be even closer once the capital was moved from Axum to the great Red Sea port of Adulis, as was planned also.

And, in any event, the long run was the long run. Antonina had no illusions that she could manipulate political and military developments over a span of centuries. She simply wanted to buy Axum twenty years of internal peace—and leave it reasonably secure at the end.

"The position of the *angabo* will be a hereditary one," she continued, "unlike the positions of the aqabe tsentsen, or the viceroys, or the commanders of the sarwen. Second only to the negusa nagast, the angabo will be accounted the highest nobleman of the realm."

She waited for a moment, letting the crowd digest that decree. The Ethiopian nobility wouldn't much like that provision, of course—but, on the other hand, it would please the sarwen commanders. Often enough, of course, the commanders *were* noblemen—but that was not the root source of either their identity or their authority within the regiments.

"The descendants of the angabo, however, may not under any circumstances assume the throne of the kingdom. They may marry into the ruling dynasty, but the children of that union will inherit the position of the angabo, not the negusa nagast. They will be, forever, the highest noblemen of Axum—but they will also be, forever, barred from the throne itself."

That was the key. She'd considered the Antonine tradition of adoption as an alternative, but both she and Garmat had decided it would be too risky. Unlike Romans, neither the Ethiopians nor the Arabs had ever used the custom of political adoption in that

manner. It would be too foreign to them. This, however, was
something everyone could understand. She'd essentially created
a Caesar alongside an Augustus—but then divided the two into
separate lineages. Instead of, as the Romans had done, making
the Caesar the designated successor to the Augustus.

Eventually, some day, one or another angabo might manage to
distort the structure enough to overthrow a dynasty. But . . . not
for at least a century, she judged. Garmat thought it would be
at least that long before anyone even seriously tried.

"They'll *like* this setup, once they get used it," he'd told her
confidently, the day before. "Ethiopians and Arabs alike. Watch
and see if I'm not right. It's almost a dual monarchy, with a senior
and a junior dynasty, which means that if you can't wheedle one,
maybe you can wheedle what you need out of the other. Good
enough—when the alternative is the risk of a failed rebellion."

Then, grinning: "Especially after they contemplate the first and
founding angabo."

Antonina paused again. By now, many sets of eyes were swiveling toward a particular person in the room. The first pair had
been those belonging to Rukaiya's father.

She was not surprised, on either count. Many of the people in
that room were extremely shrewd—none more so than Rukaiya's
father, leaving aside Garmat himself.

Best of all, to her, was the sense she got that he was immensely
relieved. A very slight sense, since the man had superb control
over his public face, but it was still definitely there. He'd be the
one person in the room who would consider this as a father,
not simply as a magnate of the kingdom—and he doted on
Rukaiya.

"To make certain that the position of the angabo and his
descendants is established surely and certainly for all to see, the
first angabo will marry Rukaiya, widow of Eon the Great and
the regent of the kingdom. Their children will thus be the half-
brothers and sisters of the negusa nagast, Wahsi."

She turned her head enough to look at Rukaiya. The girl was
staring up at her, blank-faced. The young queen was still waiting,
still keeping her expression under tight control. She'd known
for some time that she would most likely have to remarry—and
soon—as little as she looked forward to the prospect.

Now, obviously, she simply wanted . . . the *name*.

She dreaded hearing it, of course. Rukaiya was a very capable, energetic and free-spirited girl. She'd been raised by a lenient and supportive father and married to a young prince, a bibliophile himself, who'd enjoyed her intellect and encouraged her learning. Now, she faced the prospect of marriage to . . .

Whoever it was, not someone likely to be much like her father or her former husband.

Antonina had to struggle to keep her own face expressionless. *Silly girl! Did you really think I'd condemn you to such a living death? Nonsense.*

It was time to end it.

"The rest is obvious. The first angabo, like the Angabo of legend, must be a complete outsider. Neither Ethiopian nor Arab, and with no existing ties to any clan or tribe in the kingdom. Yet he must also be a famous warrior and a wise counselor. One whom all know can and has hunted and slain evil serpent-kings—as this one, in my presence once, helped my husband trap and slay the serpent-queen of Malwa. Who was the greatest, and most evil, creature in the world."

Finally, she turned to look at him squarely.

"Ousanas, the first angabo."

Ousanas would have figured it out as quickly as Rukaiya's father. By now, he had his expression completely under control.

Too bad. It was probably the only chance Antonina would ever get to make the man's jaw drop.

Noisily, Garmat cleared his throat. "Does Ousanas accept the post?"

The famous grin came, then. "What does 'accept' have to do with it?" He nodded toward Ezana, standing stone-faced on the other side of the dais. "I heard what he said, even if some others were deaf. The words were 'final' and 'absolute'—and I *distinctly* remember 'without question.' That said . . ."

For a moment, while Ousanas' grin faded away, he and Ezana stared at each other. It was not quite a contest of wills. Not quite.

Ousanas turned to the queen, sitting on the throne. "That said," he continued quietly, "I would not force this on Rukaiya. She has been very dear to me also, if not in the same way she was to Eon."

The moment Antonina had spoken the name, she'd seen Rukaiya

lower her head, as if she were solely concerned with her feeding infant. That was as good a way as any to bring herself under composure, of course.

Now, she looked up. Quickly, before lowering her head again to concentrate on Wahsi.

There might have been a hint of tears in her eyes. But all she said was: "I have no objection, Ousanas."

"*It is done!*" Ezana boomed. More forcefully than ever, the spearbutt slammed the stones. "It is *done*—and the royal regiments stand ready to enforce the decrees. As before. As always. As ever."

He glanced at Antonina. Seeing her little nod, he boomed: "All clear the chamber! There will be no further audience until the morrow."

At a small sign from Antonina, Garmat remained behind. No one would think that amiss. The old adviser's special relationship to the throne was well established and accepted. In any event, most people in the room would already have realized that he would soon be the new aqabe tsentsen, to replace Ousanas.

She would have liked to have Rukaiya's father remain. Under the circumstances, however, that might give rise to certain resentments.

Ezana stayed, also. He'd begun to leave, but even before Antonina could signal him to stay, Ousanas ordered him to do so.

Ordered him, outright. The first time he'd ever done so, in the many years the two men had known each other and worked closely together training and nurturing and protecting a young prince named Eon.

To Antonina's relief, Ezana had not seemed to bridle at all. In fact, he seemed a bit relieved himself.

In the short time that it took to clear the chamber, Antonina studied Ousanas. The man had seemed majestic to her for several years. Never more so than now.

By God, this will work.

Once the room was empty except for the five key people—six, counting the infant—Ousanas smiled ruefully.

"I will admit—again—that you are a genius, Antonina. This will work, I think. But . . ."

He looked at Rukaiya. She, back at him. There was sadness in both faces.

"I am not ready for this. Not yet. Neither is she."

There were definitely tears in Rukaiya's eyes, now. She shook her head. "No, I am not. I have . . . no objection, as I said. Sooner or later, I would have had to marry again, and I can think of no one I'd prefer. But Eon is still too close."

Ezana cleared his throat. "Yes. Of course. But I think he would be pleased, Rukaiya. And I knew him as well as any man."

She smiled, slightly. "Oh, yes. His ghost will be pleased—but not yet."

"It doesn't matter," Antonina said firmly. "We need to hold the wedding soon, but there is no reason you need to consummate the marriage immediately. In fact—"

Garmat picked up the cue, seamlessly. "It would be a bad idea," he said firmly. "We will need children from this union—*many* children, to be blunt, to give Wahsi a host of half-brothers and sisters to help him rule, since he will have no full ones. But we don't need them right now. No one will even start thinking about opposition for at least two years."

"More likely five—or ten," Ezana grunted. The smile that followed was a very cold sort of thing. "I can guarantee that much."

Garmat nodded. "Actually, the danger would be for you to have a child too *soon*. Enough time must elapse for it to have been impossible for Eon to have been the father. *Impossible*. That means waiting at least a year after his death last summer."

The relief on the faces of both Rukaiya and Ousanas was almost comical.

"Of course," Ousanas said. "Stupid of me not to have seen it instantly. Or else—three generations from now—some over-ambitious and small-brained great-grandson of mine might start claiming he was actually the great-grandson of Eon."

Smiling very gently now, he stepped forward and placed his hand on the baby's head. "In my safe-keeping, also."

He straightened. "We should do more, I think. Make it impossible the other way, also. And do so in a way that is publicly obvious, even to bedouin."

Clearly enough, his brain was back to working as well as always.

"Yes," she said firmly. This was something that Antonina and Garmat had already decided upon. "There is no need for me to remain here, and I would very much like to see my husband again. Ousanas should go with me to India, leading whatever military force Axum can add to the war."

She gave a quick glance at Ezana. "Except the three royal regiments, of course."

"We'll leave two regiments in Arabia also," said Garmat. "That will be enough. The Arabs will have no problem with Antonina's decrees on the succession."

"That will be enough," Ezana agreed. "The kingdom will be stable, and Ousanas can squeeze whatever advantage he can get for Axum from our deepened participation in the war. By the time he gets back, at least a year will have elapsed from Eon's death."

"Rukaiya?" Antonina asked.

"Yes. I agree." She also smiled gently. "And I will be ready, by then, for another husband."

"Done!" Ezana boomed. He did, however—just barely—manage to restrain himself from slamming the ferrule on the stones.

Ousanas scowled. "And, now—for the details! We'll have at least a week to squabble—more likely, two—before a suitable wedding can be organized. The *first* thing I want clearly established is that the royal regiments—*not* the otherwise-soon-to-be-impoverished mendicant family of the downtrodden angabo—have to pay for all the damage done to the floors by heavy-handed commanders."

"Ridiculous!" boomed Ezana. "The maintenance of the palace should clearly be paid for out of the angabo's coffers."

The spearbutt slammed the floor.

Chapter 11
CHABAHARI, IN THE STRAITS OF HORMUZ

Chabahari seemed like a nightmare to Anna. When she first arrived in the town—city, now—she was mainly struck by the chaos in the place. Not so long ago, Chabahari had been a sleepy fishing village. Since the great Roman-Persian expedition led by Belisarius to invade the Malwa homeland through the Indus valley had begun, Chabahari had been transformed almost overnight into a great military staging depot. The original fishing village was now buried somewhere within a sprawling and disorganized mass of tents, pavilions, jury-rigged shacks—and, of course, the beginnings of the inevitable grandiose palaces the Persians insisted on putting anywhere that their grandees resided.

Her first day was spent entirely in a search for the authorities in charge of the town. She had promised Dryopus she would report to those authorities as soon as she arrived.

But the search was futile. She found the official headquarters easily enough—one of the half-built palaces being erected by the Persians. But the interior of the edifice was nothing but confusion, a mass of workmen swarming all over, being overseen by a handful of harassed-looking supervisors. Not an official was to be found anywhere, neither Persian nor Roman.

"Try the docks," suggested the one foreman who spoke Greek and was prepared to give her a few minutes of his time. "The noble sirs complain about the noise here, and the smell everywhere else."

The smell *was* atrocious. Except in the immediate vicinity of the docks—which had their own none-too-savory aroma—the entire city seemed to be immersed in a miasma made up of the combined stench of excrement, urine, sweat, food—half of it seemingly rotten—and, perhaps most of all, blood and corrupting flesh. In addition to being a staging area for the invasion, Chabahari was also a depot where badly injured soldiers were being evacuated back to their homelands.

Those of them who survive this horrid place, Anna thought angrily, as she stalked out of the "headquarters." Illus and Cottomenes trailed behind her. Once she passed through the aivan onto the street beyond—insofar as the term "street" could be used at all for a simple space between buildings and shacks, teeming with people—she spent a moment or so looking south toward the docks.

"What's the point?" asked Illus, echoing her thoughts. "We didn't find anyone there when we disembarked." He cast a glance at the small mound of Anna's luggage piled up next to the building. The wharf boys whom Anna had hired to carry her belongings were lounging nearby, under Abdul's watchful eye.

"Besides," Illus continued, "it'll be almost impossible to keep your stuff from being stolen, in that madhouse down there."

Anna sighed. She looked down at her long dress, grimacing ruefully. The lowest few inches of the once-fine fabric, already ill-used by her journey from Constantinople, was now completely ruined. And the rest of it was well on its way—as much from her own sweat as anything else. The elaborate garments of a Greek noblewoman, designed for salons in the Roman Empire's capital, were torture in this climate.

A glimpse of passing color caught her eye. For a moment, she studied the figure of a young woman moving down the street. Some sort of Indian girl, apparently. Since the war had erupted into the Indian subcontinent, the inevitable human turbulence had thrown people of different lands into the new cauldrons of such cities as Chabahari. Mixing them up like grain caught in a thresher. Anna had noticed several Indians even in Charax.

Mainly, she just envied the woman's clothing, which was infinitely better suited for the climate than her own. By her senatorial family standards, of course, it was shockingly immodest.

But she spent a few seconds just *imagining* what her bare midriff would feel like, if it didn't feel like a mass of spongy, sweaty flesh.

Illus chuckled. "You'd peel like a grape, girl. With your fair skin?"

Anna had long since stopped taking offense at her "servant's" familiarity with her. That, too, would have outraged her family. But Anna herself took an odd little comfort in it. Much to her surprise, she had discovered over the weeks of travel that she was at ease in the company of Illus and his companions.

"Damn you, too," she muttered, not without some humor of her own. "I'd toughen up soon enough. And I wouldn't mind shedding some skin, anyway. What I've got right now feels like it's gangrenous."

It was Illus' turn to grimace. "Don't even think it, girl. Until you've seen real gangrene . . ."

A stray waft of breeze from the northwest illustrated his point. That was the direction of the great military "hospital" that the Roman army had set up on the outskirts of the city. The smell almost made Anna gag.

The gag brought up a reflex of anger, and, with it, a sudden decision.

"Let's go there," she said.

"Why?" demanded Illus.

Anna shrugged. "Maybe there'll be an official there. If nothing else, I need to find where the telegraph office is located."

Illus' face made his disagreement clear enough. Still—for all that she allowed familiarity, Anna had also established over the past weeks that she *was* his master.

"Let's go," she repeated firmly. "If nothing else, that's probably the only part of this city where we'd find some empty lodgings."

"True enough," said Illus, sighing. "They'll be dying like flies, over there." He hesitated, then began to speak. But Anna cut him off before he got out more than three words.

"I'm not insane, damn you. If there's an epidemic, we'll leave. But I doubt it. Not in this climate, this time of year. At least . . . not if they've been following the sanitary regulations."

Illus' face creased in a puzzled frown. "What's that got to do with anything? What regulations?"

Anna snorted and began to walk off to the northwest. "Don't you read *anything* besides those damned *Dispatches*?"

Cottomenes spoke up. "No one does," he said. Cheerfully, as usual. "No soldier, anyway. Your husband's got a way with words, he does. Have you ever tried to *read* official regulations?"

Those words, too, brought a reflex of anger. But, as she forced her way through the mob toward the military hospital, Anna found herself thinking about them. And eventually came to realize two things.

One. Although she was a voracious reader, she *hadn't* ever read any official regulations. Not those of the army, at any rate. But she suspected they were every bit as turgid as the regulations that officials in Constantinople spun out like spiders spinning webs.

Two. Calopodius *did* have a way with words. On their way down the Euphrates—and then again, as they sailed from Charax to Chabahari—the latest *Dispatches* and the newest chapters from his *History of Belisarius and the War* had been available constantly. Belisarius, Anna had noted, seemed to be as adamant about strewing printing presses behind his army's passage as he was about arms depots.

The chapters of the *History* had been merely perused on occasion by her soldier companions. Anna could appreciate the literary skill involved, but the constant allusions in those pages were meaningless to Illus and his brother, much less the illiterate Abdul. Yet they pored over each and every *Dispatch,* often enough in the company of a dozen other soldiers, one of them reading it aloud, while the others listened with rapt attention.

As always, her husband's fame caused some part of Anna to seethe with fury. But, this time, she also *thought* about it. And if, at the end, her thoughts caused her anger to swell, it was a much cleaner kind of anger. One which did not coil in her stomach like a worm, but simply filled her with determination.

The hospital was even worse than she'd imagined. But she did, not surprisingly, find an unused tent in which she and her companions could make their quarters. And she did discover the location of the telegraph office—which, as it happened, was situated right next to the sprawling grounds of the "hospital."

The second discovery, however, did her little good. The official in charge, once she awakened him from his afternoon nap, yawned and explained that the telegraph line from Barbaricum to Chabahari was still at least a month away from completion.

"That'll mean a few weeks here," muttered Illus. "It'll take at least that long for couriers to bring your husband's reply."

Instead of the pure rage those words would have brought to her once, the Isaurian's sour remark simply caused Anna's angry determination to harden into something like iron.

"Good," she pronounced. "We'll put the time to good use."

"How?" he demanded.

"Give me tonight to figure it out."

It didn't take her all night. Just four hours. The first hour she spent sitting in her screened-off portion of the tent, with her knees hugged closely to her chest, listening to the moans and shrieks of the maimed and dying soldiers who surrounded it. The remaining three, studying the books she had brought with her—especially her favorite, Irene Macrembolitissa's *Commentaries on the Talisman of God*, which had been published just a few months before Anna's precipitous decision to leave Constantinople in search of her husband.

Irene Macrembolitissa was Anna's private idol. Not that the sheltered daughter of the Melisseni had ever thought to emulate the woman's adventurous life, except intellectually. The admiration had simply been an emotional thing, the heroine-worship of a frustrated girl for a woman who had done so many things she could only dream about. But now, carefully studying those pages in which Macrembolitissa explained certain features of natural philosophy as given to mankind through Belisarius by the Talisman of God, she came to understand the hard practical core which lay beneath the great woman's flowery prose and ease with classical and biblical allusions. And, with that understanding, came a hardening of her own soul.

Fate, against her will and her wishes, had condemned her to be a wife. So be it. She would begin with that practical core; with concrete truth, not abstraction. She would steel the bitterness of *a* wife into the driving will of *the* wife. The wife of Calopodius the Blind, Calopodius of the Saronites.

The next morning, very early, she presented her proposition.

"Do any of you have a problem with working in trade?"

The three soldiers stared at her, stared at each other, broke into soft laughter.

"We're not senators, girl," chuckled Illus.

Anna nodded. "Fine. You'll have to work on speculation, though. I'll need the money I have left to pay the others."

"What 'others'?"

Anna smiled grimly. "I think you call it 'the muscle.'"

Cottomenes frowned. "I thought *we* were 'the muscle.'"

"Not any more," said Anna. "You're promoted. All three of you are now officers in the hospital service."

"*What* 'hospital service'?"

Anna realized she hadn't considered the name of the thing. For a moment, the old anger flared. But she suppressed it easily enough. This was no time for pettiness, after all.

"We'll call it Calopodius' Wife's Service. How's that?"

The three soldiers shook their heads. Clearly enough, they had no understanding of what she was talking about.

"You'll see," she predicted.

It didn't take them long. Illus' glare was enough to cow the official "commander" of the hospital, who was as sorry-looking a specimen of "officer" as Anna could imagine. And if the man might have wondered at the oddness of such glorious ranks being borne by such as Illus and his two companions—Abdul looked as far removed from a *tribune* as could be imagined—he was wise enough to keep his doubts to himself.

The dozen or so soldiers whom Anna recruited into the Service in the next hour—"the muscle"—had no trouble at all believing that Illus and Cottomenes and Abdul were, respectively, the *chiliarch* and two *tribunes* of a new army "service" they'd never heard of. First, because they were all veterans of the war and could recognize others—and knew, as well, that Belisarius promoted with no regard for personal origin. Second—more importantly—because they were wounded soldiers cast adrift in a chaotic "military hospital" in the middle of nowhere. Anna—Illus, actually, following her directions—selected only those soldiers whose wounds were healing well. Men who could move around and exert themselves. Still, even for such men, the prospect of regular pay meant a much increased chance at survival.

Anna wondered, a bit, whether walking-wounded "muscle" would serve the purpose. But her reservations were settled within the next hour after four of the new "muscle," at Illus' command, beat the first surgeon into a bloody pulp when the man responded to Anna's command to start boiling his instruments with a sneer and a derogatory remark about meddling women.

By the end of the first day, eight other surgeons were sporting cuts and bruises. But, at least when it came to the medical staff, there were no longer any doubts—none at all, in point of fact—as to whether this bizarre new "Calopodius' Wife's Service" had any actual authority.

Two of the surgeons complained to the hospital's commandant, but that worthy chose to remain inside his headquarters' tent. That night, Illus and three of his new "muscle" beat the two complaining surgeons into a still bloodier pulp, and all complaints to the commandant ceased thereafter.

Complaints from the medical staff, at least. A body of perhaps twenty soldiers complained to the hospital commandant the next day, hobbling to the HQ as best they could. But, again, the commandant chose to remain inside; and, again, Illus—this time using his entire corps of "muscle," which had now swollen to thirty men—thrashed the complainers senseless afterward.

Thereafter, whatever they might have muttered under their breath, none of the soldiers in the hospital protested openly when they were instructed to dig real latrines, *away* from the tents—and use them. Nor did they complain when they were ordered to help completely immobilized soldiers use them as well.

By the end of the fifth day, Anna was confident that her authority in the hospital was well enough established. She spent a goodly portion of those days daydreaming about the pleasures of wearing more suitable apparel, as she made her slow way through the ranks of wounded men in the swarm of tents. But she knew full well that the sweat that seemed to saturate her was one of the prices she would have to pay. Lady Saronites, wife of Calopodius the Blind, daughter of the illustrious family of the Melisseni, was a figure of power and majesty and authority—and had the noble gowns to prove it, even if they were soiled and frayed. Young Anna, all of nineteen years old, wearing a sari, would have had none at all.

By the sixth day, as she had feared, what was left of the money she had brought with her from Constantinople was almost gone. So, gathering her now-filthy robes in two small but determined hands, she marched her way back into the city of Chabahari. By now, at least, she had learned the name of the city's commander.

It took her half the day to find the man, in the *taberna* where he was reputed to spend most of his time. By the time she did, as she had been told, he was already half-drunk.

"Garrison troops," muttered Illus as they entered the tent that served the city's officers for their entertainment. The tent was filthy, as well as crowded with officers and their whores.

Anna found the commandant of the garrison in a corner, with a young half-naked girl perched on his lap. After taking half the day to find the man, it only took her a few minutes to reason with him and obtain the money she needed to keep the Service in operation.

Most of those few minutes were spent explaining, in considerable detail, exactly what she needed. Most of that, in specifying tools and artifacts—*more shovels to dig more latrines; pots for boiling water; more fabric for making more tents, because the ones they had were too crowded.* And so forth.

She spent a bit of time, at the end, specifying the sums of money she would need.

"Twenty solidi—a day." She nodded at an elderly wounded soldier whom she had brought with her along with Illus. "That's Zeno. He's literate. He's the Service's accountant in Chabahari. You can make all the arrangements through him."

The garrison's commandant then spent a minute explaining to Anna, also in considerable detail—mostly anatomical—what she could do with the tools, artifacts and money she needed.

Illus' face was very strained, by the end. Half with fury, half with apprehension—this man was no petty officer to be pounded with fists. But Anna herself sat through the garrison commander's tirade quite calmly. When he was done, she did not need more than a few seconds to reason with him further and bring him to see the error of his position.

"My husband is Calopodius the Blind. I will tell him what you have said to me, and he will place the words in his next *Dispatch.* You will be a lucky man if all that happens to you is that General Belisarius has you executed."

She left the tent without waiting to hear his response. By the time she reached the tent's entrance, the garrison commander's face was much whiter than the tent fabric and he was gasping for breath.

The next morning, a chest containing a hundred solidi was brought to the hospital and placed in Zeno's care. The day after that, the first of the tools and artifacts began arriving.

Four weeks later, when Calopodius' note finally arrived, the mortality rate in the hospital was less than half what it had been when Anna arrived. She was almost sorry to leave.

In truth, she might not have left at all, except by then she was confident that Zeno was quite capable of managing the entire service as well as its finances.

"Don't steal anything," she warned him, as she prepared to leave.

Zeno's face quirked with a rueful smile. "I wouldn't dare risk the Wife's anger."

She laughed, then; and found herself wondering through all the days of their slow oar-driven travel to Barbaricum why those words had brought her no anger at all.

And, each night, she took out Calopodius' letter and wondered at it also. Anna had lived with anger and bitterness for so long—"so long," at least, to a nineteen-year-old girl—that she was confused by its absence. She was even more confused by the little glow of warmth which the last words in the letter gave her, each time she read them.

"You're a strange woman," Illus told her, as the great battlements and cannons of Barbaricum loomed on the horizon.

There was no way to explain. "Yes," was all she said.

The first thing she did upon arriving at Barbaricum was march into the telegraph office. If the officers in command thought there was anything peculiar about a young Greek noblewoman dressed in the finest and filthiest garments they had ever seen, they kept it to themselves. Perhaps rumors of "the Wife" had preceded her.

"Send a telegram immediately," she commanded. "To my husband, Calopodius the Blind."

They hastened to comply. The message was brief:

ADDRESS MEDICAL CARE AND SANITATION IN NEXT DISPATCH STOP FIRMLY STOP

THE IRON TRIANGLE

When Calopodius received the telegram—and he received it immediately, because his post was in the Iron Triangle's command and communication center—the first words he said as soon as the telegraph operator finished reading it to him were:

"God, I'm an idiot!"

Belisarius had heard the telegram also. In fact, all the officers in the command center had heard, because they had been waiting with an ear cocked. By now, the peculiar journey of Calopodius' wife was a source of feverish gossip in the ranks of the entire army fighting off the Malwa siege in the Punjab. *What the hell is that girl doing, anyway?* being only the most polite of the speculations.

The general sighed and rolled his eyes. Then, closed them. It was obvious to everyone that he was reviewing all of Calopodius' now-famous *Dispatches* in his mind.

"We're both idiots," he muttered. "We've maintained proper medical and sanitation procedures *here,* sure enough. But . . ."

His words trailed off. His second-in-command, Maurice, filled in the rest.

"She must have passed through half the invasion staging posts along the way. Garrison troops, garrison officers—with the local butchers as the so-called 'surgeons.' God help us, I don't even want to think . . ."

"I'll write it immediately," said Calopodius.

Belisarius nodded. "Do so. And I'll give you some choice words to include." He cocked his head at Maurice, smiling crookedly. "What do you think? Should we resurrect crucifixion as a punishment?"

Maurice shook his head. "Don't be so damned flamboyant. Make the punishment fit the crime. Surgeons who do not boil their instruments will be boiled alive. Officers who do not see to it that proper latrines are maintained will be buried alive in them. That sort of thing."

Calopodius was already seated at the desk where he dictated his *Dispatches* and the chapters of the *History.* So was his scribe, pen in hand.

"I'll add a few nice little flourishes," his young voice said confidently. "This strikes me as a good place for grammar and rhetoric."

Chapter 12
THE THAR DESERT
NEAR THE IRON TRIANGLE

Three days later, at sunrise, Belisarius and a small escort rode into the Thar Desert. "The Great Indian Desert," as it was also sometimes called.

They didn't go far. No farther than they'd been able to travel in the three days since they'd left the Triangle. Partly, that was because Belisarius' bodyguards were by now pestering him almost constantly regarding his security. They hadn't been happy at all when he'd informed them he planned to leave the Triangle on a week-long scouting expedition of his own. The bodyguards had the not-unreasonable attitude that scouting expeditions should be done by scouts, not commanders-in-chief.

Belisarius didn't disagree with them, as a matter of general principle. Nor was this expedition one of the periodically calculated risks he took, proving to his men that he was willing to share their dangers and hardships. It was, in fact, purely and simply a scouting expedition—and not one in which he expected to encounter any enemies.

Why would he, after all? The Thar was enemy enough, to any human. With the exception of some small nomadic tribes, no one ventured into it willingly. There was no logical reason for the Malwa to be sending patrols into its interior. In any event, Belisarius had been careful to enter the desert much farther south than the most advanced Malwa contingents.

Aide wasn't any happier at the situation than the bodyguards were.

This is purely stupid. Why are you bothering, anyway? You already crossed the Thar, once before, when you were fleeing India. And don't try to deny it! I was there, remember?

Belisarius ignored him, for a moment. His eyes continued to range the landscape, absorbing it as best he could.

True, he had crossed this desert once—albeit a considerable distance to the south. Still, what he could see here was not really any different from what he'd seen years earlier. The Thar desert, like most deserts, is much of a sameness.

Yes, I remember—but my memories were those of the man who crossed this desert then. *One man, alone, on a camel rather than a horse, and with plenty of water and supplies. I needed to see it again, to really bring back* all *the memories.*

I could have done that for you, Aide pointed out peevishly. One of the crystal's seemingly-magical powers was an ability to bring back any of Belisarius' memories—while Aide had been with him, at least—as vividly as if they'd just happened.

Belisarius shook his head slightly. *It's still not the same. I need to feel the heat again, on my own skin. Gauge it, just as I gauge the dryness and the barrenness.*

He gave Abbu, riding just behind him to his left, a little jerk of the head to summon him forward.

"What do you think?" he asked the leader of his Arab scouts.

Abbu's grizzle-bearded countenance glared at the desert. "It is nothing, next to the Empty Quarter!"

Bedouin honor having been satisfied, he shrugged. "Still, it is a real desert. No oases, even, from what I've been told."

He's right, Aide chimed in. *There aren't any. The desert isn't as bad as it will become a millennia and a half from now, when the first real records were maintained. The Thar is a fairly recent desert. Still, as the old bandit says, it is indeed a real desert. And no artesian wells, either.*

Belisarius mused on the problem, for a minute or so.

Could we dig our own wells, then?

I could find the spots for you. Very likely ones, at least. The records are good, and the aquifers would not have changed much. But there are no guarantees, and . . . In a desert this bad, if even one of my estimates proves wrong, it could be disastrous.

Belisarius was considerably more sanguine than Aide, on that score. He had found many times that Aide's superhuman intellect, while it often floundered with matters involving human emotions, rarely failed when it came to a straightforward task of deduction based on a mass of empirical data.

Still, he saw no reason to take unnecessary chances.

"Abbu, if I send you and some of your men through this desert—a dozen or two, whatever you wish—along with a chart indicating the likely spots to dig wells, could you find them?"

Abbu's expression was sour. "I don't read charts easily," he grumbled. "Detest the newfangled things."

Belisarius suppressed a smile. What Abbu said was true enough—the part about detesting the things, at any rate—but the scout leader was perfectly capable of reading them well enough. Even if he weren't, he had several young Arabs who could read and interpret maps and charts as easily as any Greek. What was really involved here was more the natural dislike of an old bedouin at the prospect of digging a number of wells in a desert.

You'd be an idiot to trust him to do it properly, anyway. If you want good wells made—ones that you can depend on, weeks or months later—you'd do better to use Greeks.

Teaching your grandfather to suck eggs again? I just want Abbu to find the spots. I'll send some of my bucellarii with him to do the work. Thracians will be even better than Greeks.

After he explained the plan to Abbu, the scout leader was mollified. "Easy, then," he announced. "Take us three weeks."

"No longer?"

Abbu squinted at the desert. "Maybe a month. The Thar is three hundred miles across, you say?"

Not really, Aide chimed in. **Not today, before the worst of the desiccation has happened. Say, two hundred miles of real desert, with a fifty-mile fringe. We're still in the fringe here, really.**

"Figure two hundred miles of real desert, Abbu, with another fifty on either side like this terrain."

The old Arab ran fingers through his beard. "And you want us to use horses. Not camels?"

Belisarius nodded.

"Then, as I say, three, maybe four weeks. Coming back will be quick, with the wells already dug."

Abbu cocked his head a little, looking at Belisarius through narrowed eyes.

"What rashness are you contemplating, General?"

Belisarius pointed with his chin toward the east. "When the time comes—if the time comes—I may want to lead an expedition across that desert. To Ajmer."

"*Ajmer?*" The Arab chief's eyes almost literally bulged. "You are mad! Ajmer is the main city of the Rajputs. It would take you ten thousand men—maybe fifteen—to seize the city. Then, you would be lucky to hold it against the counterattack."

He stretched out his hand and flipped it, simultaneously indicating the desert with the gesture and dismissing everything else. "You cannot—*can not*, General, not even you—get more than a thousand men across that desert. Not even with wells dug. Not even in this fine *rabi* season—and we'll soon be in the heat of *garam*. With camels, maybe two thousand. But with horses? A thousand at most!"

"I wasn't actually planning to take a thousand," Belisarius said mildly. "I think five hundred of my bucellarii will suffice. With an additional two hundred of your scouts, as outriders."

"Against *Rajputs?*" Fiercely, Abbu shook his head. "Not a chance, General. Not with only five hundred of your best Thracians. Not even with splendid Arab scouts. We would not get within sight of Ajmer before we were overrun. Not all the Rajputs are in the Deccan with Damodara, you know. Many are not."

Belisarius nodded placidly. "A great many, according to my spies. I'm counting on that, in fact. I need at least fifteen thousand Rajputs to be in or around Ajmer when we arrive. Twenty would be better."

Abbu rolled his eyes. "What lunacy is this? You are expecting the Rajputs to become changed men? Lambs, where once they were lions?"

Belisarius chuckled. "Oh, not that, certainly. I'd have no use for Rajput lambs. But . . . yes, Abbu. If I do this—which I may well not, since right now it's only a possibility—then I expect the Rajputs to have changed."

He reined his horse around. "More than that, I will not say. This is all speculation, in any event. Let's get back to the Triangle."

✧   ✧   ✧

When they returned to the Triangle, Belisarius gave three orders.

The first summoned Ashot from the Sukkur gorge. He was no longer needed there, in command of the Roman forces, now that the Persians had established firm control over the area.

"I'll want him in charge of the bucellarii, of course," he told Maurice, "since you'll have to remain behind."

The bucellarii were Belisarius' picked force of Thracian cataphracts, armored heavy cavalrymen. A private army, in essence, that he'd maintained for years. A large one, too, numbering by now seven thousand men. He could afford it, since the immense loot from the past years of successful campaigns—first, against the Persians; and then, in alliance with them against the Malwa—had made Belisarius the richest person in the Roman Empire except for Justinian and Theodora.

Maurice had been the leader of those bucellarii since they were first formed, over ten years earlier. But, today, he was essentially the second-in-command of the entire Roman army in the Punjab.

Maurice grunted. "Ashot'll do fine. I still say it's a crazy idea."

"It may never happen, anyway," Belisarius pointed out. "It's something of a long shot, depending on several factors over which we have no control at all."

Maurice scowled. "So what? 'Long shot' and 'no control' are the two phrases that best describe this war to begin with."

Rightly said! chimed in Aide.

Belisarius gave the crystal the mental equivalent of a very cross-eyed look. *If I recall correctly,* you *were the one who started the war in the first place.*

Oh, nonsense! I just pointed out the inevitable.

The second order, which he issued immediately thereafter, summoned Agathius from Mesopotamia.

"We don't need him there either, any more," he explained to Maurice.

"No, we don't. Although I hate to think of what chaos those damn Persians will create in our logistics without Agathius to crack the whip over them. Still . . ."

The chiliarch ran fingers through his grizzled beard. "We could use him here, better. If you go haring off on this preposterous mad dash of yours, I'll have to command the troops here. Bloody fighting, that'll be, all across the front."

"Bloodier than anything you've ever seen," Belisarius agreed. "Or I've ever seen—or anyone's ever seen. The two greatest armies ever assembled in history hammering at each other across not more than twenty miles of front. And the Malwa *will* hammer, Maurice. You can be sure that Link will give that order before the monster departs. Whatever else, it will want this Roman army kept in its cage, and not able to come after it."

Maurice's grunted chuckle even had a bit of real humor. Not much, of course. "But no fancy maneuvers required. Nothing that really needs the crooked brain of Belisarius. Just stout, simple-minded Maurice of Thrace, like the centurion of the Bible. Saying to one, come, and he cometh. Saying to another, go, and he goeth."

Belisarius smiled, but said nothing.

Maurice grunted again, seeing the smile. "Well, I can do that, certainly. And I agree that it would help a lot to have Agathius here. He can manage everything else while I command on the front lines."

The third order he gave to Ashot, a few days later, as soon as he arrived.

More in the way of a set of orders, actually. Which of them Ashot chose to follow would depend on ... this and that.

"Marvelous," said Ashot, after Belisarius finished. The stubby Armenian cataphract exchanged a familiar look with Maurice. The one that translated more-or-less as: *what sins did we commit to be given such a young lunatic for a commander?*

But he verbalized none of it. Even the exchange of looks was more in the way of a familiar habit than anything really heartfelt. It was not as if he and Maurice weren't accustomed to the experience, by now.

"I don't much doubt Kungas will agree," he said. "So I should be back within a month."

Belisarius cocked an eyebrow. "That soon?"

"There are advantages to working as closely as I have with Persians, General. I know at least two dehgans in Sukkur who are familiar with the terrain I'll have to pass through to reach Kungas. They'll guide me, readily enough."

"All right. How many men do you want?"

"Not more than thirty. We shouldn't encounter any Malwa, the route I'll be taking. Thirty will be enough to scare off any bandits. Any more would just slow us down."

Ashot and his little troop left the next morning. Thereafter, Belisarius went back to the routine of the siege.

"I hate sieges," he commented to Calopodius. "But I will say they don't require much in the way of thought, once everything's settled down."

"Meaning no offense, General, but if you think *you* hate sieges, I invite you to try writing a history about one. Grammar and rhetoric can only do so much."

Antonina stared down at the message in her hand. She was trying to remember if, at any time in her life, she'd ever felt such conflicting emotions.

"That is the oddest expression I can ever remember seeing on your face," Ousanas mused. "Although it does remind me, a bit, of the expression I once saw on the face of a young Greek nobleman in Alexandria."

Stalling for time while she tried to sort out her feelings, Antonina muttered: "When did you ever know any Greek noblemen in Alexandria?"

Glancing up, she saw Ousanas was smiling, that serene little smile that was always a little disconcerting on his face.

"I have led a varied life, you know. I wasn't always shackled to this wretched little African backwater in the mountains. On that occasion—there were several—the youth fancied himself a philosopher. I showed him otherwise."

Lounging on a nearby chair in Antonina's salon, Ezana grunted. He'd taken no offense, of course, at Ousanas' wisecrack about Axum. Partly, because he was used to it; partly, because he knew from experience that the only way to deal with Ousanas' wisecracks was to ignore them.

"And *that* is what caused a peculiar expression on his face?" he asked skeptically. "I would have thought one of your devastating logical ripostes—for which the world has seen no equal since Socrates—would have simply left him aghast at his ignorance."

Ezana was no slouch himself, when it came to wisecracks—or turning a properly florid phrase, for that matter. Ousanas flashed a quick grin in recognition, and then shrugged.

"Alas, no. My rebuttal went so far over his head that the callow stripling had no idea at all that I'd disemboweled him, intellectually speaking. No, the peculiar expression came not five minutes later, when a courier arrived bearing the news that the lad's father had died in Constantinople. And that he had inherited one of the largest fortunes in the empire."

He pointed a finger at Antonina's face. "*That* expression."

She didn't know whether to laugh or scowl. In the end, she managed to do both.

"It's a letter from Theodora. Sent by telegraph to Alexandria, relayed to Myos Hormos, and then brought by a dispatch vessel the rest of the way." She held it up. "My son—his wife Tahmina, too—is coming on a tour of our allies. Starting here in Axum, of course. He'll go with us to India."

"Ah." Ousanas nodded. "All is explained. Your delight at the unexpected prospect of seeing your son again, much sooner than you expected. Your chagrin at having to delay your much-anticipated reunion with your husband. The maternal instinct of a proper Egyptian woman clashing with the salacious habits of a Greek harlot."

He and Ezana exchanged stern glances.

"You should wait for your son," Ezana pronounced. "Even if you are a Greek harlot."

Antonina gave them the benefit of her sweetest smile. "I would remind both of you that Greek women are also the world's best and most experienced poisoners. And you do not use food-tasters in Ethiopia."

"She has a point," Ousanas averred.

Ezana grunted again. "She should still wait for her son. Even if she is—"

"*Of course I'm going to wait for my son, you—you—fucking idiots!*"

The next day, though, it was her turn to start needling Ousanas.

"What? If it's that hard for you, why don't you leave now? There's no reason *you* have to wait here until Photius arrives. You can surely find some way to pass the time in Barbaricum—or

Chabahari, most like—as accustomed as you are to the humdrum life in this African backwater."

Ousanas scowled at her. For one of the rare times since she'd met him, years earlier, the Bantu once-hunter had no easy quip to make in response.

"Damnation, Antonina, it is *difficult*. It never was, before, because..."

"Yes, I know. The mind—even yours, o great philosopher—makes different categories for different things. It's convenient, that way, and avoids problems."

Ousanas ran fingers over his scalp. "Yes," he said curtly. "Even mine. And now..."

His eyes started to drift toward the window they were standing near. Then, he looked away.

Antonina leaned over and glanced down into the courtyard below, one of several in the Ta'akha Maryam. Rukaiya was still there, sitting on a bench and holding her baby.

"She is very beautiful," Antonina said softly.

Ousanas was still looking aside. "Beauty I could ignore, readily enough. I am no peasant boy." For an instant, the familiar smile gleamed. "No longer, at least. I can remember a time when the mere sight of her would have paralyzed me."

He shrugged, uncomfortably. "Much harder to ignore the wit and the intelligence, coupled to the beauty. The damn girl is even well educated, for her age. Give her ten years..."

Antonina eyed him. "I did choose her for a king's wife, you know. And not just any king, but Eon. And I chose very well, I think."

"Yes, you did. Eon was besotted with her. I never had any trouble understanding why—but it never affected me then, either."

"The wedding will be tomorrow, Ousanas. Leave the next day, if you will."

"I can't, Antonina. First, because it would look odd, since everyone now knows that you are waiting for Photius. People would assume it was because I was displeased with the girl, instead of... ah, the exact opposite."

He brought his eyes back to look at her. "The bigger problem, however, is Koutina. Which we must now discuss. Before I do anything else, I must resolve that issue. People are already jabbering about it."

Antonina winced. As pleased as she was, overall, with her settlement of the Axumite succession problem, it was not a perfect world and her solution had shared in that imperfection. Most of the problems she could ignore, at least personally, since they mainly involved the grievances and disgruntlements of people she thought were too full of themselves anyway.

But Koutina . . .

"I don't know what to do about her," she admitted sadly.

The girl had been the most faithful and capable servant Antonina had ever had. And she'd now repaid her by separating her from Ousanas, with whom she'd developed a relationship that went considerably beyond a casual sexual liaison.

"Neither do I," said Ousanas. His tone was, if anything, still sadder. "She's always known, of course, that as the aqabe tsentsen I'd eventually have to make a marriage of state. But—"

He shrugged again. "The position of concubine was acceptable to her."

"It's not possible, now. You know that."

"Yes. Of course." After a moment's hesitation, Ousanas stepped to the window and looked down.

"She approached me about it two days ago, you know," he murmured.

"Rukaiya?"

"Yes. She told me she understood my existing attachment to Koutina and would have no objection if I kept her as a concubine." He smiled, turned away from the window, and held up a stiff finger. "'Only one, though!' she said. 'Koutina is different. Any others and I will have you poisoned. Not the concubine— you!'"

Antonina chuckled. "That . . . is very much like Rukaiya."

Which, it was, although Antonina was skeptical that Rukaiya would actually be able to handle the situation that easily. Granted, the girl was Arab and thus no stranger to the institution of concubinage. Even her recent conversion to Christianity would not have made much difference, if any. Concubinage might be frowned upon by the church, but it was common enough practice among wealthy Christians also—including plenty of bishops.

Still, she'd been a queen for some time now—and Eon's queen, to boot. There had never been any hint of interest in concubines on Eon's part. Of course, with a wife like Rukaiya, that was hardly surprising. Not only was she quite possibly the most beautiful woman in the Axumite empire, she had wit and brains and a charming personality to go with it.

But it didn't matter, anyway. "Ousanas—"

"Yes, yes, I know." He waved his hand. "Absolutely impossible, given the nature of my new position as the angabo. The situation will be tricky enough as it is, making sure that the children Rukaiya will bear me have the proper relationship with Wahsi. Throw into that delicate balance yet another batch of children with Koutina . . ."

He shook his head. "It would be madness. She's not barren, either."

Koutina's one pregnancy had ended in a miscarriage. That was not particularly unusual, of course. Most likely, Koutina's next pregnancy *would* produce a child.

Suddenly, Ousanas shook his head again, but this time with rueful amusement. "Ha! It's probably a good thing Rukaiya *is* so comely and enjoyable to be around. I'm afraid there'll be no more sexual adventures on the part of the mighty Ousanas. As aqabe tsentsen, I could do most anything in that regard and only produce chuckles. As angabo, I will have to be like the Caesar's wife you Romans brag about—even if, mind you, I can't see where you've often lived up to it."

Antonina grinned. "Theodora does. Which, given her history, may seem ironic to some people. On the other hand, the one advantage to being an ex-whore—take it from me—is that you're not subject to the notion some women have that the man in some other woman's bed is much more interesting than the one in your own." She stuck out her tongue. "*Bleah.*"

"I can imagine. However . . ."

"Yes, I know. We are no closer to a solution. And the problem is as bad as it could be, because Koutina is not only losing you, she's losing *me.* I can't very well keep her on as my servant when you will be accompanying me on the same trip with . . ."

Her voice trailed off. Looking suddenly at Ousanas, she saw that his eyes had that slightly unfocused look she suspected were in her own.

"Photius would have to agree, of course," Ousanas mused. "Tahmina, rather."

Antonina tried to poke at the idea, to find any weak spots.

"It still leaves the problem that Koutina will be with us. People might think—"

"Pah!" Ousanas' sneer, when he threw himself into it, could be as magnificent as his grin. "What 'people'? The only 'people'—*person*—who matters here is Rukaiya. And she will believe me—she'll certainly believe you—when we explain it to her. For the rest..."

He shrugged. "Who cares what gossip circulates, as long as Rukaiya doesn't pay attention to it? Gossip is easy to deal with. Ignore it unless it gets too obtrusive, at which point you inform Ezana that Loudmouths Alpha, Beta and Gamma have become a nuisance. Shortly thereafter, Loudmouths Alpha, Beta and Gamma will either cease being a nuisance or will cease altogether."

The grin came. "Such a handy fellow to have around, even if he lacks the proper appreciation of my philosophical talents."

The more Antonina considered the idea, the more she liked it. "Yes. Eventually, the trip is over. So long as there are no Ousanas bastards inconveniently lounging about"—here she gave him a pointed look—"there's no problem. Koutina goes to Constantinople as one of Tahmina's maidservants, and..."

Her face cleared. "She'll do quite well. You've already started her education. If she continues it—she's very pretty, and very capable—she'll eventually wind up in a good marriage. A senatorial family is not out of the question, if she has Tahmina's favor. Which, I have no doubt she will."

For a moment, she and Ousanas regarded each other with that special satisfaction that belongs to conspirators having reached a particularly pleasing conspiracy.

Then, Ousanas frowned. "I remind you. Photius will have to agree."

Antonina's expression became—she hoped, anyway—suitably outraged. "Of course, he will! He's my *son,* you idiot!"

When Photius arrived, two weeks later, he didn't actually have an opinion, one way or the other.

"Whatever you want, Mother," in the resigned but dutiful tones of an eleven-year-old.

Antonina's older daughter-in-law, on the other hand, proved far more perceptive.

"What a marvelous idea, Mother! And do you think she'd be

willing to carry around a cuirass for me, too?" The sixteen-year-old gave her husband a very credible eyelash-batting. "I think I'd look good in a cuirass, Photius, don't you?"

Photius choked. "Not in bed!" he protested. "I'd break my hands, trying to give you backrubs."

Chapter 13
BARBARICUM, ON THE INDIAN COAST

Anna and her companions spent their first night in India crowded into the corner of a tavern packed full with Roman soldiers and all the other typical denizens of a great port city—longshoremen, sailors, petty merchants and their womenfolk, pimps and prostitutes, gamblers, and the usual sprinkling of thieves and other criminals.

Like almost all the buildings in Barbaricum, the tavern was a mudbrick edifice that had been badly burned in the great fires that swept the city during the Roman conquest. The arson had not been committed by Belisarius' men, but by the fanatic Mahaveda priests who led the Malwa defenders. Despite the still obvious reminders of that destruction, the tavern was in use for the simple reason that, unlike so many buildings in the city, the walls were still standing and there was even a functional roof.

When they first entered, Anna and her party had been assessed by the mob of people packed in the tavern. The assessment had not been as quick as the one which that experienced crowd would have normally made. Anna and her party were . . . odd.

The hesitation worked entirely to her advantage, however. The tough-looking Isaurian brothers and Abdul were enough to give would-be cutpurses pause, and in the little space and time cleared for them, the magical rumor had time to begin and spread throughout the tavern. Watching it spread—so obvious, from the curious stares and glances sent her way—Anna was simultaneously appalled, amused, angry, and thankful.

It's her. Calopodius the Blind's wife. Got to be.

"Who started this damned rumor, anyway?" she asked peevishly, after Illus cleared a reasonably clean spot for her in a corner and she was finally able to sit down. She leaned against the shelter of the walls with relief. She was well-nigh exhausted.

Abdul grunted with amusement. The Arab was frequently amused, Anna noted with exasperation. But it was an old and well-worn exasperation, by now, almost pleasant in its predictability.

Cottomenes, whose amusement at life's quirks was not much less than Abdul's, chuckled his own agreement. "You're hot news, Lady Saronites. Everybody on the docks was talking about it, too. And the soldiers outside the telegraph office." Cottomenes, unlike his older brother, never allowed himself the familiarity of calling her "girl." In all other respects, however, he showed her a lack of fawning respect that would have outraged her family.

After the dockboys whom Anna had hired finished stacking her luggage next to her, they crowded themselves against a wall nearby, ignoring the glares directed their way by the tavern's usual habitués. Clearly enough, having found this source of incredible largesse, the dockboys had no intention of relinquishing it.

Anna shook her head. The vehement motion finished the last work of disarranging her long dark hair. The elaborate coiffure under which she had departed Constantinople, so many weeks before, was now entirely a thing of the past. Her hair was every bit as tangled and filthy as her clothing. She wondered if she would ever feel clean again.

"*Why?*" she whispered.

Squatting next to her, Illus studied her for a moment. His eyes were knowing, as if the weeks of close companionship and travel had finally enabled a half-barbarian mercenary soldier to understand the weird torments of a young noblewoman's soul.

Which, indeed, perhaps they had.

"You're different, girl. What you do is *different*. You have no idea how important that can be, to a man who does nothing, day after day, but toil under a sun. Or to a woman who does nothing, day after day, but wash clothes and carry water."

She stared up at him. Seeing the warmth lurking somewhere

deep in Illus' eyes, in that hard tight face, Anna was stunned to realize how great a place the man had carved for himself in her heart. *Friendship* was a stranger to Anna of the Melisseni.

"And what is an angel, in the end," said the Isaurian softly, "but something *different*?"

Anna stared down at her grimy garments, noting all the little tears and frays in the fabric.

"In *this*?"

The epiphany finally came to her, then. And she wondered, in the hour or so that she spent leaning against the walls of the noisy tavern before she finally drifted into sleep, whether Calopodius had also known such an epiphany. Not on the day he chose to leave her behind, all her dreams crushed, in order to gain his own; but on the day he first awoke, a blind man, and realized that sight is its own curse.

And for the first time since she'd heard Calopodius' name, she no longer regretted the life that had been denied to her. No longer thought with bitterness of the years she would never spend in the shelter of the cloister, allowing her mind to range through the world's accumulated wisdom like a hawk finally soaring free.

When she awoke the next morning, the first thought that came to her was that she finally understood her own faith—and never had before, not truly. There was some regret in the thought, of course. Understanding, for all except God, is also limitation. But with that limitation came clarity and sharpness, so different from the froth and fuzz of a girl's fancies and dreams.

In the gray light of an alien land's morning, filtering into a tavern more noisome than any she would ever have imagined, Anna studied her soiled and ragged clothing. Seeing, this time, not filth and ruin but simply the carpet of her life opening up before her. A life she had thought closeted forever.

"Practicality first," she announced firmly. "It is not a sin."

The words woke up Illus. He gazed at her through slitted, puzzled eyes.

"Get up," she commanded. "We need uniforms."

A few minutes later, leading the way out the door with her three-soldier escort and five dock urchins toting her luggage, Anna issued the first of that day's rulings and commandments.

"It'll be expensive, but my husband will pay for it. He's rich."

"He's not here," grunted Illus.

"His name is. He's also famous. Find me a banker."

It took a bit of time before she was able to make the concept of "banker" clear to Illus. Or, more precisely, differentiate it from the concepts of "pawnbroker," "usurer" and "loan shark." But, eventually, he agreed to seek out and capture this mythological creature—with as much confidence as he would have announced plans to trap a griffin or a minotaur.

"Never mind," grumbled Anna, seeing the nervous little way in which Illus was fingering his sword. "I'll do it myself. Where's the army headquarters in this city? *They'll* know what a 'banker' is, be sure of it."

That task was within Illus' scheme of things. And since Barbaricum was in the actual theater of Belisarius' operations, the officers in command of the garrison were several cuts of competence above those at Chabahari. By midmorning, Anna had been steered to the largest of the many new moneylenders who had fixed themselves upon Belisarius' army.

An Indian himself, ironically enough, named Pulinda. Anna wondered, as she negotiated the terms, what secrets—and what dreams, realized or stultified—lay behind the life of the small and elderly man sitting across from her. How had a man from the teeming Ganges valley eventually found himself, awash with wealth obtained in whatever mysterious manner, a paymaster to the alien army which was hammering at the gates of his own homeland?

Did he regret the life which had brought him to this place? Savor it?

Most likely both, she concluded. And was then amused, when she realized how astonished Pulinda would have been had he realized that the woman with whom he was quarreling over terms was actually awash in good feeling toward him.

Perhaps, in some unknown way, he sensed that warmth. In any event, the negotiations came to an end sooner than Anna had expected. They certainly left her with better terms than she had expected.

Or, perhaps, it was simply that magic name of Calopodius again, clearing the waters before her. Pulinda's last words to her were: "Mention me to your husband, if you would."

By mid-afternoon, she had tracked down the tailor reputed to be the best in Barbaricum. By sundown, she had completed her business with him. Most of that time had been spent keeping the dockboys from fidgeting as the tailor measured them.

"You also!" Anna commanded, slapping the most obstreperous urchin on top of his head. "In the Service, cleanliness is essential."

The next day, however, when they donned their new uniforms, the dockboys were almost beside themselves with joy. The plain and utilitarian garments were, by a great margin, the finest clothing they had ever possessed.

The Isaurian brothers and Abdul were not quite as demonstrative. Not quite.

"We look like princes," gurgled Cottomenes happily.

"And so you are," pronounced Anna. "The highest officers of the Wife's Service. A rank which will someday"—she spoke with a confidence far beyond her years—"be envied by princes the world over."

THE IRON TRIANGLE

"Relax, Calopodius," said Menander cheerfully, giving the blind young officer a friendly pat on the shoulder. "I'll see to it she arrives safely."

"She's already left Barbaricum," muttered Calopodius. "Damnation, why didn't she *wait*?"

Despite his agitation, Calopodius couldn't help smiling when he heard the little round of laughter which echoed around him. As usual, whenever the subject of Calopodius' wife arose, every officer and orderly in the command bunker had listened. In her own way, Anna was becoming as famous as anyone in the great Roman army fighting its way into India.

Most husbands, to say the least, do not like to discover that their wives are the subject of endless army gossip. But since, in this case, the cause of the gossip was not the usual sexual peccadilloes, Calopodius was not certain how he felt about it. Some part of him, ingrained with custom, still felt a certain dull outrage. But, for the most part—perhaps oddly—his main reaction was one of quiet pride.

"I suppose that's a ridiculous question," he admitted ruefully. "She hasn't waited for anything else."

When Menander spoke again, the tone in his voice was much less jovial. As if he, too, shared in the concern which—much to his surprise—Calopodius had found engulfing him since he learned of Anna's journey. Strange, really, that he should care so much about the well-being of a wife who was little but a vague image to him.

But ... Even before his blinding, the world of literature had often seemed as real to Calopodius as any other. Since he lost his sight, it had become all the more so—despite the fact that he could no longer read or write himself, but depended on others to do it for him.

Anna Melisseni, the distant girl he had married and had known for a short time in Constantinople, meant practically nothing to him. But *the Wife of Calopodius the Blind,* the unknown woman who had been advancing toward him for weeks now, she was a different thing altogether. Still mysterious, but not a stranger. How could she be, any longer?

Had he not, after all, written about her often enough in his own *Dispatches*? In the third person, of course, as he always spoke of himself in his writings. No subjective mood was ever inserted into his *Dispatches,* any more than into the chapters of his massive *History of the War.* But, detached or not, whenever he received news of Anna he included at least a few sentences detailing for the army her latest adventures. Just as he did for those officers and men who had distinguished themselves. And he was no longer surprised to discover that most of the army found a young wife's exploits more interesting than their own.

She's *different.*

"Difference," however, was no shield against life's misfortunes— misfortunes which are multiplied several times over in the middle of a war zone. So, within seconds, Calopodius was back to fretting.

"Why didn't she wait, damn it all?"

Again, Menander clapped his shoulder. "I'm leaving with the *Victrix* this afternoon, Calopodius. Steaming with the riverflow, I'll be in Sukkur long before Anna gets there coming upstream in an oared river craft. So I'll be her escort on the last leg of her journey, coming into the Punjab."

"The Sind's not that safe," grumbled Calopodius, still fretting. The Sind was the lower half of the Indus river valley, and while it had now been cleared of Malwa troops and was under the jurisdiction of Rome's Persian allies, the province was still greatly unsettled. "Dacoits everywhere."

"Dacoits aren't going to attack a military convoy," interrupted Belisarius. "I'll make sure she gets a Persian escort of some kind as far as Sukkur."

One of the telegraphs in the command center began to chatter. When the message was read aloud, a short time later, even Calopodius began to relax.

"Guess not," he mumbled—more than a little abashed. "With *that* escort."

Chapter 14
THE LOWER INDUS
Spring, 534 AD

"I don't believe this," mumbled Illus—more than a little abashed. He glanced down at his uniform. For all the finery of the fabric and the cut, the garment seemed utterly drab matched against the glittering costumes which seemed to fill the wharf against which their river barge was just now being tied.

Standing next to him, Anna said nothing. Her face was stiff, showing none of the uneasiness she felt herself. Her own costume was even more severe and plainly cut than those of her officers, even if the fabric itself was expensive. And she found herself wishing desperately that her cosmetics had survived the journey from Constantinople. For a woman of her class, being seen with a face unadorned by anything except nature was well-nigh unthinkable. In *any* company, much less...

The tying-up was finished and the gangplank laid. Anna was able to guess at the identity of the first man to stride across it.

She was not even surprised. Anna had read everything ever written by Irene Macrembolitissa—several times over—including the last book the woman wrote just before she left for the Hindu Kush on her great expedition of conquest. *The Deeds of Khusrau,* she thought, described the man quite well. The Emperor of Persia was not particularly large, but so full of life and energy that he seemed like a giant as he strode toward her across the gangplank.

What am I doing here? she wondered. *I never planned on such as this!*

"So! You are the one!" were the first words he boomed. "To live in such days, when legends walk among us!"

In the confused time that followed, as Anna was introduced to a not-so-little mob of Persian officers and officials—most of them obviously struggling not to frown with disapproval at such a disreputable woman—she pondered on those words.

They seemed meaningless to her. Khusrau Anushirvan—"Khusrau of the Immortal Soul"—was a legend, not she.

So why had he said that?

By the end of that evening, after spending hours sitting stiffly in a chair while Iran's royalty and nobility wined and dined her, she had mustered enough courage to lean over to the emperor—sitting next to her!—and whisper the question into his ear.

Khusrau's response astonished her even more. He grinned broadly, white teeth gleaming in a square-cut Persian beard. Then, he leaned over and whispered in return:

"I am an expert on legends, wife of Calopodius. Truth be told, I often think the art of kingship is mainly knowing how to make the things."

He glanced slyly at his assembled nobility, who had not stopped frowning at Anna throughout the royal feast—but always, she noticed, under lowered brows.

"But keep it a secret," he whispered. "It wouldn't do for my noble sahrdaran and vurzurgan to discover that their emperor is really a common manufacturer. I don't need another rebellion this year."

She managed to choke down a laugh, fortunately. The effort, however, caused her hand to shake just enough to spill some wine onto her long dress.

"No matter," whispered the emperor. "Don't even try to remove the stain. By next week, it'll be the blood of a dying man brought back to life by the touch of your hand. Ask anyone."

She tightened her lips to keep from smiling. It was nonsense, of course, but there was no denying the emperor was a charming man.

But, royal decree or no, it was still nonsense. Bloodstains aplenty there had been on the garments she'd brought from Constantinople, true enough. Blood and pus and urine and excrement and every manner of fluid produced by human suffering. She'd gained them in Chabahari, and again at Barbaricum. Nor did she doubt there would be bloodstains on this garment also, soon enough, to match the wine stain she had just put there.

Indeed, she had designed the uniforms of the Wife's Service with that in mind. That was why the fabric had been dyed a purple so dark it was almost black.

But it was still nonsense. Her touch had no more magic power than anyone's. Her knowledge—or rather, the knowledge which she had obtained by reading everything Macrembolitissa or anyone else had ever written transmitting the Talisman of God's wisdom—now, *that* was powerful. But it had nothing to do with her, except insofar as she was another vessel of those truths.

Something of her skepticism must have shown, despite her effort to remain impassive-faced. She was only nineteen, after all, and hardly an experienced diplomat.

Khusrau's lips quirked. "You'll see."

The next day she resumed her journey up the river toward Sukkur. The emperor himself, due to the pressing business of completing his incorporation of the Sind into the swelling empire of Iran, apologized for not being able to accompany her personally. But he detailed no fewer than four Persian war galleys to serve as her escort.

"No fear of dacoits," said Illus, with great satisfaction. "Or deserters turned robbers."

His satisfaction turned a bit sour at Anna's response.

"Good. We'll be able to stop at every hospital along the way then. No matter how small."

And stop they did. Only briefly, in the Roman ones. By now, to Anna's satisfaction, Belisarius' blood-curdling threats had resulted in a marked improvement in medical procedures and sanitary practices.

But most of the small military hospitals along the way were Persian. The "hospitals" were nothing more than tents pitched along the riverbank—mere staging posts for disabled Persian soldiers being evacuated back to their homeland. The conditions within them had Anna seething, with a fury that was all the greater because neither she nor either of the Isaurian officers could speak a word of the Iranian language. Abdul could make himself understood, but his pidgin was quite inadequate to the task of convincing skeptical—even hostile—Persian officials that Anna's opinion was anything more than female twaddle.

Anna spent another futile hour trying to convince the officers in command of her escort to send a message to Khusrau himself. Clearly enough, however, none of them were prepared to annoy the emperor at the behest of a Roman woman who was probably half-insane to begin with.

Fortunately, at the town of Dadu, there was a telegraph station. Anna marched into it and fired off a message to her husband.

```
WHY  TALISMAN  MEDICAL  PRECEPTS  NOT
TRANSLATED  INTO  PERSIAN  STOP  INSTRUCT
EMPEROR  IRAN  DISCIPLINE  HIS  IDIOTS
STOP
```

"Do it," said Belisarius, after Calopodius read him the message.

The general paused. "Well, the first part, anyway. The Persian translation. I'll have to figure out a somewhat more diplomatic way to pass the rest of it on to Khusrau."

Maurice snorted. "How about hitting him on the head with a club? That'd be somewhat more diplomatic."

By the time the convoy reached Sukkur, it was moving very slowly.

There were no military hospitals along the final stretch of the river, because wounded soldiers were kept either in Sukkur itself or had already passed through the evacuation routes. The slow pace was now due entirely to the native population.

By whatever mysterious means, word of the Wife's passage had spread up and down the Indus. The convoy was constantly approached by small river boats bearing sick and injured villagers, begging for what was apparently being called "the healing touch."

Anna tried to reason, to argue, to convince. But it was hopeless. The language barrier was well-nigh impassible. Even the officers of her Persian escort could do no more than roughly translate the phrase "healing touch."

In the end, not being able to bear the looks of anguish on their faces, Anna laid her hands on every villager brought alongside her barge for the purpose. Muttering curses under her breath all the while—curses which were all the more bitter since she was quite certain the villagers of the Sind took them for powerful incantations.

At Sukkur, she was met by Menander and the entire crew of the *Victrix*. Beaming from ear to ear.

The grins faded soon enough. After waiting impatiently for the introductions to be completed, Anna's next words were: "Where's the telegraph station?"

```
URGENT STOP MUST TRANSLATE TALISMAN
PRECEPTS INTO NATIVE TONGUES ALSO
STOP
```

Menander fidgeted while she waited for the reply.

"I've got a critical military cargo to haul to the island," he muttered. "Calopodius may not even send an answer."

"He's my husband," came her curt response. "Of course he'll answer me."

Sure enough, the answer came very soon.

```
CANNOT STOP IS NO WRITTEN NATIVE
LANGUAGE STOP NOT EVEN ALPHABET STOP
```

After reading it, Anna snorted. "We'll see about that."

```
YOU SUPPOSEDLY EXPERT GRAMMAR AND
RHETORIC STOP INVENT ONE STOP
```

"You'd best get started on it," mused Belisarius. The general's head turned to the south. "She'll be coming soon."

"Like a tidal bore," added Maurice.

That night, he dreamed of islands again.

First, of Rhodes, where he spent an idle day on his journey to join Belisarius' army while his ship took on supplies.

Some of that time he spent visiting the place where, years before, John of Rhodes had constructed an armaments center. Calopodius' own skills and interests were not inclined in a mechanical direction, but he was still curious enough to want to see the mysterious facility.

But, in truth, there was no longer much there of interest. Just a handful of buildings, vacant now except for livestock. So, after wandering about for a bit, he spent the rest of the day perched on a headland staring at the sea.

It was a peaceful, calm, and solitary day. The last one he would enjoy in his life, thus far.

Then, his dreams took him to the island in the Strait of Hormuz where Belisarius was having a naval base constructed. The general had sent Calopodius over from the mainland where the army was marching its way toward the Indus, in order to help resolve one of the many minor disputes which had erupted between the Romans and Persians who were constructing the facility. Among the members of the small corps of noble couriers who served Belisarius for liaison with the Persians, Calopodius had displayed a great deal of tact as well as verbal aptitude.

It was something of a private joke between him and the general. "I need you to take care of another obstreperous aunt," was the way Belisarius put it.

The task of mediating between the quarrelsome Romans and Persians had been stressful. But Calopodius had enjoyed the boat ride well enough; and, in the end, he had managed to translate Belisarius' blunt words into language flowery enough to slide the command through—like a knife between unguarded ribs.

Toward the end, his dreams slid into a flashing nightmare image of Bukkur Island. A log, painted to look like a field gun, sent flying by a lucky cannon ball fired by one of the Malwa gunships whose bombardment accompanied that last frenzied assault. The Romans drove off that attack also, in the end. But not before a mortar shell had ripped Calopodius' eyes out of his head.

The last sight he would ever have in his life was of that log, whirling through the air and crushing the skull of a Roman soldier standing in its way. What made the thing a nightmare was that Calopodius could not remember the soldier's name, if he had ever known it. So it all seemed very incomplete, in a way that was too horrible for Calopodius to be able to express clearly to anyone, even himself. Grammar and rhetoric simply collapsed under the coarse reality, just as fragile human bone and brain had collapsed under hurtling wood.

The sound of his aide-de-camp clumping about in the bunker awoke him. The warm little courtesy banished the nightmare, and Calopodius returned to life with a smile.

"How does the place look?" he asked.

"It's hardly fit for a Melisseni girl. But I imagine it'll do for *your* wife."

"Soon, now."

"Yes." Calopodius heard Luke lay something on the small table next to the cot. From the slight rustle, he understood that it was another stack of telegrams. Private ones, addressed to him, not army business.

"Any from Anna?"

"No. Just more bills."

Calopodius laughed. "Well, whatever else, she still spends money like a Melisseni. Before she's done, that banker will be the richest man in India."

Luke said nothing in response. After a moment, Calopodius' humor faded away, replaced by simple wonder.

"Soon, now. I wonder what she'll be like?"

Chapter 15
LADY DAMODARA'S PALACE
KAUSAMBI

"We should go back," whispered Rajiv's little sister. Nervously, the girl's eyes ranged about the dark cellar. "It's scary down here."

Truth be told, Rajiv found the place fairly creepy himself. The little chamber was one of many they'd found in this long-unused portion of the palace's underground cellars. Rajiv found the maze-like complexity of the cellars fascinating. He could not for the life of him figure out any rhyme or reason to the ancient architectural design, if there had ever been one at all. But that same labyrinthine character of the little grottoes also made them . . .

Well. A little scary.

But no thirteen-year-old boy will admit as much to his seven-year-old sister. Not even a peasant boy, much less the son of Rajputana's most famous king.

"You go back if you want to," he said, lifting the oil lamp to get a better look at the archway ahead of them. He could see part of another small cellar beyond. "I want to see all of it."

"I'll get lost on my own," Mirabai whined. "And there's only one lamp."

For a moment, Rajiv hesitated. He could, after all, use his sister's fear and the lack of a second lamp as a legitimate justification for going back. No reflection on *his* courage.

He might have, too, except that his sister's next words irritated him.

155

"There are *ghosts* down here," she whispered. "I can hear them talking."

"Oh, don't be silly!" He took a step toward the archway.

"I *can* hear them," she said. Quietly, but insistently.

Rajiv started to make a sarcastic rejoinder, when he heard something. He froze, half-cocking his head to bring an ear to bear.

She was right! Rajiv could hear voices himself. No words, as such, just murmuring.

"There's more than one of them, too," his sister hissed.

Again, she was right. Rajiv could distinguish at least two separate voices. From their tone, they seemed to be having an argument of some sort.

Would ghosts argue? he wondered.

That half-frightened, half-puzzled question steadied his nerves. With the steadiness, came a more acute sense of what he was hearing.

"Those aren't ghosts," he whispered. "Those are people. Live people."

Mirabai's face was tight with fear. "What would *people* be doing down here?"

That was . . . a very good question. And the only answer that came to Rajiv was a bad one.

He thrust the lamp at his sister. "Here. Take it and go back. Then get the Mongoose and Anastasius down here, as quickly as you can. Mother too. And you'd better tell Lady Damodara."

The girl squinted at the lamp, fearfully. "I'll get lost! I don't know the way."

"Just follow the same route I took us on," Rajiv hissed. "Any time I didn't know which way to go, when there was a choice, I turned to the left. So on your way back, you turn to the right."

He reminded himself forcefully that his sister was only seven years old. In a much more kindly tone, he added: "You can do it, Mirabai. You *have* to do it. I think we're dealing with treachery here."

Mirabai's eyes widened and moved to the dark, open archway. "What are you going to do?"

"I don't know," he whispered. "Something."

He half-forced her to take the lamp. "Now go!"

After his sister scampered off, Rajiv crept toward the archway.

He had to move from memory alone. With the light of the lamp gone, it was pitch dark in these deep cellars.

After groping his way through the arch, he moved slowly across the cellar. Very faintly, he could see what looked like another archway on the opposite side. There was a dim light beyond that seemed to flicker, a bit. That meant that someone on the other side—probably at least one cellar farther away, maybe more—had an oil lamp.

His foot encountered an obstacle and he tripped, sprawling across the stone floor. Fortunately, the endless hours of training under the harsh regimen of the Mongoose had Rajiv's reflexes honed to a fine edge. He cushioned his fall with his hands, keeping the noise to a minimum.

His feet were still lying on something. Something . . . not stone. Not really hard at all.

Even before he got to his knees and reached back, to feel, he was certain he knew what he'd tripped over.

Yes. It was a body.

Fingering gingerly, probing, it didn't take Rajiv long to determine who the man was. Small, wiry, clad only in a loincloth. It had to be one of the Bihari slave miners that Lady Damodara was using to dig an escape route from the palace, if it was someday needed. They worked under the supervision of half a dozen Ye-tai mercenary soldiers. Ajatasutra had bought the slaves and hired the mercenaries.

Now that he was close, he could smell the stink. The man had voided himself in dying. The body was noticeably cool, too. Although the blood didn't feel crusted, it was dry by now. And while Rajiv could smell the feces, the odor wasn't that strong any longer. He hadn't noticed it at all when he entered the room, and he had a good sense of smell. Rajiv guessed that the murder had taken place recently, but not all that recently. Two or three hours earlier.

He didn't think it could have happened earlier than that, though. The body wasn't stiff yet. Some years before—he'd been about eight, as he recalled—Rajiv had questioned his father's lieutenant Jaimal on the subject, in that simultaneously horrified, fascinated and almost gleeful way that young boys will do. Jaimal had told him that, as a rule, a body stiffened three hours after death and then grew limp again after a day and a half. But Rajiv remembered

Jaimal also telling him that the rule was only a rough one. The times could vary, especially depending on the temperature. In these cool cellars, it might all have happened faster.

It was possible there'd simply been a quarrel amongst the slaves. But where would a slave have gotten the blade to cut a throat so neatly? The only tools they had were picks and shovels.

So it was probably treachery—and on the part of the Ye-tai. Some of them, at least.

Rajiv had to find out. He hadn't really followed the progress of the tunnel-digging, since it was none of his affair and he was usually preoccupied with his training. The only reason he'd had today free to do some exploring was that the Mongoose was now spending more time in the company of Dhruva and her infant.

If the tunnel was almost finished—possibly even *was* finished . . .

This could be bad. Very bad.

Rajiv moved into the next cellar, slowly and carefully.

It seemed to Mirabai that it took her forever to get out of the cellars. Looking back on it later, she realized it had really taken very little time at all. The lamp had been bright enough to enable her to walk quickly, if not run—and her brother's instructions had worked perfectly.

The most surprising thing about it all was that she got more scared when it was over. She'd never in her life seen *that* look on her mother's face. Her mother never seemed to worry about anything.

"Get Kandhik," Valentinian hissed to Anastasius. "Break all his bones if you have to."

Anastasius didn't have to break any of the Ye-tai mercenary leader's bones. As huge and powerful as he was, a simple twisting of the arm did the trick.

Kandhik massaged his arm. "I don't know anything," he insisted. The Ye-tai was scowling ferociously, but he wasn't scowling directly at Anastasius—and he was doing everything in his power not to look at Valentinian at all.

The Mongoose was a frightening man under any circumstances.

Under these circumstances, with that weasel smile on his face and a sword in his hand, he was terrifying. Kandhik was neither cowardly nor timid, but he knew perfectly well that either of the Roman cataphracts could kill him without working up a sweat.

Anastasius might need to take a deep breath. Valentinian wouldn't.

"Don't know *anything*," he insisted.

Sanga's wife and Lata came into the chamber. So did Lady Damodara.

"Three of the Ye-tai are missing," the girl said. "The other two are asleep in their chamber."

Although Ye-tai were sometimes called "White Huns," they were definitely Asiatic in their ancestry. Their only similarity to Europeans was that their features were somewhat bonier than those of most steppe-dwellers. Their complexion was certainly not pale—but, at that moment, Kandhik's face was almost ashen.

"Don't know *anything*," he repeated, this time pleading the words.

"He's telling the truth," Valentinian said abruptly. He touched the tip of the sword to Kandhik's throat. "Stay here and watch over the women. Do everything right and nothing wrong, and you'll live to see the end of this day. If my mood doesn't get worse."

With that, he turned and left the room. Anastasius lumbered after him.

Dhruva came in with the baby. She and her sister stared at each other, their eyes wide with fright.

Not as wide as Mirabai's, however. "What should we do, Mother?"

Sanga's wife looked around, rubbing her hands up and down her hips. The familiar gesture calmed Mirabai, a bit.

"May as well go to the kitchen and wait," she said. "I've got some onions to cut. Some leeks, too."

"I agree," said Lady Damodara.

After several minutes of listening from the darkness of the adjoining cellar, Rajiv understood exactly what was happening. The three Ye-tai in the next cellar were, in fact, planning to betray their employers. Apparently—it was not clear what threats or promises they'd made to do it—they'd gotten two of the Biharis to dig a side tunnel for them. It must have taken weeks to do the work, while keeping it a secret from everyone else.

And, now, it was done. But one of the Ye-tai was having second thoughts.

"—never dealt with *anvaya-prapta sachivya*. I have! And I'm telling you that unless we have a guarantee of some—"

"Shut up!" snarled one of the others. "I'm sick of hearing you brag about the times you hobnobbed with the Malwa. *What* 'guarantees'?"

The quarrel went back over familiar ground. Rajiv himself was inclined to agree with the doubter. He'd no more trust the Malwa royal clan than he would a scorpion. But he paid little attention to the rest of it.

Whether or not the doubting Ye-tai was worried about the reaction of the *anvaya-prapta sachivya*, it was clear enough he was weakening. He didn't really have any choice, after all, now that the deed was effectively done. Soon enough, he'd give up his objections and the three Ye-tai would be gone.

Then . . . within a day, Lady Damodara's palace would be swarmed by Emperor Skandagupta's troops. And the secret escape tunnel wouldn't be of any use, because the Ye-tai traitors would have told the Malwa where the tunnel exited. They'd have as many soldiers positioned in the stable as they would at the palace. And it wouldn't take them long to torture the stable-keeper—his family, more likely—into showing them where it was.

It was up to Rajiv, then. One thirteen-year-old boy, unarmed, against three Ye-tai mercenaries. Who were . . .

He peeked around the corner again.

Definitely armed. Each of them with a sword.

But Rajiv didn't give their weapons more than a glance. He'd already peeked around that corner before, twice, and studied them well enough. This time he was examining the body of the second Bihari miner, whom the mercenaries had cast into a corner of the cellar after cutting his throat also.

Not the body, actually. Rajiv was studying the miner's tools, which the Ye-tai had tossed on top of his corpse.

A pick and a shovel. A short-handled spade, really. Both of the tools were rather small, not so much because most of the Biharis were small but simply because there wasn't much room in the tunnels they dug.

That was good, Rajiv decided. Small tools—at least for someone his size—would make better weapons than large ones would have.

Until he met the Mongoose, Rajiv would never have considered the possibility that tools might make weapons. He'd been raised a Rajput prince, after all. But the Mongoose had hammered that out of him, like many other things. He'd even insisted on teaching Rajiv to fight with big kitchen ladles.

Rajiv's mother had been mightily amused. Rajiv himself had been mortified—until, by the fourth time the Mongoose knocked him down, he'd stopped sneering at ladles.

He decided he'd start with the pick. It was a clumsier thing than the spade, and he'd probably lose it in the first encounter anyway.

There was no point in dawdling. Rajiv gave a last quick glance at the three oil lamps perched on a ledge. No way to knock them off, he decided. Not spaced out the way there were.

Besides, he didn't think fighting in the dark would be to his advantage anyway. That would be a clumsy business, and if there was one thing the Mongoose had driven home to him, it was that "clumsy" and "too damn much sweat" always went together.

"Fight like a miser," he whispered to himself. Then, came out of his crouch and sprang into the cellar.

He said nothing; issued no war cry; gave no speech. The Mongoose had slapped that out of him also. Just went for the pick, with destruction in his heart.

Still many cellars away, Valentinian and Anastasius heard the fight start.

Nothing from Rajiv. Just the sound of several angry and startled men, their shouts echoing through the labyrinth.

Rajiv went to meet the first Ye-tai. That surprised him, as he'd thought it would.

When you're outmatched, get in quick. They won't expect that, the fucks.

The Ye-tai's sword came up. Rajiv raised the pick as if to match blows. The mercenary grinned savagely, seeing him do so. He outweighed Rajiv by at least fifty pounds.

At the last instant, Rajiv reversed his grip, ducked under the sword, and drove the handle of the pick into the man's groin.

Go for the shithead's dick and balls. Turn him into a squealing bitch.

The Ye-tai didn't squeal. As hard as Rajiv had driven in the end of the shaft, he didn't do anything except stare ahead, his mouth agape. He'd dropped his sword and was clutching his groin, half-stooped.

His eyes were wide as saucers, too, which was handy.

Rajiv rose from his crouch, reversed his grip again, and drove one of the pick's narrow blades into an eye. The blunt iron sank three inches into the Ye-tai's skull.

As he'd expected, he'd lost the pick. But it had all happened fast enough that he had time to dive for the spade, grab it, and come up rolling in a far corner.

He wasn't thinking at all, really, just acting. Hours and hours and hours of the Mongoose's training, that was.

You don't have time to think in a fight. If you have to think, you're a dead man.

The slumping corpse of the first Ye-tai got in the way of the second. Rajiv had planned for that, when he chose the corner to roll into.

The third came at him, again with his sword high.

That's just stupid, some part of Rajiv's mind recorded. Dimly, there was another, walled-off part that remembered he had once thought that way of using a sword very warriorlike. Dramatic-looking. Heroic.

But that was before hours and hours and hours of the Mongoose. A lifetime ago, it seemed now—and even a thirteen-year life is a fair span of time.

Rajiv evaded the sword strike. No flair to it, just—got out of the way.

Not much. Just enough. Miserly in everything.

A short, quick, hard jab of the spade into the side of the Ye-tai's knee was enough to throw off his backhand stroke. Rajiv evaded that one easily. He didn't try to parry the blow. The wood and iron of his spade would be no match for a steel sword.

Another quick hard jab to the same knee was enough to bring the Ye-tai down.

As he did so, Rajiv swiveled, causing the crumpling Ye-tai to impede the other.

Fuck 'em up, when you're fighting a crowd. Make 'em fall over each other.

The third Ye-tai didn't fall. But he stumbled into the kneeling body of his comrade hard enough that he had to steady himself with one hand. His other hand, holding the sword, swung out wide in an instinctive reach for balance.

Rajiv drove the edge of the spade into the wrist of the sword arm. The hand popped open. The sword fell. Blood oozed from the laceration on the wrist. It was a bad laceration, even if Rajiv hadn't managed to sever anything critical.

Go for the extremities. Always go for extremities. Hands, feet, toes, fingers. They're your closest target and the hardest for the asshole to defend.

The Ye-tai gaped at him, more in surprise than anything else.

But Rajiv ignored him, for the moment.

Don't linger, you idiot. Cut a man just enough, then cut another. Then come back and cut the first one again, if you need to. Like your mother cuts onions. Practical. Fuck all that other crap.

The second Ye-tai *was* squealing, in a hissing sort of way. Rajiv knew that knee injuries were excruciating. The Mongoose had told him so—and then, twice, banged up his knee in training sessions to prove it.

The Ye-tai's head was unguarded, with both his hands clutching the ruined knee. So Rajiv drove the spade at his temple.

He made his first mistake, then. The target was so tempting—so glorious, as it were—that he threw everything into the blow. He'd take off that head!

The extra time it took to position his whole body for that mighty blow was enough for the Ye-tai to bring up his hand to protect the head.

Stupid! Rajiv snarled silently at himself.

It probably didn't make any difference, of course. If the edge of the spade wasn't as sharp as a true weapon, it wasn't all that dull; and if iron wasn't steel, it was still much harder than human flesh. The strike cut off one of the man's fingers and maimed the whole hand—and still delivered a powerful blow to the skull. Moaning, the Ye-tai collapsed to the floor, half-unconscious.

Still, Rajiv was glad the Mongoose hadn't seen.

"Stupid," he heard a voice mutter.

Startled, he glanced aside. The Mongoose was there, in the entrance to the chamber. He had his sword in his hand, but it was down alongside his leg. Behind him, Rajiv could see the huge figure of Anastasius looming.

The Mongoose leaned against the stone entrance, tapping the tip of the sword against his boot. Then, nodded his head toward the last Ye-tai against the far wall.

"Finish him, boy. And don't fuck up again."

Rajiv looked at the Ye-tai. The man was paying him no attention at all. He was staring at the Mongoose, obviously frightened out of his wits.

The spade had served well enough, but there was now a sword available. The one the second Ye-tai had dropped after Rajiv smashed his knee.

No reason to waste the spade, of course. Certainly not with the Mongoose watching. Rajiv had been trained—for hours and hours and hours—to throw most anything. Even ladles. The Mongoose was a firm believer in the value of weapons used at a distance.

Rajiv would never be the Mongoose's equal with a throwing knife, of course. He was not sure even the heroes and *asuras* of the legends could throw a knife that well.

But he was awfully good, by now. The spade, hurled like a spear, struck the Ye-tai in the groin.

"Good!" the Mongoose grunted.

With the sword in his hand, Rajiv approached the Ye-tai. By now, of course, the man had noticed him. Half-crouched, snarling, clutching himself with his left hand while he tried to grab his dropped sword with the still-bleeding right hand.

Rajiv sliced open his scalp with a quick, flicking strike of the sword.

Don't try to split his head open, you jackass. You'll likely just get your sword stuck. And it's too easy to block and what's the fucking point anyway? Just cut him somewhere in the front of the head. Anywhere the blood'll spill into his eyes and blind him. Head wounds bleed like nothing else.

Blood poured over the Ye-tai's face. The sword he'd been

bringing up went, instead, to his face, as he tried to wipe off the blood with the back of his wrist.

It never got there. Another quick, flicking sword strike struck the hand and took off the thumb. The sword, again, fell to the ground.

"Don't . . . fuck . . . it . . . up," the Mongoose growled.

Rajiv didn't really need the lesson. He'd learned it well enough already, this day, with that one mistake. He was sorely tempted to end it all, but not for any romantic reason. The carnage was starting to upset him. He'd never been in a real fight before—not a killing one—and he was discovering that men don't die the way chickens and lambs do when they're slaughtered.

He'd always thought they would. But they didn't. They bled the same, pretty much. But lambs—certainly chickens—never had that look of horror in their eyes as they knew they were dying.

That same, walled-off part of Rajiv's mind thought he understood, now. The reason his father always seemed so stern. Not like his mother at all.

Father's son or mother's son, Rajiv was Mongoose-trained. So the sword flicked out five more times, mercilessly slicing and cutting everywhere, before he finally opened the big arteries and veins in the Ye-tai's throat.

"Good." The Mongoose straightened up and pointed with his sword toward a corner. "If you need to puke, do it over there. Cleaning up this mess is going to be a bitch as it is."

Anastasius pushed him aside and came into the chamber. "For the sake of Christ, Valentinian, will you give the boy a break? Three men, in his first fight—and him starting without a weapon."

The Mongoose scowled. "He did pretty damn good. I still don't want to clean up blood and puke all mixed together. Neither do you."

But Rajiv wasn't listening, any longer. He was in the corner, hands on his knees, puking.

He still had the sword firmly gripped, though—and was careful to keep the blade out of the way of the spewing vomit.

"Pretty damn good," the Mongoose repeated.

"We were very lucky," Lady Damodara said to Sanga's wife, that evening. "If it hadn't been for your son . . ."

She lowered her head, one hand rubbing her cheek. "We can't wait much longer. I must—finally—get word to my husband. He can't wait, either. I'd thought Ajatasutra would have come back, by now. The fact that he hasn't makes me wonder—"

"I think you're wrong, Lady. " Rajiv's mother was standing by the window, looking out over Kausambi. She was making no attempt to hide from sight. Even if the Malwa dynasty had spies watching from a distance—which was very likely—all they would see in the twilight was the figure of a gray-haired and plain-seeming woman, dressed in simple apparel. A servant, obviously, and there were many servants in such a palace.

"I think Ajatasutra's long absence means the opposite. I think your husband is finally making his move."

More hopefully, Lady Damodara raised her head. She'd come to have a great deal of confidence in the Rajput queen. "You think so?"

Sanga's wife smiled. "Well, let me put it this way. Yes, I think so—and if I'm wrong, we're all dead anyway. So why fret about it?"

Lady Damodara chuckled. "If only I had your unflappable temperament!"

The smile went away. "Not so unflappable as all that. When I heard, afterward, what Rajiv had done . . ." She shook her head. "I almost screamed at him, I was so angry and upset."

"He was very brave."

"Yes, he was. That is why I was so angry. Reckless boy! But . . ."

She seemed to shudder a little. "He was also very, very deadly. That is why I was so upset. At the Mongoose, I think, more than him."

Lady Damodara tilted her head. "He is a Rajput prince."

"Yes, he is. So much is fine. What I do *not* want is for him to become a Rajput legend. *Another* damned Rajput legend. Being married to one is enough!"

There was silence, for a time.

"You may not have any choice," Lady Damodara finally said.

"Probably not," Sanga's wife agreed gloomily. "There are times I think I should have poisoned Valentinian right at the beginning."

There was silence for a time, again.

"He probably wouldn't have died anyway."

"Probably not."

Chapter 16
PESHAWAR

"What if it's in the middle of *garam* season?" Kungas asked skeptically, tugging at his little goatee. "The heat won't be so bad, here in the Vale, although it will be if we descend into the Punjab. But I'm concerned about water."

Ashot started to say something, but Kungas waved him down impatiently. "Yes, yes, fine. *If* we make it to the Indus, we'll have plenty of water. Even in *garam*."

He jerked his head toward a nearby window in the palace, which faced to the south. "I remind you, Ashot, that I have well over twenty thousand Malwa camped out there, just beyond the passes. Closer to thirty, I think. I'd have to get through *them*, before I could reach the Indus—with no more than twenty thousand men of my own. Less than that, actually, since I'd have to leave some soldiers here to keep the Pathans from getting stupid ideas."

Ashot said nothing. Just waited.

Kungas went back to his beard-tugging.

"The Malwa have stopped trying to break into the Vale. For weeks, now, they've been putting up their own fortifications. So I'd have to get through *those*, too."

Tug. Tug. Tug.

"Piss-poor fortifications, true. Lazy Malwa. Also true that those are not their best troops. There are not more than three thousand Ye-tai in the lot. Still."

Tug. Tug. Tug.

167

Eventually, Kungas gave Ashot his crack of a smile. "You are not trying to persuade me, I notice. Smart man. Let me persuade myself."

Ashot's returning smile was a wider thing. Of course, almost anyone's smile was wider than that of Kungas, even when the king was in a sunny mood.

"The general is not expecting you to *defeat* those Malwa," the Armenian cataphract pointed out. "If you can, splendid. But it would be enough if he knew you could tie them up. Keep them from being used elsewhere."

Kungas sniffed. "Marvelous. I point out to you that I am *already* tying them up and keeping them from being used against him. And have to do nothing more vigorous than drink wine and eat fruit in the doing."

He matched deed to word, taking a sip from his wine and plucking a pear from a bowl on the low table in front of the settee. The sip was very small, though, and he didn't actually eat the pear. Just held it in his hand, weighing it as if it were the problem he confronted.

Ashot started to open his mouth, then closed it. Kungas' little smile widened slightly.

"Very smart man. Yes, yes, I know—the general is assuming that if he produces enough of a crisis, the Malwa will draw their troops away from the Vale to reinforce the soldiers he faces. And he wants me to stop them from doing so, which—alas—I cannot do drinking wine and eating pears."

Kungas set the pear back in the bowl, rose and went to the window. On the way, almost absently, he gave his wife's ponytail a gentle stroke. Irene was sitting on a chair—more like a raised cushion, really—at the same low table. She smiled at his passing figure, but said nothing.

Like Ashot, she knew that the best way to persuade Kungas of anything was not to push him too hard.

Once at the window, Kungas looked out over the Vale of Peshawar. Not at the Vale itself, so much as the mountains beyond.

"How certain is Belisarius that such a crisis is coming?" he asked.

Ashot shrugged. "I don't think 'certain' is the right word. The general doesn't think that way. 'Likely,' 'not likely,' 'possible,' 'probable'—it's just not the way his mind works."

"No, it isn't," mused Kungas. "As my too-educated Greek wife would put it, he thinks like a geometer, not an arithmetician. It's the angles he considers, not the sums. That's because he thinks if he can gauge the angle correctly, he can create the sums he needs."

The Kushan king's eyes lowered, now looking at the big market square below. "Which, he usually can. He'd do badly, I think, as a merchant. But he's probably the deadliest general in centuries. I'm glad he's not my enemy."

Abruptly, he turned away from the window. "Done. Tell Belisarius that if the Malwa start trying to pull troops from the Vale, I will do my best to pin them here. I make no promises, you understand. No guarantees. I will do my best, but—I have a kingdom to protect also, now that I have created it."

Ashot rose, nodding. "That will be more than enough, Your Majesty. Your best will be more than enough."

Kungas snorted. "Such phrases! And 'Your Majesty,' no less. Be careful, Ashot, or your general will make you an ambassador instead of a soldier."

The Armenian cataphract winced. Irene laughed softly. "It's not so bad, Ashot. Of course, you'll have to learn how to wear a veil."

"I'm going with you," Shakuntala announced. "And don't bother trying to argue with me. I *am* the empress."

Her husband spread his hands, smiling. A very diplomatic smile, that was.

"I would not dream of opposing your royal self."

Shakuntala gazed up at him suspiciously. For a moment, her hand went to stroke her belly, although she never completed the gesture.

"What's this?" she demanded. "I was expecting a husband's prattle about my duties as a mother. A lecture on the dangers of miscarriage."

The smile still on his face, Rao shrugged. "Bring Namadev, if you want to. Not much risk of disease, really, now that *garam* has started."

"Don't remind me," the empress said. She moved over to a window in the palace and scowled out at the landscape of Majarashtra. The hills surrounding Deogiri shimmered in the heat, from hot air rising from the baked soil.

Whatever else Indians disputed over, they all agreed that *rabi* was the best season, cool and dry as it was. One of India's three seasons, it corresponded roughly to what other lands considered winter. Alas, now that they were in what Christians called the month of March, *rabi* had ended.

Thereafter opinions diverged as to whether *garam* was worse than *khalif*, or the opposite. In Shakuntala's opinion, it was a silly argument. *Garam*, obviously! Especially here in the Great Country!

The monsoon season could be a nuisance, true enough, with its heavy rains. But she came from Keralan stock, on her mother's side, and had spent a fair part of her childhood in Kerala. Located as it was on India's southwest coast, Kerala was practically inundated during *khalif*. She was accustomed to rains far heavier than any that came here.

In any event, stony and arid Majarashtra desperately needed the monsoon's rainfall by the time it came. That began in what the Christians called "late May." What the Great Country did *not* need was the dry and blistering heat of *garam*. Not for one day, much less the three months it would last.

"I hate garam," she muttered. "Especially in the palace. It will be good for me—our son too!—to get outside for a while."

"Probably," Rao allowed. "You and Namadev will travel in a howdah, of course. The canopy will keep off the sun, and you might get some breeze."

Shakuntala turned away from the window and looked at him. "Are you really *that* sure, Rao? You are my beloved."

The expression that came to her husband's face then reminded Shakuntala forcibly of the differences between them, however much they might love each other. Where she was young, Rao was middle-aged. And, perhaps even more importantly, he was a philosopher and she was . . . not.

"Who can say?" he asked serenely.

"You are relying too much on complicated logic," she hissed. "Treacherous, that is."

"Actually, no. There is the logic of it, true enough. But, in the end . . ."

He moved to the same window and gazed out. "It is more that I am swayed by the beauty of the thing. Whatever deities exist, they care not much for logic, for they treasure their whimsy. But they do love beauty. All of them—even the most bloody—will adore the notion."

"You are mad," she stated, with the certainty of an empress.

Of course, she'd stated those words before. And been proven wrong.

"Bring the baby, too," Rao said, tranquilly. "He will be in no danger."

From the battlements on the landward side of the city, Nanda Lal and Toramana watched Damodara's great army set out on its march upriver.

Suspicion was ever-present in the Malwa empire's spymaster, and today was no exception.

"Why the Narmada?" he demanded softly. "This makes no sense to me. Why does Damodara think Raghunath Rao will be foolish enough to meet him on a river plain? He'd stay in the badlands, I would think, where the terrain favors him."

Although Nanda Lal's eyes had never left the departing army, the question was addressed at the big Ye-tai general standing next to him.

Toramana, never prone to expansive gestures, shifted his shoulders a bit. "Better to say, why not? Lord, it may be that Rao will not come down out of the hills. But he says he will, to meet Sanga in single combat. So, if he doesn't, he is shamed. The worst that happens, from Damodara's position, is that he has undermined his opponent."

Nanda Lal made a face. Raised as he was in the Malwa dynasty's traditions—not to mention the even colder school of Link—it was always a bit difficult for him to realize that other men took this business about "honor" quite seriously. Even the Ye-tai next to him, just a hair's breadth removed from nomadic savagery and with a personality that was ruthless in its own right, seemed at least partly caught up in the spirit of the thing.

So, he said nothing. And, after cogitating on the problem for a few minutes, decided that Toramana was probably right.

"Notify me if you hear anything amiss," he commanded, and left. He saw no reason to stay until the last elements of Damodara's army were no longer visible from the battlements. Let the Ye-tai barbarian, if he chose, find "honor" in that splendid vista of dust, the rear ends of animals, and the trail of manure they left behind.

Toramana did remain on the battlements until the army was no longer in sight. Not because of any demands of honor, however. He was no more of a romantic than Nanda Lal on the subject of horseshit. Or any other, for that matter.

No, he did so for two other reasons.

First, to be certain he had suppressed any trace of humor before he was seen by any of Nanda Lal's spies in the city. Or even good cheer, of which the Ye-tai general was full.

Damodara had said nothing to him, of course. Neither had Narses, beyond the vaguest of hints. It didn't matter. Toramana, from his own analysis of the situation, was almost certain that Damodara had decided the time had come. The reason he was full of good cheer was because, if he was right, that meant both Damodara and Narses had great confidence in him. They were relying on Toramana to do what was necessary, without needing to be told anything.

He'd know, of course, if his assessment was correct. There would be one sure and simple sign to come.

So, he foresaw a great future for himself. Assuming he survived the next few months. But, if he did—yes, a great future.

And an even greater future for his children.

Of course, producing those children also depended on surviving the next few months. But Toramana was a confident man, and on no subject so much as his own prospects for survival.

That led him to his other reason for remaining on the battlements, which was the need to make a final decision on the second most important issue he faced.

He came to that decision quickly. More quickly than he had expected he would. Odd, perhaps. Toramana was not generally given to experimental whimsy. On the other hand, new times called for new measures.

Odder still, though, was the sense of relief that decision brought also.

Why? he wondered. Fearing, for a moment, that he might have been infected with the decadence he saw around him. But he soon decided that there was no infection. Simply . . .

And how odd that was! He was actually looking forward to it. New times, indeed.

That evening, as he had done every evening since she'd arrived in Bharakuccha, Toramana presented himself at the chambers where his intended had taken up residence in the great palace.

Outside the chambers, of course. Betrothed or not, there would be no question of impropriety. Even after Indira appeared and they began their customary promenade through the gardens, she was followed by a small host of wizened old chaperones and three Rajput warriors. Clansmen of Rana Sanga's, naturally.

For the first few minutes, their talk was idle. The usual meaningless chitchat. Meaningless, at least, in its content. The real purpose of these promenades was simply to allow a groom and his future bride to become at least somewhat acquainted with each other. As stiff as they were, even Rajputs understood that the necessary function of a wedding night was simplified and made easier if the spouses didn't have to grope at each other's voices as well as bodies.

After a time, Toramana cleared his throat. "Can you read?"

Indira's eyes widened. Toramana had expected that. He was pleased to see, however, that they didn't widen very much, and the face beneath remained quite composed. To anyone watching, she might have been mildly surprised by a comment he made concerning an unusual insect.

His hopes for this wife, already high, rose a bit further. She would be a splendid asset.

"No," she replied. "It is not the custom."

Toramana nodded. "I can read, myself. But not well. That must change. And I will want you to become literate also. I will hire tutors for us."

She gazed at a nearby vine. The slight widening of the girl's eyes was gone, now. "There will be some talk. My brother's wife can read, however, even if somewhat poorly. So probably not all that much talk."

"Talk does not concern me," Toramana said stiffly. "The future concerns me. I do not think great families with illiterate women will do so well, in that future."

The smile that spread across her face was a slow, cool thing.

The very proper smile of a young Rajput princess hearing her betrothed make a pleasant comment regarding a pretty vine.

"I agree," she said. "Though most others would not."

"I am not concerned about 'most others.' Most others will obey or they will break."

The smile spread just a bit further. "A few others will not break so easily."

"Easily, no. Still, they will break."

The smile now faded quickly, soon replaced by the solemn countenance with which she'd begun the promenade. As was proper. A princess should smile at the remarks of her betrothed, to be sure, but not too widely and not for too long. They were not married yet, after all.

"I am looking forward to our wedding," Indira said softly. Too softly for the wizened little horde behind them to overhear. "To the marriage, even more."

"I am pleased to hear it."

"It is not the custom," she repeated.

"Customs change. Or they break."

Before nightfall, the promenade was over and Toramana returned to his own quarters.

No sooner had the Ye-tai general entered his private sleeping chamber than the one sure and simple sign he'd expected made its appearance.

Like a ghost, emerging from the wall. Toramana had no idea where the assassin had hidden himself.

"I'm afraid I'll need to sleep here," Ajatasutra said. "Nanda Lal has spies almost everywhere."

Toramana's lip curled, just a bit. "He has no spies here."

"No, not here."

"When?"

"Four days. Though nothing will be needed from you immediately. It will take at least two days for Damodara to return."

Toramana nodded. "And then?"

The assassin shrugged. "Whatever is necessary. The future is hard to predict. It looks good, though. I do not foresee any great difficulty."

Toramana began removing his armor. It was not extensive,

simply the half-armor he wore on garrison duty. "No. There should be no great difficulty."

There was a thin, mocking smile on Ajatasutra's face, as there often was. On another man's face, that smile would have irritated Toramana, perhaps even angered him. But the Ye-tai general was accustomed to it, by now.

So, he responded with a thin, mocking smile of his own.

"What amuses you?" Ajatasutra asked.

"A difficulty I had not foreseen, which I just now remembered. Nanda Lal once promised me that he would attend my wedding. And I told him I would hold him to it."

"Ah." The assassin nodded. "Yes, that is a difficulty. A matter of honor is involved."

The armor finally removed and placed on a nearby stand, Toramana scratched his ribs. Even half-armor was sweaty, in garam.

"Not *that* difficult," he said.

"Oh, certainly not."

He and Ajatasutra exchanged the smile, now. They got along very well together. Why not? They were much alike.

Agathius was on the dock at Charax to greet Antonina and Photius and Ousanas when the Axumite fleet arrived.

So much, Antonina had expected. What she had not expected was the sight of Agathius' young Persian wife and the small mountain of luggage next to her.

"We're going with you," Agathius announced gruffly, as soon as the gangplank was lowered and he hobbled across.

He looked at Ousanas. "I hear you have a new title. No longer the keeper of the fly whisks."

"Indeed, not! My new title is far more august. 'Angabo,' no less. That signifies—"

"The keeper of the crutches. Splendid, you can hold mine for a moment." Agathius leaned his weight against the rail and handed his crutches to Ousanas. Then, started digging in his tunic. "I've got the orders here."

By the time Antonina stopped giggling at the startled expression on Ousanas' face, Agathius was handing her a sheaf of official-looking documents.

"Right there," he said, tapping a finger on the name at the

bottom. "It's not a signature, of course. Not in these modern times, with telegraph."

He seemed to be avoiding her eyes. Antonina didn't bother looking at the documents. Instead, she looked at Agathius' wife, who was still on the dock and peering at her suspiciously.

"I'll bet my husband's orders don't say anything about Sudaba."

Agathius seemed to shrink a little. "Well, no. But if you want to argue the matter with her, *you* do it."

"Oh, I wouldn't think of doing so." Honey dripped from the words. "The children?"

"They'll stay here. Sudaba's family will take them in, until we get back." The burly Roman general's shoulders swelled again. "I insisted. Made it stick, too."

Antonina was trying very hard not to laugh. Sudaba had become something of a legend in the Roman army. What saved Agathius from being ridiculed behind his back was that the soldiery was too envious. Sudaba never henpecked Agathius about anything else—and precious few of *them* had a young and very good-looking wife who insisted on accompanying her husband everywhere he went. The fact that Agathius had lost his legs in battle and had to hobble around on crutches and wooden legs only augmented that amatory prestige.

Ousanas grinned and handed back the crutches. "'Angabo' does *not* mean keeper of the crutches. It also doesn't mean 'nursemaid,' so don't ask me to take in your brats when you return. They'll be spoiled rotten."

In a cheerier mood, now that he knew Antonina wouldn't object to Sudaba's presence, Agathius took back the crutches. "True. So what? They're already spoiled rotten. And we'll see how long that grin lasts. The Persians insist on a huge festival to honor your arrival. Well—Photius' arrival, formally speaking. But you'll have to attend also."

The grin vanished.

There had never been a grin on the face of the Malwa assassination commander, or any of his men. Not even a smile, since they'd arrived at Charax.

Any assassination attempt in Egypt had proven impossible, as they'd surmised it would be. Unfortunately, the situation in Charax was no better. The docks were still under Roman authority, and the security there was even more ferocious than it had been in Alexandria.

True, for the day and half the festival lasted, their targets were under Persian protection. But if the Aryans were slacker and less well-organized than the Romans, they made up for it by sheer numbers. Worst of all, by that invariant Persian snobbery, only Roman officials and Persian grandees and *azadan*—"men of noble birth"—were allowed anywhere in the vicinity of the Roman and Axumite visitors.

With the resources available, in the time they had, there was no way for the assassins to forge documents good enough to pass Roman inspection. As for trying to claim noble Aryan lineage . . .

Impossible. Persian documents were fairly easy to forge, and it would be as easy for some of the assassins to pass themselves off as Persians as polyglot Romans. But if Persian bureaucrats were easy to fool, Persian retainers were not. Tightly knit together by kinship as the great Persian families were, they relied on personal recognition to separate the wheat from the chaff—and to those keen eyes, the Malwa assassins were clearly chaff. If nothing else, they'd certainly insist on searching their luggage, and they'd find the bombard—a weapon that had no conceivable use except assassination.

"No help for it," the commander said, as he watched the Axumite war fleet leaving the harbor, with their target safely aboard the largest vessel. "We'll have to try again at Barbaricum. No point even thinking about Chabahari."

His men nodded, looking no more pleased than he did. Leaving aside the fact that this mission had been frustrating from the very start, they now had the distinctly unpleasant prospect of voyaging down the Gulf in an oared galley. It was unlikely they'd be able to use sails, traveling eastbound, with monsoon season still so far away. And—worst of all—while they'd had enough money to afford a galley, they hadn't been able to afford a crew beyond a pilot.

Malwa assassins were expert at many things. Rowing was not one of them.

"Our hands'll be too badly blistered to hold a knife," one of them predicted gloomily.

"Shut up," his commander responded, every bit as gloomily.

Chapter 17
THE INDUS

The attack came as a complete surprise. Not to Anna, who simply didn't know enough about war to understand what could be expected and what not, but to her military escort.

"What in the name of God do they think they're *doing*?" demanded Menander angrily.

He studied the fleet of small boats—skiffs, really—pushing out from the southern shore. The skiffs were loaded with Malwa soldiers, along with more than the usual complement of Mahaveda priests and their mahamimamsa "enforcers." The presence of the latter was a sure sign that the Malwa considered this project so near-suicidal that the soldiers needed to be held in a tight rein.

"It's an ambush," explained his pilot, saying aloud the conclusion Menander had already reached. The man pointed to the thick reeds. "The Malwa must have hauled those boats across the desert, hidden them in the reeds, waited for us. We don't keep regular patrols on the south bank, since there's really nothing there to watch for."

Menander's face was tight with exasperation. "But what's the *point* of it?" For a moment, his eyes moved forward, toward the heavily shielded bow of the ship where the *Victrix*'s firecannon was situated. "We'll burn them up like so many piles of kindling."

But even before he finished the last words, even before he saw the target of the oncoming boats, Menander understood the truth. The fact of it, at least, if not the reasoning.

"*Why?* They're all dead men, no matter what happens. In the name of God, she's just a woman!"

He didn't wait for an answer, however, before starting to issue his commands. The *Victrix* began shuddering to a halt. The skiffs were coming swiftly, driven by almost frenzied rowing. It would take the *Victrix* time to come to a halt and turn around; time to make its way back to protect the barge it was towing.

Time, Menander feared, that he might not have.

"What should we do?" asked Anna. For all the strain in her voice, she was relieved that her words came without stammering. A Melisseni girl could afford to scream with terror; she couldn't. Not any longer.

Grim-faced, Illus glanced around the barge. Other than he and Cottomenes and Abdul, there were only five Roman soldiers on the barge—and only two of those were armed with muskets. Since Belisarius and Khusrau had driven the Malwa out of the Sind, and established Roman naval supremacy on the Indus with the new steam-powered gunboats, there had been no Malwa attempt to threaten shipping south of the Iron Triangle.

Then his eyes came to rest on the vessel's new feature, and his tight lips creased into something like a smile.

"God bless good officers," he muttered.

He pointed to the top of the cabin amidships, where a shell of thin iron was perched. It was a turret, of sorts, for the odd and ungainly looking "Puckle gun" that Menander had insisted on adding to the barge. The helmeted face and upper body of the gunner was visible, and Illus could see the man beginning to train the weapon on the oncoming canoes.

"Get up there—*now*. There's enough room in there for you, and it's the best armored place on the barge." He gave the oncoming Malwa a quick glance. "They've got a few muskets of their own. Won't be able to hit much, not shooting from skiffs moving that quickly—but keep your head down once you get there."

It took Anna a great deal of effort, encumbered as she was by her heavy and severe gown, to clamber atop the cabin. She couldn't have made it at all, if Abdul hadn't boosted her. Climbing over the iron wall of the turret was a bit easier, but not much. Fortunately, the gunner lent her a hand.

After she sprawled into the open interior of the turret, the hard edges of some kind of ammunition containers bruising her back, Anna had to struggle fiercely not to burst into shrill cursing.

I have got to design *a new costume. Propriety be damned!*

For a moment, her thoughts veered aside. She remembered that Irene Macrembolitissa, in her *Observations of India,* had mentioned—with some amusement—that Empress Shakuntala often wore pantaloons in public. Outrageous behavior, really, but . . . when *you're* the one who owns the executioners, you can afford to outrage public opinion.

The thought made her smile, and it was with that cheerful expression on her lips that she turned her face up to the gunner frowning down at her.

"Is there anything I can do to help?"

The man's face suddenly lightened, and he smiled himself.

"Damn if you aren't a prize!" he chuckled. Then, nodding his head. "Yes, ma'am. As a matter of fact, there is."

He pointed to the odd-looking objects lying on the floor of the turret, which had bruised Anna when she landed on them. "Those are called cylinders." He patted the strange looking weapon behind which he was half-crouched. "This thing'll wreak havoc, sure enough, as long as I can keep it loaded. I'm supposed to have a loader, but since we added this just as an afterthought . . ."

He turned his head, studying the enemy vessels. "Better do it quick, ma'am. If those skiffs get alongside, your men and the other soldiers won't be enough to beat them back. And they'll have grenades anyway, they're bound to. If I can't keep them off, we're all dead."

Anna scrambled around until she was on her knees, then seized one of the weird-looking metal contraptions. It was not as heavy as it looked. "What do you need me to do? Be precise!"

"Just hand them to me, ma'am, that's all. I'll do the rest. And keep your head down—it's *you* they're after."

Anna froze for a moment, dumbfounded. "Me? *Why?*"

"Damned if I know. Doesn't make sense."

But, in truth, the gunner did understand. Some part of it, at least, even if he lacked the sophistication to follow all of the reasoning of the inhuman monster who commanded the Malwa empire. The gunner had never heard—and never would—of a man named Napoleon. But he was an experienced soldier, and not stupid even if his formal education was rudimentary. *The moral is to the material in war as three-to-one* was not a phrase the man would have ever uttered himself, but he would have had no difficulty understanding it.

Link, the emissary from the new gods of the future who ruled the Malwa in all but name and commanded its great army in the Punjab, had ordered this ambush. The "why" was self-evident to its superhuman intelligence. Spending the lives of a few soldiers and Mahaveda priests was well worth the price, if it would enable the monster to destroy *the Wife* whose exploits its spies reported. Exploits which, in their own peculiar way, had become important to Roman morale.

Cheap at the price, in fact. Dirt cheap.

THE IRON TRIANGLE

The battle on the river was observed from the north bank by a patrol of light Arab cavalry in Roman service. Being Beni Ghassan, the cavalrymen were far more sophisticated in the uses of new technology than most Arabs. Their commander immediately dispatched three riders to bring news of the Malwa ambush to the nearest telegraph station, which was but a few miles distant.

By the time Belisarius got the news, of course, the outcome of the battle had already been decided, one way or the other. So he could do nothing more than curse himself for a fool, and try not to let the ashen face of a blind young man sway his cold-blooded reasoning.

"I'm a damned fool not to have foreseen the possibility. It just didn't occur to me that the Malwa might carry *boats* across the desert. But it should have."

"Not your fault, sir," said Calopodius quietly.

Belisarius tightened his jaws. "Like hell it isn't."

Maurice, standing nearby, ran fingers through his bristly iron-gray hair. "We all screwed up. I should have thought of it, too. We've been so busy just being entertained by the episode that we didn't think about it. Not seriously."

Belisarius sighed and nodded. "There's still no point in me sending the *Justinian*. By the time it got there, it will all have been long settled—and there's always the chance Link might be trying for a diversion."

"You *can't* send the *Justinian*," said Calopodius, half-whispering. "With the *Victrix* gone—and the *Photius* down at Sukkur—the Malwa might try an amphibious attack on the Triangle. They could get past the mine fields with a lot of little boats, where they couldn't with just their few ironclads."

He spoke the cold truth, and every officer in the command center knew it. So nothing further was said. They simply waited for another telegraph report to inform them whether Calopodius was a husband or a widower.

THE INDUS

Before the battle was over, Anna had reason to be thankful for her heavy gown.

As cheerfully profligate as he was, the gunner soon used up the preloaded cylinders for the Puckle gun. Thereafter, Anna had to reload the cylinders manually with the cartridges she found in a metal case against the shell of the turret. Placing the new shells *into* a cylinder was easy enough, with a little experience. The trick was taking out the spent ones. The brass cartridges were hot enough to hurt her fingers, the first time she tried prying them out.

Thereafter, following the gunner's hastily shouted instructions, she started using the little ramrod provided in the ammunition case. Kneeling in the shelter of the turret, she just upended the cylinders—carefully holding them with the hem of her dress, because they were hot also—and smacked the cartridges loose.

The cartridges came out easily enough, that way—right onto her lap and knees. In a lighter gown, a less severe and formal garment, her thighs would soon enough have been scorched by the little pile of hot metal.

As it was, the heat was endurable, and Anna didn't care in the least that the expensive fabric was being ruined in the process. She just went about her business, brushing the cartridges onto the floor of the turret, loading and reloading with the thunderous racket of the Puckle gun in her ears, ignoring everything else around her.

Throughout, her mind only strayed once. After the work became something of a routine, she found herself wondering if her husband's mind had been so detached in battles. Not whether he had ignored pain—of course he had; Anna had learned that much since leaving Constantinople—but whether he had been able to ignore his continued existence as well.

She suspected he had, and found herself quite warmed by the thought. She even handed up the next loaded cylinder with a smile.

The gunner noticed the smile, and that too would become part of the legend. He would survive the war, as it happened; and, in later years, in taverns in his native Anatolia, whenever he heard the tale of how the Wife smote down Malwa boarders with a sword and a laugh, he saw no reason to set the matter straight. By then, he had come to half-believe it himself.

Anna sensed a shadow passing, but she paid it very little attention. By now, her hands and fingers were throbbing enough to block out most sensation beyond what was necessary to keep reloading the cylinders. She barely even noticed the sudden burst of fiery light and the screams that announced that the *Victrix* had arrived and was wreaking its delayed vengeance on what was left of the Malwa ambush.

Which was not much, in truth. The gunner was a very capable man, and Anna had kept him well supplied. Most of the skiffs now drifting near the barge had bodies draped over their sides and sprawled lifelessly within. At that close range, the Puckle gun had been murderous.

"Enough, ma'am," said the gunner. "It's over."

Anna finished reloading the cylinder in her hands. Then, when the meaning of the words finally registered, she set the thing down on the floor of the turret. Perhaps oddly, the relief of finally not having to handle hot metal only made the pain in her hands—and legs, too, she noticed finally—all the worse.

She stared down at the fabric of her gown. There were little stains all over it, where cartridges had rested before she brushed them onto the floor. There was a time, she could vaguely remember, when the destruction of an expensive garment would have been a cause of great concern. But it seemed a very long time ago.

"How is Illus?" she asked softly. "And the others? The boys?"

The gunner sighed. "One of the boys got killed, ma'am. Just bad luck—Illus kept the youngsters back, but that one grenade . . ."

Vaguely, Anna remembered hearing an explosion. She began to ask which boy it was, whose death she had caused, of the five urchins she had found on the docks of Barbaricum and conscripted into her Service. But she could not bear that pain yet.

"Illus?"

"He's fine. So's Abdul. Cottomenes got cut pretty bad."

Something to do again. The thought came as a relief. Within seconds, she was clambering awkwardly over the side of the turret again—and, again, silently cursing the impractical garment she wore.

Cottomenes was badly gashed, true enough. But the leg wound was not even close to the great femoral artery, and by now Anna had learned to sew other things than cloth. Besides, the *Victrix's* boiler was an excellent mechanism for boiling water.

The ship's engineer was a bit outraged, of course. But, wisely, he kept his mouth shut.

THE IRON TRIANGLE

The telegraph started chattering. Everyone in the command bunker froze for a moment. Then, understanding the meaning of the dot-dashes faster than anyone—even the operator jotting down the message—Calopodius slumped in his chair with relief. The message was unusually long, with two short pauses in the middle, and by the time it was completed Calopodius was even smiling.

Belisarius, unlike Calopodius, could not quite follow the message until it was translated. When he took the message from the hand of the operator and scanned it quickly, he understood the smile on the face of the blind young officer. He grinned himself.

"Well, I'd say she's in good form," he announced to the small crowd in the bunker. Then, quoting:

"ALL FINE EXCEPT COTTOMENES INJURED AND
RAFFI DEAD. RAFFI ONLY TWELVE YEARS OLD.
FEEL HORRIBLE ABOUT IT. MENTION HIM IN
DISPATCHES. PLEASE. ALSO MENTION PUCKLE
GUNNER LEO CONSTANTES. SPLENDID MAN. ALSO
INSTRUCT GENERAL BELISARIUS MAKE MORE
PUCKLE GUNS. SPLENDID THINGS. ALSO—"

"Here's where the pause was," explained the general. His grin
widened. "It goes on:

"OPERATOR SAYS MESSAGE TOO LONG. OPERATOR
REFUSES GIVE HIS NAME. MENTION NAMELESS
OPERATOR IN DISPATCHES. STUPID OFFICIOUS
ASININE OBNOXIOUS WORTHLESS FELLOW."

"Why do I think someone in that telegraph station has a
sword at his throat?" mused Maurice idly. "Her bodyguards are
Isaurians, right? Stupid idiot." He was grinning also.

"MENANDER SAYS WILL ARRIVE SOON. WILL
NEED NEW CLOTHES."

Belisarius' grin didn't fade, exactly, but it became less purely
jovial. His last words were spoken softly, and addressed to Calopodius rather than to the room at large.

"Here was the second pause. The last part of the message
reads:

"AM EAGER TO SEE YOU AGAIN. MY HUSBAND."

Chapter 18
THE NARMADA RIVER

The Malwa army drawn up on the open plain just south of the Narmada was terrifying. Looking over them from a distance, perched in her howdah with the baby, Shakuntala finally understood—*really* understood—why her husband had been so cautious in his tactics from the very beginning.

It might be better to say, cautious in his strategy. When the Panther did strike, he struck hard and fast. But he'd carefully avoided getting anywhere near the Malwa lion's jaws and talons.

"Impressive, aren't they?" Rao called up to her. He was riding a horse alongside the elephant that bore her and Namadev.

Until that morning, two maidservants had been in the howdah with them. But Shakuntala had insisted they remain behind, when the Maratha army moved out at dawn to meet Damodara and his forces. The empress still suspected treachery. For that reason, she had one of the best horses in India following behind, in case she and Namadev had to flee precipitously into the badlands of the Great Country. On that horse, she was confident she could elude even Rajput cavalry. On an elephant, hopeless to do so.

She stared down at her husband. Amazingly, to all appearances, he was in as sunny a mood as she'd ever seen him.

Rao raised himself a little in his stirrups—by now, the Roman innovations were ubiquitous—to get a better view of the enemy.

186

"The best army the Malwa have, for a certainty." He pointed with his finger, and then slowly swept it across the front lines of the enemy. They were still a thousand yards away.

"See how Damodara has his artillery units scattered among the infantry? You won't see that in any other Malwa army. No lolling about in the comfort of the rear for *his* kshatriya."

The finger jabbed; here, there, there.

"Notice, also, the way he has the Ye-tai units positioned with respect to the main force of Rajput cavalry. In the center, most of them, forming his spearhead while the Rajputs are concentrated on the flanks. His Ye-tai will lead the charge, here, not stay behind to drive forward badly trained and ill-motivated peasant foot soldiers."

The finger lowered. "Of which," he concluded cheerily, "Damodara doesn't have that many in any event. They're back guarding the supply wagons, I imagine. Along with the mahaveda priests, of course, who control the munitions supply. That last feature is about the only way in which Damodara's army still resembles a Malwa force."

"Rao . . ." Shakuntala said hesitantly.

"Oh, yes, my dearest. You're quite right." Still standing in the stirrups, Rao swiveled his upper body back and forth, studying his own army.

The Maratha army was barely half the size of the enemy force across the field. And didn't bear so much as a fourth the weight of fine armor, fine swords and lances—and not a tenth the weight of firearms and gunpowder.

"Oh, yes," he repeated, his voice still as sunny-toned as ever, "if I were idiotic enough to meet them on this field, they'd hammer us flat. Be lucky if a third of my army survived at all."

"Rao . . ."

"Be still, dearest. This is not a field where two armies will meet. Simply two souls. Three, actually, counting Damodara. Perhaps four, if we count Narses as well. Which I think we must."

She took a deep, slow breath. "Your soul is as great as any I have ever known. But it is not great enough to do *this*."

He laughed. "Of course not! It's not *my* soul I'm counting on, however."

He reached up and extended his hand. "Touch me, dearest. Not for the last time! Simply—a gift."

She did so, briefly clutching the strong fingers. Strong and large. Rao had the hands of a man half again his size.

Then, he was gone, trotting his horse onto the open field between the armies.

Sitting on his own mount at the very front and center of the Malwa army, Rana Sanga watched him come.

At first, he simply assumed it was Raghunath Rao, from the logic of the matter. Even the keen eyes of the man who was probably India's greatest archer could not distinguish features at the distance of a thousand yards. The more so, when he had not seen the features themselves in over two decades. The famous duel between him and Rao had happened when they were both young men.

Long ago, that was. A thousand years ago, it seemed to the greatest king of Rajputana. Between then and now lay a gulf that could not be measured in simple years. The young Sanga who had faced a young Rao so long ago had been sure and certain in his beliefs, his creed, his duty, his loyalties, and his place in the universe. The middle-aged man who was about to meet him again was no longer sure of anything.

Except in his prowess as a warrior, of course. But Rana Sanga knew full well that was the least of the things that were meeting today on a new field of battle. Something much greater was at stake now. He only wished he knew exactly what it was. But the only thought that came to his mind was . . .

Onions.

It was bizarre, really. All he could think of was onions, peeling away. With every horse's pace the distant figure shortened between them, Sanga could sense another peel, falling.

Soon enough—still long before he could recognize the features—he knew it was Rao.

"I'd half-forgotten," he murmured.

Next to him, Damodara raised a questioning eyebrow.

"How frightening an opponent he is," Sanga explained.

Damodara squinted at the coming figure, trying to discern what Sanga seemed to see in it. Damodara himself was . . .

Unimpressed, really. Given the reputation of the Panther—or the Wind of the Great Country, as he was also known—he'd been expecting some sort of giant of a man. But the Maratha warrior approaching across the field seemed no more than average size.

Very wide in the shoulders, true. So much was obvious even at a distance, and Damodara didn't think it was due to the armor Rao was wearing. It was not elaborate armor, in any event. Just the utilitarian gear than any hill-fighter might bring into battle.

But as Rao neared, he began to understand. It was a subtle thing, given that the man was on horseback. Still, after a time, it became apparent enough.

"The way he moves, even riding a horse . . ."

Sanga barked a harsh laugh. "Hope you never see him move up close, with a blade or his iron-clawed gauntlet! Not even the Mongoose is so fast, so sure. Always so balanced. I remember thinking I was facing an asura under the human-seeming flesh."

The Rajput king eased his sword out of the scabbard. Just an inch or so, making sure it was loose. Then, did the same with the lance in its scabbard by his knee.

Then, drew his bow. He'd start with that, of course. With a bow, Sanga out-matched Rao. With a lance also, probably, especially now with the added advantage of stirrups.

Still, given Rao, it would probably end with them on foot. The last time they'd met, they'd fought for an entire day with every weapon they'd possessed. And then, too exhausted to move, had finished by exchanging philosophical barbs and quips.

"Wish me well, Lord," he said. Then, spurred his own horse into a trot.

A great roar went up from the Malwa army. Matched, a moment later, by one from the Marathas across the field.

"Oh, splendid," murmured Ajatasutra. He and the assassin he'd kept with him exchanged a little smile.

"Let's hope they keep it up." The assassin glanced at one of the nearby munitions wagons. The mahaveda head priest and the two mahamimamsa who guarded it were standing, their eyes riveted on the two combatants approaching each other. They were paying no attention at all to the men who, in the nondescript and patchy armor of common infantrymen, were quietly spreading through the munitions wagons.

"You will give the signal?"

Ajatasutra pinched his hawk nose, smiling more widely under the fingers. "If need be, yes. But unless I'm much mistaken, that won't be necessary. The thing will be, ah, quite obvious."

The assassin cocked his head slightly, in a subtle question.

"Look at it this way. The two most flamboyant men in India are about to meet. True, one is the sternest of Rajputs and the other is reputed to be a great philosopher. Still, I don't think subtlety will be the end result."

Narses just watched, perched on his mule. Whatever he could do, he had done. The rest was in the hands of whatever God existed.

So, although he watched intently, he was quite calm. What would happen, would happen. There remained only the anticipation of the outcome. The greatest game of all, the game of thrones.

For the rest—whatever God might be—Narses was quite sure he was damned anyway. But he thought he'd have the satisfaction, whatever happened, of being able to thumb his nose at all the gods and devils of the universe, as he plunged into the Pit.

Which, he reminded himself, might still be some decades off anyway.

Damodara was far less relaxed. He was as tense and as keyed up as he'd ever been, on the edge of a battle.

It could not be otherwise, of course. It was he who would, as commanders must, gauge the right moment.

Once Sanga and Rao were within seventy yards of each other, Rao drew up his horse.

Sanga did likewise. He already had the bow in his left hand. Now, relinquishing the reins, he drew and notched an arrow with the right.

Then, waited. Gallant as ever, the Rajput king would allow the Maratha chieftain and imperial consort to ready his own bow.

Titles had vanished, on this field. Everything had vanished, except the glory of India's two greatest warriors meeting again in single combat.

Rao grinned. He hadn't intended to, but the sight of Sanga's frown—quite obvious, even at the distance, given the open-faced nature of Rajput helmets—made it impossible to do otherwise.

Always strict! Sanga was obviously a bit disgruntled that Rao had been so careless as not to have his own bow already in hand. Had the great Maratha warrior grown senile?

"The last time," Rao murmured, "great king of the Rajputs, we began with bows and ended with philosophy. But we're much older now, and that seems like such a waste of sweat. So let's start with philosophy, shall we? Where it always ends, anyway."

Rao slid from his horse and landed on the ground, poised and balanced on his feet.

First, he reached up, drew his lance from the saddle scabbard, and pitched it aside. Then, did the same with the bow. Being careful, of course, to make sure they landed on soft patches of soil and far from any rocks. They were good weapons, very well made and expensive. It would be pointless extravagance to damage them. From a philosophical standpoint, downright grotesque.

The arrow quiver followed. Holding it like a vase, he scattered the arrows across the field. Then, tossed the quiver aside. He was less careful where they landed. Arrows were easy enough to come by, and the utilitarian quiver even more so.

Armed now only with a sword and hand weapons, Rao began walking toward Sanga. After ten steps, the sword was pitched to the ground.

Laid on the ground, rather, and carefully at that. It was an excellent sword and Rao didn't want to see it damaged. Still, it was all done very quickly.

The dagger, likewise.

His iron-clawed gauntlet being a sturdier thing, he simply dropped it casually as he moved on.

He walked slowly. Not for the sake of drama, but simply because unlacing and removing armor requires some concentration.

The helmet was the easiest, so it went first. Tough and utilitarian, like the gauntlet, it was simply dropped from one pace to the next. The rest took a bit of time. Not much, given Rao's fingers.

By the time he was done, he stood thirty yards from Sanga. And wore nothing but a loincloth.

And, still—he hadn't meant to, but couldn't resist—that same grin.

Shakuntala held her breath. The baby squalled, so tightly was she clutching him. But she never heard.

Damodara rolled his eyes. Just for a moment, praising the heavens.

True, he'd expected *something*. That was why he had waited. But he hadn't expected Rao to make it the simplest task he'd probably ever confront, as the emperor of Malwa.

He spurred his horse forward. No slow trot, this, either.

Sanga stared. Paralyzed.

There was no way—not even Rao!—that any man could survive against him, standing there and in that manner.

He didn't know what to do.

No, worse.

He *did* know what to do. And couldn't.

Not though his very soul was screaming at him. As was the soul of his wife, whether she was dead or not.

And, still, all he could think of was onions. Not peeling away now, though. He could sense the shadow of his wife, throwing them at him.

"King of Rajputana! Stop!"

The voice came as an immense relief. Swiveling in his saddle, Sanga stared at Damodara. For years now, the man coming toward him had been his commander. At first, Sanga had obeyed of necessity; then, with acceptance; finally, with great pleasure.

Never greater than now.

For the first time in his life, Sanga realized, he had a true and genuine lord. And, desperately, wanted his master's guidance.

Ajatasutra glanced up at the priest atop the wagon he was now standing beside. The mahaveda was scowling, of course. But, if anything, had his attention more riveted in the distance than ever.

Oh, splendid.

As soon as Damodara drew alongside the Rajput king, he nodded toward Rao.

"You cannot survive this, Sanga," he said softly. "When glory and honor and duty and necessity all clash together, on the same field, no man can survive. Not even the gods can do so."

The Rajput's dark eyes stared at him.

"Lord . . ." he said slowly.

"Yes, well." Damodara cleared his throat. Awkward, that. But he did need to keep a straight face. Even if that maniac's grin thirty yards away was infectious.

"Yes, well. That's actually the point. You may recall that I once told you, on the banks of the Tigris, that the day might come when I would need to remind you of your oath."

"Yes, Lord." The eyes seemed darker yet. "I swore an oath—as did all Rajputs—to the Emperor of Malwa."

"Indeed so. Well, I just discovered—"

He had to clear his throat again. No choice. *Damn that Maratha rascal!*

"Amazing news. Horrifying, actually. But Narses ferreted out the plot. It seems that—two generations ago, if you can believe it—"

Damodara had insisted on that, overriding the eunuch's protests, even though it made the forgeries far more difficult. He did not think it likely his father and mother would survive what was coming, despite Narses' assurances. So be it. They were elderly, in any event. But he would not have them shamed also.

"—unscrupulous plotters in the dynasty substituted another baby for the rightful heir. Who was my grandfather, as it happens. The rightful heir to the throne, that is. Which means that Skandagupta is an impostor and a fraud, and his minion Nanda Lal is a traitor and a wretch. And, well, it seems that *I* am actually the Emperor of Malwa."

By now, he wished he could *strangle* that still-grinning Maratha ape. Even though he'd gotten it all out without choking once.

Alas. The only man who could possibly manage that feat was Rana Sanga.

Who was still staring at him, with eyes that now seemed as dark as eternity.

Carefully keeping his gaze away from Rao and his blasted grin, Damodara spoke as sternly as he could manage.

"So, King of Rajputana. Will you honor your oath?"

❖   ❖   ❖

It all fell into place for Sanga, then. As if the last shadow onion, hurled by his shadow wife, had struck him on the forehead and abruptly dispelled all illusions.

He looked away from Damodara and gazed upon Rao.

He always understood, Sanga realized. *And, thus, understood me as well.*

Sanga remembered the silvery moon over tortured Ranapur, that he had turned away from out of his duty. And knew, at last, that the duty had been illusion also. Already, then, nothing but illusion.

He remembered Belisarius holding a jewel in his hand, and asking the Rajput king if he would exchange his plain wife for a beautiful one. The answer to that question had been obvious to Sanga at the time. Why, he wondered now, had he not seen that the same answer applied to all things?

He remembered Belisarius' exact words, speaking of the jewel in his hand. How stupid of Sanga, not to have understood then!

This, too, is a thing of pollution. A monster. An intelligent being created from disease. The worst disease which ever stalked the universe. And yet—

Is he not beautiful? Just like a diamond, forged out of rotting waste?

For years, Sanga had held tightly to the memory of his duel with Rao. Had held to that memory, as he'd seen the glory of his youth slide into what seemed an endless pit of vileness and corruption.

Looking upon Raghunath Rao today, standing almost naked before him—naked and unarmed—Sanga knew that he was already defeated. But also understood that, out of this defeat, would come the victory he had so desperately sought for so many years.

So stupid.

How could he have been so blind, not to have seen the truth? Not to have seen the way in which, out of the filth and evil of the Malwa dynasty, had emerged the true thing? There was no excuse, really, since Sanga had been there to bear witness, every step of the way. Had been there himself, and witnessed, as a short, fat—fat then, at least—and unassuming distant cousin of the emperor had shown Sanga and all Rajputs that their sacred vows had not and would not be scorned by the gods of India.

An onion, peeled away by divine will to show the jewel at the center.

Even Narses had seen it. And if the Roman eunuch had chosen forgery and duplicity to peel away the illusion, Sanga had no need of such artificial devices.

The truth was what it was. The great land of India needed a great emperor. And now it had one, despite the schemes of an alien monster. No, not even *despite* the monster. Though never meaning to do so and never recognizing its own deed, the monster itself had created that true emperor, because it had created the need for him.

In a manner that the Roman traitor would never understand, his forgeries were simply a recognition of the truth.

"Of course, Emperor," he said.

Damodara had seen Sanga smile before. Not often, true, by the standards of most men. Still, he'd seen him smile. Even grin, now and then.

Never, though, in a manner you might almost call *sly*.

"Of course," Sanga repeated. "You forget that I am also a student of philosophy. If not"—he jerked his head toward Rao—"with the same extravagance as that one. But enough to understand that truth and illusion fade into each other, when the cycle comes. I remember pondering that matter, as I listened to the screams of dying Ranapur."

There was no humor in the last sentence. Nor in the next.

"And did I not understand, my wife would explain it to me. If she could."

"Oh." Damodara felt like an idiot. "Sorry. I forgot. Narses uncovered another plot. It seems—"

"*Please*, Lord. She has been my life. She and my children."

"Still is, still is. So are they." Damodara drew the little knife from the pouch, and handed it to the Rajput. "She said—told Narses, through Ajatasutra—that you'd recognize this. Asked that you be given an onion, too."

He drew that forth also, feeling like an idiot again. What sort of emperor serves up onions?

But since the answer was obvious, he didn't feel like much of an idiot.

Successful emperors, that's who.

Sanga stared down at the knife and the onion, though he made no attempt to take them. No way he could have, without relinquishing the bow and the arrow.

"Yes, I recognize it. And the message in the onion. I felt its shadow strike me, but a minute ago."

For an instant, the Rajput's eyes flicked toward the Malwa army. *"Narses,"* he hissed, sounding like a cobra. A very, very angry cobra.

That had to be deflected. "Later, Sanga. For the moment . . ."

Damodara's jaws tightened. He was still quietly furious at Narses himself.

"He probably kept us all alive. And in the meantime, there are other matters to deal with."

Sanga took a slow deep breath. "Yes." Another such breath, by the end of which the tall and powerful figure on the horse next to Damodara seemed quite relaxed.

Poised rather, in the manner of a great warrior.

"What do you command, Emperor?"

"Let's start by ridding ourselves of those pestiferous priests, shall we? Along with their pet torturers. I decree the Mahaveda cult an abomination. All the cult's priests and mahamimamsa are under immediate sentence of death. None will be spared."

"My great pleasure, Lord of Malwa."

And, so, India was given a new legend, after all. Whatever regrets the warriors who watched might have had, that the great duel between Sanga and Rao never happened, they were mollified by the bow shot.

The greatest ever, all would swear, since Krishna the charioteer drove Arjuna and his great bow onto the ancient battlefield of Kurukshetra. Hundreds of yards, that arrow flew, to strike like a thunderbolt.

For one of the few times in his life, Ajatasutra was quite amazed. The arrow went right through the chief priest, striking the perfect bowman's target—just above the breastbone—and severing the great arteries as it passed. The chief priest collapsed on the wagon like a puppet with cut strings, blood gushing as if from a fountain. The arrow might even have severed the spine, from the way the priest was still thrashing.

"You see?" he demanded.

But the assassin was already onto the wagon, cutting the first mahamimamsa.

Ajatasutra saw no reason to follow. The assassins he'd assembled, over the months, were very good. Not as good as he was, of course. But quite good enough—any one of them—to be more than a match for twice their number of torturers.

Besides, he had other duties. Sanga was coming, driving his horse like another thunderbolt, and with his lance in hand. The Ye-tai were paralyzed, for the moment, but the Rajputs were not hesitating at all.

There were twenty thousand Rajput cavalrymen on that field, now curling from the flanks onto the munitions train like two great waves. Even with the best of discipline, they were likely to shatter the wagons unless Ajatasutra had them clearly under control.

A small disaster, that. There was still a war to be fought and won.

He put away his dagger and drew the sword. If the scabbard that sword had been concealed in was shabby, the sword was that of a commander.

"*Guard the wagons!*" he shouted at the infantrymen, standing around, their mouths agape. "Swing them into a circle. Now, you idiots!"

They obeyed, almost instantly. Even those illiterate and provincial peasants could figure out the equation.

The mahaveda and mahamimamsa were all dead or dying.

Ajatasutra seemed to know what he was doing.

Twenty *thousand* Rajputs were on the way. The hooves of their horses seem to make the very ground shake.

By the time the Rajputs arrived, Ajatasutra had the wagons in a rough circle. With, in a still wider circle around them, the corpses of priests and torturers tossed out. As if they were so many sacrificial offerings.

Which . . . they were. Even the Rajputs were satisfied.

Throughout, neither the Ye-tai nor the kshatriya artillerymen moved at all. This was Rajput business, even if Damodara had obviously given it his blessing.

Good enough. No doubt an explanation would be forthcoming. For the moment, wisdom and sagacity both called for the tactics of mice in the presence of predators.

Stillness and silence, lest one be noticed. Let the hawks feed on the priests and torturers. True, they were already carrion, but raptors are not fussy.

And who cared, anyway?

After the years of victory with Damodara, the years of battles and maneuvers in the course of which their commander had showed himself worthy of his men, *who cared?*

When the announcement was finally made to the entire army, the Ye-tai and kshatriya simply grunted their satisfaction.

Of course he was the emperor. Stupid of them, really, not to have realized it sooner. All that wasted time.

Still worse, the endless miles of pointless marching back and forth across central Asia—when Kausambi was so close.

That came later, however. For the moment, Damodara had more pressing business.

After Sanga was gone, thundering off, Damodara trotted over to Rao.

The grin was gone, at least.

"I am the new Emperor of Malwa. I did not start this war, I would now finish it."

Rao nodded. "I want the border set on the crest of the Vindhyas. *And* we get the crest—with the right to build forts on it."

Damodara thought about it, for a minute.

That was reasonable, he decided. In the nature of things, it would always be northern India with its teeming population in the Ganges valley that posed a threat to the realms of southern India. Forts along the crest of the Vindhyas in the hands of Marathas could serve to defend the Deccan. There was really no way they could ever serve as invasion routes onto the Gangetic plain.

"Agreed," he said. "In return, I want Bharakuccha to be an open city. I will need a large seaport on the west coast."

It was Rao's turn to consider.

"The population is mostly Maratha," he pointed out.

"It was once. Not any longer. It's twice the size it was at the conquest, and as polyglot as any city in the world. No more than a third of the populace is Maratha, these days."

Rao grunted. "Still."

"I do not insist on a Malwa garrison. But I don't want it garrisoned by Andhra, either. Or Persians."

"On that last, we are agreed," Rao said, scowling. "There'll be no way to keep the greedy arrogant bastards out of the Sind, of course, thanks to you idiots. Not now. But that's as close as I want them, and closer than I imagine you do."

"Yes. And I don't want Romans, either. They're too powerful."

Rao scratched his jaw. "Well, that's true. Friends now—ours, if not yours—but who knows what the future will bring?"

Damodara made the final move. "An Axumite garrison, then, just big enough to maintain order. Axum is powerful at sea but too small to pose a military threat to any major realm of India. But *not* Axumite territory. An open city, with its own government—we'll thrash that out later—and neutral to all parties."

"You understand they'll insist on the right to collect the tolls? To maintain the garrison."

"For Axum, that matters. For us, it does not. Let them skim the trade. The trade itself flows in and out of India. North as well as south."

Rao nodded. "Agreed, then. That leaves the Malwa armies in the Deccan outside of the Great Country. There's still a huge garrison in Amaravati, and large ones elsewhere. Since you're the Goptri of the Deccan, they're officially under your command. What happens, now that you're the Emperor?"

Damodara shrugged. "Ask me in a few months. If I take Kausambi and depose Skandagupta, they will obey me. I will then order them to come home. Until then, however, I'd just as soon they stayed where they are. I've never had much dealings with them, and I don't know which way they'd go so long as things are unsettled."

Rao studied the Malwa army. It was collapsing inward, leaving units of Ye-tai and kshatriya in place while the Rajputs came in to slaughter the priests. If they weren't already slaughtered, which . . .

Rao now studied the new Malwa emperor.

They probably were. If Damodara had none of the overween-ing ambition of Malwa's previous dynasts, Rao was quite sure he concentrated in his short person more capability than any of them—and at least as much in the way of ruthlessness.

But it was a very intelligent ruthlessness, the sort that didn't confuse means with ends and didn't prize ruthlessness for its own sake.

Rao could live with that. More importantly, his son—and his son, and his son—could live with it too. The Deccan could live with it. There would always be a great empire in northern India, that southern India would have to deal with. That being so, better to deal with an empire founded by such as Damodara.

"Done. It would take me two months anyway—at least—to march on Amaravati. But I warn you that I will, if you fail."

"If I fail, what do I care? And if I don't, it won't be neces-sary." Damodara smiled. "Or do you think that the garrison at Amaravati will suddenly get ambitious? With me above them, and you at the gates?"

Rao returned the smile. It would be pleasant, in the years to come, to deal with this man. Not easy, of course. But . . .

Yes, pleasant.

He nodded, and started to walk away.

Damodara called him back. "Rao—one thing more."

"Yes?"

"If I succeed, I would like your sadhu to visit Kausambi."

"Bindusara? Why?"

The new emperor seemed to shiver a little. "It is not enough to cut the throats of the mahaveda. For generations, now, they have been a poison in India. I think we need to consider an antidote."

It was the only thing that happened that day that surprised Rao. He had never—not once—considered the possibility that the new emperor of Malwa might actually be wise.

"I have no objection. But I can't speak for Bindusara. He's a sadhu, you know. Stubborn, as the real ones always are."

"Yes. Why I want him."

Rao nodded, again, and walked away.

Much more than simply pleasant, then.

Of course, that would also make it less easy. But Rao had never expected the universe to be easy. In truth, he didn't want it to be. With too much ease, came softness; and with softness, came rot.

It took him a while, to return. First, because he had to settle down some eager and jittery units of his own army. It was always hard for soldiers to restrain themselves, seeing what appeared to be an enemy in confusion.

That was accomplished easily enough. A few shouts and gestures did the trick. Rao's position was unquestioned, after all.

It took longer to collect the weapons and armor he'd discarded. Nor was he tempted to ignore the business. In truth, he didn't even think of doing so. Legend or not, consort of an empress or not, Raghunath Rao was Maratha born and bred. Like hill people the world over, they were a thrifty lot.

Eventually, though, he made his way back to the howdah and looked up at his beloved wife.

"See?" he demanded.

"I never doubted you once, husband," she lied.

Chapter 19
THE IRON TRIANGLE

There was no reception for Anna at the docks, when she arrived at the Iron Triangle. Just a small gang of men hurrying out from the bunker to catch the lines thrown from the *Victrix* and the barge.

She was a bit surprised. Not disgruntled, simply . . .

Surprised.

Menander seemed to understand. "We do this as quickly as possible these days," he explained apologetically. "The Malwa have spotters hidden in the reeds, and they often fire rocket volleys at us whenever a convoy arrives."

As if his words were the cue, Anna heard a faint sound to the north. Vaguely, like a snake hissing. Looking up, she saw several rockets soaring up into the sky.

After a moment, startled, she realized how far away they were. "I didn't know they were so big."

"They have to be. Those are fired from the Malwa lines, miles to the north. At first, the spotters would fire small ones from the reeds. But that's just pure suicide for them. Even the Malwa, after a while, gave it up."

Too uncertain to know whether she should be worried or not, Anna watched the rockets climb higher into the sky.

"They're headed our way, girl," Illus said gruffly. He pointed toward the low bunker toward which they were being towed. The

202

roof of the bunker was just tall enough for the *Victrix* to pass underneath. "I'd feel better if you moved into the bow. That'll reach the shelter first."

"Yes. I suppose." Anna gathered up the heavy skirts and began moving forward. Illus followed her, with Abdul helping Cottomenes limp along. Behind them came the four boys.

Glancing back, she saw that Menander had remained in his place. He was still watching the rockets. From his apparent lack of concern, she realized they must be veering off.

"Keep moving, girl," Illus growled. "Yes, the damn things are completely inaccurate. But they don't always miss—and any rocket that big is going to have a monster of a warhead."

She didn't argue the point. Illus was usually cooperative with her, after all, and this was his business.

Still, most of her mind was concentrated on the sound of the coming rockets. Between that, the deep gloom of the approaching bunker, and the need to watch her feet moving across the cluttered deck, she was caught completely by surprise when the fanfare erupted.

That happened as soon as the bow passed under the overhang of the ship bunker.

Cornicens, a lot of them, and some big drums. She wasn't very familiar with cornicens. They were almost entirely a military instrument.

"Oh," she said. "Oh."

Illus was grinning from ear to ear. "I was starting to wonder. Stupid, that. When you're dealing with the general."

By the time the fanfare ended and the bow of the ship bumped gently against the wharf inside the bunker, Anna thought she might be growing deaf. Cornicens were *loud.* Especially when the sound was reflected from such a low ceiling.

The cheers of the soldiers even seemed dim, in her ears. They couldn't be, of course. Not with that many soldiers. Especially when they started banging the hilts of their swords on their shields as well.

She was startled by that martial salute almost as much as she'd been by the cornicens.

She glanced at Illus. He had a peculiar look on his face. A sort of fierce satisfaction.

"Do they always do that?" she asked, almost shouting the words.

He shook his head. That gesture, too, had the air of satisfaction. "No, girl. They almost never do that."

When she saw the first man who came up the gangplank, after it was laid, Anna was startled again. She'd learned enough of Roman uniforms and insignia to realize that this had to be Belisarius. But she'd never pictured him so. The fact that he was tall and broad-shouldered fit her image well enough. But the rest . . .

She'd read all of Macrembolitissa's work, so she knew a great deal about the general. Despite that knowledge—or perhaps because of it—she'd imagined some sort of modern Nestor. Wise, in a grim sort of way; not old, certainly—abstractly, she knew he was a young man—but still somehow middle-aged. Perhaps a bit of gray in his hair.

She'd certainly never thought he would be so handsome. And so very young, to have done all that he had.

Finally, as he neared, she found an anchor. Something that matched the writings.

The general's smile *was* crooked. She'd always thought that was just Macrembolitissa, indulging herself in poetic license.

She said as much.

Belisarius smiled more crookedly still. "So I'm told. Welcome to the Iron Triangle, Lady Saronites."

The general escorted her off the *Victrix*. Anna was relieved that he didn't offer her a hand, though. She'd be in far more danger of tripping over the long and ragged skirts without both hands to hold them.

She had to concentrate so much on that task that she wasn't really looking at anything else.

They reached the relatively safe footing of the wharf.

"Lady Saronites," said the general, "your husband."

She looked up, startled again.

"Oh," she said. "Oh."

There came, then, the most startling thing of all that day. For the first time in years, Anna was too shy to say a word.

✧   ✧   ✧

"It's not much," said Calopodius apologetically.

Anna's eyes moved over the interior of the little bunker where Calopodius lived. Where she would now live also. She did not fail to notice all the little touches here and there—the bright, cheery little cloths; the crucifix; even a few native handcrafts—as well as the relative cleanliness of the place. But . . .

No, it was not much. Just a big pit in the ground, when all was said and done, covered over with logs and soil.

"It's fine," she said. "Not a problem."

She turned and stared at him. Her husband, once a handsome boy, was now a hideously ugly man. She had expected the empty eye sockets, true enough. But even after all the carnage she had witnessed since she left Constantinople, she had not once considered what a mortar shell would do to the *rest* of his face.

Stupid, really. As if shrapnel would obey the rules of poetry, and pierce eyes as neatly as a goddess at a loom. The upper half of his face was a complete ruin. The lower half was relatively unmarked, except for one scar along his right jaw and another puckerlike mark on his left cheek.

His mouth and lips, on the other hand, were still as she vaguely remembered them. A nice mouth, she decided, noticing for the first time.

"It's fine," she repeated. "Not a problem."

A moment later, Illus and Abdul came into the bunker hauling her luggage. What was left of it. Until they were gone, Anna and Calopodius were silent. Then he said, very softly:

"I don't understand why you came."

Anna tried to remember the answer. It was difficult. And probably impossible to explain, in any event. *I wanted a divorce, maybe* . . . seemed . . . strange. Even stranger, though closer to the truth, would be: *or at least to drag you back so you could share the ruins of my own life.*

"It doesn't matter now. I'm here. I'm staying."

For the first time since she'd rejoined her husband, he smiled. Anna realized she'd never really seen him smile before. Not, at least, with an expression that was anything more than politeness.

He reached out his hand, tentatively, and she moved toward him. The hand, fumbling, stroked her ribs.

"God in Heaven, Anna!" he choked. "How can you *stand* something like that—in this climate? You'll drown in sweat."

Anna tried to keep from laughing; and then, realizing finally where she was, stopped trying. Even in the haughtiest aristocratic circles of Constantinople, a woman was allowed to laugh in the presence of her husband.

When she was done—the laughter was perhaps a bit hysterical—Calopodius shook his head. "We've got to get you a sari, first thing. I can't have my wife dying on me from heat prostration."

Calopodius matched deed to word immediately. A few words to his aide-to-camp Luke, and, much sooner than Anna would have expected, a veritable horde of Punjabis from the adjacent town were packed into the bunker.

Some of them were actually there on business, bringing piles of clothing for her to try on. Most of them, she finally understood, just wanted to get a look at her.

Of course, they were all expelled from the bunker while she changed her clothing—except for two native women whose expert assistance she required until she mastered the secrets of the foreign garments. But once the women announced that she was suitably attired, the mob of admirers was allowed back in.

In fact, after a while Anna found it necessary to leave the bunker altogether and model her new clothing on the ground outside, where everyone could get a good look at her new appearance. Her husband insisted, to her surprise.

"You're beautiful," he said to her, "and I want everyone to know it."

She almost asked how a blind man could tell, but he forestalled the question with a little smile. "Did you think I'd forget?"

But later, that night, he admitted the truth. They were lying side by side, stiffly, still fully clothed, on the pallet in a corner of the bunker where Calopodius slept. "To be honest, I can't remember very well what you look like."

Anna thought about it, for a moment. Then:

"I can't really remember myself."

"I wish I could see you," he murmured.

"It doesn't matter." She took his hand and laid it on her bare belly. The flesh reveled in its new coolness. She herself, on the other hand, reveled in the touch. And did not find it strange that she should do so.

"Feel."

His hand was gentle, at first. And never really stopped being so, for all the passion that followed. When it was all over, Anna was covered in sweat again. But she didn't mind at all. Without heavy and proper fabric to cover her—with nothing covering her now except Calopodius' hand—the sweat dried soon enough. That, too, was a great pleasure.

"I warn you," she murmured into his ear. "We're not in Constantinople any more. Won't be for a long time, if ever. So if I catch you with a courtesan, I'll boil you alive."

"The thought never crossed my mind!" he insisted. And even believed it was true.

Chapter 20
BARBARICUM

As they walked down the gangplank from their ship to the dock at Barbaricum, where a crowd waited to greet them, Ousanas gave Antonina a sly little smile. "Brace yourself. I realize it's a shock for you, not being the most famous woman in the area."

Antonina sniffed. "It's a relief, frankly. Give them someone else to gossip about."

Ousanas shook his head. "The other woman in question being a saint and the model of virtue, your own notoriety will simply stand out in contrast. The gossip will be fiercer than ever. Especially—"

He swelled out his chest. A chest which needed no swelling to begin with, as muscular as it so obviously was under the flashy but sparse Axumite regalia. "—arriving, as you do, in the company of such a magnificent male."

Throughout, he'd kept a solemn expression on his face. As they neared the pack of notables on the dock, the expression became positively lugubrious. He tilted his head toward her, murmuring: "Within a day, tales will be sweeping the city of the orgy you held on the ship, from the moment it left Adulis."

"Ridiculous." She lifted her head slightly, to augment her dignified bearing. "That same reputation will shield me. Everyone knows that if *I'd* been holding an orgy, you wouldn't be able to walk off this ship in the first place. 'Magnificent male.' Ha. Weaklings, all of you."

They were almost at the docks. The front line of the crowd consisted of Roman officials, Persian noblemen and Axumite troop leaders. Quite an august body, really. So Antonina's next words were spoken almost in a whisper.

"I grant you, if we had any stallions or bulls on the ship, I'd be in trouble. But we didn't bring any."

It was all she could do not to stick out her tongue at him. Getting the best of Ousanas in that sort of repartee was something of an accomplishment.

The ceremonies that followed were the usual tedious business. Fortunately, Antonina was spared the worst of it, thanks to Photius and Tahmina. Their own transfer from the ship to the dock had been no simple matter of walking down a gangplank. The Roman officials and Persian grandees had vied with each other to see who could produce the most absurdly elaborate palanquins for the purpose.

"I was scared the gangplank would collapse under the weight," Photius confided to her later. "Tahmina—did you *see* the idiotic thing they carried her off in?—was downright petrified."

The most interesting part of the day, perhaps ironically, was the tour of the new hospital. The one *the Wife* had established.

It wasn't hers, really. Anna Saronites might have been wealthy enough—her husband Calopodius, at any rate—to commission the building of a brand-new hospital. But she simply hadn't been in Barbaricum long enough, before she began her voyage up the Indus.

But, from what Antonina could determine, that didn't seem to matter. The young Roman noblewoman had struck the existing hospital like the monsoon. Leaving plenty of wreckage in her wake, as the monsoon does. But—also like the monsoon—leaving a greener land behind. One with life, where there had been death.

"I'm impressed," Ousanas admitted. For once, not joking at all. "I wouldn't have thought even the Emperor of Iran and all his executioners could have swept aside this much stupidity and carelessness. In that short a time, anyway."

Antonina eyed a nearby member of the Wife's Service, standing solemnly in the doorway to the next ward. Despite the purple uniform, he bore approximately the same resemblance to a "nurse" as a tavern bouncer bears to an "usher."

"She knew the trick," Antonina murmured. "I'm a little flattered, actually."

Ousanas cocked his head.

"Don't you see? She patterned the Service after the Hospitalers. That's what it takes, for something like this. People will simply evade the rulings of officials. Much harder to evade the strictures of a militant mass order."

"You're quite right," came a voice from behind. Turning her head, Antonina saw the chief of the Service in Barbaricum. Psoes, his name was. She hadn't realized he was following them closely enough to have overheard.

"You're quite right," he repeated. "She told me she got the idea from reading Irene Macrembolitissa's account of your exploits in Alexandria."

Antonina chuckled. "Irene's fables, you mean. She was long gone from Alexandria and on her way to India before all that happened. That account she wrote was entirely after the fact, and based on hearsay."

"*Your* hearsay, to make it worse," Ousanas grunted. "Told to her in one of your scandalous drinking bouts."

He surveyed the ward again, before they passed on to the next. This one was devoted to men recovering from amputations of the lower extremities, where the one they'd passed through earlier was given over to men who'd suffered more severe trauma. The harshly practical mind of the Wife was evident even in the hospital's new design. Triage, everywhere. Partly to keep diseased men from infecting men who were simply injured. Mostly, because the Wife accepted that some men would die, but saw no reason that other men should die unnecessarily.

In times past, hospitals simply heaped men wherever they happened to have a space, with no more forethought than a wind driving leaves against a fence. In such haphazard piles, a man suffering a simple amputation might die from neglect, simply because he was in a ward most of whose occupants were dying anyway.

Agathius came limping up. He'd lagged behind to reassure one of the soldiers from his own personal experience that while wooden legs were certainly a nuisance, they didn't seriously interfere with copulation. Once they were removed, anyway.

"Horrible," he muttered. "Thank God Sudaba remained in the palace and didn't see this."

Antonina lifted an eyebrow. "She never struck me as being particularly squeamish."

"She's not." Agathius glowered around the room. "That's what I'm worried about. She's already hard enough to control. Once she meets this cursed 'Wife' . . ."

The glower came to Antonina. "I'm blaming you, mostly. You and that damned Macrembolitissa. Hadn't been for your example— hers, even worse!—none of this would be happening."

"Men's lives *are* being saved," Ousanas pointed out mildly.

The glower never wavered. "Who cares? All men die sooner or later anyway. But in the good old days, whatever years we had given to us, we didn't have to spend half of them arguing with the women. It's your fault, Antonina."

That evening, over dinner at the palace that had been turned over to them for the duration of their short sojourn in Barbaricum, Antonina recounted the day's activities to those who had remained behind.

Sudaba wasn't interested in the official ceremonies. As a girl whose father was merely a dehgan, she might have been. As a young woman who'd now been married to the top Roman official in Mesopotamia for almost two years and had attended more official ceremonies than she could remember, she wasn't in the least.

What she *was* interested in hearing about—at length—was the hospital.

"I can't wait to meet this woman," she said.

Antonina smiled at Agathius. "Oh, stop glaring at the roast. It's already overcooked as it is."

"*Your* fault, I say it again."

It was odd, really, the comfort the stable-keeper took from the presence of the giant Roman soldier. Under any other circumstances, the man—Anastasius, his name—would have terrified him. The stable-keeper was Bengali. Despite the years he'd lived in Kausambi, he'd never really gotten accustomed to the size of western barbarians. The Ye-tai were bad enough. But no Ye-tai the stable-keeper had ever seen was as big and powerful-looking as this Roman.

Anastasius still did frighten the stable-keeper. But since he was so much less terrifying than his companion, the stable-keeper was almost relieved to have him around. He liked to imagine that the giant one would restrain the other—Valentinian, he was called, with another of those bizarre western names—in the all-too-likely event that the man reverted to the predator nature he so obviously possessed.

"Stop bullying the poor man, Valentinian," the giant rumbled.

"I'm not bullying him. I'm simply pointing out the facts of life."

The stable-keeper avoided both their gazes. Squatting on the floor of one of his stables and staring at the ground, he whimpered: "Why did I ever agree to this?"

"Why?" The one named Valentinian leaned over and casually spit on the ground. He was standing, not squatting, and leaning against a nearby stall. "Four reasons. First, you were stupid enough to catch the eye of somebody powerful—today, if not then—when he came through here some years ago, and impressed him with your competence and sterling character. Fucking idiot. You're what—almost fifty years old? And you still haven't learned that no good deed shall go unpunished?"

The stable-keeper whimpered again. "I didn't know who he was."

"Stupider still, then. The second reason is that this stable is about the right distance. Close enough that we could dig to it, far enough away that nobody will connect it to the palace once we blow the tunnel. It's even more or less in the right direction—away from the river."

He spat again. "Just bad luck, that. The next two reasons were your own fault, though. To begin with, you were greedy enough to accept our money."

The whimper that came out now was considerably louder. "You didn't explain exactly what you were doing," he protested.

"You didn't ask either, did you? Like I said, too greedy."

The weasel-faced Roman fell silent, his eyes idly wandering about the gloom of the stable.

The stable-keeper was hoping he wouldn't continue with the explanation.

But, of course, he did.

"The fourth and final reason is that if you don't do what we tell you to do, I'll kill you. Then I'll kill every member of your family after raping your wife and daughters and nieces. Your mother's too old and your sister has bad breath. I'll save the baby for last. He looks pretty tender and I'm sick of lamb."

The giant rolled his eyes. "Oh, for the love of God, Valentinian!"

He squatted down next to the stable-keeper and placed a huge hand on his skinny shoulder. Then, gave him a friendly and reassuring smile.

"He's lying," he assured the stable-keeper. "Valentinian won't rape the women before he kills them. And all he'll do to the baby is just cut his throat."

The stable-keeper believed him. Most insane of all was that he *did* find that a relief.

"How is that last reason my fault?" he whined.

Valentinian gave him that horrible weasel smile. "You weren't born big enough and tough enough and mean enough to fight back against the likes of me, and not rich enough to hire a small army to do it for you. Maybe in your next life, you won't be so careless."

Valentinian and Anastasius spent several hours in the tunnel, on the way back, checking and inspecting everything.

More precisely, Anastasius pretended to check the timbers and shoring, while Valentinian gave the Bihari miners and their remaining Ye-tai guards that level and dark-eyed stare that could intimidate a demon. Neither Valentinian nor Anastasius were miners, after all, so they really had no good idea what to look for. True, they had considerable experience at siege work—as both defenders and attackers—but neither of them had ever been used as sappers. That was specialty work, and not something that cataphracts generally got involved in.

"Ignore him," Anastasius assured the miners. "He just likes to stay in practice."

In a half-crouch due to the low ceiling, Anastasius planted his hands on his knees and smiled at the chief of the miners. "It looks good to me. But we don't want it to be *too* good. There are three doglegs we might need to use, and all three of them have to collapse if we set off the charges. Collapse for dozens of yards, too. Won't do us any good just to cave in a few feet. The Malwa can dig, too."

After giving Valentinian a quick, nervous glance, the Bihari nodded vigorously. "Not a problem! Not a problem! Look here!" He scurried over to one of the nearby wood pillars that held up the roof and began jabbing with his finger. Here, there—everywhere, it seemed.

"See how the wedges are set? The charges will blow them all loose. Without the wedges, everything will come down. We put all the doglegs deep, too. Deeper than the rest of the tunnels. With that much weight of earth above them—especially the first dogleg, near the river, with all that muddy soil—they'll come right down."

Anastasius swiveled a bit, to be able to look at Valentinian. "Looks good to me. You have a problem with anything?"

Valentinian was in a half-crouch also, although in his case he was leaning his rump against one of the pillars to support his weight rather than using hands on knees. He wasn't as tall as Anastasius, but he was still much too tall to stand upright in the low tunnel. Even the short Bihari miners had to stoop a little.

"Not really," he said, "beyond the general principle that something's bound to get fucked up." He gave the miner a little nod of the head. "It's not as if I really distrust him and his men. If it doesn't work, they're dead meat along with the rest of us."

The miner nodded his head, maybe a dozen times. "Yes! Yes! And if it works, we get our freedom and a big bonus. The lady promised. And—ah—"

He left off the rest, since it was a bit awkward. What was more to the point was that Valentinian had agreed to the lady's promise, and done so to their faces. For all that he frightened the miners—and frightened the Ye-tai even more, probably—there was an odd way in which they all trusted Valentinian. A man that murderous simply didn't need to stoop to petty treachery, when all was said and done.

Rajiv's fight with the three traitors had cemented Valentinian's reputation with those men. Especially the Ye-tai, who were experienced warriors themselves. "The Mongoose" might be a legend, inflated and overblown as legends often are. A man so deadly he could train a thirteen-year-old boy to kill three mercenaries—with jury-rigged weapons, to boot—was a living, breathing human cobra in their midst.

They were scared of Anastasius, also. But for all his size and strength and the fact they knew him to be an experienced fighter, he just didn't have the same dark aura about him. If anything, like the stable-keeper, they found his presence alongside Valentinian something of a relief.

Besides, there was hope as well as fear. Freedom and enough money to set themselves up well, for the slave miners. For the Ye-tai who had remained loyal, the chance to join an imperial bodyguard, with all its perks and privileges.

That presumed, of course, that the scheme worked. By now, all of them knew the gist of the thing, since there was no point in trying to keep any of it a secret any longer. But if it didn't work, they were all dead anyway. So why not dream?

When the two cataphracts got back to the palace late in the afternoon and reported to Lady Damodara, she expressed some doubts.

"This is all so risky. We're depending on the loyalty of a man we don't know at all, simply because of a message sent by a man who is our enemy."

Anastasius shrugged. "I've met Holkar. Know him pretty well, actually. I really don't think this is the sort of thing he'd get tricky about. If he vouches for the character of the stable-keeper, I think we can trust him. Don't forget that the life of Holkar's daughters is at stake, too."

Valentinian started to spit on the floor. Then, remembering where he was, swallowed the phlegm. "Besides, we're not trusting the stable-keeper. I'm threatening him. Big difference."

Lady Damodara shook her head disapprovingly. "You shouldn't bully him so. He does seem like a nice man, after all."

"So? When this is all over, he's still a nice man. Except he's a nice man with the favor of the new emperor instead of a dirt-poor stable-keeper with no friends worth talking about. He'll have the fanciest stable in India. His biggest problem will be keeping the help from stealing the jewels encrusting the imperial saddles and howdahs."

Lady Damodara laughed softly. "I'm not sure I've ever met anyone with quite your view of life, Valentinian. I don't know how to describe it, exactly."

"Stripped to the bone," Valentinian supplied. He jerked a thumb at his huge companion. "This one can prattle about Plato and Aristotle all he wants. My philosophy is simple. Moralize like a miser."

Still later that evening, it was Dhruva's turn to chide Valentinian.

"You're spoiling him again!"

Valentinian studied the infant in his arms. Baji was grinning at him, his hands waving about for another sweet to suck on.

"Goo!"

"I know." He was silent for a while, playing tug-of-war with Baji over his finger. "Terrific grip. I've got hopes for the kid."

"Give him to me," Dhruva insisted. "He needs to eat real food. He can't live on sweets."

After handing him over, Valentinian sighed. "I know I spoil him. Maybe it's my way of making amends."

"For what?"

He waved his hand vaguely. "I don't know. Me."

Dhruva started to feed the baby. "That's silly. You're not so bad."

Valentinian chuckled. "You're one of the few people I know who'd say that."

She shrugged with only one arm and shoulder, the other being occupied with the baby at her breast. "Most people haven't been Maratha slave whores in a Malwa brothel."

She said it almost serenely. After a while, she looked up. "I have never asked. Does that bother you?"

"No. It's like I told Lady Damodara. I'm pretty well stripped to the bone."

She nodded and looked back down at Baji. "Yes. You must have done something right in your former life."

Valentinian watched her, for a time. "I think maybe I did."

Chapter 21
BHARAKUCCHA

The soldiers along the battlements were so excited they weren't even trying to maintain disciplined formations. The closer Lord Damodara's army came to the gates of Bharakuccha, they more excited they got. By now, most of them were shouting.

Malwa's soldiers hated service in the Great Country. The war against the Marathas had been a savage business. But now, it seemed, it was finally over.

"A great victory, clearly," commented Toramana to Nanda Lal. "Look at those skin-sacks! Dozens of them. That must be Raghunath Rao's, floating from Rana Sanga's lance."

Nanda Lal squinted into the distance. "Yes, probably . . ."

It was frustrating! A properly prepared skin-sack had all its holes sewed up, so the skin could be filled with air. Thus buoyant and bloated, it swung gaily in the breeze, like a paper lantern. Best of all, the features could be distinguished. Grossly deformed, of course, but still made out clearly enough. Even all these years later, the face of the former emperor of Andhra was recognizable, where he hung in the great feasting hall of the imperial palace at Kausambi.

These skin-sacks, however, were limp and flaccid. Simply the flayed pelts of men, flapping like streamers and quite unrecognizable as individuals. No way to avoid it, of course. A field army like Damodara's simply wasn't equipped to do the work properly.

Flaying skin came naturally enough to soldiers. Careful sewing did not.

No matter, in and of itself, as long as the skins weren't too badly damaged. Once the sacks arrived in the city, they could be salvaged and redone correctly. Nanda Lal was simply frustrated because he was a man who liked to *know*, not guess.

The Malwa spymaster squinted at the other skin-sacks hanging from the lances toward the fore of the army. Even without being properly inflated, the dugs of a female sack should be easy enough to discern. Damodara and Rana Sanga and the lead elements of the army were quite close, now. In fact, the gates to the city were already opening.

Toramana had apparently spotted the same absence. "Shakuntala must have escaped. If she was even there at all."

Nanda Lal grunted. He was . . .

Not happy, he realized.

Why? It was indeed a great victory. If Raghunath Rao's skin was among those—and who else's would be hanging from Rana Sanga's own lance?—the Maratha rebellion that had been such a running wound in the side of Malwa was effectively over. No doubt, small and isolated bands of rebels would continue to fight. But with Rao dead and the main Maratha army broken, they would soon degenerate into simple banditry. No more than a minor nuisance.

Even assuming that Shakuntala had escaped, that was no great problem either. With her rebellion broken, she would simply become one of the world's petty would-be rulers, of which there were a multitude. In exile at Constantinople, she would be no threat to anyone beyond Roman imperial chambermaids.

And, who knew? With the lapse of enough time, it might be possible for a Malwa assassination team to infiltrate the Roman imperial compound, kill her, and smuggle out the corpse. The day might come when Shakuntala's skinsack hung also from the rafters of Skandagupta's feasting hall, swaying in the convivial breeze of the celebrants below alongside her father's and mother's.

Yet, he was *not* happy. Definitely not.

The death of a couple of his telegraph operators bothered him, for one thing. That had happened two days ago. A simple tavern killing, to all appearances. Eyewitnesses said the men got into a drunken brawl over a prostitute and stabbed each other. But . . .

A sudden fluke of the wind twisted the skinsack hanging from Sanga's lance. For the first time, Nanda Lal was able to see the face clearly.

He froze. Paralyzed, for just that moment.

Toramana spotted the same thing. A warrior, not a spymaster, he reacted more quickly.

"*Treachery,*" he hissed. The sword seemed to fly into his hand. "Lord, we have a traitor among us."

"Yes," snarled Nanda Lal. "Close the gates. Call—"

There was no pain, really. Or, perhaps, agony so great it could not register as such.

Nanda Lal stared down at the sword Toramana had driven into his belly. So deeply, he knew the tip must be sticking out from his back. Somewhere about the kidney area. The long-experienced torturer's part of his mind calmly informed him that he was a dead man. Two or three vital organs must have been pierced.

With a jerk of his powerful wrist, Toramana twisted the sword to let in air and break the suction. Then, his left hand clenched on Nanda Lal's shoulder, drew the blade back out. Blood spilled down and out like a torrent. At least one artery must have been severed.

That *hurt*. But all Nanda Lal could do was gasp. He still seemed paralyzed.

Unfairest of all, he thought, was that Toramana had stepped aside so deftly that only a few drops of the blood had spattered his tunic and armor.

Nanda Lal saw the sword come up, for a mighty blow. But could not move. Could only clutch the great wound in his stomach.

"Your head'll do," said Toramana. He brought the sword around and down.

Sanga had been watching, from under the edge of his helmet. The moment he saw Toramana strike, he spurred his horse forward. An instant later, the two hundred Rajputs who followed him did likewise.

By the time they reached the gate, now standing wide, they were at a full gallop. The dozen or so Malwa soldiers swinging open the gates gaped at them.

Not for long. Hundreds of war horses approaching at a gallop at a distance measured in mere yards is a purely terrifying sight. Even to soldiers braced and ready for the charge, with pikes in their hands. These garrison soldiers, expecting nothing but a celebration, never thought to do anything but race aside.

By then, Toramana was bringing his Ye-tai contingents under control. They were caught just as much by surprise, since he'd taken none of them into his confidence.

But it didn't matter, as he'd known it wouldn't. Confused men—soldiers, especially—will automatically turn to the nearest authority figure for guidance. With Nanda Lal dead—many of them had seen the killing—that meant . . .

Well, Toramana. The commander of the entire garrison.

And Lord Damodara, of course. The Goptri of the Decca, whom they could even now see passing through the gates behind Rana Sanga and the lead Rajputs.

"*Treason!*" Toramana bellowed, standing on the battlements where the soldiers could see him easily. "Nanda Lal was planning treason! The murder of Lord Damodara!"

He pointed with the sword in his hand to the figure of Damodara, riding into the city. "All rally to the Goptri! Defend him against assassins!"

In response, Lord Damodara waved his hand. It was a rather cheery gesture, actually. Then, twisted in his saddle and gave Toramana something in the way of a salute.

It took no more that. The soldiers were still confused, the Ye-tai as much as any of them. But, if anything, the confusion made them even more inclined to obey unquestioningly.

And why not? For years, for that army, their real commanders had been soldiers like Damodara. Toramana, for the Ye-tai; Sanga for the Rajputs.

Nanda Lal was simply a mysterious and unsettling figure from far-off Kausambi. Neither known nor popular. And, if somewhat fearsome, not nearly as fearsome as the commanders who had once even beaten Belisarius in battle.

The reaction of two Ye-tai soldiers was typical. Drawing his sword, one of them snarled at a nearby squad of regular troops.

"You heard him, you piglets! Spread out! Watch for assassins!"

As the squad scurried to obey, the Ye-tai's companion leaned over and half-whispered: "What do you think—"

"Who gives a shit?" the first Ye-tai hissed.

He stabbed his sword toward the distant body of Nanda Lal. The headless corpse had sprawled to the edge of the parapet. By now, most of the blood had drained from the neck, leaving a pool on the ground below.

"If you care that much, go ask *him*."

The other Ye-tai stared at the corpse. Then, at the head lying some yards from the parapet wall. It had bounced, twice, and then rolled, after it hit the ground.

He drew his own sword and lifted it high. "Long live the Goptri! Death to traitors!"

Some time later, once he was sure the city was under control, Toramana returned to the parapet wall and retrieved Nanda Lal's head. After brushing off the dirt, he held it up.

"A bit dented. But you'll do."

Sanga came up.

"Lord Damodara wants the wedding this evening, if possible. The Ye-tai seem solid, but the wedding will seal the thing."

"Yes. Not just my clan, either. All of them." Toramana continued to admire the head. "I told Indira to be ready several days ago, for a quick wedding. You know your sister."

Sanga's dark eyes studied him, for a moment. "Yes, I do. I hadn't realized you did, so well."

Toramana smiled. "Nothing improper! If you don't believe me, ask that mob of old women. But you can talk about other things than flowers and insects in a garden, you know. And she's smart. Very, very smart."

"Yes, she is." The dark eyes went to the severed head. "I approve of a man who keeps his promises. On a spike?"

Toramana shook his head. "Bit of a nuisance, that. It's garam, don't forget."

Sanga made a face. "Flies."

"A horde of them. Even more than those old women. I think a clear jar will do fine." The Ye-tai commander finally lowered the head. "I promised him he'd be *at* the wedding. I made no guarantees he'd be able to flatter the bride."

❖   ❖   ❖

By sundown, Sanga was satisfied that all the mahaveda and mahamimamsa in the city had been tracked down and slaughtered. There might be a handful surviving in a corner here and there. Bharakuccha was a huge city, after all.

But, he doubted it—and knew for a certainty that even if there were, they wouldn't survive long anyway. The Mahaveda cult had never sunk roots into India's masses. Had never, for that matter, even tried to win any popular support. It was a sect that depended entirely on the favor of the powerful. That favor once withdrawn—here, with a vengeance—the cult was as helpless as a mouse in a pen full of raptors.

Most of the time, the Rajputs hadn't even needed to hunt down the priests and torturers. At least a third of the populace was still Maratha. The majority of the inhabitants might not have hated them as much, but they hated them nonetheless. The only face the cult had ever turned to the city's poor was that of the tithe-collector. And a harsh and unyielding one, at that. Most of the priests and mahamimamsa who went under the swords of the Rajputs were hauled to them by the city's mobs.

The telegraph and radio stations were secured almost immediately. Ajatasutra's assassins had seen to the first, with the telegraph operators whom Narses had already suborned.

The Ye-tai commander of the unit guarding the radio station had not been privy to Toramana's plans. But the Ye-tai general had selected the man carefully. He was both smart and ambitious. It hadn't taken him more than thirty seconds to realize which way the new wind was blowing—and that it was blowing with all the force of a monsoon. By the time Toramana and Damodara got to the radio station, the operators had all been arrested and were being kept in an empty chamber in the palace.

Damodara studied them. Huddled in a corner, squatting, the radio operators avoided his gaze. Several of them were trembling.

"Don't terrify them any further," he instructed Toramana's lieutenant. "And give them plenty of food and water. By tomorrow, I'll need at least one of them to be cooperative."

"Yes, Lord."

Damodara gave him an impassive look. It didn't take the lieutenant—smart man—more than half a second to remember the announcement.

"Yes, Emperor."

"Splendid."

The wedding went quite smoothly. More so than Sanga had feared, given the hastiness of the preparations.

Not *that* hasty, he finally understood. His sister took firm charge of it, driving right over the protests of the old women who'd expected a traditional Rajput wedding. Within an hour, it became obvious to Sanga that she and Toramana must have planned this, too.

He'd never think of promenades in a garden the same way, he realized ruefully.

The ceremony was a hybrid affair. Half-Rajput, half-Ye-tai, with both halves almost skeletal.

Good enough, however. More than good enough.

"Don't you think?" he asked the head in a glass jar.

Nanda Lal's opinion remained unspoken, but Sanga was quite sure he disapproved mightily. The Malwa dynasty had maintained its rule, among other things, by always keeping a sharp and clear boundary between the Rajputs and the Ye-tai. Able, thus, to pit one against the other, if need be.

True, under the pressure of the Roman offensive, the Malwa had begun to ease the division. The dynasty had agreed to this wedding also, after all. But Sanga knew they'd never intended to ease it very far.

Damodara was simply tossing the whole business aside. He'd base his rule—initially, at least—on the oldest and simplest method. The support of the army. And, for that, he wanted the two most powerful contingents within the army tied as closely together as possible. The marriage between Toramana and Indira would only be the first of many.

Sanga understood the logic. For all the many things that separated the Rajputs and the Ye-tai, they had certain things very much in common.

Two, in particular.

First, they were both warrior nations. So, whatever they disliked about the other—for the Rajputs, Ye-tai crudity; for the Ye-tai, Rajput haughtiness—there was much to admire also.

Second, they were both nations still closely based on clan ties and allegiances. The fact that the Rajputs draped a veil of Hindu mysticism over the matter and called their clan chieftains "kings" was more illusion than truth. Sanga had known since he was a boy that if you scratched the shiny Rajput veneer, you'd find more than a trace of their central Asian nomadic origins.

Clan ties meant blood ties. Which were brought by marriages. Within three generations, Rajput and Ye-tai clans would be so intermingled as to make the old divisions impossible.

Not conflict, of course. Clan wars could be as savage as any. But they were not the stuff—*could* not be the stuff—that would tear northern India into pieces.

The Malwa methods had been determined by their goal of world conquest. For Damodara, having given up that grandiose ambition, everything else followed. He would build a new empire that would not go beyond northern India. But, within those limits—which were still immense, after all—he would forge something far more resilient, and more flexible, than anything the dynasty had done before.

More resilient and flexible, for that matter, than anything the Maurya or Gupta empires had accomplished either. Sanga was beginning to suspect that Damodara would someday have the cognomen "the Great" attached to his name.

Not in his own lifetime, though. He was far too canny for that.

Before the wedding was halfway over, Sanga realized he was in an excellent mood. He even participated in the dancing.

"Good thing I stopped the duel," Damodara told him afterward. "That too-clever-by-half Maratha bandit probably would have insisted on a dancing contest as part of it."

Sanga grimaced.

"Oh, yes. We'd have found your body strewn all over. Speaking of which—" He glanced around. "What happened to Nanda Lal's head?"

"My brother-in-law felt that propriety had been satisfied enough by his presence at the wedding, and there was no need to keep him around for the festivities. I believe he gave it to some Ye-tai boys. That game they play. You know, the one where—"

"Oh, yes. Of all my many cousins, I think I disliked him the most except Venandakatra. Well. Hard to pick between Nanda Lal and Skandagupta, of course. Isn't that the game where they use dogs to retrieve the lost balls?"

"Yes, Emperor."

"Splendid."

Chapter 22
BHARAKUCCHA

Early the next morning, Damodara commanded Sanga to meet him in the radio station.

"Why here, Emperor?" Sanga asked, as soon as he arrived. The room was empty, except for the two of them and the bizarre equipment. "I thought you planned to use the telegraph."

Damodara looked a bit haggard, as if he hadn't slept well. "I did," he said, tugging at his chin. "But I thought about it most of the night. And I think . . ."

He was interrupted by a small commotion at the door. A moment later, two burly Ye-tai came in, with a much smaller man between them. They weren't guiding him in so much as simply carrying him by the armpits.

Once in the room, they set him down. "Lord Toramana says this one, Emperor."

Damodara nodded. "Leave us, then."

For a moment, the Ye-tai seemed taken aback.

Damodara smiled, looking upon the radio operator. He was but a few inches over five feet tall, and couldn't have weighed more than one hundred and twenty pounds. Wearing nothing but a loincloth, it was also obvious that he was scrawnily built.

Damodara flicked his fingers toward Sanga. "I dare say that with the Rajput king present, this desperate fellow will restrain his assassin's impulses."

He gave the radio operator a winning smile. "Am I not correct?"

226

The man bobbed his head like a small bird pecking at grains.

"You will make no attempt upon my life?"

The man shook his head so fast it seemed to vibrate.

"I thought not." He gave the two guards a cold eye, and they departed.

After they were gone, Damodara pointed to the chair in front of the complex apparatus. "Sit," he commanded.

The operator did so.

"Is there a code you must use, when you transmit?"

Again, that vibrating head-shake.

"I'd really much prefer it if you spoke, man," Damodara said mildly.

The operator swallowed. Then, managed to croak out: "No, sir. There's no code."

Sanga frowned fiercely. "None? I warn you not to lie! It makes no sense to me—"

"But there *isn't*, Lord," the operator protested desperately. "I swear it. She—"

He broke off. Almost seemed to be choking.

Damodara sighed. "As I suspected. And feared." He leaned forward a bit. "I want nothing but the truth. This 'she.' Of whom do you speak?"

The operator stared at him, his eyes very wide with fear. He looked more like trapped rodent than anything else.

"You're speaking of Great Lady Sati, yes?"

The operator swallowed again. "Yes," he whispered. "But that's supposed to be a secret. I'm not supposed—"

He broke off again, this time because of the sight and sound of Sanga's sword coming out of the scabbard. The Rajput king held the sword blade in front of the man's face. So close he had to look at it cross-eyed.

"I suggest you have much deeper concerns now than whether you are violating an oath of secrecy," Damodara pointed out. "Tell me."

Still looking cross-eyed at the blade, the man began to speak softly but quickly.

"All the operators know it, Lord. We do, at least. I don't know about the telegraph men. When we make the transmissions, Great Lady Sati is always at the other end. Herself in person. She—she—she—"

"Yes, I know. She's a witch. A demoness."

"She *is*," he half-moaned. "It was part of our training. We had to spend a few minutes with her. She—she—she—"

Careful to avoid the blade, he brought up a shaky hand to wipe his brow. He was sweating profusely.

Damodara straightened up. "Put away the sword, Sanga. He's telling the truth."

Sanga did as commanded. His own face was very stiff. Like Damodara—and now, it seemed, this insignificant radio operator—Sanga had spent time alone in the presence of one of the females of the dynasty who served as the vessel for Link. Great Lady Holi, in his case. But he knew it made no difference.

Damodara went to the door and opened it. The two Ye-tai were standing just beyond. "Take the operator elsewhere, for a time. I need to speak with Sanga in private. Don't take him far, though. And summon Narses."

After they were alone, Damodara sat in the chair. He stared at the mechanism whose workings he barely understood at all.

"*Now* you understand the problem. It came to me in the middle of the night. Like a nightmare."

"Yes, Emperor."

When Narses arrived and was informed, he shook his head.

"No, I had no idea. They always kept the radio men carefully sequestered. I was able to suborn most of the telegraph operators, but I couldn't even get close to these fellows. That's why Toramana and I finally decided just to use their Ye-tai guard contingent to secure the radio."

Damodara nodded. He hadn't thought Narses had known, or the shrewd old eunuch would long since have seen the problem. Their entire plan had just gone up in smoke.

For his part, Sanga grunted sourly. The look he gave Narses was more sour still. The Rajput king was still angry at the Roman traitor for the way he'd manipulated all of them. But after he'd learned from Narses that the eunuch had been instructed by Skandagupta and Great Lady Sati to murder his family outright, his sheer fury toward him had dissipated.

He didn't doubt the eunuch was telling the truth, either. Link was the ultimate source of that plot, and Sanga had met the monster. The plot Narses described was exactly the sort of thing it would have designed. It was cold-blooded beyond any sense of the term "cold" that either a reptile or a glacier would have understood.

Narses glared at the radio apparatus. "Maybe we could just use the telegraph—"

But he was already shaking his own head when Damodara interrupted him. "No point in that," the new emperor said. "Link will expect a radio transmission also. The fact that none took place last night will make it suspicious already. Perhaps there was a thunderstorm, of course, even if that's unlikely this time of year. Two nights in a row, impossible. It will immediately know something is wrong."

The eunuch took a deep, almost shuddering breath. "Damnation. It never occured to me that she might *personally* take the transmissions."

Damodara shrugged heavily. "There's a logic to it. I always wondered, a bit, why we were putting so much effort into these huge radio towers. The telegraph works well enough, for most purposes—and has fewer security problems. Now I know. Look where they are: Kausambi, the Punjab, and here. Nowhere else."

"Are we sure of that?" asked Sanga.

"Yes," growled Narses. "That much I am sure of. They're planning two more. One in Amaravati and one in Tamralipti. But they haven't even started building them yet."

"It makes perfect sense, Sanga," Damodara continued. "The basic function of these towers is to enable Link to control the empire. Well, not 'control' it so much as enable it to be sure if rebellion has begun."

Narses was still glaring at the apparatus. "I fooled that stinking bitch once. I bet I can . . ."

The words trailed off.

"Don't be stupid, old man," he muttered, to himself as much as to the other men in the room. "First, you don't know how to use the gadget. Even if you tried to learn—in a few hours?—you'd fumble something. The bitch would know right away someone other than one of her operators was at the other end. And even if you could do it, the last time you weren't trying to lie to her."

Sanga frowned at the door. "If we calmed down the operator . . ."

But, like Narses, he rebutted his own half-advanced plan. "Impossible. There'd be *some* sign of his agitation. Nothing we'd notice—or he himself, even—but the monster would."

He ran fingers through his thick, still-black hair. "Yes, that explains the radio towers. The telegraph is now too common, too widely spread. There's no way she could personally monitor even most of the transmissions, much less all of them. But with a few towers, located only in the empire's critical regions, she can. And there is no way—no way—to lie to her. To *it,* that is both greater and less than human."

He fell silent. Damodara rose from the chair he'd been sitting on and began pacing. He, also, was silent.

Eventually, Narses spoke.

"No help for it, then. We were planning to begin the march upcountry tomorrow, anyway. We'll just have to send telegraph messages saying there's a terrible—very unseasonal—storm, and the radio won't work for a while. She'll suspect something, of course. But with the problems she has in the Punjab anyway, she won't *know.*"

He spread his hands. "I grant you, it won't buy us more than a few days. But it's the best we can do."

Damodara stopped his pacing. "No."

He strode over to the apparatus, moving almost eagerly. "Your man Ajatasutra had it right. Then—and now. We will do this like an assassin, not a torturer. Quick and deadly, in the sunlight, not lingering over it in a cellar."

Narses frowned at him. "What are you talking about?"

Sanga was frowning also. Suddenly, his brow cleared, and he barked a laugh. Again, hissing its way like a snake, the blade came out of the scabbard.

"*Yes!*" the Rajput king bellowed. He tilted the sword toward Damodara in a salute. "Emperor of Malwa! True and pure!"

Narses looked from one to the other. "Have you both gone mad?"

Damodara gave him an impassive look.

"Ah. Sorry. Your Majesty, have you gone mad?"

"I don't believe so," replied the new emperor cheerily. "And if I am, you have only yourself to blame. Aren't you the one who told me, after all, that there is another radio in India?"

After a second, Narses shot to his feet. "You're out of your fucking mind!"

The look Sanga gave him was not impassive in the least. Even Narses shrank a little.

"Ah. Sorry. Your Majesty, I submit to you that you need to consider the possibility that when the traitors substituted the false emperor in the crib of your grandfather, that they also poisoned him."

Damodara, fortunately, was in an expansive mood. "I see. Some slow-acting poison, I take it? Doesn't show its effects for two generations, when the grandson turns into a blithering fool."

"Yes, Your Majesty. That one."

Ajatasutra, on the other hand, thought it was a marvelous plan, when it was explained to him less than an hour later.

"Don't see why not," he commented, smiling at Narses. "Stop glaring at me, old man."

"How many times do I beat you at chess?"

"The game of thrones is not really a chess game—a saying, as I recall, that you are quite fond of." The assassin shrugged. "Narses, what does it matter? Even by the old plan, the people in Kausambi would have been in danger long before we could arrive."

"This will strike them even quicker and harder," Narses pointed out darkly.

Since the people involved were not his—except, perhaps, the two girls, in a way—Ajatasutra looked at Damodara and Sanga.

Damodara's face was tight, but Sanga seemed quite relaxed.

"I fought the Mongoose, remember. He will react quickly enough, I think. And if he can't, no man can anyway."

Damodara wiped his face. "True. I watched from close by. He is very, very, very quick. And what's probably more important, he's ruthless enough not to hesitate."

He dropped the hand. "We have no real choice, anyway. Narses, your alternative has only negative virtues. My plan, risky at it is, brings us something."

"Maybe," Narses said gloomily. "Maybe."

"We'll know soon enough. Sanga, make sure the army is ready to leave at daybreak. We'll start sending the messages at dusk."

"Yes, Emperor."

Chapter 23
THE IRON TRIANGLE

Maurice was actually grinning. Thinly, true. But it was still a genuine grin, full of nothing but amusement.

"Yes, General, he's late again. Like he has been for every shift since she got here."

Belisarius glanced at the empty chair where Calopodius normally sat. The scribes at the table were in their seats, with their implements in hand. But they were simply chatting casually, waiting for their boss to arrive.

They didn't seem any more disgruntled than Maurice, however. Calopodius was popular with the men who staffed Belisarius' headquarters bunker.

"I thought she'd hit this place like a storm," Belisarius mused. "I know for a fact that the medical staff was trembling in their boots. What I hadn't foreseen was that Calopodius would absorb most of it."

"His pallet, rather—and thank God I'm not one of the straws. Be bruised and battered bloody, by now."

"Don't be crude, Maurice."

"I'm not being crude. Just recognizing that once you strip away the mysticism about 'the Blind Scribe' and 'the Wife,' what you're really dealing with are newlyweds—for all practical purposes—neither of whom is twenty years old yet. Ha! Randy teenagers. Can't keep their hands off—"

He coughed, and broke off. Calopodius was hurrying into the bunker.

"Hurrying" was the word, too. Blind he might be, but by this time Calopodius had the dimensions of the bunker and the location of everything in it committed to memory. And he had an excellent memory.

The position of the people in the bunker, of course, was less predictable. But, by now, they'd learned to keep out of his way. Belisarius watched as one of the staff officers, grinning, sidestepped Calopodius as he half-raced to the table.

"Sorry I'm late, General," the young man muttered, as he sat down. "Anna—ah—had a bit of trouble with her uniform."

Under the circumstances, that was perhaps the worst excuse he could have come up with. The entire staff in the bunker—Belisarius and Maurice included—burst into laughter.

Calopodius flushed. As the laughter continued, the flush deepened until he was almost literally red-faced. But the expression on his face also became subtly transmuted into something that was ultimately more smug than chagrinned. Most young men, after all—even ones raised in Constantinople's haughty aristocratic circles—are not actually embarrassed by having a reputation for being able to keep their wives in their beds, and happy to be there.

As the laughter faded away, Luke and Illus came into the bunker. They were both smiling, too, as they took their accustomed places on chairs near the entrance.

"Accustomed," at least, for Luke. Illus was still settling into his new role as one of Calopodius' staff. Officially, he was a bodyguard; just as, officially, Luke was a valet. In practice, Calopodius used either or both of them in whatever capacity seemed needed. Fortunately, the two men seemed to get along well enough.

"Right," Calopodius said briskly. He turned his head toward the scribe to his right. "Mark, I think we should—"

The radio began its short-and-long buzzing noises. The noise was different from the typical click-clack made by the telegraph, when it received an incoming message, but had a basic similarity. Aide—like Link—had not tried to design anything more complex than a spark gap radio system. So the radio used the same "Morse code" that the telegraph did.

The Malwa used the same code, except when they were

transmitting encrypted messages. That was not really so odd, since that code was the common one in the history of the universe that had produced both Aide and Link.

"—start with the dispatches—"

—bzzz-bz-bzzz-bzzz-bz-bz-bzzz—

"—regarding . . ." He trailed off, his head swiveling toward the radio. Calopodius, unlike Belisarius, could translate Morse code instantly. It was by now a language he was as fluent in as he was in Greek or Latin.

—bzzz-bz-bz-buzz-bz-bzzz-bz-bz-bzzz—

"General . . ." Calopodius rose to his feet.

Belisarius, frowning, tried to interpret the messages. There was something . . .

Yes! Yes! Yes! Aide was doing the equivalent of shouting. **It's starting!**

What's starting? I can't—

Be quiet. I'll translate for you, starting from the beginning.

> **GENERAL BELISARIUS STOP THIS IS EMPEROR DAMODARA STOP I AM TRUE AND RIGHTFUL EMPEROR OF MALWA STOP NARSES UNCOVERED PLOT THAT STOLE MY BIRTHRIGHT STOP I MARCH ON KAUSAMBI AT DAWN STOP WILL OVERTHROW THE USURPER SKANDAGUPTA STOP**

Calopodius was translating the same words aloud, for everyone else in the bunker.

"I will be damned," murmured Maurice, shaking his head. "You were right all along. I never really thought you were."

> **RANA SANGA AND HIS RAJPUTS WITH ME STOP TORAMANA AND HIS YE-TAI WITH ME STOP ENTIRE DECCAN ARMY WITH ME STOP**

"Calopodius!" Belisarius half-shouted, waving his hand in summons. "Let someone else translate. I need your assistance. Now."

He moved toward the radio. "Over here." The blind young officer came away from the table and followed him. So did Maurice.

BHARAKUCCHA IN MY HANDS STOP NANDA LAL
EXECUTED STOP MAHAVEDA CULT OUTLAWED
STOP ALL MAHAVEDA AND MAHAMIMAMSA
UNDER SENTENCE OF DEATH STOP

Calopodius was not the only one in the bunker who was fluent in Morse. One of his scribes had picked up the translation
almost without a pause.

"He's not fooling around, is he?" said Maurice.

MADE PEACE WITH RAO STOP VINDHYAS THE
NEW BORDER STOP BHARAKUCCHA TO BE FREE
CITY STOP NEED AXUMITE TROOPS FOR GAR-
RISON STOP

"Smart," said Belisarius. "Very smart. Calopodius, Antonina's
still in Barbaricum with Ousanas, isn't she?"

"Yes. They weren't going to start up the Indus until tomorrow
or the day after."

"Good. Send her a message immediately telling her to stay there
until she hears from me. Better use the telegraph rather than the
radio, though. No reason to let the Malwa overhear—"

"They won't anyway," came Justinian's voice from the entrance.
Belisarius turned and saw the former emperor moving into the
bunker. "Don't you pay attention to *anything* I tell you?"

He didn't seem more than mildly aggrieved, though. Justinian
always enjoyed explaining how clever he was. When it came to
artisanship, anyway, if not politics.

"I designed this system so that we *wouldn't* be intercepted."
Lousy old braggart, grumbled Aide. **He didn't design the
system. *I* did. He just followed my instructions. But he's right.
The position and length of the antennas—everything—were set
up so we could send signals without the Malwa overhearing
us as long as we do it right. They'll intercept anything we
receive, of course. No way to prevent that. But we can transmit in secret.**

"Explain," Belisarius commanded. "Explain *clearly,* so a dimwit
like me can understand it."

Justinian snorted. "Such unwonted modesty! It's like this, my
not-so-stupid General." Justinian began moving his hands, as if

he were shaping a cat's cradle with no string. "With directional radio, the signal has two strong ... call them beams. The strongest, by far, is the forward signal. But there's also a back signal that can often be picked up. The side signals, however—the lobes—are undetectable."

By any technology either we or the Malwa have, anyway, Aide agreed.

Belisarius thought about it. "In other words, any signal I sent to Damodara in Bharakuccha would probably be picked up by Link."

"Yes. The monster's radio tower, our radio installation, and the Malwa tower in Bharakuccha are almost in a direct line. Not quite, but close enough that we don't want to risk it. *Barbaricum,* on the other hand—"

"Is off to the side, yes. Far enough?"

Yes.

"Yes," said Justinian simultaneously. "Link won't hear anything you send to Barbaricum. And *they,* in turn—"

But Belisarius had already figured it out. "I understand. We can't signal Damodara in secret, but Barbaricum can with their radio. So we set up a triangle of communications—and the only part of the leg Link can pick up is what we receive. But not what we send."

Yes.

"Yes."

Belisarius scratched his chin. While they'd been talking, the radio had kept up its beeping and whooping.

Bring me current, Aide, while I think. What's Damodara saying now?

Most of it's pretty pointless, in my opinion. A lot of grandiose declarations about the sterling character of the Ye-tai—talk about a pile of nonsense—and even more stuff—really grisly, this part—about the penalties to be meted out to mahaveda priests and mahamimamsa.

The jewel sounded more than a little miffed. **I don't understand why he's taking up so much precious radio time just to specify what order in which to tear off their limbs and what animals are permitted to feed on the corpses. That last business started with jackals and he's been working his way down from there. Right now he's talking about how beetles should** be used to finish up the odd bits and ends. Do you think he's a sadist, maybe? That could be a problem.

Belisarius chuckled. Even after all these years, Aide—who was vastly more intelligent than humans when it came to many things—could still fumble at the simplest emotional equations.

No, he's just very clever. Since he decided to launch his rebellion openly—and that's interesting, right there, don't you think?—he's taking advantage of the opportunities as well as the problems. First, he's making crystal clear to the Ye-tai that if they acquiesce to the new regime, they won't be penalized. I'll bet he's been sprinkling Toramana's name all through, yes?

"Showering" his name, more like. All right, I can understand that. But why—

The business with the priests? They're hated all through India, to begin with, so it's another way to rally popular support. What's probably more important, at least immediately, is that the mahaveda and mahamimamsa are Malwa's first line of enforcers.

Along with the Ye-tai. But . . . oh.

Belisarius smiled. *I know you can feel "fear" yourself, Aide, but it's always a fairly calm thing for you, isn't it? Almost an intellectual business. No trembling, no sweating, no bowels loosening.*

Don't be silly. Protoplasmic nonsense, that is. You're saying he's trying to panic the mahaveda?

Scare them shitless, Belisarius agreed. *Don't forget that the mahaveda and mahamimamsa, unlike the Ye-tai, aren't a different race or ethnic line.*

Yes, you're right. Most of them are Malwa, but not all—and Malwa aren't racially distinct from any other north Indians anyway. So?

So what's to stop a priest or torturer from throwing away their identifying garments and paraphernalia and just vanishing? Worse comes to worst, even a beggar in a loincloth is better off than a dismembered corpse feeding beetles.

Oh. True. "Dismembering" is the least of it, really. He spent more time talking about the red hot tongs that are to be used to pull out intestines. I still don't understand the point of it. He's obviously doing this in the open because he thinks Link is receiving the radio transmissions directly.

Yes. That's got to be the explanation. Belisarius had to suppress a little shudder, remembering the one time he'd met Link himself. *No way to fool that monster, even over a radio transmission.*

No, there isn't. Even human radio and telegraph operators, with experience, can recognize who's on the other end. Everyone has a distinctive "fist," as they call it. But . . .

You're thinking that if Link is at the receiving end—here in the Punjab, if not in Kausambi—it'll simply suppress the transmission. No one in Malwa India will hear it.

Of course, it will! Even in Kausambi, that radio station has to be under iron control.

Belisarius was smiling broadly, now. *And why do you think Damodara is only using the radio? I'll bet you—if you had anything to wager—that this same message is going over every telegraph line in India. And, by now, there are far too many telegraph stations for Link to be able to keep them quiet. The only reason Damodara is using the radio at all is to communicate with us.*

Silence, for a moment.

Then: **Oh.**

Then: **It's not fair. I'm just a crystal. Lost in this protoplasmic scheming and trickiness. A lamb among wolves.**

Aide started to add another complaint, but broke off. **He's starting to say something to us again. Here it is:**

PROPOSE GRAND ALLIANCE STOP IRAN TO KEEP THE SIND STOP JOINT OCCUPATION OF THE PUNJAB STOP KUSHANS TO KEEP THE HINDU KUSH STOP AXUM TO GARRISON KEY NEUTRAL SEAPORTS STOP INDEPENDENT CITIES BUT AXUM MAY COLLECT TOLLS STOP IS THIS AGREED STOP

Belisarius turned to Calopodius. "Do you have Barbaricum on the line, yet?"

"Yes. Antonina hasn't arrived in the station, though. Neither has Ousanas. But they're on the way."

"We'll wait till they arrive. What about Sukkur?"

"Same story. I've got the Persians on the line, but Khusrau is somewhere else. He's in the city, however, so they say it won't take long."

"Good. Have you instructed the radio operators in Barbaricum to send a relay signal to Bharakuccha—and *only* to Bhara-kuccha?"

"Yes, General. I—ah—made the last part quite clear."

Maurice grinned. So did Justinian. "I will say your wife has done wonders for your assertiveness," said the former emperor.

Justinian turned to Belisarius. Faced in his direction, rather. As was often the case with blind people, he had a good sense of other peoples' locations in the room, but didn't know exactly where their faces were.

"And what about you? I trust we're not going to see a sudden lapse into timid modesty. 'It's not my place, whine; I'm just a general, whine.'"

Belisarius grimaced. "Theodora is *not* going to like it. She's already accusing me of giving away everything."

"So what? She's in Constantinople—and, more to the point, the *Emperor* of Rome is in Barbaricum. Probably at your wife's elbow."

That's a dirty rotten lawyer's trick, for sure, said Aide. **Of course, he *is* the Empire's top lawyer.**

"She's still the Empress Regent," Belisarius pointed out. "Until he attains his majority, Photius doesn't technically have the authority to order most anything."

"So what, again? Difficult times, difficult measures. Unfortunately, the raging thunderstorm"—here Justinian waved at the entrance to the bunker, beyond which could be heard the faint sounds of people enjoying a pleasant and balmy evening—"made it impossible to communicate with Constantinople by radio. And the telegraph—all those pestiferous relays—just wasn't fast enough. Given that a decision had to be made *immediately*."

Justinian's smile was unusually cheerful, for him. "I can assure you that, as the Grand Justiciar, I will be forced to rule in your favor if Theodora presses the matter."

Belisarius returned the smile, scratching his chin. "No qualms, yourself?"

Justinian shrugged. "We've been together a long time, she and I. It's not likely she'll have me poisoned. And I'm right and she's wrong—and no one knows it better than you. In another universe, I kept you at war for years out of my overreaching ambition, and had nothing to show for it in the end except exhaustion and ruin. Let's not do it again, shall we?"

He's right.

Yes, of course he is. Rome doesn't need more territory. It'd just bring grief with it. Even the enclave I'll insist on here in the Triangle is for purely political reasons. But you—*o craven crystal*—*will remain huddling in your pouch while I* have *to bear the brunt of Theodora's wrath.*

Seems fair to me. You're the general. I'm just the hired help. Grossly underpaid, to boot.

"Antonina's on the line, General," said Calopodius. "And they're telling me Khusrau has arrived at the telegraph station in Sukkur."

"Let's do it, then."

The communication with Antonina went quickly.

```
PHOTIUS  AGREES  TO  DAMODARA  TERMS  STOP
WANTS  TO  KNOW  IF  EXILE  POSSIBLE  IN
TRIANGLE  TO  ESCAPE  THEODORA  STOP  HE
WORRIES  TOO  MUCH  STOP  LOVE  YOU  STOP
```

"Ask her about—"

"It's already coming in," Calopodius interrupted him.

```
OUSANAS  AGREES  TO  DAMODARA  TERMS
ALSO  STOP  WILL  TAKE  FLEET  AND  ARMY
IMMEDIATELY  TO  BHARAKUCCHA  STOP  WHAT
YOU  WANT  ME  AND  PHOTIUS  DO  STOP
```

"Have her and the boy go with them," Maurice suggested. "They'll be much safer in Bharakuccha than up here, with everything breaking loose. And what would they do here, anyway?"

It didn't take Belisarius long to decide that Maurice was right. If Antonina still had her Theodoran Cohort with her, she might be able to play a useful military role in the Triangle. But she'd left them behind in Alexandria. If just she and Photius and Tahmina came to the Triangle—with a huge flock of servants, to make things worse—they'd be nothing a distraction and a nuisance to Maurice.

And Belisarius himself wouldn't be there at all, if his plans worked.

"Yes, I agree. Leaving aside the safety problem, she'll probably be useful in Bharakuccha anyway. That populace will need to be settled down, and she's a lot better at that than Ousanas would be. Calopodius, tell her and Photius to accompany Ousanas to Bharakuccha."

Two last messages came back:

WHEN WILL SEE YOU AGAIN STOP

Then, after a brief pause:

NEVER MIND STOP STUPID QUESTION STOP
BE WELL STOP LOVE YOU STOP

The warmth that last message gave him dissipated soon enough. The negotiations with Khusrau were neither brief nor cordial.

Eventually, Belisarius broke it off altogether. "I haven't got time for this nonsense," he snarled. "Tell him an assault just started and I have to leave. Damodara's terms are important and need a quick answer. This is just mindless Aryan pig-headed greed."

As the telegraph operator did as instructed, Belisarius stalked over to the radio. "I can't believe it. Khusrau's not usually that stupid. Wasting time with endless quibbles over a few square miles of the Punjab, for God's sake!"

Maurice was running fingers through his beard, as he often did when thinking. "I'm not sure that's it," he said slowly. "Menander told me almost all the Persian grandees are assembled in Suk-kur now. Sahrdarans and vurzurgans crawling all over the place. Members of all seven great families except the Suren. Baresmanas stayed behind to more or less run the empire for Khusrau, but he's about the only one."

Still too irritated to think clearly, Belisarius shook his head. "What's the point, Maurice?"

"The point is that he's playing to an audience. You know the great houses aren't happy at all with the way he's using small dehgans as imperial officials to administer the Sind. Menander says they're howling like banshees, insisting that they deserve a big share of the Punjab."

Belisarius rolled his eyes. "Just what's needed! A herd of idiot feudal magnates pouring into . . ."

His eyes came down, squinting at Maurice. "Jesus," he hissed. "Could he be *that* ruthless?"

Sure he could, said Aide. **It'd be one quick way to break feudalism in Persia. Lead the magnates into a slaughter. No feudalists, no feudalism.**

"Maybe," said Maurice. He gestured with his thumb toward the radio. "But why don't you let me worry about that, if need be? You've got Damodara to deal with."

"So I do." He looked around. "Calopodius, are you ready?"

The young signals officer hurried up. "Yes, General. Sorry. I just wanted to make sure the scribes were set."

The smile he gave Belisarius was half apology and half sheer anticipation.

"Sorry," he repeated. "I've got the soul of an historian. And this is . . . history."

Belisarius chuckled. "Not yet. But let's see if we can't make it so. The first message is—"

Chapter 24
BHARAKUCCHA

Damodara stared at the message that had just been handed to him. Idly, some part of his mind noted that the radio operator had perhaps the best handwriting he'd ever seen. Artistic calligraphy, almost—yet he'd seen the man jot down the message as rapidly as it came in.

He tilted the paper in his hand, so that Rana Sanga and Narses could read it also.

```
THIS MESSAGE RELAYED THROUGH BARBARICUM
STOP SATI CANNOT HEAR IT STOP SATI
WILL HEAR ANY MESSAGE SENT TO US STOP
ROMANS AND AXUMITES ACCEPT TERMS STOP
CANNOT SPEAK TO KUSHANS DIRECTLY BUT
FORESEE NO DIFFICULTY THEIR PART STOP
PERSIANS USUAL SELVES STOP WILL WORK
ON THEM STOP
```

"Persians," Narses sneered. "That's why I was able to manipulate them so easily, in my days in Rome. Every border dehgan fancies himself the Lord of the Universe, because he's got a few more goats than his neighbor. It might help if he could read."

Rana Sanga shrugged. "I don't see where the Persians on their own can be much of a problem. Well..."

"Except in the Punjab," said Damodara.

The radio operator handed him another message.

```
TERMS  FOR  PUNJAB  AGREEABLE  TO  ROME
STOP  BUT  WANT  IRON  TRIANGLE  MAINTAINED
AS  ROMAN  ENCLAVE  STOP  KEEP  THE  PEACE
STOP
```

"He's probably right," said Sanga. "The Rajputs can live with a small Roman territory in the fork of the Indus and the Chenab, easily enough. Probably even be good for us, in terms of trade. And he might keep the Persians from pushing north."

"Why do you care, anyway?" demanded Narses. "*Let* the Persians have part of the Punjab, for pity's sake. Just insist on two things. First, they have to stay west of the Indus as far north as Multan; then, west of the line formed by the Chenab and the Jhelum. To make sure they stick to it, expand the Roman enclave. Let the Romans have the whole area in the fork of the Indus and the Chenab all the way up to Multan—and give them Multan."

Sanga was starting to look outraged. "You'd give the Persians almost half—"

"Oh, nonsense! It's not more than a third of the Punjab—and most of it, once you get north of Multan, is desert and badlands. Almost useless, except to the hill tribes. So let the Persians deal with the cantankerous bastards. As far as the expanded Roman enclave goes, yes, that's fertile territory. But it's still not all that much—and you can't stop them from taking it anyway, if Link's—"

He glanced at the radio operator. "If Great Lady Sati's army collapses. Which we're counting on, because if it doesn't we're for exile anyway. Assuming we survive at all."

"He has a point, Sanga," said Damodara mildly. "There's another advantage, too, which is that giving the Aryans everything west of the Jhelum brings *them* up against the Kushans in the north."

Sanga thought about it, briefly. "True. And that means the Persians and the Kushans—not us—would have to deal with the Pathans and the other hill tribes. An endless headache, that is."

He gave Narses a not-entirely-admiring look. "And what's the second thing?"

The old eunuch's smile was very cold. "I should think it was obvious. The Persians can have that area—*if* they can take it."

After a moment, Damodara laughed harshly. "Yes. Let them bleed. Done, Narses."

In the Iron Triangle, it was Belisarius' turn to stare at a message. Then, tilt it so that Maurice could see. He also spoke the words aloud, for the benefit of Justinian and Calopodius.

```
PROPOSE  ROMAN  ENCLAVE  BETWEEN  INDUS  AND
CHENAB  EXPANDED  NORTH  TO  MULTAN  STOP
ROMANS  MAY  HAVE  MULTAN  STOP  PERSIANS
MAY  HAVE  PUNJAB  WEST  OF  INDUS  TO
MULTAN  STOP  NORTH  OF  MULTAN  MAY  HAVE
PUNJAB  WEST  OF  CHENAB  AND  JHELUM  STOP
IF  THEY  CAN  TAKE  IT  FROM  SATI  ARMY
STOP
```

"It's nice to see our new ally isn't an idiot," mused Justinian. "Unlike the old one."

The Grand Justiciar got a look on his face that could have been called "dreamy-eyed," if he'd still had eyes.

"Forget it," said Belisarius, half-chuckling. "We are *not* going to form a pact with Damodara to attack Persia and carve it up between us."

"Probably a bad idea," admitted Justinian. "Still, you have to admit it's tempting."

Maurice had ignored the byplay. By now, having read the message perhaps five times, he was scowling fiercely. "Fine and dandy for you and Damodara—Khusrau's probably in on it, also—to scheme up ways to bleed Persia's aristocracy dry. But I remind you that *I* will have to be the one to deal with them. And I'm damned if I'm going to go along with any foolhardy plans to launch a massive frontal assault on the Malwa here. Their fortifications aren't much weaker than ours, you know."

"I doubt that'll be a problem," Belisarius said, shaking his head. "If you're guessing right about Khusrau's plans, he'll probably insist that you remain here while he leads a glorious Aryan sweeping maneuver against the right flank of the enemy. He'll want you to keep some pressure on, of course."

Maurice grunted. "We're doing that anyway, just being here."

"Multan's what? About a hundred miles north of here?" asked

Justinian. His face still had traces of dreaminess in it. "And at that point, the distance between the two rivers must be at least fifty miles."

Belisarius drew up a mental image of a map of the Punjab. "Yes, that's about right."

"So our 'enclave'—using the term very loosely, now—would contain something like two thousand square miles."

"Um . . . Probably closer to fifteen hundred," countered Maurice. "That's an awfully narrow triangle."

"Still. Even fifteen hundred square miles is a fair amount of breathing room. The land here is all fertile, too, even as arid as it is, because of the rivers. We could support a million people, easily. Some enclave!"

Belisarius couldn't help but smile. Justinian might insist that he'd given up his wicked old imperial ways of looking at the world, but it never took much to stir the beast up again.

"That's as may be," he said, a bit brusquely. "It's certainly a good deal for us, at least in the short run—and, better yet, might go a long way to mollifying Theodora. In the long run . . . hard to say. We'd be completely dependent on maintaining trade routes through either Persian or Indian territory, don't forget. We wouldn't even have a common border with the Kushans."

Justinian started to say something, but Belisarius drove over him. "Enough of that, however. We *still* have a war to win."

He turned to Calopodius. "Draft another message telling Damodara we agree. And add the following—"

—*bz-bzzz-bz-bz-bzzz-bzzz-bz-bz-bzzz*—

"I purely *detest* that sound," snarled Narses. "My ears are too old to be inflicted with it."

But he made no move to leave. Didn't so much as twitch a muscle.

The message finished, the operator handed it to Damodara. Again, the new Malwa emperor tilted it so both Narses and Rana Sanga could read the contents.

```
AGREE  TO  ALL  TERMS  STOP  THINK  PERSIANS
WILL  ALSO  STOP  BELISARIUS  CAN  CROSS
THE  THAR  WITH  FIVE  HUNDRED  MEN  STOP
```

PROBABLY REACH AJMER IN A FORTNIGHT
STOP WELLS ALREADY DUG STOP IF YOU
CAN SEND AUTHORIZATION BY THAT TIME
CAN PUT RAJPUT FORCE IN THE FIELD TO
INTERCEPT SATI STOP KUSHANS WILL DELAY
HER AS LONG AS POSSIBLE STOP

By the time they finished the message, all three pairs of eyes were very wide.

"God damn him," said Narses tonelessly. "No man should be that smart. Not even me."

Damodara shook his head, just slightly. "He *planned* for this, and months ago. There are no wells in the Thar—so he had them dug in advance."

"Months?" Sanga's headshake was a more vigorous affair. "I think not, Emperor. I think he has been planning this for years."

His gaze grew unfocused, as he pulled on his beard. "All along, I think . . . If you consider everything, from the beginning. He never planned to defeat the Malwa Empire by outright conquest. Never once. Instead, he pried it apart. Worked at all the weaknesses until it erupted. Forged alliances with Axum and Persia—the latter, an ancient Roman enemy—not so much to hammer us but so that he could support and supply a Maratha rebellion. Which he fostered himself. And then . . ."

"We *did* beat him at the Pass," pointed out Damodara.

Sanga left off the beard-pulling, and grimaced.

Damodara chuckled, quite humorlessly. "Yes, I know. A tactical victory only. You could even argue it was a strategic defeat. Still, as an army we were never defeated by him. Not even badly battered, really."

"Well, of course not," said Narses, in the same toneless voice. "He planned that, too. All through that campaign—if you recall it again, from this angle—he was careful to keep our casualties to a minimum. His army's, as well, of course. We thought at the time that was simply because he needed it intact to take Charax. But, as usual, there was a second string to the bow. He wanted *your* army intact also. So that, some day, you could do what you're doing now."

His old eyes were pure slits, now, glaring at the message. "That bastard! I should have had him assassinated when I could."

Sanga's lips twisted. "And when was that, exactly?"

"I could have done it when he was still six years old," replied Narses gloomily. "Of course, he was nobody then, so it never occured to me. Just another scion of minor Thracian nobility, with pig shit on his bare feet."

"Enough!" snapped Damodara. "I, for one, am glad he's here." He held the message up, inclining it toward Sanga. "What's the answer? *Can* we get someone to Ajmer in time to meet him? Someone the Rajputs there will listen to—but it can't be you, Sanga. We've got our own forced march to make, with a great siege at the end."

The Rajput king went back to beard-pulling. "A fortnight ... That's the problem. I'll send Jaimal and Udai, with fifty men. Neither of them are kings, but they're both well-known and much respected. Also known to be among my closest lieutenants. The Rajputs will listen to them."

A smile came, distorted by a sharp yank on the beard. "Ha! After these years, Belisarius is something of a legend among the Rajputs also—and we are a people who adore our legends. The truth, Emperor? If Jaimal and Udai are there to vouch for him, most Rajput warriors will flock to his banner. Especially the young ones."

"No problem with the oath?"

"No, not really. The old men will quibble and complain and quarrel, of course. But who cares? It won't be old men that Belisarius leads toward the headwaters of the Ganges, to meet a monster on the field of battle. Young men, they'll be. With no love for Skandagupta, an interpretation of the oath that's good enough—since it was good enough for me—and a commander out of legend."

He lowered his hand. "Yes, it'll work. *If* Jaimal and Udai can reach Ajmer in time."

He looked around. "I need to summon them. Also need a map. One moment."

He went to the door, opened it, and barked the orders.

Damodara leaned over the radio operator's shoulder. "How much longer can we transmit?"

"Hard to say, Your Majesty. The best time, at this distance, is around sunrise and sunset. But, especially once the sun is down, the window—that's what we call it—can stay open for hours. All night, sometimes."

"We'll just have to hope for the best. If necessary, we can send the final message in the morning. For now, send the following. *Exactly* as I give it you, understand? Great Lady Sati will be receiving it also, and she mustn't be able to understand what it means."

The operator's nod was nervous, but not the terrified gesture it had been hours earlier. As time had passed, the man had come to conclude that while the new self-proclaimed emperor was a scary man—the tall Rajput and the evil-looking old eunuch, even worse—he was not as scary as Nanda Lal had been.

Not even close. The truth was that the radio operator had no more love for the old dynasty than anybody. Certainly not for their stinking priests and torturers.

The buzzing was brief.

"Here's all there is, General," Calopodius said apologetically. "I thought there'd be more. And what there is doesn't make much sense."

Belisarius looked at the message.

```
AGREE   IN   PRINCIPLE   STOP   RETURN   OF
PEDDLER  EMERALD  MAY  BE  DELAYED  STOP
```

He needed a moment himself, to decipher it. "Very clever. Sanga must have found that peddler, after all."

"What peddler?" demanded Justinian. "And what kind of peddler has an emerald to begin with?"

"A very happy peddler—although I imagine his joy vanished once Sanga caught him."

Belisarius handed the message back to Calopodius. "Years ago, when I fled India, I finally shook off Sanga and his men at Ajmer. I traded my horses for three camels and all the water and supplies I needed to cross the desert. To clinch the deal, I gave the peddler one of the emeralds that had been part of Skandagupta's bribe and told him there'd be another one for him if he delivered a message in Bharakuccha to a Captain Jason, commanding a vessel named the *Argo*."

Maurice already knew the story, so he simply smiled. Calopodius and Justinian laughed aloud.

"That peddler must have thought I was crazy, giving him an emerald for camels. But it did the trick. Sanga and his men followed the horse tracks—I'd nicked one of the hooves to make it distinctive—and by the time they could have run down the peddler and realized what happened, I was well into the Thar. No way to catch me then."

He looked at Calopodius. "How much longer before the window closes?"

The blind young officer shrugged. "There's really no way to predict it, General. It may never close at all."

"Well enough, even if it does. It'll take me half the night anyway to get the men ready to leave. By morning, we'll know."

"Get some sleep, woman," Ousanas said gruffly. "There's nothing you can do here on the docks, anyway. The fleet will be ready to sail at dawn, be sure of it."

"Ready to row, you should say."

"Don't remind me!" In the dim lighting thrown off by the lanterns along the docks, Ousanas' dark features were hard to make out. But the scowl on his face was ferocious enough to be quite evident.

"Your husband! It's his fault. If he was clever enough to manipulate everyone to this ridiculous state of affairs, why didn't he time it *properly*? Two or three more months and we'd be in monsoon season. Sail all the way, lolling in comfort and drinking wine."

"He's only mortal," replied Antonina, smiling despite herself. Even though she wouldn't be working an oar, she was not looking forward to the voyage to Bharakuccha any more than Ousanas was. It would be long and slow and . . . hot.

"I hope the Hindus are right," grumbled Ousanas. "For this idiot stunt, Belisarius deserves to come into his next life as a lizard. Perched on a rock in the desert in the middle of garam, so he can fry—instead of us."

Hands on hips, his gaze swept back and forth across the row of Axumite galleys. Even in the near-darkness, every one of them was a beehive of activity as the Ethiopian sailors and marines made ready for the voyage. What Antonina couldn't see, she could hear.

"They don't seem to be complaining as much as I expected," she said.

"That's because of my awesome new title. In the olden days, when I was but the modest keeper of the fly whisks, I'd have had a mutiny on my hands. Be swinging from a gibbet, by now. Disemboweled, too. My entrails dangling just inches above the water, so the Axumite marines could bet on the sharks competing for them."

Antonina couldn't help but laugh. When he was in the mood, Ousanas did histrionic gloom as well as he did anything else. If he'd been alive in the days of Cassandra, probably no one would remember her at all.

"Stop exaggerating. They'd only have beaten you to a senseless pulp and placed bets on the alley dogs."

Ousanas' grin flashed in the night. A moment later, more seriously, he added: "They're not really disgruntled at all, in truth. Yes, the voyage to Bharakuccha at this time of year will be a miserable business. We'll be lucky if we have the sails up more than a few hours every other day. Row, row, row and sweat buckets while we do it. But . . ."

He took a long, slow breath. "But there is Bharakuccha for them, at the end. The same city where Eon left us, and whose harbor they destroyed in their vengeance. This time, with its gates opening wide."

Antonina felt a pang of grief. She remembered that harbor very well herself. She had been sitting next to Eon when he died, reading to him from the Bible.

"Best of all, it'll be garrison duty. In one of the world's largest and busiest seaports. Dens of vice and iniquity on every street. No more fighting, dying and bleeding. Let the Hindu heathens fight it out amongst themselves, from now on. For Axum, the war is over—and what remains are the pickings."

The grin flashed again. "Great pickings, too. There are even more merchant coffers in Bharakuccha than taverns and brothels. Just skimming the tolls—even the light ones we'll maintain—will make Axum rich. Richer still, I should say."

He basked in that happy thought, for a moment. Then the scowl came back.

"And *will* you get some sleep, woman? You'll need to be wide awake and alert tomorrow morning."

"Whatever for? *I'm* not pulling an oar." Half-righteously and half-apologetically, she added: "I'm too small. It'd be silly."

"Who cares about that? I remind you that it will be your responsibility—not mine!—to oversee the transfer of your emperor son and his sahrdaran wife aboard ship. Especially her. God only knows what absurd contrivance the Persians will come up with, for the purpose. But I'm sure it'll involve elephants."

Antonina didn't quite scamper from the docks. Not quite.

"You're certain?"

"Yes," replied Jaimal. Udai nodded his agreement.

Sanga's lieutenant traced a line on the map. "We can follow the rivers, most of the way, east of the Aravalli mountains. Basically, it's the same route we took years ago, when we tried to catch up with Belisarius by sea. That time, it took us almost three weeks. But we had tired horses, after that long chase, where this time we'll be starting with fresh ones. And . . . well . . ."

Sanga smiled thinly. "Yes, I know. Last time, I wasn't really driving the matter, since I knew it was hopeless anyway."

He straightened up from the map. "Well enough. Be out of the city as soon as possible. Try to make it in two weeks. But don't be foolish!" He held up an admonishing finger. "Better to use half the day—most of it, if need be—to make sure you've got the best horses in Bharakuccha. You'll make up the difference within five days."

The admonition was simply a symptom of Sanga's tension, so Jaimal and Udai took it in good enough spirits. On its face, of course, it was insulting. Teach a Rajput about horses!

The final message was also brief.

EMERALD READY IN TIME FOR TRANSACTION

"I'm off, then," said Belisarius. "At first light."

Chapter 25
KAUSAMBI

Lady Damodara came into the chamber that served Dhruva and Lata as something in the way of a modest salon. There was no expression on her face, but her features seemed taut.

"Valentinian? I'm not certain—neither is Rajiv—but . . ."

Even after all these months, Dhruva could still be surprised at how quickly Valentinian moved when he wanted to. Before she quite knew what was happening, he'd plopped the baby he'd been playing with into her lap and was at the side of the one window in the room.

His finger moved the curtain. Just slightly, and very briefly, as if a breeze had fluttered it.

"It's starting," he said, turning away from the window.

Lady Damodara was startled. "But you only glanced—"

Then, seeing the look on Valentinian's face, she smiled wryly. "Yes, I know. Stupid to question an expert."

Valentinian waved at Dhruva and Lata, who was perched on another settee. "Out, now. Into the tunnel. Lata, you make sure all the other maids and servants on this floor are moving. Don't let them dilly-dally to pack anything, either. They're supposed to be packed already."

Anastasius came into the room, scowling. "If you can tear yourself away from—oh. You know, I take it?"

Valentinian scowled right back at him. "Why is it that philosophy

253

never seems to help you with anything useful? Of course, I know. What's the majordomo up to?"

"He's getting everyone out of the kitchens. Rajiv and Khandik are rousting the rest of the servants on the floor above."

Valentinian nodded, and turned to Lady Damodara. "It will help if you and Lady Sanga take charge of the evacuation. Anastasius and I and the Ye-tai—and Rajiv—need to concentrate on the delaying action."

The tautness came back to Lady Damodara's face. "Rajiv, too?"

"*Especially* Rajiv," said Valentinian. He gave her what he probably thought was a reassuring look. Even in the tension of the moment, Dhruva had to fight down a laugh. On *his* face, it didn't look reassuring so much as simply sanguine.

"We need him, Lady," added Anastasius. "Rajiv's more cool-headed than the Ye-tai. We've been training him to handle the charges."

"Oh." The tautness faded. "You won't have him in the front?"

Valentinian started to say something that Dhruva was pretty sure would come out as a snarl, but Anastasius hastily interrupted.

"That'd be silly, wouldn't it? What I mean is, those tunnels aren't wide enough for more than two men at the front, and what with me and Valentinian—" He waved a huge hand at his glowering comrade. "No room for Rajiv there, anyway."

"We're wasting time," snarled Valentinian. "The boy goes with us, Lady Damodara. No way I want some damn Ye-tai deciding when to blow the charges."

By the time Dhruva and Lata got all the servants and maids chivvied into the cellars, some order had been brought to the initial chaos.

Quite a bit, actually. Between them, the wives of Damodara and Rana Sanga practically oozed authority, and the majordomo was always there to handle the little details. Most of the cooks and servants and maids were now being guided into the tunnel by the Bihari miners.

That, too, had been planned long before. One miner for every four servants. True, they were now short the two murdered miners—and shorter still, in terms of the Ye-tai mercenaries who were supposed to oversee the whole operation. Still, there was no trouble. Khandik and one of the other two remaining mercenaries were staying in the cellars to help with the evacuation. The third one was upstairs with the two Roman cataphracts and Rajiv.

Things were even orderly enough for Lata to do a quick count.

"We're missing one of the maids, I think. That one—I can't remember her name—who helps with the washing."

Dhruva scanned the faces, trying to place her. The two sisters hadn't had much contact with the servants on the upper floors, as a rule. But because Lady Damodara insisted that all clothes washing had to be done indoors, they did encounter the ones who came to the laundry.

"I don't know her name either, but I know you who mean. The one . . . Well. She's pretty stupid, from what I could tell."

They saw the majordomo walking quickly toward Lady Damo-dara and Sanga's wife, who were standing in the center of the big cellar watching over everything. From the frown on his face, Dhruva was pretty sure he'd just finished his own head count and had come to the same conclusion.

A moment later, he and the two ladies were talking. All of them were now frowning. The two sisters couldn't hear the words, but the subject was fairly obvious.

"I better help," Lata said. "Will you be all right with the baby?"

"Yes. I'll wait till the last. Be careful."

Lata hurried over. Sanga's wife spotted her coming almost instantly. A faint look of relief came to her face.

As Lata neared, Lady Sanga interrupted the majordomo. "Yes, fine." She pointed at Lata. "We can send her upstairs to find out what happened to the girl."

Lady Damodara looked at Lata and gave her a quick nod. An instant later, she was scampering up the stairs.

Even before she got to the main floor, Lata could hear the dull booming. The Malwa soldiery must be trying to batter down the main entrance door. Over the months, as discreetly as possible, Lady Damodara had had iron bars placed over all the windows on the palace's ground floor. To stymie thieves, she'd claimed, the one time a Malwa city official had investigated. He'd probably thought the explanation was silly, since that wealthy part of Kausambi with its frequent military patrols was hardly a place that any sensible thief would ply his trade. But he hadn't pursued the matter.

Now, that official would probably lose his head for negligence. Or be impaled on a stake, if the secret police decided that more than negligence was involved. The only way into the palace for troops trying to storm it quickly was through the main entrance. And that wasn't going to be quick, even with battering rams, as heavy and well-braced and barred as it now was.

Lata reached the landing and scampered toward the sound of the booming. The cataphracts would be there, of course.

So, indeed, they were. Along with Rajiv and the third Ye-tai mercenary, they were standing in a small alcove at the far end of the great entry vestibule. The same alcove that Lata entered, since it was the one that led to the basement floor and the cellars below.

"One of the maids is—"

Anastasius waved her down, without turning his head. "We know, Lata. She's over there."

Lata looked past him. Sure enough, the missing maid was cowering against a far wall of the vestibule.

"Come here, girl!" Rajiv shouted. "There's still time!"

There was plenty of time, in fact. The main door shook again, booming fiercely as whatever battering ram the soldiery had smashed into it. But, beyond loosening one of the hinges, the blow seemed to have no impact. The door would stand for at least another minute or two. More than enough time for the maid to saunter across to the alcove and the safety beyond, much less run.

But it didn't matter. The girl was obviously too petrified to think at all, even if she weren't dim-witted to begin with. She'd been overlooked in the initial evacuation, and now ...

"Step aside, Rajiv," Valentinian said harshly.

Lata could see the shoulders of the young Rajput prince tighten. He didn't move from his position at the front of the alcove.

"Obey me, boy."

Rajiv took a shuddering little breath; then, moved aside and flattened himself against the wall.

Valentinian already had an arrow notched. The bow came up quickly, easily; the draw, likewise. Lata wasn't astonished, even though Valentinian had once let her draw that bow when she'd expressed curiosity.

Try to draw it, rather. She might as well have tried to lift an ox.

She never really saw the arrow's flight. Just stared, as the poor stupid maid was pinned to the far wall like a butterfly. Only a foot or so of the arrow protruded from her chest. The arrowhead had passed right through her and sunk into the thick wood of the wall.

Valentinian had no expression on his face at all. Another arrow was already out of the quiver and notched.

"It was quick, Rajiv," said Anastasius quietly. "In the heart. We can't leave anyone behind who might talk, you know that. And we need you now on the detonator."

Tight-faced, Rajiv nodded and came toward Lata. Looking down, Lata saw an odd-looking contraption on the floor not more than three feet away from her. It was a small wooden box with a wire leading from it into the wall of the alcove, and a knobbed handle sticking up from the middle. A plunger of some kind, she thought.

Rajiv didn't look at Valentinian as he passed him. He seemed surprised to see Lata. And, from the look on his face, a bit frightened.

"You have to go below!" He glanced back, as if to look at Valentinian. "Quickly."

"I just came up to see what happened to her. We took a count and . . ."

Turning his head slightly, Valentinian said over his shoulder: "Get below, Lata. Now."

Once she was back in the cellar, she just shook her head in response to the question in Lady Damodara's raised eyebrows.

The lady seemed to understand. She nodded and looked away.

"What happened?" Dhruva hissed.

"Never mind. She's dead." Lata half-pushed her sister toward the tunnel. "We're almost the last ones. Let's get in there. We're just in the way, now."

There were two Bihari miners left, still standing by the entrance. One of them came to escort them.

"This way, ladies. You'll have to stoop a little. Do you need help with the baby?"

"Don't be silly," Dhruva replied.

The upper hinge gave first. Once the integrity of the door was breached, three more blows from the battering ram were enough to knock it completely aside.

By the time those blows were finished, Valentinian had already fired four arrows through the widening gap. Each one of them killed a Malwa soldier in the huge mass of soldiery Rajiv could see on the street beyond.

Anastasius fired only once. His arrow, even more powerfully shot, took a Malwa in the shoulder. Hitting the armor there, it spun him into the mob.

The Ye-tai mercenary fired also. Twice, Rajiv thought, but he wasn't paying him any attention. He was settling his nerves from the killing of the maid by coldly gauging the archery skill of the two cataphracts against his father's.

Anastasius was more powerful, but much slower; Valentinian, faster than his father—and as accurate—but not as powerful.

So, a Rajput prince concluded, his father remained the greatest archer in the world. In India, at least.

That was some satisfaction. Rajput notions concerning the responsibility of a lord to his retainers were just as stiff as all their notions. Even if, technically, the maid was simply a servant and not one of Rajiv's anyway, her casual murder had raised his hackles.

Don't be silly, part of his mind said to him. *Your father would have done the same.*

Rajiv shook his head. *Not so quickly!* he protested. *Not so—so—*

The voice came again. *Uncaringly? Probably true. And so what? She'd have been just as dead. Don't ever think otherwise. To you, he's a father and a great warrior. To his enemies, he's never been anything but a cold and deadly killer.*

And you are his son—and do you intend to flinch when the time comes to push that plunger? Most of the men you'll destroy when you do so are peasants, and some of them none too intelligent. Does a stupid maid have a right to live, and they, not?

The door finally came off the hinges altogether and smashed—what was left of it—onto the tiles of the huge vestibule. Malwa soldiers came pouring in.

Valentinian fired three more times, faster than Rajiv could really follow. Anastasius, once; the Ye-tai, once. Four Malwa soldiers fell dead. One—the Ye-tai's target—was merely wounded.

Valentinian stepped back quickly into the shelter of the alcove. Anastasius and the Ye-tai followed, an instant later.

"Now," commanded Valentinian.

Rajiv's hand struck down the plunger.

The charges carefully implanted in the walls of the vestibule turned the whole room into an abattoir. In the months they'd had to prepare, the majordomo had even been able to secretly buy good drop shot on the black market. So it was real bullets that the mines sent flying into the room, not haphazard pieces of metal.

Rajiv supposed that some of the soldiers in the room must have survived. One or two, perhaps not even injured.

But not many. In a split second, he'd killed more men than most seasoned warriors would kill in a lifetime.

Somewhere on the stairs leading to the cellars, Rajiv uttered his one and only protest.

"I didn't hesitate. Not at all."

Anastasius smiled. "Well, of course not."

Valentinian shook his head. "Don't get melancholy and philosophical on me, boy. You've still got to do it twice more. Today."

For some reason, that didn't bother Rajiv.

Maybe that was because his enemies now had fair warning.

He said as much.

Anastasius smiled again, more broadly. At the foot of the stairs, now in the cellar, Valentinian turned around and glared at him.

"Who cares about 'fair warnings'? Dead is dead and we all die anyway. Just do it."

Anastasius, now also at the bottom of the stairs, cleared his throat. "If I may put Valentinian's viewpoint in proper Stoic terms, what he means to say—"

"Is exactly what the fuck I said," Valentinian hissed. "Just do it."

He glanced up the stairs. "In about ten minutes, at a guess."

His guess was off, a bit. Rajiv didn't blow the next charges for at least a quarter of an hour.

Whether because he'd satisfied himself concerning the ethics of the issue, or simply because Valentinian's cold-blooded murderousness was infectious, he wasn't sure. For whatever reason, Rajiv had no trouble waiting until the cellars were full of Malwa soldiery, probing uncertainly in the torch-lit darkness to find whatever hole their quarry had scurried into.

From the still greater darkness of the tunnel, Rajiv gauged the moment. He even out-waited Valentinian.

"Now, boy."

"Not yet."

Two minutes later, he drove in the next plunger. The same type of shaped-charge mines implanted in the walls of the cellars turned those underground chambers into more abattoirs.

"Quickly, now!" urged Anastasius, already lumbering at a half-crouch down the tunnel. "We've got to get to the shelter as soon as possible. Before they can figure out—"

He continued in that vein, explaining the self-evident to people who already knew the plan by heart. Rajiv ignored him. Looking ahead, down the tunnel, he could see the figure of the Ye-tai already vanishing in the half-gloom thrown out by the few oil lamps still in place. Valentinian was close on his heels.

"You're doing good, boy," said the Mongoose. "Really, really good."

All things considered, Rajiv decided the Roman cataphract was right.

To be sure, this was not something he'd ever brag about. On the other hand . . .

When did you ever hear your father brag? came that little, back-of-the-mind voice.

The answer was: *Never.*

Rajiv had noticed that, in times past. Now, finally, he thought he understood it. And, for the first time in his life, came to feel something for his father beyond love, admiration and respect.

Simple affection. Nothing fancy. Just the sort of fondness that a man—a woman too, he supposed—feels when he thinks about someone who has shared a task and a hardship.

When they reached the shelter, even Valentinian took a deep breath.

"Well," he muttered, "this is where we find out. God damn all Biharis—miners down to newborn babes—if it doesn't."

The Ye-tai just looked blank-faced. Anastasius' eyes flicked about the small chamber, with its massive bracing. "Looks good, anyway."

It seemed fitting, somehow, for Rajiv to finally take charge. "Place the barrier." It seemed silly to call that great heavy thing a "door."

He pointed to it, propped against the entrance they'd just come through. "Anastasius, you're the only one strong enough to hold it in place. Valentinian, you set the braces. You"—this to the Ye-tai—"help him."

The work was done quickly. The last of it was setting the angled braces that supplemented the great cross-bars and strengthened the door by propping it against the floor.

There was no point in waiting. The shelter would either hold, or they'd all be crushed. But there'd be no point to any of it if Rajiv didn't blow the last charges before the surviving Malwa in the palace that was now over a hundred yards distant as well as many feet above them had time to realize what had happened.

"I guess you'd better—" Valentinian started to say, but Rajiv's hand had already driven home the plunger.

"Well, shit," he added, before the earthquake made it impossible to talk at all.

The Malwa general in command of the entire operation had remained outside the palace. After he was knocked off his feet, he stared dumbfounded as the walls of the palace seemed to erupt all around the base.

The palace came down, like a stone avalanche.

Some of those stones were large, others were really pieces of wall that had somehow remained intact.

Some were blown a considerable distance by the explosion. Others bounced, after they fell.

Scrambling frantically, the general managed to avoid all the

ones sent sailing by the blast. But as close as he'd been standing, he didn't escape one section of wall—a very big section—as
it disintegrated.

A few minutes later, his second-in-command and now successor was able to finally piece together the few coherent reports
he could get.

There weren't many, and they weren't all that coherent. Only
three of the soldiers who had gone into the palace were still
alive, and one of them was too badly injured to talk. None of
the soldiers who'd gone into the cellar had survived, of course.

But he was pretty sure he knew what had happened, and hastened to make his report to Emperor Skandagupta.

In his own far greater palace, the emperor waited impatiently
for the officer to finish.

When he was done, Skandagupta shook his head. "They all
committed suicide? That's nonsense."

He pointed at the officer. "Execute this incompetent."

Once that was done, the emperor gave his orders. They were
not complicated.

"Dig. Remove all the rubble. There's an escape tunnel there
somewhere. I want it found."

Carefully—very carefully—none of his advisers allowed any of
their dismay to show. Not with the emperor in such a foul and
murderous mood.

Not one of them wanted to draw his attention. It would take
days to clear away all that rubble. Long, long days, in which
the emperor would probably have at least one or two more men
executed for incompetence.

At least. As the advisers assigned to the task of excavation
started filing out of the imperial audience chamber, Skandagupta
was already giving orders to discover which incompetent—no,
which traitor—in charge of the capital's munitions supply had
been so corrupt or careless—no, treasonous—to allow such a
huge quantity of gunpowder to slip through his fingers.

After the advisers reached the relative safety of the streets
outside the palace, they went their separate ways to begin orga-
nizing the excavation project.

All but one of them, that is. That one, after he was certain no one was watching him, headed for Kausambi's northern gate.

The city was still in a state of semi-chaos, so soon after the word of Damodara's rebellion had spread everywhere from the telegraph stations, despite the secret police's attempts to suppress the news. The destruction of Lady Damodara's palace, right in the middle of the imperial quarter, would simply add to it.

The adviser thought he had a good chance of slipping out of the city unnoticed, if he moved immediately. He had no choice, in any event, if he had any hope of staying alive himself or keeping his wife and children alive.

True, the adviser had no connection to Kausambi's munitions depot. But one of his first cousins was in charge of it, and the adviser knew perfectly well the man was not only corrupt but careless. He had no doubt at all that an investigation would soon discover that Lady Damodara's agents had simply *bought* the gunpowder. Probably had it delivered to the palace in the munitions depot's own wagons.

Fortunately, his wife and two children had remained in their home town farther down the Ganges. With luck he could get there in time to get them out. He had enough money on his person to bribe the guards at the gate and even hire transport. There was considerably more money in their mansion. With that, they might be able to escape into Bengal somewhere ...

Beyond that, he thought no further. There was no point in it. He could feel the Malwa Empire cracking and breaking under his feet. With that greatest of all the world's certainties shaking, what man could possibly foresee the future?

He made it out of the city. But, within a day, was captured by a cavalry patrol. The emperor had soon considered that possibility also, and had placed a ban on any officials leaving Kausambi without written orders. By then, his savage punitive actions had terrified the city's soldiery enough that the guards at the gate whom the adviser had bribed prattled freely to the secret police.

Before noon of the next day, the adviser's body was on a stake outside Skandagupta's palace. Four days later, the bodies of his wife and two children joined him. The soldiers had some trouble fitting the boy, since he was only three.

Not much, however. By then, Skandagupta's fury was cutting through the imperial elite like a scythe, and small stakes were being prepared. Plenty of them.

"He's hysterical," Lady Damodara said, pinched-faced, after getting the latest news from one of the stable-keeper's sons. "Even for Skandagupta, this is insane."

Sanga's wife shifted a bit on her cushions. The cushions were thinner than she was used to, and—worse—their quarters were extremely crowded. The entire staff from the palace was crammed into the last stretch of the tunnel while they waited for the first search of the city to run its course. So were over a dozen miners. But she knew that even after they were able to move into the stables, in a few days, the conditions wouldn't improve all that much.

As places of exile went, the stables would be utterly wretched. As a place of refuge from the Malwa madness sweeping the city and leaving hundreds of people staked outside the imperial palace, however, it would be superb.

She gave the stable-keeper's son a level look. "Are you frightened, Tarun?"

The twelve-year-old boy swallowed. "Some, Lady. Not too much, though. The soldiers who searched the stables this morning were irritated, but they didn't take it out on us, and they didn't search all that seriously. They didn't really search at all in the stable that has the hidden door leading to this tunnel. Since then, our parents and our sisters stay out of sight, but my brother and I can move around on the streets easily enough. The soldiers even answer our questions, usually. They really aren't paying much attention to . . . Well. People like us."

Lady Damodara chuckled, humorlessly. "So Narses predicted. 'You'll be lost in Kausambi's ocean of poverty,' were his exact words. I remember. Damn his soul."

"No," said Rajiv forcefully. "Damn Malwa's soul."

Both ladies gave him a level look.

"The false Malwa, I mean," added Rajiv hastily.

Lady Damodara's chuckle, this time, had a bit of humor in it. "Look at it this way, Rajiv. When it's all over, if we survive, we can look at Skandagupta on a stake."

"You think so?" asked Rajiv.

"Oh, yes," said the lady serenely.

Lady Sanga sniffed. "Maybe. By the time he gets here, Rajiv, your father's temper will be up. They'll need toothpicks. I doubt if even Lord Damodara will be able to restrain him enough to keep some portion of Skandagupta's body suitably sized for a stake."

"He probably won't even try," allowed Lady Damodara. "Now that I think about it."

Chapter 26
THE PUNJAB

"I am leaving you in charge, General Samudra," said Great Lady Sati. To the general's relief, the tone and timber of the voice was that of the young woman Sati appeared to be, not . . .

The thing for which it was really just a vessel.

The god—or goddess—he should say. But Samudra was beginning to have his doubts on that issue. Desperately, he hoped that the thing inside Great Lady Sati could detect none of his reservations.

Apparently not, since she said nothing to the special assassins positioned against the walls of her caravan. Perhaps that was simply because Samudra's general anxiety overrode anything specific.

He didn't *want* to be left in charge of the Malwa army in the Punjab. That was not due to any hesitations concerning his own military abilities, it was simply because the situation was obviously beginning to crumble for political reasons, and Samudra was wary of the repercussions.

Samudra had always stayed as far away as he could from political matters. Insofar as possible, at least, within the inevitable limits of the Malwa dynastic system of which he was himself a member. He was one of the emperor's distant cousins, after all. Still, he'd done his very best throughout his life to remain a purely military figure in the dynasty.

But all he said was: "Yes, Great Lady."

"I will take thirty thousand troops with me, from here, and

another ten from Multan. No artillery units, however. They will slow me down too much and I can acquire artillery once I reach the Ganges plain. Have them ready by early morning, the day after tomorrow. You may select them, but I want good units with Ye-tai security battalions. *Full* battalions, Samudra."

He managed not to wince. The problem wasn't the total number of soldiers Sati wanted to take back to Kausambi with her. Thirty thousand was actually lower than he'd expected. The problem would be filling out the ranks of the Ye-tai. Few of the security battalions were still up to strength. The defection of so many Kushans to Kungas and his new kingdom had forced the Malwa to use Ye-tai as spearhead assault troops. As brave as they were, the Ye-tai had little of the Kushan experience with that role. Their casualties had been very heavy, this past two years.

Samudra knew he'd have no choice but to strip the needed reinforcements out of all the other security battalions. And with only one full day to do the work, it would be done hastily and haphazardly, to boot, with not much more in the way of rhyme or reason than what he might accomplish with a lottery.

Gloomily, Samudra contemplated the months of fighting ahead of him here in the Punjab. The morale of the great mass of the soldiery was already low. The departure of Great Lady Sati, forty thousand troops—and a disproportionate percentage of the Ye-tai security forces—would leave it shakier still.

On the brighter side, the Romans seemed content to simply fight a siege. If Great Lady Sati . . .

Her next words brought considerable relief.

"I do not expect you to make any headway in my absence," she said. "Nor is it needed. Simply keep Belisarius pinned here while I attend to suppressing Damodara's rebellion. We will resume offensive operations next year."

"Yes, Great Lady." Samudra hesitated. The next subject was delicate.

"No artillery units, understood. But of the thirty thousand, how many . . . ah . . ."

"Cavalry? Not more than three thousand. Enough to provide me with a screen, that's all. You understand that none of the cavalry may be Rajputs, I assume?"

Samudra nodded. Although there'd been no open mutinies among the Rajputs yet—aside from the huge number already with Rana Sanga—no Malwa top commander could place much reliance on them until Damodara's rebellion was crushed.

Sati shrugged, in an oddly human gesture. "Without using Rajputs, we cannot assemble a large force of cavalry that I could depend upon. Since I'll need to use mostly infantry, I may as well make it a strong infantry unit with only enough cavalrymen to serve as scouts and a screen. It shouldn't matter, anyway. I don't expect to encounter any opposition until I've almost reached Kausambi. Damodara will probably reach the capital before I do, but he'll be stymied by the fortifications until I arrive. By then, after I've reached the plain, I'll have been able to assemble a huge army from the garrisons in all the major cities along the Ganges. With me as the hammer and the walls of Kausambi as the anvil, Damodara will be crushed."

"Yes, Great Lady."

"*Here?*" exclaimed Dasal. The oldest of the Rajput kings in the chamber rolled his eyes and stared at the ceiling.

"All it needed," he muttered. From the expressions on their faces, it was obvious the other six kings present in the chamber—they were all elderly, if none quite so old as Dasal—shared his gloomy sentiments.

His younger brother Jaisal rose from his cushion and moved to a nearby window, walking with the creaky tread of a man well into his seventies. Once at the window, he stared out over the city of Ajmer.

The capital of the Rajputs, that was—insofar as that fractious nation could be said to have a "capital" at all. Dasal found himself wondering whether it would still be standing, a year from now.

"Where are they being kept?" he asked.

The Rajput officer who'd brought the news to the council shook his head. "I was not given that information. Nor will I be, I think. They may not even be in Ajmer, at all."

Dasal lowered his eyes. "They're here somewhere," he snorted. "Be sure of it."

"We *could* find them . . ." ventured one of the other kings. Chachu was his name, and his normally cautious manner was fully evident in the questioning tone of the remark.

Simultaneously, one sitting and one still standing at the window, the brothers Dasal and Jaisal shook their heads.

"What would be the point of that?" demanded Jaisal. "Better if we can claim we never knew the location of Damodara's parents."

Gloomy silence filled the chamber again. The seven kings in that room formed what passed for a Rajput ruling council. None of them, singly or together, had any illusion that if Damodara's rebellion was crushed, Rajputana would retain even a shred of its semi-autonomy. Direct Malwa rule would be imposed—harshly—and each and every one of them would be questioned under torture.

Still, it was easier to deny something under torture that was a false accusation. Very narrowly defined, of course—but these were men grasping at straws.

"That madman Rana Sanga," Chachu hissed. But even that remark sounded as if it were punctuated by a question mark.

"It's not much," said one of their kidnappers apologetically. "The problem isn't even money, since we were given plenty. But Ajat—ah, our chief—told us to remain inconspicuous."

Damodara's father finished his inspection of the room. That hadn't taken long, as sparsely furnished as it was. It would be one of many such rooms in many such buildings in Ajmer. The city was a center for trade routes, and needed to provide simple accommodations for passing merchants, traders and tinkers.

He spent more time examining the man who had spoken. An assassin, obviously. Lord Damodara recognized the type, from his adventurous youth.

A very polite assassin, however, as all of them had been since they seized Damodara's parents from the bedroom of their palace and smuggled them into the night.

Better to think of them as bodyguards, he decided wryly.

"I'm exhausted," his wife said. She gazed longingly at the one bed in the room. It had been a long trip, especially for people of their advanced years.

"Yes, we need sleep," her husband agreed. He nodded to the assassin. "Thank you."

The man gave a bow in return. "We will be in the next room, should you need anything."

After he was gone, closing the door behind him, Damodara's mother half-collapsed on the bed. She winced, then, feeling the thin pallet.

"Not much!" she exclaimed, half-laughing and half-sobbing.

Her husband made a face. "A year from now we will either be skin-sacks hanging from Emperor Skandagupta's rafters or be sleeping in one of the finest chambers in his palace."

The noise his wife emitted was, again, half a sob and half a laugh. "Your son! I told you—years ago!—that you were letting him think too much."

There were times—not many—that Agathius was thankful he'd lost his legs at the Battle of the Dam.

This was one of them. Being an obvious cripple might deflect some of the Persian fury being heaped upon his unoffending person, where the strength of Samson unchained would have been pointless.

"—*not be cheated, I say it again!*"

Khusrau punctuated the bellow with a glare ferocious enough to be worthy of . . .

Well, an emperor, actually. Which he was.

The mass of Persian noblemen packed into Khusrau's audience chamber at Sukkur growled their approval. They sounded like so many hungry tigers.

Not a dehgan in the lot, either, so far as Agathius could tell. That broad, lowest class of the Iranian *azadan*—"men of noble birth"—hadn't been invited to send representatives to this enclave. The only men in the room were sahrdaran and vurzurgan.

Agathius shifted his weight on his crutches. "Your Majesty," he said mildly, "I just arrived here from Barbaricum. I have no idea beyond the sketchiest telegraph messages—which certainly didn't mention these issues—what the general has planned in terms of a postwar distribution of the spoils. But I'm quite sure he has no intention of denying the Iranians their just due."

Another surge of muttered growls came. The phrase *he'd better not!* seemed to be the gist of most of them.

"He'd better not!" roared Khusrau. His clenched fist pounded the heavy armrest of his throne. Three times, synchronized with *bet-ter-not*.

"I'm sure the thought has never crossed his mind," said Agathius firmly. He contemplated a sudden collapse on the floor, but decided that would be histrionic. He wasn't *that* crippled, after all. Besides, he'd said the words with such complete conviction that even the angry and suspicious Persians seemed a bit mollified.

And why not? The statement was quite true. Agathius was as certain as he was of the sunrise that the thought of swindling the Persians out of their rightful share of the postwar spoils had not, in fact, "crossed" Belisarius' mind.

Been planted there like a sapling, yes. Been studied and examined from every angle, to be sure. Weighed, pondered, appraised, considered, measured, gauged, adjudged, evaluated, assessed—for a certainty.

Crossed, no.

Belisarius studied the telegram.

"Pretty blistering language, sir," Calopodius said apologetically, as if he were somehow responsible for the intemperate tone of the message.

"Um." Belisarius scanned over it quickly again. "Well, I agree that the verbs 'cheat' and 'rob' are excessive. And there was certainly no need to bring up my ancestry. Still and all, it could be worse. If you look at it closely—well, squint—this is really more in the way of a protest than a threat."

He dropped the Persian emperor's message onto the table. "And, as it happens, all quite unnecessary. I have no intentions of 'cheating' the Persians out of their fair share of the spoils."

He turned to Maurice, smiling. "Be sure to tell Khusrau that, when he arrives."

Maurice scowled back at him. "You'll be gone, naturally."

"Of course!" said Belisarius gaily. "Before dawn, tomorrow, I'm off across the Thar."

Before Maurice could respond, Anna stalked into the headquarters bunker.

She spoke with no preamble. "Your own latrines and medical facilities are adequate, General. But those of the Punjabi natives are atrocious. I *insist* that something be done about it."

Belisarius bestowed the same gleeful smile on her. "Absolutely! I place you in charge. What's a good title, Maurice?"

The chiliarch's scowl darkened. "Who cares? How about 'Mistress of the Wogs'?"

Anna hissed.

Belisarius clucked his tongue. "Thracian peasant. No, that won't do at all."

He turned to Calopodius. "Exercise your talent for rhetoric here, youngster."

Calopodius scratched his chin. "Well . . . I can think of several appropriate technical titles, but the subtleties of the Greek language involved wouldn't mean anything to the natives. So why not just call her the Governess?"

"That's silly," said Maurice.

"My husband," said Anna.

"Done," said Belisarius.

A full hour before sunrise, Belisarius and his expedition left the Triangle. To maintain the secrecy of the operation, they were ferried south for several miles before being set ashore. By now, Roman patrols had scoured both banks of the Indus so thoroughly that no enemy spies could be hidden anywhere.

As always with water transport, the horses were the biggest problem. The rest was easy enough, since Belisarius was bringing no artillery beyond mortars and half a dozen of the rocket chariots.

By mid-morning, they were completely out of sight of the river, heading east into the wasteland.

At approximately the same time, Sati started her own procession out of the Malwa camp to the north. There was no attempt at secrecy here, of course. What can be done—even then, with difficulty—by less than a thousand men, cannot possibly be done by thirty thousand. So huge was that mass of men, in fact, that it took the rest of the day before all of them had filed from the camps and started up the road.

Preceded only by a cavalry screen and one Ye-tai battalion, the Great Lady herself led the way. Since the infantry would set the pace of the march, she would ride in the comfort of a large howdah suspended between two elephants.

The "howdah" was really more in the way of a caravan or a large sedan than the relatively small conveyance the word normally denoted. The *chaundoli,* as it was called, was carried on heavy poles suspended between two elephants, much the way a litter is carried between two men. Its walls and roof were made of thin wood, with three small windows on each side. The walls and roof were covered with grass woven onto canes and lashed to the exterior. The grass would be periodically soaked with water during the course of the journey, which would keep the interior cool as the breeze struck the chaundoli.

Since none of the Great Lady's special bodyguards or assassins were horsemen, those of them who could not be fit into her own chaundoli rode in a second one just behind her. They could have marched, of course. But the thing which possessed the body of the Great Lady had no desire to risk its special assistants becoming fatigued. Link didn't expect to need them, but the situation had become so chaotic that even its superhuman capacity for calculation was being a bit overwhelmed.

Lord Samudra watched Great Lady Sati's army depart from the great complex of fortresses and camps which had by then been erected facing the Roman lines in the Iron Triangle. Come evening, he returned to his own headquarters—which was, in fact, built much the same way as a chaundoli except the walls were of heavy timber. The water-soaked grass wasn't quite as effective a cooling mechanism with such a massive and stationary structure. But it was still far superior to the sweltering heat of a tent or the sort of buried bunkers the Roman generals used.

Idiots, they were, in Samudra's opinion. The only reason they needed bunkers was because of their flamboyant insistence on remaining close to the fighting lines. Samudra's own headquarters was several miles beyond the farthest possible range of Roman cannons or rockets.

"Have more water poured on the grass," Samudra commanded his majordomo. "And be quick about it. I am not in a good mood."

Chapter 27
THE IRON TRIANGLE

At least Emperor Khusrau had enough sense to leave his Persian army on the west bank of the Indus, when he came storming into Maurice's bunker on the Iron Triangle. In point of fact, Maurice wouldn't have allowed him to bring them across—and he, not the Persians, controlled the rivers. The Iranians had nothing to match the Roman ironclad and fireship.

Still, even Khusrau alone—in his current mood—would have been bad enough. Surrounded as he was with enough sahrdaran to pack the bunker, he was even worse. And the fact that Maurice was sure the Persian emperor was mostly playing to the audience didn't improve his own mood at all.

"—not be cheated!"

Maurice had had enough. "*Cheated?*" he demanded. "Who is 'cheating you,' damnation?" He had just enough control of his temper left to add: "Your Majesty."

Maurice pointed to the west wall of the bunker. "Take as much as you can over there, for all I care! But don't expect *me* to do your fighting for you!"

Several of the sahrdaran hissed angrily, one of them very loudly. That was a sahrdaran in his early forties whose name was Shahrbaraz. He was the oldest son of the leader of the Karin family, which was one of the seven great sahrdaran houses and perhaps the most influential after the Suren.

Maurice glared at him, still pointing at the west wall. "Why are you here, hissing at me—instead of fighting to take the land you claim is yours?"

Shahrbaraz started to respond angrily, but the emperor waved him down.

"Be silent!" Khusrau commanded. He gave Maurice a fine glare of his own. "May I then assume that you will not object if I launch my own offensive?"

"Not in the least."

"And you will not object if we retain the land we conquer?"

Maurice snatched up the messages on the center table and shook them at the emperor. Those were copies of the exchange between Belisarius and Damodara that had taken place days earlier. "How many times do I need to show this to you? Your Majesty. Whatever you can take west of the river is yours. As far north as you can manage to get."

"To the Hindu Kush!" shouted one of the other sahrdaran. Maurice couldn't remember his name, but he was a prominent member of the house of the Spandiyads.

By a mighty struggle, Maurice managed not to sneer. "I'd recommend you stop at the *foot* of the Hindu Kush. Keeping in mind that King Kungas counts the Vale of Peshawar as part of it. Everything north of Kohat Pass and west of Margalla Pass belongs to him, he says. But if you think you can roll over the Kushans as well as the Malwa, so be it."

"And when have the Aryans cared—"

"Be silent!" Khusrau roared again. This time, thankfully, it was the Spandiyad who was the recipient of his imperial glare. "We are not at war with the Kushans," he stated. "All of the west Punjab *to* the Hindu Kush. We will stop once we have reached the passes into the Vale of Peshawar held by our allies the Kushans."

The emperor glanced down at the half-crumpled pile of messages. "As all have now agreed," he finished, more softly.

When he looked up at Maurice, he seemed considerably calmer. "Will your gunships provide us with protection from the Malwa ironclads?"

Maurice shook his head. Not angrily, but firmly nonetheless. "We can't, Your Majesty. I'm sorry, but we just *can't*. Neither the *Justinian* nor the *Victrix* is a match for them. Not even one of them, much less the two they have stationed on the Indus. That's why we laid the mine fields across the rivers. Once you move north of those minefields, you'll be on your own. I recommend you keep your army away from the rivers. Far enough away to be out of range of the ironclads' guns."

Khusrau didn't seem surprised by the response. Or angry, for that matter. He simply grunted softly and turned away.

"To the Hindu Kush!" he bellowed, striding toward the exit of the bunker.

Within a minute, they were all gone.

"Thank God," muttered Maurice. "Can't stand Persians. Never have liked the arrogant bastards. Think their shit doesn't stink."

"It certainly *does*," sniffed Anna. She'd happened to be present in the bunker, visiting her husband, when the Persian delegation arrived. "I've visited their camps, on the way up here. Their sanitary practices would cause a hyena to tremble."

Maurice chuckled. "Worse than the natives here?"

"Yes, as a matter of fact," Anna replied stiffly. "Even before I started governessing them. Today, the Punjabi habits are much better. A week from now—well, a month—there'll be no comparison at all."

Maurice didn't doubt it, although he thought Anna's estimate of one month was wildly optimistic. The difficulty wasn't so much native resistance—perhaps oddly, the Punjabis seemed quite taken by their new "Governess"—as it was the sheer scale of the problem.

Malwa armies were always notorious for their rough habits with local populations. The huge Malwa army dug in to the north of the Triangle was behaving especially badly, as packed in as those soldiers were and suffering all the miseries and frustrations of siege warfare. The Iron Triangle had become a refuge for untold thousands of Punjabis in the area. They came across the rivers, on small skiffs or even swimming through the minefields.

By now, the population density of the Triangle was almost that of a huge city. Worse, really, since most of the land area had to be left available for farming. The Triangle got much of its supplies from the Sind, brought up by the river boats, but it still had to provide the bulk of its own food. Controlling the raw sewage produced by such a population was enough to make Hercules' legendary cleaning of the Augean Stables look like an afternoon's easy chore.

"You'll see," said Anna.

✧   ✧   ✧

"There'll be enough, General," said Ashot. "Just barely."

Belisarius nodded, after he finished wiping his face with a cloth. That was to clean off the dust, mostly. Despite the heat, the Thar was so dry that sweat didn't have time to really accumulate.

He was careful not to let his worry show. This was the third well they'd reached, and all of them had had just enough water—just barely—for his expedition. They had almost no reserve left at all. If even one of the wells was empty, or near-empty . . .

But there was no point in fretting over the matter. The long war with the Malwa was nearing its end, and there remained only to drive home the lance—or die in the attempt. It was in the hands of Fate, now.

"Let's be off," he said. He glanced at the horizon, where the dawn was beginning. "There's still enough time for three hours' travel before the sun's up high enough to force us to camp for the day."

"I feel like a bat," complained Ashot. "Live by night, sleep by day."

He said it fairly cheerily, though. Ashot had plenty of experience with desert campaigns, and knew perfectly well that no sane man traveled through an area like the Thar when the sun was up. Like all the cataphracts on the expedition, he was wearing loose-fitting Arab-style robes instead of armor—the only difference being that Ashot knew how to put them on without help from one of Abbu's men.

"Something's happening," Kujulo stated. Slowly, he swept the telescope across the terrain below the pass. "I'm not sure what, but there's too much movement down there."

"Are they preparing another attack?" asked one of the other Kushans.

"After the way we butchered the last one? Doubt it," grunted Kujulo. "No, I think they're pulling out some of their forces. And I think—not sure about this at all—that there's some sort of troop movement in the far distance. But it doesn't seem to be reinforcements."

He lowered the telescope. Awkwardly, since it was big and clumsy; it was one of the eyeglasses newly made in Begram's fledgling optical industry, not one of the sleek Roman devices.

"Let the king know," he commanded. "This may be what he's expecting."

Miles away, a squad of Ye-tai had a much better view of what was happening. They were serving as sentries for the Malwa army positioned against the Kushans—and none too happy about it, either. In times past, it would have been Kushans themselves who'd be detached for this rigorous duty. But Kushans could no longer be relied upon, what few of them were still left in the Malwa forces. Their army's commander hadn't dared used common troops for the purpose. Kushans were much too good at mountain warfare to depend on levied infantry to serve as outlying sentries.

"Tell me again," said the squad leader.

The new member of the squad shrugged. He'd only arrived the day before. "Don't believe me, then. Great Lady Sati is on her way to the capital. With forty thousand troops. Seems there's a big rebellion."

"Why were *you* traveling with them?"

"I wasn't. I was just part of a troop sent by Samudra up here. We only marched with the Great Lady's expedition for a short distance. She's headed up the Sutlej, of course."

"I wish we were too," muttered one of the other squad members.

Again, the newcomer shrugged. "So do I. But they're leaving some of the Ye-tai they brought with them here—me among them, worse luck—while they take back to the Punjab almost ten thousand regular troops."

"Why do the two of you wish you were going back to the plain?" demanded the squad leader. "So we could get lost in a whirlpool in the Ganges? Don't be stupid."

Their camp was perched on a rise that looked directly onto Margalla Pass, which divided the Vale of Peshawar from the Punjab proper. From the distance, the squad leader couldn't see any of the Kushan troops who were holding the pass. But he imagined he could almost see the blood the Malwa army had left on those slopes, in the course of four defeated assaults.

They were being ground up here. On level ground, the Ye-tai squad leader would have faced Kushans without worrying too much. Up here, in the hills and mountains, fighting them was like fighting crocodiles in a river.

"I'm half-Sarmatian," he murmured. "Mother's side."

None of his mates so much as curled a lip, despite the absurdity of the statement. There hadn't been any Sarmatians in centuries.

It didn't matter, since that wasn't the point of the statement. Within a few seconds, all of the squad members were eyeing the new arrival.

Fortunately for him, he wasn't stupid. "The war's lost," he said, softly but clearly. "That's what I think, anyway."

The squad leader grinned. "What's your name?"

The new man grinned back. "Prabhak. I know, it sounds funny. It's a Sarmatian name. Given to me by my mother."

At that, the whole squad laughed. "Welcome, brother," said one of them. "Would you believe that all of us are half-Sarmatian?"

That brought another little laugh. When it died down, Prabhak asked: "When? And which way?"

The squad leader glanced at the sun, which was now setting. "As soon as dark falls. There'll be a half moon. Good enough. And we'll head for the Kushans."

Prabhak winced, as did most of the squad members.

"Don't be stupid," growled the squad leader. "You want to spend the rest of your lives living like goats?"

Put that way . . .

"They say King Kungas isn't a bad sort," mused one of the squad members.

The squad leader chuckled humorlessly. "Nobody says anything of the sort. He's a demon and his witch wife is even worse. Which is fine with me. Just the sort of rulers who can keep us alive, in what's coming."

The first fortress in the Vindhyas that Damodara's army reached was deserted. Its garrison had fled two days before, they were told by some of the natives.

So was the second, and the third.

The fourth fortress, far down from the crest, was still manned. Either the garrison or its commander was more stalwart.

They were stalwart enough to last for exactly eight minutes, once Sanga launched the assault, before they tried to surrender.

Tried, and failed. Sanga was giving no quarter.

Even if he'd been inclined to, which he wasn't—not with his wife and children in Kausambi—Lord Damodara had commanded a massacre.

Emperor Damodara, rather. As a mere lord, Damodara had always been noted for his comparative leniency toward defeated enemies, by Malwa standards. But the garrison of the fortress which had dared to resist him were no longer simply "enemies." They were traitors and rebels.

Of course, Sanga allowed some of the garrison to escape. That, too, had been commanded by Emperor Damodara. There was no point in slaughtering garrisons if other garrisons didn't learn of it.

By the next day, Damodara's army was out of the mountains and marching up the Chambal river. The Chambal was the main tributary of the Yamuna, whose junction was still five hundred miles to the north. Once they reached that junction, they'd still have three hundred miles to march down the Yamuna before reaching Kausambi.

Even with every man in his army mounted, either as cavalry or dragoons, Damodara could not hope to make faster progress than twenty miles a day—and the long march would probably go slower than that. True, now that they were out of the Vindhyas, the countryside was fertile and they could forage as they went. But his army still numbered some forty thousand men. It was simply not possible to move such a huge number of soldiers very quickly.

Six weeks, at least, it would take them to reach Kausambi. Conceivably, two months—and if they had to fight any major battles on the way, longer than that. They could not afford to be delayed by any of the fortresses along the way.

The first fortress they encountered on the river was deserted.

So was the next.

So was the next.

"They've heard of us, it seems," said Rana Sanga to the emperor.

"I prefer to think it's the majestic aura of my imperial presence."

"Yes, Your Majesty. Though I'm not sure I understand the difference."

Damodara smiled. "Neither do I, as it happens. You'd think I would, since I believe I'm now semi-divine. Maybe even three-quarters."

✧ ✧ ✧

The Bihari miner straightened up from his crouch. "They're getting close, master. I think so, anyway. It's hard to tell, because of all the echoes."

The term "echoes" seemed strange to Valentinian, but he understood what the miner meant. At the first dogleg, they'd dug two short false tunnels in addition to the one that led—eventually—to the exit in the stables. What the miner was hearing were the complex resonances of the sounds being made by the Malwa miners as they neared the end of clearing away the rubble that the Romans had left behind when they blew the charges.

"Will you know when they break through?"

"Oh, yes. Even before the charges go off."

The miner grimaced as he made the last statement. As someone who had spent all of his adult life and a good portion of his childhood working beneath the earth, he had an automatic sympathy for men who would soon be crushed in a series of cave-ins. Enemies or not.

Valentinian didn't share any of his sentiments. Dead was dead. What difference did it make if it came under tons of rock and soil, the point of a lance—or just old age?

He turned to Rajiv. "Are you willing to do this? Or would you prefer it if I did?"

The young Rajput prince shrugged. "If everything works right, the charges will go off automatically, anyway. I won't have to do anything."

" 'If everything works right,' " Valentinian jeered. "Nothing ever works right, boy. That's the cataphract's wisdom."

But Valentinian proved to be wrong.

When their miners finally broke through the rubble into a cleared area, two Malwa officers pushed them aside and entered the tunnel. For all the risk involved, they were both eager. Emperor Skandagupta had promised a great reward for whatever officers captured Damodara's family.

Both of them moved their torches about, illuminating the area. Then, cursed together.

"Three tunnels leading off!" snarled the superior officer. "But which is the right one?"

His lieutenant gestured with his torch to the tunnel ahead of him. "I'll explore this one, if you want. You take one of the others. We can leave some men to guard the third, until we have time to investigate it."

"As good a plan as any, I guess." The captain swiveled his head and barked some orders. Within a minute, three guards had entered the tunnel along with one of the mining engineers.

"Make a diagram of the three tunnels," he commanded the engineer. "Nothing fancy. Just something that shows us—the emperor—what direction they lead."

He ordered the guards to remain at the head of the third tunnel, while he and the lieutenant explored the other two.

The engineer was done with his task in less than two minutes. "Nothing fancy," the man had said—and the engineer didn't want to stay there any longer than he had to. His sketch completed, he crawled back through the opening into the area that had now been cleared of the rubble left behind by the great explosions.

He straightened up with a great sense of relief.

The lieutenant spotted the booby trap in his tunnel just in time to keep his foot from triggering the trip-wire.

His superior was less observant.

The charges in all three tunnels were wired together, of course. So the lieutenant's greater caution only gave him a split-second longer lifespan, before the tunnels collapsed. The guards at the third tunnel were just as surely crushed.

The engineer was knocked off his feet by the explosion, and then covered with the dust blown through the opening. He had just enough presence of mind to keep a grip on the sketch he'd made and protect it from harm.

That caution, also, proved to be of no value.

"This is useless," snarled Skandagupta, after a quick study of the sketch. "They could have gone anywhere."

The emperor crumpled up the sketch and hurled it at the engineer. "Impale him," he commanded.

Chapter 28
KAUSAMBI

"They'll be doing another search of the city," Anastasius said. "For sure and certain."

Lady Damodara looked around the stall in the stable that had been turned into her personal chamber. Then, she smiled very crookedly.

"Who would have thought the day would come that I'd regard a stable stall as luxurious surroundings?"

Lady Sanga was smiling just as crookedly. "Living in a tunnel gives you a sense of proportion. Anything is better than that. Still, Anastasius is right. We can't take the risk."

Lady Damodara sighed. "Yes. I know. The next search might be more thorough. There's really no way to keep soldiers out of this stable if they insist on coming in. As it is"—she gave Valentinian a sly glance—"we'll have to work hard and fast to remove any traces that we were here."

Valentinian returned the glance with a scowl. He'd argued against moving into the stable at all, preferring to remain the whole time in the enlarged tunnel below. Eventually, he'd given in, for the sole reason that providing the hideaways with enough edible food was too difficult if they stayed for very long in the tunnels.

The problem wasn't money. Lady Damodara had a fortune in coins and jewels, and had brought all of it with her into the tunnels. She had more than enough money to feed them all with the world's finest delicacies for years.

The problem was that large purchases of anything beyond simple foodstuffs would eventually be noticed by the city's authorities. And, unfortunately, the sort of cheap and readily available food that the stable-keeper's family could purchase without notice needed to be *cooked*.

Cooking in a stable was easy. Cooking in a tunnel was not.

Valentinian had then had to wage a mighty struggle to keep the Indians from decorating the stable so much that it would be impossible to disguise their occupancy.

Anastasius was more sanguine. "No problem. One full day of horse shit will disguise anything."

Both women laughed. The horses who'd formerly occupied that stable had been moved into adjoining ones, of course, but they could be moved back quickly and easily.

The stable-keeper had explained to the one customer who'd inquired that the move was due to his doubts regarding the structural soundness of the stable. Doubts which, truth be told, weren't entirely faked. The stable that the refugees were using as a hiding place *was* the most wretched and rickety building in the compound. Of course, that meant it was also the one it was impossible to see into, because of the extra bracing and shoring.

"No help for it," Lady Damodara stated firmly, when she was done laughing. "We'll make the move back into the tunnel this evening. And stop scowling, Valentinian! If we tried to move immediately, we'd be too careless in covering up all the signs that we've been here for weeks."

That was true enough, but it didn't stop Valentinian from scowling.

"Something will go wrong," he predicted.

In the event, nothing did go wrong. Skandagupta ordered another major search of the city. But, as with the initial search, the effort was undone by its very ambition.

"Scour Kausambi" was an easy order to give, from the imperial palace. From the viewpoint of the mass of soldiers on the ground who had to carry it out, the task looked very different. All the more so because they were never given any clear instructions or explanations as to exactly what they were looking for, beyond "the Lady Damodara and her entourage." Most of the soldiers who conducted the search were peasants, other than the Ye-tai, who were usually semi-barbarians and almost as likely to be illiterate. Their assumptions concerning where a "great lady" could expect to be found hiding simply didn't include stables.

A squad of soldiers searched the stables, to be sure. But their investigation was perfunctory. They didn't even enter the stall where the entrance to the tunnels below was located, much less give it the kind of search that might have uncovered the well-hidden trapdoor.

Not surprising, of course. That stall had more manure in it than any of them.

Still, Valentinian insisted that everyone stay below for three days following the search. Only after Tarun, the stable-keeper's oldest son, reported that the search seemed to have ended all over the city, did Valentinian let the people from the palace come up to enjoy the relative comforts of the stable.

"See?" demanded Anastasius, grinning.

Valentinian's scowl was just as dark as ever. "Don't be an idiot. This isn't going as well as we'd thought it would."

"What are you talking about?" Still grinning, Anastasius waved a huge hand in the direction of the imperial palace. "Tarun says they added four more heads to Skandagupta's collection, perched on pikes outside the palace gates. He thinks one of them was even a member of the dynasty."

"All that philosophy has rotted your brains. What do you think will happen *next*, Anastasius? I'll tell you what'll happen. Whoever the new batch of officers are in charge of the search, they'll throw still more men at digging out the rubble. Put enough hands to the work, and they could dig up the whole city. We're only a few hundred yards from the lady's palace, you know. That's really not that far, no matter how much we confused them with the doglegs."

The grin faded from Anastasius' face. "You think?"

"You're damn right 'I think.' I didn't worry about it, before, when we first came up with this scheme. Most of the tunnel passes under other buildings. To find out which direction it goes, once we collapsed the beginning of it, they can't just dig up soil. They have to level whole city blocks, in their own capital. Who's going to do that?"

Valentinian was literally chewing on his beard. "But I never expected Skandagupta to carry out this kind of reign of terror. I figured he'd be satisfied with one or two searches, and then give it up, figuring the lady had somehow managed to get out of the city altogether."

"Stop chewing on your beard. It's disgusting." As if to give his fellow cataphract a better example, Anastasius started tugging on his own beard. "How soon do you think Damodara and Sanga can get here?"

Valentinian shrugged. At least the gesture dislodged the beard from his mouth. "Who knows? Be at least another month. And even when they do get here, so what? They *still* have to get into the city. There's no way to break down these walls without siege guns—and there's no way Damodara could have brought them with him from the Deccan."

"I'm sure he has a plan," said Anastasius. Uncertainly.

"Sure he does," sneered Valentinian. "Use his new imperial semi-divine aura to overawe the garrison." Again, he shrugged. "It might even work, actually. But not quickly enough to save our necks. We've got to come up with a new plan."

"What?"

"I don't know. I'm thinking."

By the next morning, he had his plan. Such as it was.

Everyone agreed with the first part of the plan. The Bihari miners were sent back underground to prepare new false tunnels—with charges in them, naturally—at the two remaining doglegs.

They made no protest, other than technical ones. Even leaving aside the fact that they were intimidated by Valentinian, the miners knew full well that their lives were now completely bound up with that of Lady Damodara and her entourage. If the Malwa caught them, they'd be staked alongside the others.

"Where will we get the wood?" asked the chief miner. "There's no way to shore tunnels without wood. Even flimsy tunnels we're planning to blow up."

"Don't be stupid." Valentinian swept his head in a little half-circle. "We're in a stable, if you hadn't noticed. Several stables, in fact. Take the wood from the stalls. Just use every other board, so the horses can't get out."

✧   ✧   ✧

The stable-keeper protested, but that was more a matter of form than anything heartfelt. He, too, knew what would happen to himself and his entire family if the Malwa found them.

It was the second part of Valentinian's plan that stirred up the ruckus. Especially the part about Rajiv.

Rajiv himself, of course, was thrilled by the plan.

His mother was not.

"He's only thirteen!"

"That's the whole point," stated Valentinian. "Nobody notices kids. Especially if they're scruffy enough." He gave Rajiv a pointed look, to which the youngster responded with a grin.

"I can do 'scruffy.' Tarun will help."

The fourteen-year-old Tarun smiled shyly. He wasn't quite as thrilled by the plan as Rajiv, being a Bengali stable-keeper's son rather than a Rajput prince. But he had the natural adventurousness of a teenage boy, to which had been added something close to idol worship. Despite being a year older than Rajiv, Tarun was rather in awe of him—and delighted beyond measure that the Rajput prince had adopted him as a boon companion in time of trouble.

His parents, naturally, shared Lady Sanga's opinion.

"He's only fourteen!" wailed Tarun's mother.

"And small for his age," added his father.

"He's only a *little bit* small for his age," countered Rajiv. "But he's stronger than he looks—and, what's more important, he's very quick-witted. I don't have any hesitation at all about Tarun's part in the plan."

Tarun positively beamed.

Before the argument could spin around in another circle, Lady Damodara spoke. Hers was ultimately the authoritative voice, after all.

"Let's remember that there are *two* parts to Valentinian's plan, and it's the second part that everyone's arguing about. But we may never have to deal with that, anyway. So let's concentrate today on the first part, which is the only part that involves the two boys. Does anybody really have any strong objection to Rajiv joining Tarun in his expeditions into the city?"

Lady Sanga took a deep breath. "No." But the hostile look she gave Valentinian made her sentiments clear. Like all mothers since the dawn of time, Lady Sanga knew perfectly well that the difference between "part of the way" and "all of the way," when dealing with a teenage son, could not be measured by the world's greatest mathematicians. Or sorcerers, for that matter.

No more than Valentinian, did she think that *we may never have to deal with that* was an accurate prediction of the future.

Neither did Rajiv.

"It can be done," he told Valentinian four days later, after he and Tarun had finished their first round of scouting. "By you, at least. But not easily."

"I didn't think it would be *easy.*" Valentinian and Anastasius exchanged a glance. Then, turned to stare at Khandik and the other two Ye-tai mercenaries.

Khandik grinned, rather humorlessly. "Why not? Five against a hundred."

"More like eighty," qualified Rajiv.

"Eighty-three," specified Tarun.

Everyone stared at him. "I can count!" protested the Bengali boy. "You have to be able to count, running a stable."

Anastasius grunted. "Still, it's odds of sixteen or seventeen to one. All garrison troops, of course." He spit on the floor of the stable, as if to emphasize his low opinion of garrison soldiers.

"It's not that bad," said Valentinian. "At least half of them will be off duty."

"On *that* day?" demanded Khandik. "With tens of thousands of Rajputs howling at the gates? I don't think so."

Valentinian grimaced. "Well . . . true." He tugged at his beard. "But the way Rajiv and Tarun report the layout of the gate, we'd only have to deal with some of them."

"If we move fast enough," agreed Rajiv.

Now, it was everyone's turn to stare at Rajiv.

"What's this 'we' business?" demanded Anastasius.

Rajiv squared his shoulders. "It'll go easier if I'm already inside."

"Me too!" said Tarun proudly. "Rajiv and me already figured it out."

Valentinian slanted his head skeptically. "And just why would you be invited in? Other than to be a catamite, which I don't recommend as a way to augment your princely status."

Rajiv made a face. So did Tarun, who stuck out his tongue in the bargain. *"Uck!"*

"It's not that," said Rajiv. For a moment, he had an uncertain expression on his face. An uncomfortable one, actually. "The soldiers are pretty friendly, to tell you the truth. Even their leaders, except for the captain. He's a kshatriya, but the rest are just peasants, including the four sergeants. Most of them Bengalis, just like Tarun. They've got their wives and kids in the barracks with them, too, remember. Lots of kids, and all ages—and the barracks are almost part of the gate itself. After a while, if Tarun and I spend enough time there, nobody will notice us coming or going."

"On *that* day?" asked Khandik skeptically.

Rajiv shrugged. "I think especially on that day. Who's going to pay any attention to me—when my father is on the other side of the gate, making threats and issuing promises?"

That brought a round of soft laughter to the small group of soldiers clustered in a corner of the stable.

"Well," said Khandik. "That's true."

Hearing the laughter, Lady Sanga scowled. She and Lady Damodara were perched on cushions in another part of the stable.

"See?" she demanded.

Her companion made a wry face. "I'm glad my son is only seven."

Lady Sanga sniffed. "Guard him carefully. Or the next thing you know, Valentinian will have him practicing with sticks."

Lady Damodara looked startled. Just the other day, she'd noticed . . .

"He wouldn't!"

"He would."

But even the two ladies were in a better mood, nine days later.

Ajatasutra showed up. At last!

"Wasn't hard," he said cheerfully. "They're still not screening anyone at the city's gates very thoroughly. Skandagupta's an idiot, trying to suppress the news of the rebellion the way he is. The rumors are flying all over already—ten times more so, once the emperor reaches the Yamuna, which he should be doing pretty soon. But since nothing is officially confirmed by Skandagupta and his officials, and no clear orders are being given, the soldiers are still going about their business as usual. They're mostly peasants, after all. None of their business, the doings of the high and mighty."

"You look tired," said Dhruva. Hearing the concern in her voice, Valentinian frowned. Seeing the frown, Anastasius had to fight down a grin.

Valentinian, jealous. Would wonders never cease?

Smiling—tiredly—Ajatasutra shrugged. "Well, yes. I've come something like seven hundred miles in less than two weeks, since I left the emperor. Even as much time as I've spent in the saddle in my life, my legs feel like they're about to fall off. Best we not discuss at all the state of my buttocks."

Once the emperor reaches the Yamuna. Since I left the emperor.

Lady Damodara almost shivered, at the casual and matter-of-fact manner of those statements. When she'd last seen her husband, he'd been simply the man she'd known and come to love since their wedding. They'd been but teenagers, at the time. He, sixteen; and she, a year younger.

Now, today . . .

"Oh, forgot." Ajatasutra started digging in his tunic. "Rana Sanga—the emperor also, once he saw—asked me to bring you gifts. Nothing fancy, of course, traveling as lightly as I was."

His hand emerged, holding two small onions. One, he gave to Lady Sanga; the other, to Lady Damodara.

Rana Sanga's wife burst into tears. Lady Damodara just smiled.

She even managed to keep the smile on her face a minute later. Ajatasutra had addressed her as "Your Majesty" from the moment he arrived, and had done so throughout the long report he'd given them. But she hadn't really thought much of it. That just seemed part of the project of disguise and deception she'd been involved with for over a year, now. Hearing him—so casually, so matter-of-factly!—refer to her as *the Empress* to Lady Sanga, was a different thing altogether.

After Ajatasutra left her part of the stable, to confer with the soldiers in their own corner, Lady Damodara gave vent to her confusion and uncertainty.

"I don't *feel* any different."

Her companion smiled. Rana Sanga's wife had become Lady Damodara's close friend, over the past months. The closest friend she'd ever had, in fact.

"Oh, but you are. Your semi-divine aura is quite noticeable now."

"Even when I shit?" Lady Damodara pointed to a chamber pot not more than five feet away. "Damn this stable, anyway."

Sanga's wife grimaced. "Well. Maybe you need to work on that part. On the other hand, why bother? Before too long, you'll either be dead or be crapping in the biggest palace in the world. With fifty chambermaids to carry out the results, and twenty spies and three executioners to make sure they keep their mouths shut about the contents."

Lady Damodara laughed.

A few minutes later, hearing the soft laughter coming from the knot of soldiers in the corner of the stable, she frowned.

"My son's not over there, is he?" But, looking around, she spotted him playing with two of the other small boys in a different part of the stable. So, her frown faded.

Lady Sanga's frown, on the other hand, had deepened into a full scowl.

"No. But my son *is*."

"Only fifteen-to-one odds," said Khandik with satisfaction, "now that Ajatasutra's here."

Young Tarun shook his head. "Thirteen-to-one. Well. A bit more."

The glare bestowed upon him by the Ye-tai mercenary was a half-and-half business. On the one hand, it was unseemly for a mere stable-boy—a wretched Bengali, to boot—to correct his superior and elder. On the other hand . . .

"Thirteen-to-one," he said, with still greater satisfaction.

His two mates weren't even half-glaring. In fact, they were almost smiling.

Under normal circumstances, of course, thirteen-to-one odds would have been horrible. But those Ye-tai mercenaries were all veterans. The kind of fighting they were considering would not be the clash of huge armies on a great battlefield, where individual prowess usually got lost in the sheer mass of the conflict. No, this would be the sort of small-scale action out of which legends were made, because legends mattered.

The Mongoose was already a legend. His huge Roman companion wasn't, but they had no difficulty imagining him as such. "Bending horseshoes," with Anastasius in the vicinity, was not a phrase to express the impossible.

As for Ajatasutra . . .

"Some people think you're the best assassin in India," said one of the Ye-tai.

"Not any Marathas," came the immediate rejoinder. Smiling, Ajatasutra added: "But I think even Marathas might allow me the honor of second-best."

Chapter 29
THE IRON TRIANGLE

"It's just impossible," said Anna wearily, leaning her head against her husband's shoulder. "That great mass of people out there isn't really a city. It's a huge refugee camp, with more people pouring into it every day. Just when I think I've got one problem solved, the solution collapses under the weight of more refugees."

Calopodius stroked her hair, listening to the cannonade outside the bunker. The firing seemed a lot heavier than usual, on the Malwa side. He wondered if they might be getting nervous. By now, their spies were sure to have reported that a large Persian army had been camped briefly just across the river from the Iron Triangle.

But he gave only a small part of his mind to that matter. He had much more pressing and immediate things to deal with.

"Have you given any thought as to what you'd like to do, after the war? With the rest of your life, I mean."

Anna's head stirred. "Some," she said softly.

"And what did you decide?"

Now, her head lifted off his shoulder entirely. He knew she was looking at him sideways.

"Do you care?" she asked, still more softly.

He started to respond with "of course," but the words died before they were spoken. He'd spent quite a bit of time thinking about Anna, lately, and knew full well that "of course" was not an answer that would have even occured to him a few months ago.

So, he simply said: "Yes. I do."

There was a pause for a few seconds. Then, Anna's head came back to nestle on his shoulder again. "I think I'd like to keep the Service going. Somehow or other. I like healing people."

Calopodius kissed her hair. It felt rich and luxurious to him; more so now, than when he'd been able to see it.

"All right," he said. "That shouldn't be too hard."

Anna issued a sound halfway between a snort and a chuckle. "Not too hard! It's *expensive*, husband. Not even your family's rich enough to subsidize medical charity on that scale. Not for very long. And once the war is over, the money Belisarius and the army have been giving me will dry up."

It was Calopodius' turn to hesitate. "Yes, I know. But . . . how would you feel about remaining here in India?"

"I wouldn't mind. But why India?"

"Lots of reasons. I've been thinking about our situation myself. But let's start with three. One that matters—I think—to you. One that matters to me. And one that would matter to my family. Perhaps more to the point, my family's coffers."

Her head came back off his shoulder and, a moment later, Calopodius could feel her shifting her weight entirely. Within a few seconds, she was no longer lying beside him on their pallet but was sitting on it cross-legged, facing him. He knew the sensation quite well. Whenever they had something to really talk about, Anna preferred to be sitting up.

"Explain."

"Let's start with you. You already know that if our world keeps the same historical pattern with regard to disease as the one we diverged from, a terrible plague is 'scheduled' to start in eight years or so. By the time it's over, millions of people in the Mediterranean world will be dead."

"It might have already started, in fact," Anna mused. "Somewhere in China. Where the death toll will be just as bad."

Calopodius nodded. He wasn't surprised that she'd remembered that part of the future history that Belisarius had imparted to them.

"Yes. It'll enter the Roman Empire in Alexandria, in the year 541. But it almost certainly got transmitted through India."

He heard Anna draw in a sharp breath. "I hadn't thought of that."

"Then I think you should start thinking about it. If you move fast enough—fast enough and with enough money and authority—between your Service and the Hospitalers in Alexandria, it might be possible to forestall the plague. Reduce its effects, anyway."

"There's no cure for it," she said. "And no . . . what's the word?"

"'Vaccine,'" Calopodius supplied.

"Yes. No vaccine. Not anything we could make in time, in sufficient quantities."

Calopodius shrugged. "True. But from what Belisarius told me Aide said to him, it wasn't really a medical 'cure' that defeated the plague in the future, anyway. It was mostly just extensive and thorough public health and sanitation. Stuff as simple and plebeian as good sewers and clean drinking water. That *is* within our technological capacity."

He listened to Anna breathing, for a while. Then she said: "It would take a lot of money, and a lot of political influence."

"Yes. It'd be a life's work. Are you willing?"

She laughed abruptly. "*I'm* willing. But is the money willing? And . . ." Her voice lowered. "I really don't want to do anything that you wouldn't be happy with."

He smiled. "Not to worry! What *I* want to do is write histories and public commentaries. But what do I write about, once the war is over?"

He moved right on to supply the answer: "Write about India, that's what. Just think of it, love. An entire *continent*. One that Rome knows almost nothing about and with a history even longer than Rome's."

Silence.

"Your life's work, then," Anna mused. Then, issued that same abrupt laugh. "So where's the money to come from?"

His smile widened, becoming very close to a grin. "Well, we'll have to keep it hidden from your family. Even from mine, the rough details. But you and I are about to found a branch of the Saronites enterprises, here in India. Crude stuff, I'm afraid. Manufacturing, mostly."

He wasn't surprised at all that the woman his wife had become did not even stumble over the prospect. "Manufacturing what?"

"I thought we'd start with medical supplies and equipment. Also pharmaceuticals. Nothing fancy, though. Mostly soap, dyes and cosmetics, at the beginning. Belisarius told me those were the substances that were the big money-makers for the chemical industry when it got really started in the future. In what he calls the 'industrial revolution.' Once the business gets rolling, we can expand into medicines."

"And exactly which one of us is going to oversee and organize this grand scheme of yours?" she demanded.

"Neither of us. We just front the money—I can get enough to start from my father—and we—mostly you—provide the political influence. I figured we could bring up your banker from Barbaricum—"

"Pulinda?"

"Yes, him. He's shrewd as they come, and he knows India. For running the technical end, we'll use Eusebius."

"If he agrees. He might not—"

"I already asked him. He says he'd love to. He's tired of figuring out new ways to kill people."

"You *already* asked him?"

"Yes. And I think Justinian will go for it, too. Not directly, of course. He's got to get back to Constantinople as soon as the war's over or Theodora will send out the executioners. But he's intrigued by the idea and says he's sure he can siphon us some imperial financing—provided he gets to play with the gadgets at his end."

The pallet lurched. Calopodius knew that Anna had risen to her feet. Jumped to her feet, more like.

"You asked the Emperor of Rome to be our business partner in a manufacturing scheme? *Are you out of your mind?*"

"He's not the emperor any longer, dear," Calopodius pointed out mildly. "Photius is."

"Still!"

"He's the Grand Justiciar. And you know how much he loves to play with gadgets."

"My husband!" Anna burst into laughter that was not abrupt at all.

Kungas came to his decision and moved away from the window looking out over Peshawar. "All right," he said, "we'll do it."

He gave the small group of Ye-tai deserters a gaze that wasn't cold so much as simply impassive. The way a glacier contemplates so many rocks who might be in its way when it ground forward to the sea. More indifferent than icy, since the outcome was inevitable.

The Ye-tai were squatting on the floor of his private audience chamber. They seemed like so many rocks, indeed, as motionless as they were. And for good reason. First, they were disarmed. Second, the Kushan soldiers standing around and guarding them were armed to the teeth. Third, there was no love lost between Kushans and Ye-tai to begin with. Hadn't been for a century, since the invading Ye-tai had broken the Kushan kingdom that Kungas had re-created.

"If you're lying, of course, you're dead men."

The Ye-tai squad leader made a shrug that was as minimal as any Kungas himself might have made. "Why would we lie?"

"I can't think of any reason myself. Which is why I decided to believe you." Kungas' crack of a smile came. "Besides, Sarmatians are noted for their honesty. Even half-Sarmatians."

That little joke brought a ripple of laughter in the room, as much from the Kushan guards as the Ye-tai prisoners. For the first time since they'd been ushered into the chamber—frog-marched, more like—the Ye-tai visibly relaxed.

Although his thin smile had remained, Kungas had not joined the laughter. When it ended, he shook his head.

"I'm not joking, really. You six are the founding members of my new military unit. If you're not lying—and I'm assuming you aren't—then you won't be the last Malwa deserters coming over to us. So I think I'll enroll all of you in the . . . What to call it?"

Irene piped up, sitting on a chair to one side. "The Royal Sarmatian Guards."

"That'll do nicely." Kungas turned to his lieutenants. "Get the army formed up. I want to march out tomorrow morning, early. Leave five thousand men in the capital."

"I won't need that many," said Irene. "Three thousand is plenty to maintain order and keep the hill tribes from getting any ideas."

Kungas thought about it, and decided she was right. He could leave the additional two thousand men with the five thousand already garrisoning the forts in the passes at Margalla and Kohat. That would secure the gates to the kingdom and leave him almost twenty thousand men to do . . .

Whatever. He didn't know yet. He was quite sure the Ye-tai deserters weren't lying. But that didn't necessarily mean their assessment of things was all that accurate, either.

Still, he thought it was probably was. Close enough, anyway. Kungas had been fighting almost since he was a boy. There was that smell in the air, of an enemy starting to come apart.

When Jaimal caught his first glimpse of the walls of Ajmer, he felt the greatest exhilaration he'd ever felt in his life. Even though he was also completely exhausted.

He glanced at Udai Singh, riding next to him at the head of the small Rajput cavalry column, and saw the same gleaming smile he must have had on his own face.

"A ride of legend!" Udai shouted. Half-croaked, rather.

Shouted or croaked, it was true. And the ragged chorus of that same half-croaked shout coming from the fifty cavalry- men following told Jaimal that their men knew it as well as they did.

Rajputana was a land of horsemen, as well as warriors. A great horse ride would become a thing of renown just as surely as a great feat of arms.

Emperor Damodara and Rana Sanga had asked them to accom- plish the incredibly difficult task of riding from Bharakuccha to Ajmer in two weeks. If possible.

They'd done it in eleven days. Without losing more than nine of their horses.

"A ride of legend!" he shouted himself.

But there was no need for that, really. Already, he could see the gates of the city opening, and cavalrymen issuing forth. Hundreds of them. Even from the great distance, just seeing the way they rode, he knew they were all young men. Seeking their own place in legends.

Jaimal and Udai would give it to them.

Standing on the walls of Ajmer and watching the way the young warriors who had poured out of the city were circling the new arrivals—there were at least a thousand of them, now, with more sallying from the gates every minute—the oldest and therefore wisest king of Rajputana knew it was hopeless. That was a whirlwind of celebration and excitement, out there.

Caution and sagacity would soon become so many leaves blown by the monsoon.

"Perhaps . . ." began Chachu.

Dasal shook his head. Standing next to him, his brother Jaisal did likewise.

"Not a chance," said Jaisal curtly. "*Look* at them, out there."

"We don't even know what it's about, yet," whined Chachu. One of the other kings who formed the council grunted something in the way of agreement.

Dasal shrugged. "Don't be foolish. No, we don't know *exactly* what news—or instructions—that cavalry column is bringing. But the gist of it is obvious."

He nodded toward the column, which was now advancing toward the gates with over a thousand other Rajput cavalrymen providing them with what was, for all practical purposes, an escort of honor.

"The new emperor sent them. Or Rana Sanga. Or both. And they will be demanding the allegiance of all Rajputs. So what do we say?"

He had no answer, himself. The Rajput heart that beat within him was just as eager as any of those young warriors out there. But that heart had now beaten for almost eighty years, each and every year of which had hammered caution into his mind, whatever his heart might feel.

"Let's return to the council chamber and await them there," suggested Jaisal.

That might help. A bit.

"Yes," Dasal said.

But when they returned to the council chamber, they discovered it had been preempted from them already. The seven thrones had been removed from their accustomed places in a half-circle at the elevated dais. They were now resting, still in a half-circle, *facing* the dais.

On the dais itself, sat only one chair. A smaller and less ostentatious chair, as it happened, than the seven chairs of the kings. And the man who sat in it was smaller—certainly more rotund—than any of the kings.

But it hardly mattered. Dasal understood who he was before he even spoke.

Chachu, as usual, had to be enlightened.

"I am Great Lord Damodara," the short, fat old man said. "The emperor's father. I am the new viceroy of Rajputana. And you will obey me."

Behind him, in a row, stood half a dozen Malwa bodyguards. Assassins, to call things by their right name. More to the point, at least fifty young Rajput warriors were standing alongside the walls of the chamber. Each and every one of whom was glaring at the seven kings.

Suddenly, the plump face of Great Lord Damodara broke into a smile. The expression made him seem a much friendlier sort of fellow.

"But, please!" he exclaimed, waving his hand at the seven chairs before him. "Take your seats, Kings of Rajputana."

Dasal considered the courtesy. Then, considered the titles. Finally, considered the chairs.

The chairs made the decision. They were the same chairs, after all. Very august ones. Not to mention comfortable.

He felt relief more than anything else. Clearly enough, the new regime in the land of the Rajputs was willing to accommodate the status—if not the authority—of the old one.

He was almost eighty years old, after all. Even the youngest of the seven kings of the council was past seventy.

"Yes, Great Lord." Dasal moved forward and sat in his accustomed chair. He gave his half dozen fellows an abrupt nod, commanding them to follow.

They did so, readily enough. Only Chachu made a token protest.

"I don't understand," he whined. "If you're still alive, why aren't *you* the new emperor instead of your son?"

The smile on the Great Lord's face stayed in place, but it got an ironic twist.

"Good question. I'll have to take it up with my headstrong son when we meet again. For the moment, I ascribe it to the monsoon times we're living in."

The smile became serene. "But I don't imagine I'll argue the point with him. Actually, it might make for a good tradition. When emperors—and kings—get too old, they tend to get too set in their ways. Best to have them retire and take up some prestigious but less demanding post, while their son assumes the heavier responsibilities. Don't you think?"

The smile was friendly. But the assassins were still there, not smiling at all. And the young warriors were still glaring.

"Indeed, Great Lord," said Dasal.

His brother echoed him immediately. Chachu, thankfully, kept his mouth shut.

Or, at least, kept his mouth shut until the two leaders of the newly arrived cavalry column finished their report.

"That's madness!" Chachu exclaimed. "*Belisarius?*"

But Dasal had come to the opposite conclusion. The great lord was right. Old men *should* retire, when the time comes.

Especially when presented with such a fine way to do so.

"It's brilliant," he rebutted, rising to his feet. "And I will lead the force that goes into the Thar to find him."

His brother came to his feet also. "I'll go with you."

"You're too old!" protested Chachu.

The two brothers glared at him, with the combined indignation of one hundred and fifty-six years of life.

"I can still ride a horse!" snarled Dasal. "Even if *you* can't ride anything other than a chair any longer."

They left the following evening, just after sunset. No sane man rides into the desert during the day. Dasal and Jaisal had one hundred and fifty-six years of sanity between them.

The young warriors were impatient, of course. All seven thousand of them.

Especially impatient were the six thousand that the two kings had insisted ride on camels, carrying the water and other supplies that they were quite sure Belisarius needed. Leave it to an idiot Roman to try to cross the desert without camels. Relying on wells! In the Thar!

Most impatient of all were the ten thousand—with more coming into the city every day—whom Dasal had insisted remain behind. With, fortunately, the agreement and approval of the new viceroy of Rajputana. They would just be a nuisance in the expedition, and a new Rajput army had to be formed.

Formed quickly. The monsoon was coming.

Fortunately, Rana Sanga's two lieutenants Jaimal and Udai Singh had the authority and experience for the task. They needed a rest anyway, after their ride of legend. By the time Jaisal and

Dasal returned to Ajmer with Belisarius, the new army would be ready.

For ... whatever. Given Belisarius, it would be a thing of legend. Dasal only hoped he would live long enough to see it.

Assuming the idiot Roman was still alive. Crossing the Thar on horses! Relying on wells!

When the Malwa assassination team finally rowed their ship into the great harbor at Bharakuccha, they knew another moment of frustration and chagrin.

"Look at that!" snarled one of them.

The captain of the team just shook his head. The docks and piers of the city seemed practically covered with a carpet of people, all of them come down to greet the Axumite fleet escorting the Emperor of Rome.

The fleet was already anchored. As they drew closer, the Malwa assassins could see the Roman imperial party being escorted to the great palace of the Goptri by a small army of Ethiopian sarwen.

Even if they'd been in position, there would have been no way to get to the boy emperor. And once he was in the palace ...

The captain of the assassination team and his lieutenant were both familiar with the great palace of the Goptri. As the palace of a conquering viceroy in a hostile land, serving a dynasty famous for its paranoia, it had been *designed* to thwart assassins. Unless the guards were utterly incompetent ...

"Ethiopian sarwen," the lieutenant grumbled. "And you can be sure that Raghunath Rao will be there to advise them."

The captain spent a moment adding up the miles he and his team had traveled, to carry out an assignment that always seem to recede before them in the distance. It had been like trying to assassinate a mirage in the desert.

From Kausambi to Bharakuccha to Alexandria to Constantinople. And then back again, almost all the way.

Something like ten thousand miles, he thought. Who could really know?

"Nothing for it," he said. "We'll sell the ship as soon as we can, since we're almost out of money. Then ... we'll just have to see what we can do."

❖   ❖   ❖

Finding a buyer for the ship was easy. Whether rightly and wrongly—and, more and more, the captain was beginning to wonder if they weren't right—the merchants of Bharakuccha seemed quite confident that the old Malwa empire was gone from the Deccan and that trade would soon be picking up.

They even got a better price than the captain had expected.

That was the first and last thing that went as planned. No sooner had they emerged from the merchant clearinghouse than a harried-looking official accosted them. Accompanied, unfortunately, by a large squad of soldiers.

Not regular Malwa soldiers, either, to make things worse. Marathas, from their look, newly impressed into the city's garrison. It seemed the new Axumite commander had given orders to form units from all residents of the city.

The captain sized them up. Eight of them there were, and tougher-looking than he liked. He didn't doubt that he and his four assassins could overcome them. But not without suffering casualties—and then what?

Five Malwa assassins in today's Bharakuccha, many if not all of them wounded, would be like so many pieces of bloody meat in shark waters.

"There you are!" the official exclaimed. "You *are* the trade delegation just returned from Rome, yes?"

That had been their official identity. The captain wondered how an official in Bharakuccha—the place was a madhouse!—had managed to keep track of the records and identify them so soon after their return.

He brought down a savage curse on all hard-working and efficient bureaucrats. A silent curse, naturally.

"Come with me!" the official commanded. "I've been instructed to send a courier team to catch up with the emperor"—he didn't even bother to specify the "new" emperor—"and you're just the men for the job!"

"I can't believe this," muttered his lieutenant. Very softly, of course.

The next morning, they were riding out of the city on excellent horses, carrying dispatches for Damodara. Along with a Maratha cavalry platoon to provide them with a safe escort out of the Deccan. The assassins were obviously Malwa—some sort of north Indians, at any rate—and despite the new truce between the Malwa and Andhran empires, it was always possible that a band of Maratha irregulars in the hills wouldn't obey it. Or would have simply turned to banditry, as some soldiers always do at the end of a war.

That same escort, needless to say, also made it impossible for them to return to Bharakuccha and continue their assignment. Not, at least, until they'd passed the crest of the Vindhyas—at which point, they have to return *another* hundred miles or so, and do it without being spotted by Maratha patrols.

The only bright spot in the whole mess was that their luggage hadn't been searched. If it had been, the bombard would have been discovered—and they'd have had a very hard time explaining why and how a "trade delegation" had been carrying an assassination device. A bombard of that size and type was never used by regular military units, and it would have been even more useless for trade delegates.

That night, around their campfire and far enough from the Maratha escort not to be overheard, the five assassins quietly discussed their options.

"It's hopeless," the captain concluded. "We've done our best. Let's just give it up and return to Kausambi for a new assignment."

His lieutenant finally said it. "That's assuming we don't find a new emperor when we get there. Then what?"

The captain shrugged, and spit into the fire.

More cheerily, one of the other assassins said: "Well, there's this. Whoever the emperor is when we get there, one thing's for sure. We won't be reporting failure to Nanda Lal. No matter what."

That was true. Perhaps the only certainty left in their lives. They'd all seen Nanda Lal's head perched on a pike outside the Goptri's palace. There hadn't been much left of it. But the captain and the lieutenant had recognized the nose. Broken, years ago, by the boot of Belisarius. Battered, at the end, by boys in their play.

Chapter 30
THE THAR DESERT

Belisarius finally managed to force his eyes somewhere else. Staring at the empty well wouldn't make it fill up.

Not that he found the sight of the desert any prettier.

"So, I gambled and lost," he said to Ashot and Abbu, standing next to him.

Ashot was still scowling down into the well. Abbu was scowling at the desert, his eyes avoiding the general's.

"It's not your fault, Abbu."

The old bedouin grimaced. "This well was one of the best!" he protested. "I was worried about the last one. And another one some twenty miles farther. Not this one!"

Finally, Ashot straightened up. "Wells are finicky in a desert like this. If the water table was reliable, we wouldn't have had to dig our own. There'd have been wells already here."

The Armenian cataphract wiped the dust off his face with a cloth. "What do we do now, General? We don't have enough water left to make the crossing to the next well. Not the whole expedition, for sure. A few dozen could make it, maybe, if they took all the water we still have."

"For what purpose?" Belisarius demanded. Not angrily, just wearily.

He leaned over the well again, gauging the dampness at the very bottom. There wasn't much.

There were two decisions to be made. One was obvious to probably everyone. The other was obvious to him.

"No," he said. "We'll send a very small force—five men—with all the water they need to cross the rest of the Thar without stopping. They might be able to reach Ajmer in time to bring a Rajput relief expedition, if Rana Sanga's already gotten the word there."

Ashot winced. Abbu shook his head.

"That's a lot of 'ifs,' General," said the Armenian. "*If* they can cross in time. *If* the Rajputs are already prepared. *If* they'll listen to a handful of men in the first place. *If* they can get back in time with water before the rest of us are dead."

"The first 'if' is the easiest, too," Abbu added. "And it stinks. Five men, crossing as fast as they can . . . It would still take them at least five days. Another week—at least—before they could get back with enough water to make a difference. That's twelve days, General, at best."

Belisarius had already figured out the deadly arithmetic. If anything, Abbu was being optimistic—one of the few times Belisarius could ever remember him being so. Belisarius himself thought the minimum would be two weeks.

In the desert, in the hot season, a man without water could not survive for more than two days before he started to die. And he died quickly, thereafter. Maybe three days, depending on the temperature. That assumed he found shelter from the sun and didn't exert himself. If he did, death would come much sooner.

If the Roman expedition shared all their remaining water evenly—and gave none to the horses—they'd run out in three days. At most, the moisture still seeping into the bottom of the well might provide them with another day's water. Then . . .

They might last a little over a week, all told. Not two weeks, certainly. Probably not even twelve days.

There was no way to go back or to go forward, either. The last well was four days behind them, and it would be almost dry anyway after their recent use of it. The next well was at least two and a half days' travel, according to Abbu, for a party this size. Since they had to water the horses also, while traveling, they'd run out within the first day. The last two days they'd be without water.

So would the horses.

They'd never make it. Not in the Thar, in the hot season.

"I understand the arithmetic," Belisarius said harshly. "It's still our only chance."

The second decision, then.

"You'll lead the party, Ashot. Abbu, you go with him. Pick three of your bedouin for the remaining men."

Ashot's eyes widened, a little. Abbu's didn't.

"You're not going yourself?"

"No. I'll stay here with the men."

"But—"

"Be off, Ashot. There's no time to waste. And there will be no argument. No discussion at all."

He turned and started walking away from the well.

Are you sure? asked Aide, uncertainly.

Yes. These men have been with me for years. I'm not leaving them to die. Not that, whatever else.

Aide said nothing. His own survival was not at stake. There were things that could destroy Aide, Belisarius knew, although the jewel had always been reticent about explaining exactly what they were. But merely being without water for a few weeks—or even a few years—was not one of them.

When Ashot returned, most likely he would find Aide in a pouch hanging from a corpse's neck. But the jewel would be as alive as ever.

Working through Ousanas would be the easiest for you, I think, Belisarius mused. *But he's probably not influential enough. You might try Rao, although there might be the same problem. The best would be Damodara, if you could reach him.*

I don't want to talk about it.

I understand. Still—

I don't want to talk about it.

Ashot and Abbu left after sundown. Once they were gone, Belisarius addressed his bucellarii and the remaining Arab scouts.

"We don't have much of a chance, men. But it'll be improved if we set up good shelters from the sun. So let's work on that tonight. Also, we want to eat as little as possible. Eating uses up water, too."

One of the cataphracts asked: "Are you going to set up a rationing system?"

Several of the Arabs who heard the question started shaking their heads.

"No," said Belisarius firmly. "Once we make an even division of what's left, drink whenever you're thirsty. If fact, after a few hours, drink something even if you're not thirsty."

That cataphract and a few others seemed confused. Apparently, they didn't have much experience with the desert.

"Rationing water as a way of staying alive in the desert is a fable," Belisarius explained. "It does more harm than good. You're only going to live as long as your body has enough water, no matter what you do. All rationing does is weaken you quicker. So drink as much as you want, whenever you want. The bigger danger, actually, is that you won't drink often enough."

One of the bedouin grunted his agreement. "Listen to the general."

"Oh, sure," said the cataphract hastily. "I was just wondering."

Later that night, after the camp was made, Aide spoke for the first time since the decision had been made.

They seem so confident.

They're not, really. But since I stayed with them, they have a barrier to fear.

Yes. I understand. I always wondered.

Wondered what?

Why Alexander the Great poured onto the sand a helmet full of water that one of his soldiers had offered him, in that terrible retreat from India through the desert. It just seemed flamboyant, to me.

Belisarius smiled. *Well, it* was *flamboyant. But that was the nature of the man. I'd have just told the soldier to return the water to the common share. That difference aside, yes, that's why he did it. His men might have died anyway. But by refusing the water, Alexander made sure they didn't panic. Which would have killed them even quicker.*

I understand now.

We still need to talk about the future. Your future. If you can reach Damodara—

I don't want to talk about that.

After a while, he added: **I'm not ready.**

I understand. We have some days yet.

✧   ✧   ✧

Meeting Raghunath Rao in the flesh was perhaps the oddest experience Antonina had ever had. That was not so much because she already knew a great deal about him, but because of one specific thing she knew.

In another world, another future, another time, another universe, she had met the man. Had known him for decades, in fact, since he'd been Belisarius' slave.

In the end, she'd been murdered by the Malwa. Murdered, and then flayed, so her skin-sack could serve as another trophy. In his last battle in that universe, Belisarius had rescued her skin, and taken it with him when he leapt into a cauldron.

She knew the story, since her husband had told her once. And she also knew that it had been Rao who washed the skin, to cleanse it of the Malwa filth, before her husband took it into the fire.

What did you say to a man who had once washed your flayed skin?

Nice to finally meet you?

That seemed . . . idiotic.

But the time had come. Having exchanged greetings with the Empress of Andhra, Antonina was now being introduced to her consort.

Rao bowed deeply, then extended his hands.

She clasped them, warmly.

"It's nice to finally meet you," she said. Feeling like an idiot.

"Use the mortars," Kungas commanded. "As many as we've got."

"We've got a *lot* of mortars," Kujulo pointed out.

"I know. Use all of them."

Kungas pointed at the Malwa army scrambling away from the pass. Obviously, whatever else they'd expected, they hadn't thought Kungas would come plunging out of the Hindu Kush with twenty thousand men. Like a flash flood of steel.

"They're already panicked. Pound them, Kujulo. Pound them as furiously as you can. I don't care if we run out of gunpowder in a few minutes. Mortars will do it."

Less than an hour later, the way out of the Peshawar Vale was clear. The Malwa army guarding Margalla pass had broken like a stick. Splintered, rather, with pieces running everywhere.

"No pursuit," Kungas commanded. "It'll take the Malwa days to rally them. That gives us time to reach the headwaters of the Sutlej before an army can reach us from Multan."

Kujulo cocked his head. "You've decided, then?"

"Yes. We'll take the gamble. I want that bitch dead. With us coming behind her, right on her heels, we can drive her into the trap."

"What trap?"

"The one Belisarius will be setting for her."

Kujulo cocked his head the other way. Kungas had to fight down a chuckle. With the plume on his helmet, he reminded the king of a confused bird.

"Ah. You've been told something."

"No," said Kungas. "I'm just guessing."

His head still cocked, Kujulo winced. "Big gamble. Based on a guess."

"Kushans love to gamble."

"True."

After Kujulo left to organize the march, Kungas summoned the Ye-tai deserters. They'd been standing nearby, garbed in their fancy new uniforms. Irene had had them made up quickly by her seamstresses, substituting flamboyance where time hadn't allowed good workmanship.

The armor, of course, was the same they'd been wearing when they arrived in Peshawar. The well-worn and utilitarian gear looked especially drab, against that colorful new fabric and gaudy design.

"You're promoted," he told the squad leader. "I think we'll use Greek ranks for the Royal Sarmatian Guards. That'll make you sound exotic. Exciting."

"Whatever you say, Your Majesty."

"You're a tribune. The rest are hecatontarchs."

The squad leader pondered the matter, briefly.

"What do those titles mean, exactly? Your Majesty."

"I'd say that's up to you, isn't it? Get me some deserters. Lots of them." He waved a hand at the low hills around them, much of their slopes now shadowed by the setting sun. "They'll be out there."

"Ye-tai only?"

Kungas shrugged. "You won't find many other than Ye-tai bold enough to come in. But it doesn't matter. Anyone who's willing to swear his mother was Sarmatian."

After the king left, the tribune turned to his mates.

"You see?" he demanded.

When the Emperor of Malwa reached the door leading into the inner sanctum of the imperial palace—the ultimate inner sanctum; the real one—he paused for a moment, his lips tightly pursed.

That was partly because he'd have to submit to a personal search, the moment he entered, at the hands of Link's special Khmer guards. It was the only time the divine emperor suffered such an indignity. As the years had passed, Skandagupta found that increasingly distasteful.

But that was only part of the matter, and probably not the largest part. The emperor hadn't come down here in well over a year. Entering the inner sanctum below the palace was always disturbing, in a way that dealing with Malwa's overlord through one of the Great Ladies who served as its sheath was not.

He wasn't sure why. Perhaps because the machines in the chambers beyond were completely unfathomable. A cold, metallic reminder that even the Malwa emperor himself was nothing but a device, in the hands of the new gods.

He wasn't even sure why he had come, this day. He'd been driven simply by a powerful impulse to do so.

Skandagupta was not given to introspection, however. A few seconds later, he opened the door.

There was no lock. He'd had to pass through several sets of guards to get down here, and the chamber immediately beyond the door had more guards still. Those quiet, frightening special assassins.

The personal inspection was brief, but not perfunctory in the least. Feeling polluted by the touch of the guards' hands, Skandagupta was ushered into the inner sanctum.

Great Lady Rani was there to greet him. She would be Great Lady Sati's replacement, whenever the time came. Standing against a nearby wall, their heads submissively bowed, were the four Khmer women who attended her, simultaneously, as servants, confidants—and, mostly, tutors. They were trained in the cult's temple in far-off Cambodia, and then trained still further by Link itself once they arrived in Kausambi.

"Welcome, Emperor," said Great Lady Rani, in that eight-year-old girl's voice that was always so discordant to Skandagupta.

No more so than Sati's had once been, of course. Or, he imagined, Holi's in times past, although he himself was not old enough to remember Holi as a small girl. Link's sheaths, once selected, were separated from the dynastic clan and brought up in ways that soon made them quite unlike any other girls. Link would not consume them until the time came, once their predecessor had died. But the overlord communed with them frequently beforehand, using the machines—somehow—to instill its spirit into their child's minds. By the time they were six, they were no longer children in any sense of that term that meant anything.

"What may I do for you?"

The emperor didn't answer for a moment, his eyes moving across the machines in a corner. He did not understand those machines; never had, and never would. He did not even understand how Link had managed to bring them here from the future, all those many years ago. Malwa's overlord had told him once that the effort had been so immense—so expensive, in ways of calculating cost that Skandagupta did not understand either—that it would be impossible to duplicate.

"What may I do for you?" she repeated.

The emperor shook his head impatiently. "Nothing, really. I just wanted . . ."

He couldn't find the conclusion to that sentence. He tried, but couldn't.

"I just wanted to visit, " he finally said, lamely. "See how you were."

"How else would I be?" The eyes in the eight-year-old face belonged to no woman at all, of any age. "Ready, as I have always been."

Skandagupta cleared his throat. "Surely it won't come to that. Not for many years. Great Lady Sati is still quite young."

"Most likely. But nothing is certain."

"Yes. Well."

He cleared his throat again. "I'll be going, now."

When he reached the landing of the stairs that led down to the inner sanctum, he was puffing heavily from the climb and not for the first time wishing he could make the trip in a palanquin carried by slaves.

Impossible, of course. Not only was the staircase much too narrow, but Link would have forbidden it anyway.

Well, not exactly. Link would allow slaves to come down to the inner sanctum. It had done so, now and then, for an occasional special purpose.

But then the Khmer assassins killed them, so what was the point? The emperor would *still* have to climb back up.

He was in a foul mood, therefore, when he reached his private audience chamber and was finally able to relax on his throne.

After hearing what his aides had to report, his mood grew fouler still.

"They blew up the tunnels *again*?" Angrily, he slapped the armrest of the throne. "That's enough! Tear down every building in that quarter of the city, within three hundred yards of Damodara's palace. Raze it all to the ground! Then dig up everything. They can't have placed mines everywhere."

He took a deep breath. "And have the commander of the project executed. Whoever he is."

"He did not survive the explosion, Your Majesty."

Skandagupta slapped the armrest again. "Do as I command!"

His aides hurried from the chamber, before the emperor's wrath could single out one of them to substitute for the now-dead commander. Despite the great rewards, serving Skandagupta had always been a rather risky proposition. If not as coldly savage as his father, he was also less predictable and given to sudden whims.

In times past, those whims had often produced great largesse for his aides.

No longer. The escape of Damodara's family, combined with Damodara's rebellion, had unsettled Skandagupta in ways that the Andhran and Persian and Roman wars had never done. For weeks, his whims had only been murderous.

"This is madness," murmured one aide to another. He allowed himself that indiscretion, since they were brothers. "What difference does it make, if they stay in hiding? Unless Damodara can breach the walls—if he manages to get to Kausambi at all—what does it matter? Just a few more rats in a cellar somewhere, a little bigger than most."

They were outside the palace now, out of range of any possible spies or eavesdroppers. Gloomily, the aide's brother agreed. "All the emperor's doing is keeping the city unsettled. Now, the reaction when we destroy an entire section . . ."

He shook his head. "Madness, indeed."

But since they were now walking past the outer wall of the palace, the conversation ended. No fear of eavesdroppers here, either. But the long row of ragged heads on pikes—entire rotting bodies on stakes, often enough—made it all a moot point.

Obey or die, after all, is not hard to understand.

Abbu returned the next day, with his Arab scouts.

"Ashot stayed behind, with the Rajputs," he explained tersely. "Just keep out of the sun and don't move any more than you must. They'll be here tomorrow. Thousands of camels, carrying enough water to fill a lake. We won't even lose the horses."

Belisarius laughed. "What an ignominious ending to my dramatic gesture!"

Now that salvation was at hand, Abbu's normally pessimistic temperament returned.

"Do not be so sure, General! Rajputs are cunning beasts. It may be a trap. The water, poisoned."

That made Belisarius laugh again. "Seven thousand Rajputs need poisoned water to kill five hundred Romans?"

"You have a reputation," Abbu insisted.

Chapter 31
THE PUNJAB,
NORTH OF THE IRON TRIANGLE

"This is the craziest thing I've ever seen," muttered Maurice. "Even for Persians."

Menander shook his head. Not because he disagreed, but simply in . . .

Disbelief?

No, not that. Sitting on his horse on a small knoll with a good view of the battlefield, Menander could *see* the insane charge that Emperor Khusrau had ordered against the Malwa line.

He could also see the fortifications of that line itself, and the guns that were spewing forth destruction. He didn't even want to think about the carnage that must be happening in front of them.

He could remember a time in his life when he would have thought that furious charge might carry the day. However insane it was, no one could doubt the courage and the tenacity of the thousands of Persian heavy cavalrymen who were hurling themselves and their armored horses against the Malwa. But, even though he was still a young man, Menander had now seen enough of gunpowder warfare to know that the Persian effort was hopeless. If the Malwa had been low on ammunition, things might have been different. But the fortifications they'd erected on the west bank of the Indus to guard their flank against just

315

such an attack could be easily resupplied by barges crossing the river. In fact, he could see two such barges being rowed across the Indus right now.

Against demoralized troops already half-ready to surrender or flee, the charge might have worked. It wouldn't work here. The morale of the Malwa army had suffered a great deal, to be sure, from their defeats over the past two years. But they were still the largest and most powerful army in the world, and their soldiers knew it.

They knew something else, too. They knew that trying to surrender to—or flee from—an assault like the Persians had launched, was impossible anyway. If they broke, they'd just get butchered.

It didn't help any, of course, that the Persians were shouting the battle cry of *Charax!* as they charged. Whether because their emperor had ordered it or because of their own fury, Menander didn't know. But he knew—and so did the Malwa soldiers manning the fortresses—that the Persians might as well have been using the battle cry of *No Quarter.*

"Let's go, lad," said Maurice quietly. "We made an appearance as observers, since Khusrau invited us. But now that the diplomacy's done, staying any longer is just pointless. This isn't really a battle, in the first place. It's just an emperor ridding himself of troublesome noblemen."

He turned his horse and began trotting away. Menander followed.

"You think?" asked Menander.

"You've met Khusrau. Did he strike you as being as dumb as an ox?"

Menander couldn't help but smile, a little. "No. Not in the least."

"Right." Maurice jerked a thumb over his shoulder. "Not even an ox would be dumb enough to think that charge might succeed."

Maurice was slandering the Persian emperor, actually. It was true that breaking the power of the sahrdaran and vurzurgan families was part of the reason Khusrau had ordered the charge. But it wasn't the only reason. It wasn't even the most important reason.

There would be no way to eliminate the great families simply through one battle, after all. Not all of their men had come to

India, even leaving aside the Suren, and not all of them would die before the walls of the Malwa.

Not even most of them, in fact. Khusrau was no stranger to war, and knew perfectly well that no battle results in casualties worse than perhaps one-quarter of the men engaged, unless they get trapped, and many of those would recover from their wounds. It was amazing, really, how many men survived what, from a distance, looked like a sheer bloodbath.

There was no chance of a trap here, nor of enemy pursuit once the Persian cavalrymen finally retreated. Many sahrdaran and vurzurgan would die this day, to be sure. But most of them wouldn't. He'd bleed the great families, but he wouldn't do more than weaken them some.

So, the emperor hadn't even stayed to watch, once he ordered the assault. Quietly, almost surreptitiously—and far enough from the Malwa lines not to be observed—he'd slipped away from his camp with two thousand of his best imperial cavalry.

Light cavalry. Over half of them Arabs, in fact.

He'd be gone for several days. Khusrau didn't believe in cavalry charges against heavy fortifications any more than Maurice did. But since he came from a nation that had always been a cavalry power, he'd given much thought to the proper uses of cavalry in the new era of gunpowder.

Assaults against fortresses were pointless. Raids against a specific target, were not.

Two days later, he was vindicated.

"You see?" he demanded.

Next to him, also sitting on a horse carefully screened from the river by high reeds, the chief of the emperor's personal cavalry smiled.

"You were right, Your Majesty. As always."

"Ha! Coming from you!"

Almost gloating, the emperor looked back to the target of the raid. One of the two ironclads had its engines steaming, but it was still tied to the dock like the other. From the casual manner of the sailors and soldiers moving about on the docks, Khusrau thought the engines were running simply as part of routine care. What the Roman naval expert Menander called "maintenance." Khusrau didn't know much about the newfangled warships, but he knew they needed a lot of it. The things were cantankerous.

"No point in trying to capture them," he said, regretfully.

The Persians had no one who could operate the things. Even the Roman experts would need time to figure out the different mechanisms—and time was not going to be available. Khusrau was quite sure his two thousand cavalrymen could break through the small garrison protecting the Malwa naval base and burn the ships before reinforcements could arrive. But it would have to be done very quickly, if they were to survive themselves. They'd had to cross a ford to get to this side of the Indus, far upstream from the battlefield—upstream from the naval base, in fact—and they'd have to cross the same ford to make their escape.

With his superb light cavalry, the emperor thought they could do it. But not if they dawdled, trying to make complex foreign equipment work.

And why bother? These were the only two ironclads the Malwa had built on the Indus. Once they were destroyed, the Malwa had no way—no quick and easy way, at least—to bring their ironclads from the other rivers. All of the rivers in the Punjab connected to the Indus eventually—but only at the Iron Triangle.

Which was held by the Romans. Who had an ironclad of their own. Which they had not dared to use because of these two ironclads. Which would shortly no longer exist.

"Do it," the emperor commanded.

He did not participate personally in the charge and the battle that followed. He was brave enough, certainly, but doing so was unnecessary—would even be even foolish. Persians did not expect their emperors to be warriors also.

What they *did* expect was that their emperors would present them with victories.

The ironclads burned very nicely. Khusrau had worried, a bit, that they might not. But the Malwa built them the same way the Romans did, just as Menander and Justinian had said they would. An iron shell over a wooden hull.

Burned very nicely, indeed.

Almost as nicely as the emperor's victory would burn in the hearts of his soldiers, after he returned to his camp. Where the sahrdaran and vurzurgan who had *insisted* on that insane assault—the emperor himself had been doubtful, and made sure everyone knew it—would be low-spirited and shamefaced.

As well they should be.

"I don't care if those sorry bastards up north are getting hammered by the Kushans!" General Samudra shouted at the mahaveda priest. Angrily, he pointed a finger to the west. "I've got Persians hammering on me right here! They just destroyed our ironclads on the Indus!"

The priest's face was stiff. He was one of several such whom Great Lady Sati had left behind to keep an eye on the military leadership. Without, however, giving them the authority to actually override any military decisions made by Samudra.

From the priests' point of view, that was unfortunate. From Samudra's point of view, it was a blessing. What priests knew about warfare could be inscribed on the world's smallest tablet.

"Absolutely not!" he continued, lowering his voice a little but speaking every bit as firmly. "I've already sent couriers with orders to the expedition I sent in relief to turn back. We need them here."

The priest wasn't going to give up that easily. "The Kushans are out of the Margalla Pass, now!"

"So what?" sneered Samudra. "Fifteen thousand Kushans—twenty at most, and don't believe that nonsense about fifty thousand—can't do anything to threaten us here. Sixty—maybe seventy—thousand Romans and Persians *can*."

"They can threaten Great Lady Sati!"

For a moment, that caused Samudra to pause. But only for a moment, before the sneer was back.

"Don't meddle in affairs that you know nothing about, priest. If you think the Kushans are going to leave their kingdom unprotected while they hare off trying to intercept the Great Lady—"

He shook his head, the way a man does upon hearing an absurd theory or proposition. "Ridiculous. Besides, by now she'll have reached the headwaters of the Sutlej. That's a hundred miles from the Margalla Pass. It would take an army of twenty thousand men—assuming they have that many to begin with—a week and a half to cover the distance."

He cleared his throat sententiously. "Had you any experience in these matters, you would understand that a large army cannot travel faster than ten miles a day."

He hoped the words didn't ring as false to the priest as they did to him, the moment he said them. That ten mile a day average was . . .

An average. No more, no less. It did not apply to *every* army. Samudra had had Kushan forces under his command, in times past, and knew that a well-trained and well-led Kushan army could march two or three times faster than that—even while fighting small battles and skirmishes along the way.

Still . . .

"By the time they got to the headwaters of the Sutlej—assuming they were foolish enough to make the attempt in the first place—Great Lady Sati's forces will have already reached the headwaters of the Ganges. It's conceivable, I suppose, that the Kushans might be mad enough to venture so far into the northern Punjab, but no enemy force—not that size!—will be lunatic enough to enter the Ganges plain. The garrison at Mathura alone has forty thousand men!"

The priest stared at him from under lowered brows. Clearly enough, he was not persuaded by Samudra's arguments. But, just as clearly, he did not have the military knowledge to pick apart the logic. So, after a moment, he turned and walked away stiffly.

Samudra, however, did have the knowledge. And, now that he thought upon the matter more fully, be was becoming more uneasy by the minute.

The northern Punjab had not been ravaged much by the war, and it was the most fertile portion of the Punjab because it got more rain during the monsoon season than the rest of the province. If the Kushans were willing to abandon their logistics train and cut across the area relying on forage, they could cover possibly thirty miles a day. Twenty, for a surety.

The terrain was good, too. Excellent, from the standpoint of a marching army. From Peshawar ran the ancient trade route known as the Uttar Path or North Way, which crossed into the Ganges plain and ran all the way to the Bay of Bengal on the other side of the subcontinent. That was the same route that Great Lady Sati herself planned to take in her return to Kausambi, once she reached it by following the Sutlej.

By now, Samudra was staring to the north, not really seeing anything except in his mind. A fast-moving Kushan army, unrestrained by a logistics train, marching down the Uttar Path from the Margalla hills with no army in their way any longer . . .

They *could* intercept Great Lady Sati.

Possibly. It depended on how fast her own march had been. But Samudra knew full well that with the size of the army she'd taken with her, mostly infantry and with elephant-borne chaundoli, she wouldn't be moving all that quickly.

He opened his mouth, about to issue orders—that army coming back would curse him, for sending them north yet again, but better the curses of soldiers—far better—than—

A horrific chain of explosions shattered his purpose.

Gaping, Samudra spun around, now facing south by southwest.

"*What happened?*" The chain of explosions was continuing. As loud as it was, it seemed strangely muffled. Samudra detected what might be . . .

Fountains, in the distance?

One of his aides coughed. "General, I think the Romans are blowing up their mine field in the river."

"That's ridiculous! Our ironclads—"

He broke off so suddenly the last word ended in a choke.

"They're only blowing the mine field in the Indus," the same officer continued, his tone apologetic. "Not the one in the Chenab."

The Malwa had no ironclads left in the Indus. The Persians had destroyed them. There was nothing to stop the Roman warships from sallying up the river, firing at troops who had no way to shoot back except with small arms and light cannon. Great Lady Sati had dismantled the heavy batteries that had once been positioned along the east bank of the Indus, once the ironclads came into service, in order to move them across the river as a shield against a possible Roman flank attack.

They could be turned around to face the river, but that would take at least a full day—and Samudra was quite sure the Romans or Persians or both would be attacking those forts again as soon as the Roman ironclad got up there and started firing on them.

Perhaps the heavy batteries at Multan could be brought down . . .

His earlier intentions completely forgotten, Samudra began issuing a blizzard of new orders.

"Let's hope this works," Menander muttered to himself, as the *Justinian* steamed at full speed up the river. "If the engine breaks down . . ."

He eyed the engine house warily. The damn gadget was more reliable than it had been when the former emperor after whom the ironclad had been named designed it, but it was still very far from being what anyone in his right mind would call "dependable."

Not for the first time, Menander contemplated ruefully the odd twists of fate that had wound up putting him in charge of the Roman army's brown-water naval forces, instead of becoming a simple cataphract liked he'd planned to be.

When he said as much to his second-in-command, the newly promoted former Puckle gunner, Leo Constantes laughed.

"*Today?* Be glad you're not a cataphract—or you'd be taking part in the crazy charge Sittas is leading."

Menander winced. "Point."

Sittas himself was downright gleeful. He'd been frustrated for months, ever since the battle on the north lines of the Iron Triangle had settled down into a siege. There was really no place for heavy cavalry in such a fight, except to stay in reserve in the unlikely event of a Malwa breakthrough. Now, finally—!

He was tempted to step up the pace, but managed to resist with no huge difficulty. Sittas was too experienced a horseman not to know that if he arrived with blown horses at the Malwa fortifications that had driven back the Persians a few days before, he might as well not have come at all.

Besides, they were nearing the Persian lines. Sittas didn't like Persians, and never had. No Roman he knew did except Belisarius—who was hopelessly eccentric—and those who had married Persian women, who at least had a reasonable excuse. Not even Sittas would deny that Persian women were attractive.

The men, on the other hand—*pah!*

"Look smart, lads!" he bellowed over his shoulder. "A fancy trot, now! Let's rub salt into their wounds!"

The Persian sahrdaran and vurzurgan glared at the Roman cavalrymen the whole way through their camp. The dehgans who fell in behind Sittas' cavalry, on the other hand, seemed more philosophical about the matter. Or perhaps they were simply more sanguine. This time it would be Romans leading the charge against those damn Malwa guns. It remained to be seen how cocky they'd still be in a few hours.

"All right," Maurice said to his top officers, gathered in the command bunker. "Remember: make the sallies as threatening as you can, *without* suffering heavy casualties. We've got no more chance of storming the Malwa lines facing us here than they have of storming the Iron Triangle. All we've got to do is pin them, so Samudra can't pull out troops to reinforce his right flank. Any questions?"

"What if *they* make a sally?" one of the officers asked. "If they break through anywhere, we don't have Sittas and his thousands of cavalrymen to drive them back."

Maurice shrugged. "We'll scramble, that's all."

When the *Justinian* came in sight of the Malwa fortifications on the west bank, Menander let out a whoop of exultation. The Punjabi peasants who'd managed to escape the labor gangs and desert to the Romans had told them that the Malwa hadn't positioned any guns on the river side of the fortifications. What they hadn't said—or hadn't been asked—was that they'd also never bothered to put up walls sheltering the guns from the river, either. Why bother, when they had the ironclads?

The gun ramps and platforms were completely exposed. The thousands of Malwa gunners and riflemen manning the lines would have no shelter at all from the *Justinian*.

"Load case shot!" he bellowed.

As his gun crews went about the labor, his eyes scanned the east bank of the river. There were some Malwa fortifications there also, but nothing substantial. What was more important was that he couldn't see any sign of big guns. A few small pieces, here and there, but the *Victrix* could handle those well enough. The fireship wasn't an ironclad, but her thick wooden walls should be able to handle anything the Malwa had on the spot. And by the time they could bring up heavy artillery, the *Victrix* would have done her job and gotten back downriver and out of range.

And quite a job it would be, too. Menander contemplated the mass of barges tied up to the wharves. There were only two crossing the river. The rest . . .

"You're kindling, boys," he gloated. "I'd recommend you get ashore quickly."

He turned to the signalman. "Tell the *Victrix* to come up."

A few seconds later, the signal flags having done their work, he saw heavy steam pouring out of the *Victrix*'s funnel. She'd be here very shortly.

But he had his own work to do. By now, the *Justinian* was just coming abreast of the first fortress. There was something almost comical about the way the Malwa soldiers were frantically trying to move the big guns facing landward and get them turned around.

It was a pointless effort, of course. But what else were they to do, except gape in consternation? The handguns and small artillery they had would just bounce off the Roman ironclad.

They wouldn't bounce off Menander, on the other hand. Constantes and the signalman had already retreated into the pilot's armored turret. Hurriedly, Menander followed them.

Once inside, he leaned over the speaking tube.

"Let 'em have it, boys."

Sittas waited until the *Justinian* had steamed completely past the fortifications, shelling them as it went.

"Now!" he bellowed, and sent his horse into the charge. Six thousand Roman cataphracts came after him—and after them, over twice that number of Persian dehgans.

"Back again," Menander commanded. The *Justinian* had finished its turn. That was always a slow and delicate business, in the relatively narrow confines of the river. He'd had to be more careful than usual, too, since he didn't have good charts of this stretch of the Indus.

But the work was done, and the enemy was about to get savaged again. They were still as defenseless as ever. More so, actually, since he could see they were starting to panic.

And well they might. By now, close to twenty thousand heavy cavalrymen would be thundering at them. If they'd still had their big guns intact, they could have sneered at that charge, as they'd done a few days earlier.

Now . . .

None of the guns had been dismounted, true enough, since Menander hadn't used anything heavier than case shot. Nor would he again, since the plan was to capture the guns intact. But he'd inflicted heavy casualties on the crews and ammunition carriers, and even managed to blow up one of the smaller ammunition dumps that had been overly exposed. They'd be in no shape to resist the kind of charge Sittas would press, all the more so since they'd have to do so with Menander firing on them again from their rear.

The barges across the river were making a nice conflagration, too. And—wonder of wonders—the wind was blowing the smoke away from the river. Menander had worried that if the smoke blew the other way he might find himself blinded.

"It's a miracle, lads," he said cheerfully to the other men in the turret. "The one and only time in my life I've seen a military operation work exactly according to plan."

The engine coughed. The *Justinian* lurched.

Coughed again. Coughed again.

Silence. The *Justinian* glided gently downriver with the current, its engine dead.

"Idiot!" Menander hissed at himself. "You had to go and say it!"

Sighing, he studied the riverbank for a moment. "Can you keep her steady in midriver?"

"Yes, sir," replied the pilot.

"All right, then." He leaned over the speaking tube again. "Relax, boys. All that happens until the engineers get the engines running again is just that we have more time to aim. Let 'em have it."

The fighting that afternoon at the front lines was brutal, but the casualties never got bad enough for Maurice to start worrying. And the Malwa never tried any sallies at all.

Samudra was too preoccupied to order any. All his attention was concentrated on the desperate effort to get reinforcements to the Indus in time to keep the Romans and Persians from crossing. It was bad enough that he'd lost the forts on the opposite bank. It wouldn't take the enemy long to turn the guns around and built new berms to shelter them. The Persians and Romans were already working like bees to get it done. As it was, he'd henceforth be pressed on his western flank as well as the southern front. But let them get a toehold on *his* side of the river . . .

Samudra managed to stave off that disaster. But it took two days to do so.

It wasn't until the morning of the third day that he remembered the Kushans at Margalla Pass. By which time it was too late to do anything.

Chapter 32
NEAR MAYAPUR, ON THE GANGES

"It's them, Great King," said the Pathan scout, pointing to the east. "Must be. No general—not even a Malwa—would be leading a large army from a chaundoli."

"How close are they to the Ganges?"

"For us, Great King, a day's march. For them, two. By mid-afternoon on the day after tomorrow, they will have reached Mayapur. They will need to wait until the next day to ford the river. The Ganges is still quick-moving, just coming out of the Silawik hills and the rapids. They would be foolish—very foolish—to cross it after sundown."

"Unless they were forced to . . ." Kungas mused. "Do you know if there's high ground nearby?"

"Yes, Great King. I have been to the shrines at Mayapur, to see the Footstep of God."

Kungas was not surprised. The Pathans were not Hindus, but like tribesmen in many places they were as likely to adopt the gods of other people as their own. Mayapur—also known as Gangadwara— was an ancient religious site, which had drawn pilgrims for centuries. It was said that Vishnu had left his footprint there, at the exact spot where the holy Ganges left the mountains.

The Pathan's hands moved surely in the air, sketching the topography. "Here, below, is the Ganges. Here—not far—there is a ridge. Very steep. There is a temple on the crest. I have been to it."

"Is the river within mortar range of the ridge?"

"Yes. The big mortars, anyway. And the flatland by the river is wide enough to hold the whole Malwa army, while they wait to cross." The Pathan grinned fiercely. "They will be relaxed and happy, now that they are finally out of the hills and entering the plain. You will slaughter them like lambs, Great King."

As he studied the distant hills, Kungas pondered the man's use of the title *Great King*. That was no title that Kungas himself had adopted or decreed, and this scout was not the first Pathan whom Kungas had heard use the expression. From what he could tell, in fact, it seemed to have become—or was becoming, at least—the generally accepted term for him among the tribesmen.

Great King.

There were subtleties in that phrase, if you knew—as Kungas did—the ways of thought of the mountain folk. People from lands accustomed to kings and emperors would think nothing of it. "Great" was simply one of many adjectives routinely attached to such rulers. A rather modest one, in fact, compared to the "divine" appellation of Indian tradition. Even the relatively egalitarian Axumites, when they indulged themselves in formal oratory, plastered such labels as "He Who Brought The Dawn" onto their monarchs.

Something else was involved here. *Great* king—where the Kushans themselves simply called him "king." The title added a certain necessary distance, for the Pathans. Kungas was not *their* king. Not the authority to whom they directly answered, who were their own clan leaders. But they would acknowledge that he was the overlord of the region, and would serve him in that capacity.

Good enough, certainly for the moment.

Kujulo was frowning slightly, looking at the Pathan. "Are you sure—"

Kungas waved his hand. "If a Pathan scout says it's Great Lady Sati, it's Great Lady Sati."

The man looked very pleased. Kungas' following question, however, had him frowning also.

"How large is her army?"

The Pathan's hands moved again, but no longer surely, as if groping a little. "Hard to say, Great King. Very large army. Many hundreds of hundreds."

Kungas left off further questioning. The Pathan was not only

illiterate, but had a concept of arithmetic that faded away somewhere into the distance after the number "one hundred." Even
that number was a borrowed Greek term. And, although the
man was an experienced warrior, he was the veteran of mountain
fights. Feuds between clans, clashes with expeditions from the
lowlands—none of them involving forces on the scale of battles
between civilized nations. Any estimate he gave of the size of
Sati's army would be meaningless.

He nodded, dismissing the scout, and turned to Kujulo. "We'll
need some of our own soldiers to do a reasonably accurate count.
Send off a party guided by the scout."

"And in the meantime? Continue the march?"

"No. As hard as we've pressed them the past few days, the
men need a rest." He glanced at the sky, gauging the sun. "I'll
want a long march tomorrow, though, and it'll be a hard one,
followed by a night march after a few hours rest. I want to be
at that ridge before Sati can cross the river."

Kujulo started to move off. Kungas called him back.

"One other thing. By now, the bitch will be suspicious because
we've cut the telegraph lines. Take three thousand men and march
immediately. Stay to the south. She'll send back a scouting expedition. Three thousand should be enough to drive them off—but
make sure you draw their attention to the *south*."

Kujulo nodded. "While you march by night and slip past them
to the north."

"Yes. If it works, we'll come onto the ridge opposite the river.
They won't know we're there until they start crossing."

Kujulo's grin was every bit as savage as the Pathan's. "A big
army—tens of thousands of soldiers—in the middle of a river
crossing. Like catching an enemy while he's shitting. Good thing
you made us wait to get more ammunition for the mortars, before
we left Margalla Pass."

"We only lost a day, thanks to Irene's efficiency, and I knew
we'd make it up in the march."

"True. Best quartermaster I ever saw, she is. Stupid Pathans.
If they had any brains, they'd know it was just plain and simple
'king'—but with a very great queen."

He hurried off, then, leaving Kungas behind to ponder the
question of whether or not he'd just seen his royal self deeply
insulted.

Being an eminently sane and rational man who'd begun life as a simple soldier, it took him no more than a second to dismiss the silly notion. But he knew his grandson—great-grandson, for sure—would think otherwise. There were perils to claiming Alexander and Siddhartha Gautama as the ancestors of a dynasty. It tended to produce a steep and rapid decline in the intelligence of the dynasty's succeeding generations.

But that was a problem for a later decade. In the coming few days, Kungas would be quite satisfied if he could tear the flanks of the army escorting Malwa's overlord to what he thought was its final battle.

He probably couldn't manage to destroy the monster itself, unfortunately. But if Kungas was right, Belisarius was waiting to pounce on the creature somewhere down the Ganges. He'd kill the monster, if it was already bleeding.

"Another splendid speech," said Jaimal approvingly.

Next to him, Udai Singh nodded. "I knew—I remembered—that your Hindi was excellent. But I didn't know you were an orator, as well."

Belisarius glanced at the men riding beside him. Over the days of hard marches since they'd left Ajmer, a subtle change had come in the way Jaimal acted toward the Roman general. Udai Singh, also.

In the beginning, they'd both been stiffly proper. Their new emperor and Rana Sanga had ordered them to place the Rajputs under Belisarius' command, and they had done so dutifully and energetically. But it had been clear enough that some hostility lurked beneath the polite surface.

Belisarius had wondered about that. He'd found it surprising. True, they'd been enemies until very recently. But the clashes between Belisarius' army and Damodara's had been gallant affairs, certainly by the standards of the Malwa war. He hadn't thought there'd be any real grudges left, now that they were allied. There'd certainly been no indication of personal animosity from either Damodara himself or Rana Sanga, when Belisarius met them for a parlay in the midst of their campaign in Persia.

Now that the harsh pace the Roman general had set his Rajput army had brought them to the Yamuna thirty miles north of Mathura the hostility seemed to have vanished. Belisarius had led an army of twenty thousand men on a march of well over two hundred miles in nine days—something Rajputs would boast about for generations. But he didn't think it was that feat alone that accounted for the change, much less the inspiring speeches he'd given along the way. Jaimal and Udai Singh were both well educated. Their praise of his rhetoric had the flavor of aesthetes, not soldiers.

The march had been ruthless as well as harsh. Ruthless toward everyone. Lamed horses were left behind, injured men were left behind—and the fields they passed through plundered and stripped of anything edible to either man or horse. The villages too, since at this time of year most of the foodstuffs were stored.

There had been no atrocities, as such, committed upon the peasantry. But that hardly mattered. Those poor folk lived close to the edge of existence. Stripped of the stored foodstuffs they depended upon until the next harvest, many of them would die. If not of starvation in their little villages, of disease and exposure after they desperately took to the roads to find refuge elsewhere.

If the war was won quickly, Belisarius would urge Damodara to send relief to the area. But there was no way to know if that would ever happen. Despite that uncertainty, Belisarius had ordered it done. In a life that had seen many cruel acts, including the slaughter of the Nika revolt, he thought this was perhaps the cruelest thing he'd ever done.

And . . . Jaimal and Udai Singh's veiled anger had faded with each day they witnessed it.

He thought he understood, finally. The two were among Rana Sanga's closest aides. They would surely have been with Sanga when he pursued Belisarius across India after his escape from Kausambi.

Three years ago, that had been.

"So," he said to them, "have you finally forgiven me for the butchered couriers?"

Both Rajputs seemed to flush. After a moment, Jaimal said softly: "Yes, General. I thought at the time it was just savagery."

"It *was* savagery," said Belisarius. "The couriers—even more, the soldiers at the station—were just common folk. Boys, two of them. I remember. The memory plagues me, still, especially when I see children."

He swept his head in a little half-circle. "Complete innocents. No different, really, than the peasants I have been condemning to death these past days. I did it then, I do it now, and whatever my regrets I will make no apologies. Even less today, than I would have then. Because today—"

He drew his sword and pointed forward with it, in a gesture that did not seem histrionic at all. Neither to him nor to the two men he rode beside.

"Three years ago, I behaved like a beast to escape a monster. Today—finally—I do so to kill the thing."

Both Jaimal and Udai Singh tightened their jaws. Not in anger, but simply in determination.

"Here, do you think?" asked Jaimal. "Or on the Ganges?"

"Somewhere between here and the Ganges, most likely. The monster would not have crossed to the headwaters of the Yamuna, I don't think. With the Rajputs beginning to revolt, there'd have been too much risk. Better to take the longer but surer northerly route and cross to the Footstep of God. But once into the great plain, it'll want the garrison at Mathura for reinforcements before it goes on to meet Damodara at Kausambi."

That brought some good cheer. All three turned in the saddle and looked behind them. There was nothing to see except an ocean of horsemen and dust, of course.

"Mathura," gloated Udai Singh. "Which is *behind* us. The Malwa beast will have to face us with what it has."

"It was a great march, General Belisarius," added Jaimal.

So it had been. Great enough, even, to wash away great sins.

"It is unseemly for a woman to lead warriors!" That came from one of the five Pathan chiefs sitting across from Irene in the throne room and glaring at her. He was the oldest, she thought. It was hard to know. They all looked liked ancient prunes to her, dried too long in the sun.

"Unthinkable!" she agreed. The vigorous headshake that followed caused her veil to ripple in reverse synchrony to her ponytail. "The thought is impossible to even contemplate. No, no. I was thinking that *you* should lead the armies when they march out. You and the rest of the clan chiefs."

The five chiefs continued to glare at her.

First, because they suspected her of mockery. "Armies" was a ridiculous term—even to them—to apply to separate columns of Pathan horsemen, not one of which would number more than six or seven hundred men. Clan rivalries and disputes made it difficult for Pathans to combine their forces closely.

Second, because she'd boxed them, and they knew it. The young clansmen were becoming more boisterous and insistent with every passing day. Lately, even disrespectful.

Their Great King—another term to cause old chiefs to scowl—was adding to his glory and where were the Pathan warriors?

Were they to hide in their villages?

It would not be long, the five old chiefs knew, before the ultimate insult was spoken aloud.

Old women! Our chiefs—so-called—are nothing but old women!

"We have no mortars," grumbled one of the chiefs. "How are we to fight Malwa armies without mortars?"

"Of course you do," Irene disagreed, in a cheerful tone of voice. "The new mortars of the Pathans have become famous."

That wasn't . . . exactly true. They were indeed famous, in a way, simply because the Kushans were astonished that illiterate and ignorant Pathans had managed to built mortars at all. But no Kushan soldier in his right mind would trust one enough to fire the thing.

Irene found it rather amazing. When it came to anything else, Pathans were as hostile to innovation as so many cats would be to the suggestion they adopt vegetarianism. But show them a new weapon—one that was effective, anyway—and within a very short time they would be modeling their own after it. Much more effectively than she'd ever imagined such a primitive folk could do.

Before the old chiefs could take further umbrage, she added: "What you lack is *ammunition.* Which I can supply you."

Boxed again. The glares darkened.

"Oh, yes, lots of ammunition." She pointed her finger out the palace window, toward the new arsenal. "It's made over there. By old women. Many old women."

Boxed again.

After they stalked out of the palace, Irene summoned her aides. "Send a telegraph message to the station at Margalla Pass. Tell them to send couriers after Kungas."

"Yes, Your Majesty. And the message to be taken to the king?"

By now, Irene had taken off her veil. The smile thus displayed was a gleaming thing. "Tell the king that I have persuaded the Pathans to provide us with troops to help guard the passes. They say ten thousand, but let's figure seven. Two thousand will go to Margalla Pass, the rest to Kohat Pass. If there's any threat, it's more likely to come from the south."

One of the aides frowned. "They won't stay in the passes, Your Majesty. They'll set off to raid the lowlands."

"Of course they will. Better yet. We'll have a screen all over the northern Punjab of thousands of cavalrymen, who'll warn us of any large approaching enemy force. They'll scamper back to the passes when we need them, rather than face Malwa regulars in the open. Pathans are ignorant beyond belief, but they're not actually stupid. Not when it comes to war, anyway."

She leaned back in her chair, basking in self-admiration. Not so much because she'd just relieved her husband of a great worry, but simply because—once again—she'd outfoxed clan chiefs.

"Tell the king he needn't worry about guarding his kingdom. With Pathan reinforcements, I can hold the passes against any Malwa army likely to be sent against us. He's free to do whatever his judgment dictates is the best course."

She detested those old men. Absolutely, completely, thoroughly, utterly detested them.

"Ha!" she barked. "If they'd sent their old women to negotiate, I'd have been lost!"

Emperor Skandagupta goggled at the telegraph message in his hand.

"Mathura? *Mathura?* How did an enemy army get to Mathura?"

The senior of the three generals facing him swallowed. His life and those of his two subordinates hung by a thread. As each week had passed since the beginning of Damodara's rebellion, the emperor's fury had become more savage. By now, there were over seven hundred heads or corpses impaled on the palace walls.

Still, he didn't dare lie. "We're not sure, Your Majesty. Some of the reports we've gotten describe them as Rajputs."

Skandagupta crumbled the message and hurled it to the floor.

"Why would Rajput rebels be moving *north* of Mathura? You idiot! If they came from Rajputana, they'd be trying to join up with Damodara."

He pursed his lips and spit on the general. "Who has still not been stopped by my supposedly mighty armies! You don't even know where he is, any longer!"

"Still far south of the Yamuna, surely," said the general, in as soothing a tone as he could manage. "A large army cannot move quickly, as you know. From your own great military experience."

In point of fact, Skandagupta had no military experience at all, beyond sitting in a huge pavilion and watching his armies reduce rebel cities. But he seemed slightly mollified by the compliment.

"True," he grunted. "Still . . . why have the reports been so spotty?"

The general didn't dare give an honest answer. *Because most of the garrisons—and telegraph operators—flee before Damodara arrives at their towns and forts.*

Instead, he simply shook his head sagely. "War is very chaotic, Your Majesty. As you know from your own experience. Once the fighting starts, information always becomes spotty."

Skandagupta grunted again. Then, pointed to the crumpled message. "Give me that."

One of the slaves attending him hastened to obey. After reopening the message and studying it for a moment, Skandagupta snarled.

The general and his two subordinates struggled not to sigh with relief. The snarl was familiar. Someone was about to die—but it wouldn't be them.

"Send a telegraph message to the governor at Mathura. The commander of the garrison is to be executed. The sheer incompetence of the man! If not—who knows?—treachery. Why didn't he march out at once in pursuit of the enemy?"

As one man, the generals decided to take that as a rhetorical question. To do otherwise would have been mortal folly. *Because you ordered all garrisons to stay at their post no matter what, Your Majesty . . .*

Would not be a wise thing to say to Skandagupta in a rage.

"Whichever officer replaces him in command is ordered to lead an expedition out of Mathura—immediately and with the utmost haste—to deal with this new enemy. Whoever it is."

"How many men from the garrison should he take, Your Majesty?"

Skandagupta slapped the throne's armrest. "Do I need to decide *everything*? As many as he thinks necessary—but not fewer than thirty thousand! Do you understand? I want this new threat crushed!

That would strip the garrison of three-fourths of its soldiers. More than that, really, since the new commander was sure to take all his best troops with him. His best cavalry and foot soldiers, at least. The experienced artillerymen would remain behind, since there would be no way to haul great guns up the roads by the Yamuna without making the phrase *immediately and with the utmost haste* a meaningless term. But artillerymen alone could not possibly defend a city as large as Mathura.

None of the generals was about to say that to the emperor, however. As many heads and bodies as there were perched on the palace walls, there were twice as many still-bare stakes waiting. Skandagupta had ordered the walls festooned with the things.

"Yes, Your Majesty."

Damodara and his army reached the Yamuna forty miles downstream of Mathura. They were met there by a small contingent of Ye-tai deserters from the garrison, who'd decided that the phrase *Toramana's Ye-tai* were words of wisdom.

"Yes, Lord—ah, Your Majesty," said the captain in command of the contingent. "Lord Shankara—he's the new garrison commander—led most of the troops out of the city three days ago. They're headed north, after another army that's invading—ah, rebelling—ah, rightfully resisting—"

Damodara waved the man's fumbling words aside. "Enough, enough. How many did he leave behind?"

"Not more than eight thousand, Your Majesty."

One of the other Ye-tai, emboldened by Damodara's relaxed demeanor, added: "Most of them are piss-poor troops, Your Majesty. Except the artillerymen."

Damodara turned his head and grinned at Rana Sanga. "See? You doubted me! I *told* you I'd find siege guns—somewhere—and the troops to man them."

He swiveled his head back, bringing the grin to bear on the Ye-tai. "They'll be cooperative, yes?"

The Ye-tai captain gave one of his men a meaningful glance. That worthy cleared his throat and announced:

"My cousin commands one of the batteries. I'll show you the gate it protects."

"They'll cooperate," growled his captain.

Damodara now bestowed the grin on Toramana. "I think these men will fit nicely in your personal regiment, don't you?"

"Oh, yes," agreed Toramana. "But I'm thinking I'll need to form another, before too long."

Chapter 33
MAYAPUR

Kungas waited until the lead elements of Great Lady Sati's army had crossed the river and her chaundoli was just reaching the opposite bank of the Ganges. He'd had to struggle mightily with himself not to give the order to open fire when there was still a chance to catch Sati herself.

But that would have been stupid. The river was within reach of the big mortars, but the range was too great for any accuracy. They'd likely have missed Sati's chaundoli altogether—while leaving her close enough to the main body of her army to rejoin it and provide her soldiers with sure and decisive leadership.

"Open fire!"

The whole ridge above Mayapur erupted with mortar fire.

This way, the Malwa army would be almost as effectively decapitated as if they'd killed the bitch herself. She'd be stranded on the opposite bank of the river with her own bodyguard and the advance contingents, while the bulk of her army would be caught on this side.

As Kungas had commanded, the mortar shells began landing, most of them in the river itself. The Ganges was too deep to be forded here, this early in garam, except by using guideropes. The soldiers in mid-crossing were moving very slowly and painstakingly. They had not even the minimal protection of being able to evade the incoming shells. They were caught as helplessly as penned sheep.

Explosions churned the river. A river which, within seconds, was streaked with red blood.

Kungas waited until the mortars had fired two more volleys. *"The near bank, now! Big mortars only!"*

He didn't have *that* much ammunition. Even to the near bank, the range was chancy for the small mortars. He wanted to save their ammunition for the charge that would soon be coming.

Clumps of the soldiers packed on the near bank waiting their turn to ford the river were hurled aside by exploding mortar rounds. The casualties as such were fairly light. But, as Kungas had expected, the soldiers were already showing signs of panic. Being caught in the open as they were, by an attack that came as a complete surprise, was unnerving.

He held his breath. This was the critical moment. If that Malwa army had the sort of officers trained by such generals as Belisarius, Damodara, or Rao—or Kungas himself—he was in real trouble. They'd organize an immediate counterattack, leading columns of men up the ridge. Kungas was confident that he'd be able to fend off such a counterattack long enough to make a successful retreat. But he'd suffer heavy casualties, and this whole risky gamble would have been for nothing.

After a few seconds, he let out the breath. Thereafter, he continued to breathe slowly and deeply, but the tension was gone.

The Malwa officers, instead, were reacting as he had gambled they would. Surely, yes; decisively, yes—but also defensively. They were simply trying to squelch the panic and force the men back into their ranks and lines.

Which, they did. Which, of course, simply made them better targets.

"Idiots," hissed the king's second-in-command, standing next to him atop the ridge.

Kungas shook his head. "Not fair, Vima. Simply officers who've spent too much time in much too close proximity to a super-human monster. Too many years of rigidity, too many years of expecting perfect orders from above."

The next few minutes were just slaughter. Even the very first rounds had struck accurately, most of them. Kushans were hill-fighters and had adopted the new mortars with something approaching religious fervor. Where other men might see in a Cohorn mortar nothing but an ugly assemblage of angular metal,

Kushans lavished the same loving care on the things that other warrior nations lavished on their horses and swords.

Finally, Kungas saw what he was expecting. Several horsemen were driving their mounts recklessly back across the river. Couriers, of course, bringing orders from the Great Lady.

"Well, it was nice while it lasted," chuckled Vima harshly. "How long do you want to hold the ridge?"

"We'll hold it as long as we can keep killing ten of them to one of us. After that—which will be once they get too close for mortars—we'll make our retreat. Nothing glamorous, you understand?"

Vima smiled. "Please, Your Majesty. Do I look like a Persian sahrdaran?"

"The battery is secure, Emperor," said Toramana.

"I think your Ye-tais should do the honors, then."

Toramana nodded. "Wise, I think. Rajputs pouring through the gate into Mathura would probably make the soldiers of the battery nervous."

After he was gone, Rana Sanga said sourly: "What has the world come to? That men would prefer to surrender to Ye-tai than Rajputs?"

Damodara just smiled.

Within two hours, Mathura was his—and the great siege guns with it.

Only one battery and two barracks of regular troops put up any resistance, once the garrison saw that Damodara's army had gained entry into the city through treachery.

All the soldiers in those two barracks were massacred.

The Ye-tai contingent that served as a security unit for the recalcitrant battery were also massacred. Toramana led the massacre personally, using nothing but Ye-tai troops.

After they surrendered, the surviving artillerymen were lined up. One out of every ten, chosen at random, was decapitated. Damodara thought that would be enough to ensure the obedience of the rest, and he didn't want to waste experienced gunners.

He'd need them, at Kausambi. Soon, now.

✧   ✧   ✧

Valentinian straightened up and rubbed his back. "Enough," he growled. "I've stared at this sketch till I'm half-blind."

"It's a good sketch!" protested Rajiv.

"I didn't say it wasn't. And I don't doubt that you and Tarun measured off every pace personally. I just said I've stared at it enough. By now, I've got it memorized."

"Me, too," grunted Anastasius, also straightening up on his stool.

The huge cataphract turned to the assassin squatting on the stable floor next to him. "You?"

Ajatasutra waved his hand. "What does it matter? *I* won't be one of the poor fellows sweating and bleeding in this desperate endeavor."

Easily, gracefully, he came to his feet. "I'm just a messenger boy, remember?"

The two Roman soldiers looked at each other. Anastasius seemed reasonably philosophical about the matter. Valentinian didn't.

But Valentinian wasn't inclined to argue the point, any more than Anastasius. They'd miss the assassin's skills—miss them mightily—when the time came. But long hours of discussion and argument had led all of them to the same conclusion:

Nothing would matter, if Sanga wasn't there at the right time. That meant someone had to get word to him, across a north Indian plain that was turning into a giant, sprawling, chaotic, confused battlefield.

A simple courier's job—but one that would require the skills of an assassin.

"You don't have to gloat about it!" snapped Valentinian.

Ajatasutra just smiled.

"You don't have to gloat!" complained Photius.

Tahmina gave him that half-serene, half-pitying look that was the single habit of his wife's that the eleven-year-old emperor of Rome positively hated. Especially because she always did it looking down at him. Even while they were sitting.

"Stop whining," she said. "It's not my fault if you make elephants nervous. They seem to like *me.*"

Gingerly, Photius leaned out over the edge of the howdah and gazed at the Bharakucchan street passing below.

Very, very far below.

"It's not natural," he insisted.

Tahmina just smiled.

"Tempting, isn't it?" said Maloji.

From their position on the very crest of the Vindhyas, Rao and Maloji gazed out over the landscape of northern India, fading below them into the distance. Visibility was excellent, since they were still some weeks from the monsoon season.

Rao glanced at Maloji, then at the hill fortress his Maratha soldiers were building some dozens of yards away.

"I won't deny it. We'd still be fools to accept that temptation."

He looked back to the north, pointing with his chin. "For the first few hundred miles, everything would go well. By now, between them, Damodara and Belisarius will have turned half the Ganges plain into a whirlpool of war. Easy pickings for us, on the edges. But then?"

He shook his head. "There are too many north Indians. And regardless of who wins this civil war, soon enough there will be another empire solidly in place. Then what?"

"Yes, I know. But at least we'd get some of our own back, after all the killing and plundering the bastards did in the Deccan. For that matter, they've *still* got a huge garrison in Amaravati."

"Not for long, they won't. Shakuntala got the word a few days ago. All of our south Indian allies have agreed to join us in our expedition to Amaravati, once we've finished this line of hill forts. The Cholas and Keralans even look to be sending large armies. Within two months—perhaps three—that garrison will be gone. One way or the other. So will all the others, in the smaller towns and cities. They'll march their bodies out of the Deccan, or we'll scatter their ashes across it."

" 'Allies,' " Maloji muttered.

In truth, the other realms of south India had played no role at all in the actual fighting, up till now. As important as the alliance was for the Andhran empire for diplomatic reasons, most of Shakuntala's subjects—especially the Marathas—were contemptuous of the other Deccan powers.

"Patience, Maloji, patience. They were disunited, and the Malwa terrified them for decades. Now that we've shown they can be beaten, even if Damodara's rebellion fails and Skandagupta keeps the throne the rest of the Deccan will cleave to us. They'll have no choice, anyway. But with our foreign allies—all the aid we can expect through Bharakuccha, if we need it—they'll even be sanguine about it."

"Bharakuccha," Maloji muttered.

Rao laughed. "Oh, leave off! As great an empire as Andhra has now become, we can well afford to give up one city. Two cities, if you count the Axumite presence in Chowpatty. What do we care? There are other ports we can expand, if we desire it. And having the Ethiopians with their own interests in the Indian trade, we'll automatically have their support also, in the event the Malwa start the war up again."

"They're not that big."

"No—which is exactly why we agreed to let them have Bharakuccha. They're no threat to *us*. But they probably have the most powerful navy in the Erythrean Sea, today. That means the Malwa won't be able to prevent the Romans from sending us all the material support we need."

Judging from the expression on his face, Maloji was still not entirely mollified. "But would they?"

"As long as Belisarius is alive, yes," replied Rao serenely. "And he's still a young man."

"A young man leading an army into the middle of the Gangetic plain. Who's to say he's even still alive?"

Rao just smiled.

Belisarius himself was scowling.

"As bad as Persians!" He matched the old Rajput kings glare for glare. "You've heard the reports. Sati will have at least thirty thousand infantry, half of them armed with muskets and the rest with pikes. We have no more chance of breaking them with cavalry charges that we do riding our horses across the ocean."

As indignant as they were, the kings were quite familiar with warfare. The two brothers Dasal and Jaisal looked away, still glaring, but no longer at Belisarius. One of the other kings, Chachu, was the only one who tried to keep the argument going.

"You have rockets," he pointed out.

Belisarius shrugged. "I've got eight rocket chariots with no more than a dozen rockets each. That's enough to harass the Malwa. It's not the sort of artillery force that would enable me to smash infantry squares."

Chachu fell silent, his angry eyes sweeping across the landscape. It was quite visible, since the command tent they were standing under was no more than an open pavilion. Just enough to shelter them from the hot sun. They were out of sight of the Yamuna, by now, marching north toward the Ganges. Well into garam season, the flat plain was parched and sere.

"It is dishonorable," he muttered.

Belisarius felt his jaws tighten. There was much to admire about Rajputs. There was also much to despise. He thought it was quite typical that Rajput kings would be solely concerned with their honor—when what bothered Belisarius was the destruction he'd soon be visiting upon innocent peasants.

"We . . . have . . . no . . . choice," he said, rasping out the words. "The tactical triangle is simple."

He held up his thumb. "Cavalry cannot break infantry armed with guns, so long as they remain in tight formations and keep discipline. You can be sure and certain that an army led by Malwa's overlord will do so."

His forefinger came up alongside the thumb. "Artillery *can* smash infantry squares—but we have no artillery worth talking about."

Another finger. "On the other side, Sati has only enough cavalry to give her a scouting screen. Not enough—not nearly enough—to drive us off."

He lowered his hand. "So, we keep the pressure on them—from a bit of a distance—and force them to remain in formation. That means they move slowly, and cannot forage. And there's nothing to forage anyway, because we will burn the land bare around them. Once their supplies run out, they're finished."

In a slightly more conciliatory tone, he added: "If you were mounted archers in the manner of the Persians, I might try the same tactics that defeated the Roman general Crassus at Carrhae. But—we must be honest here—you are not."

Chachu's head came back around. "Rajput archers are as good—!"

"Oh, be quiet!" snapped Dasal. The oldest of the Rajput kings shifted his glare from the landscape to his fellow king.

"I have seen Persian dehgans in combat. You haven't. What the Roman general is talking about is not their individual skill as bowmen—although that's much greater than ours also, except for a few like Sanga. Those damn Persians grow up with bows. He's talking about their tactics."

Dasal took a deep breath and let it out slowly. "We do not fight in that manner, it is true. Rajputs are a nation of lancers and swordsmen."

Belisarius nodded. "And there's no way to train an army in such tactics quickly. My own bucellarii have been trained to fight that way, but there are only five hundred of them. Not enough. Not nearly enough."

Chachu's face looked as sour as vinegar. "Where did you learn such a disgraceful method?"

Belisarius' chuckle was completely humorless. "From another Roman defeat, how else? I propose to do to Sati's Malwa army exactly what the Persians did to the army of the Roman Emperor Julian, when he was foolish enough to march into the Mesopotamian countryside in midsummer with no secured lines of supply."

Belisarius' gaze moved across the same landscape. It was richer than that of Mesopotamia, but every bit as dry this time of year. Just more things to burn.

"Julian the Apostate, he was called," Belisarius added softly. "A brilliant commander, in many ways. He defeated the Persians in almost every battle they fought. But he, too, was full of his own inflated sense of glory. I am not. And, Roman or no, *I* command this army. Your own emperor has so decreed."

He let the silence settle, for a minute. Then, brought his eyes back to the assembled little group of kings. "You will do as I say. As soon as our scouts make the first contact with Sati's army, we will start burning the land. Behind her as well as before her. On both sides of the Ganges, so that even if she manages to find enough boats, it will do her no good."

After the kings had left the pavilion, Belisarius turned to Jaimal and Udai Singh.

"And you?"

Udai shrugged. "It is a low tactic, no doubt about it. But who cares, when the enemy is Malwa?"

Jaimal just smiled.

✧   ✧   ✧

Two days after the battle at Mayapur—such as it was—Kungas and his army had covered thirty-five miles in their retreat to Peshawar. It was a "retreat," of course, only in the most technical sense of the term. They'd left Sati in command of the battlefield, true enough. But they'd accomplished their purpose, and it was now time to hurry back lest the Malwa take advantage of their absence to invade the Vale.

The first of Irene's couriers reached them while they were still in the hills.

Kungas read her message several times over, before showing it to Vima and Kujulo.

"What do you want to do?" asked Vima.

Kungas was already looking back toward the east. After a moment, he turned and gazed at the distant peaks of the Himalayas.

So far off, they were. So majestic, also.

He decided it was an omen.

"We'll go back," he said. "I want that bitch dead. No, more. I want to *see* her dead."

After traveling perhaps a hundred miles north of the Vindhyas, following the route Damodara and his army had taken, the captain of the assassination team had had enough.

"This is a madhouse," he said to his lieutenant. "Half the garrisons vanished completely, leaving the countryside open to bandits. What's worse, the other half is roaming the countryside like bandits themselves."

"And there's only five of us," agreed his subordinate gloomily. "This whole assignment has turned into one stinking mess after another. What do you want to do?"

The captain thought for a moment. "Let's start by getting away from the area Damodara passed through. We'll go east, first, and then see if we can work our way up to Kausambi from the south. It'll take longer, but there'll be less chance of being attacked by dacoits."

The lieutenant nodded. "I can't think of anything better. By the time we get to Kausambi, of course, Damodara will have it under siege. Which will be a fitting end to the most thankless task we've ever been given."

"We can probably make it through the lines," the captain said, trying to sound confident. "Then . . ."

"Report? To who? Nanda Lal's dead and—I don't know about you—but I really don't want to have to tell the emperor that we've traveled ten thousand miles to accomplish exactly nothing. He's foul-tempered in the best of times."

The captain just smiled. But it was a sickly sort of thing.

Chapter 34
THE IRON TRIANGLE

"Keep the pressure on," said Maurice firmly. "We'll do *that*. But that's all we'll do."

He ignored the sour look on Sittas' face. That was a given, and Maurice saw no point in getting into another argument with him. Sittas was the most aggressive commander in the Roman army, a trait that was valuable when it came time for headlong cavalry charges. But that same trait also made him prone to recklessness. The Romans and Persians had been able to seize the Malwa fortresses upstream on the west bank of the Indus simply—and solely—because Menander and his warships had been able to launch an attack on their unprotected rear. No such advantage existed if they tried to carry the fight across to the east bank of the river.

Menander was also looking sour-faced, however, and that Maurice did have to deal with.

"All right," he growled. "You can keep making your sorties up the river—*until* you spot any signs that the Malwa are bringing over ironclads from the other rivers—"

"And how will they do that?"

"Don't be stupid. They'll do it in the simplest way possible. Just pick them up and haul the damn things there."

"That'd take—"

"A mighty host of slave laborers and ruthless overseers. Which is exactly what the Malwa have."

348

Maurice decided it was time for a moderate display of temper. He gave a quick glance at Agathius and then slammed his fist onto the table in the command bunker.

"God damn it! Have you all lost your wits so completely that one single victory turns you into drooling babes?"

"Take it easy," said Agathius soothingly. As Maurice had expected, the crippled cataphract commander picked up the cue instantly. He'd been a tremendous asset ever since he arrived in the Triangle.

"There's no need to lose our tempers. Still, Maurice is right. It'll take them some time, but the Malwa *will* get those iron-clads into the Indus. One, at least—and you've already admitted, Menander, that the *Justinian* probably can't handle even one of them."

Menander still looked sour-faced, but he didn't try to argue the point. The *Justinian* had been designed mainly to destroy Malwa shipping. Its guns were probably as heavy as anything the Malwa ironclads had, but it wasn't as well armored. The ironclads had been designed to do one thing and one thing only—destroy the *Justinian,* if it ever came out against them.

Agathius swiveled on his crutches to face Sittas. "And will you *please* leave off your endless pestering? To be honest, I'm as sick of it as Maurice is. Sittas, even if you could get your cataphracts across the river in the face of enemy fire—"

"We could go—"

"Upstream? Where? Anywhere below here and Multan, the Malwa now have fortifications all along the Indus. And if you try to take your cavalry north of Multan . . ."

He shrugged. "Leave that to the Persians. We need the cavalry here in case the Malwa manage to penetrate our lines some-where."

For all his stubbornness, Sittas wasn't actually stupid. After a moment, the anger faded from his face, leaving an oddly rueful expression.

"It's not fair!" he said, half-chuckling. "Once again, that damned Belisarius grabs all the glory work for himself and leaves me to hold the fort."

Unexpectedly, Calopodius spoke up from his communications table. He normally kept silent during these command conferences, unless he was asked to do something.

"Is a shield 'false,' and only a sword 'true'?"

All of the commanders peered at him.

"What does that mean?" demanded Sittas.

Calopodius smiled and pointed a finger—almost exactly in the right direction—at his servant Luke, sitting inconspicuously on a chair against a far wall, next to Illus.

"Ask him."

The commanders peered at Luke.

"Ah . . ." said that worthy fellow.

Antonina took a slow turn on her heels, admiring the huge audience chamber of the Goptri's palace in Bharakuccha.

"Pretty incredible," she said. "You'd think the weight of encrusted gems in the walls alone would collapse the thing."

Ousanas shared none of her sentiments. "Incredible nuisance," he grumbled. He gave Dadaji Holkar a look from under lowered brows. The peshwa of Andhra was standing just a few feet away from them. "Mark my words, Antonina. No sooner will this current world war end than a new one will begin, every nation on earth fighting for possession of this grotesque monument to vanity."

She chuckled softly. "Don't exaggerate. The fighting will be entirely between you and the Marathas. The empires of Rome and Persia and Malwa will only send observers."

Dadaji made a face. Ousanas sneered.

"Ha! Until they observe the obscene wealth piled up here themselves. At which point great armies will be marching. Mark my words!"

Still slowly turning, Antonina considered the problem. To be sure, Ousanas was indulging himself in his beloved Cassandra impersonation. But there did remain a genuine core of concern, underneath.

What *were* they to do with the Goptri's palace? Except for the palace of the emperor himself at Kausambi, it was the most splendiferous edifice ever erected by the Malwa. And the interior was an even greater source of greed and potential strife than the glorious shell. For every gem encrusted in the walls, there were twenty in the chests piled high in the vaults below. Along with other chests of gold, silver, ivory, valuable spices—everything, it seemed, that a viceroy could flaunt before a conquered half-continent.

There'd been skin-sacks, too, but those the Ethiopian soldiers and Maratha irregulars had taken down immediately, once they took possession of the palace. Since then, they'd simply glared at each other over the rest.

By the time she finished the turn, she had the answer.

"Give it to me," she said. "To my Hospitalers, rather. And to Anna Saronites, and her Wife's Service."

She lowered her eyes to look at Dadaji. "Surely you—or Bindusara, more likely—can devise an equivalent body for Hindus. If so, you will get an equal share in the palace. An equal share in the wealth in the vaults, as well as equal space in the palace itself."

Thoughtfully, Holkar tugged at his ear. "And for the Kushans? Another equal share, if they create a Buddhist hospital service?"

"Why not?"

"Hm." He kept tugging at his ear, for a few more seconds. Then, shrugged. "Why not?"

Ousanas' eyes widened, half with outrage and half with . . . something that seemed remarkably like amusement.

"Preposterous! What of we Axumites? We get *nothing?*"

"Nonsense," said Antonina. "The Hospitalers are a *religious* order, not an imperial one. Nothing in the world prevents Ethiopians from joining it. Or creating your own hospital service, if you insist on maintaining your sectarian distinction."

Holkar's hand fell from his ear, to rise again, with forefinger pointing rigidly. "Absolutely not! You Christians already have two hospital services! Three is too many! You would take half the palace!"

"Nonsense," Antonina repeated. "The Wife's Service has no religious affiliation at all. True—so far—all of its members are probably Christians. But they've given medical care to Persians and Indians just as readily as they have to Christians."

The accusing forefinger went back to tugging the ear. "Hm. You propose, then, that every religion be given a share of the palace, provided they create a medical service. And then one other—the Wife's Service—which is free of any sectarian affiliation altogether. Yes?"

"Yes."

"Hm." She began to fear for his earlobe. "Interesting. Keep the kings and emperors at arm's length."

"Arm's length, with the hand holding a pole," Ousanas grunted. "Very long pole. Only way it will work. Kings and emperors are greedy by nature. Let them get within smelling distance of gold and jewels . . . might as well throw bloody meat into a pond full of sharks."

"True," mused Holkar. "Monks and priests will at least resist temptation for a generation or two. Thereafter, of course—"

"Thereafter is thereafter," said Antonina firmly. "There is a plague coming, long before that 'thereafter' will arrive."

By now, the three of them had drifted closely together, to what an unkind observer might have called a conspiratorial distance.

"Major religions only," insisted Ousanas. "No sects, no factions. Or else the doctrinal fanatics in Alexandria alone would insist their eighty-seven sects were entitled to the entire palace and its vaults—and demand that eighty-six more be built."

Holkar chuckled. "Be even worse among Indians. Hindus are not given to heresy-hunts, but they divide over religious matters even more promiscuously than Christians."

"Agreed," said Antonina, nodding. "One for the Christians, one for the Hindus, one for the Buddhists, and one for the Zoroastrians if the Persians want it. And one nondenominational service."

After a moment, she added: "Better offer a share to the Jews, too, I think. Half a share, at least."

"There aren't that many Jews," protested Ousanas.

"And almost none in India," added Holkar.

"True—and beside the point. One-third of the populace of Alexandria is Jewish. And it will be through Alexandria that the plague enters the Mediterranean."

Ousanas and Holkar stared at her. Then, at each other. Then, back at Antonina.

"Agreed," said Ousanas.

"A half-share for the Jews," added Holkar. "But if we're going to do that, we'll need to offer a half-share to the Jains, as well."

Ousanas frowned. "What is this adding up to?"

"Six shares all told," Antonina answered. She'd been keeping track. "One of the shares to be divided evenly between the Jews and the Jains."

Now it was her turn to hold up the rigid forefinger of

admonition. "But only if they all agree to form hospitals and medical services! We don't need this palace crawling with useless monks and priests, squabbling over everything."

"Certainly don't," said Ousanas. His eyes swept the great room. "One-sixth of this . . . and the vaults below . . ."

He grinned, then. That great, gleaming Ousanas grin.

"I do believe they will accept."

Ajatasutra had no difficulty at all getting out of Kausambi. The guards at the gates were carefully checking everyone who sought to leave the city, but they were only looking for someone who might fit the description of "a great lady and her entourage."

Even dressed at his finest, Ajatasutra bore no resemblance to such. Seeing him dressed in the utilitarian garb of an imperial courier and riding a very fine but obviously spirited horse, the guards didn't give him more than a glance. Great ladies traveled only in howdahs and palanquins. Those armed peasants didn't know much, but they knew that. Everybody knew that.

Nor did the assassin have any trouble in the first two days of his journey. Mid-morning of the third day, he began encountering the first refugees fleeing from Mathura.

Thereafter, the situation became contradictory. On the one hand, the ever-widening flow of refugees greatly impeded his forward progress. On the other hand, he was cheerfully certain that whatever progress he made was indeed forward.

Only two things in the world could cause such an immense flow of refugees: plague, or an invading army. And none of the refugees looked especially sick.

Frightened, yes; desperate, yes; ill, no.

Damodara was somewhere up ahead. And no longer far away at all.

"He's within a hundred miles, you—you—!"

Skandagupta lapsed into gasping silence, unable to come up with a word or phrase that properly encapsulated his sentiments toward the generals standing before him.

No longer standing, of course. They were prostrate, now, hoping he might spare their lives.

Stupid-incompetent-worthless-craven-fumbling-halfwitted-stinking-treacherous dogs—

Would have done it. But he was too short of breath to even think of uttering the phrase. Never in his worst nightmares had he imagined Damodara would penetrate the huge Malwa empire this far. All the way from the Deccan, he'd come, in less than two months. Now . . .

Within a hundred miles of Kausambi!

Only a supreme effort of self-control enabled Skandagupta to refrain from ordering the three generals impaled immediately. He desperately wanted to, but there was a siege coming. As surely and certainly as the sunrise. He could not afford to lose his remaining top generals on the eve of a siege.

Could . . . not . . . afford . . . it.

Finally, his breathing slowed. "See to the city's defenses!" he barked. "Leave me, you—you—dogs!"

The generals scuttled from the audience chamber.

Once outside, one of them said to the others: "Perhaps we should have told him that Damodara will surely be bringing the big guns from Mathura . . ."

"Don't be a fool," hissed one of the others.

"He'll hear them anyway, once they start firing."

The third general shook his head. "Don't be so sure of that. Within a day he'll be hiding below the palace in the deep bunkers. They say—I've never been down there myself—that you can't hear anything, so deep."

You couldn't, in fact. That evening, Skandagupta went down to the inner sanctum. Seeking . . .

Whatever. Reassurance, perhaps. Or simply the deep silence there.

He got none, however. Neither reassurance, nor silence. Just a stern command, in the tones of an eight-year-old girl, to return above and resume his duties.

Now.

He did so. The girl was not yet Link. But someday she would be. And, even today, the special assassins would obey her.

Belisarius studied the sketch that one of the Pathan trackers had made in the dirt. It was a good sketch. Pathans served the Rajput kings as scouts and skirmishers, just as Arabs did for

Roman emperors. The man was even less likely to be literate than an Arab, but he had the same keen eye for terrain, the same superb memory for it, and the same ability to translate what he'd seen into symbols drawn in dirt with a knife.

"Two days, then," Belisarius mused. "It would take the monster at least that long to retreat to the Ganges, with such a force."

The Pathan, naturally, had been far less precise in his estimate of the size of Link's army. It could be anywhere between twenty and sixty thousand men, Belisarius figured. Splitting the difference would be as good a guess as any, until he had better reports.

Forty thousand men, then. A force almost twice as large as his own.

Almost all infantry, though. That had been suggested by the earliest reports, and the Pathan scout was able to confirm it. If the man could not tell the difference between five thousand and ten thousand, he could easily distinguish foot soldiers from cavalry. He could do that by the age of four.

"Start burning today?" asked Jaimal.

Belisarius shook his head. "I'd like to, but we can't risk it. The monster could drive its men back across two days' worth of ashes. Even three days' worth, I think."

"With no water?" Jaisal asked skeptically.

"They'll have some. In any event, there are streams here and there, and we can't burn the streams."

"Not much water in those streams," grunted Dasal. "Not in the middle of garam. Still . . . the monster would lose some men."

"Oh, yes," agreed Belisarius. Then, he shrugged. "But enough? We're outnumbered probably two to one. If we let them get back to the Ganges, they'll be able to cross eventually."

"No fords there. Not anywhere nearby. And we will have burned all the trees they could use for timber."

"Doesn't matter. First of all, because you *can't* burn all the trees. You know that as well as I do, Jaisal. Not down to the heartwood. And even if you could, what difference would it make? A few days' delay, that's all, while the monster assembled some means to cross. It would manage, eventually. We could hurt them, but not kill them. Not with so great a disparity in numbers. They'd get hungry, but not hungry enough—and they'd have plenty of water. Once they were on the opposite bank of the Ganges, they'd be able to make it to Kausambi. Nothing we could do to stop them."

"By then, Damodara might have taken Kausambi," pointed out Jaimal.

"And he might not, too," said Dasal. The old Rajput king straightened up. "No, I think Belisarius is right. Best to be cautious here."

A day later, three more Pathan scouts came in with reports. Two from the south, one from the north.

"There is another army coming, General," said one of the two scouts in the first party. He pointed a finger to the south. "From Mathura. Most of the garrison, I think. Many men. Mostly foot soldiers. Maybe five thousand cavalry. Some cannons. Not the great big ones, though."

"They're moving very slowly," added the other scout.

Belisarius nodded. "That's good news, actually—although it makes our life more complicated."

Jaisal cocked his head. "Why 'good' news?"

His brother snorted. "Think, youngster. If we've drawn the garrison at Mathura to leave the safety of the city's walls to come up here, we've opened the door to Kausambi for Damodara."

"Oh." Jaisal looked a bit shame-faced.

Belisarius had to fight down a smile. The "youngster" thus admonished had to be somewhere in his mid-seventies.

"Yes," he said. "It makes our life more difficult, of course."

He began to weigh various alternatives in his mind. But once he heard the second report, all those alternatives were discarded.

"*Another* army?" demanded Dasal. "From the *north*?"

The scout nodded. "Yes. Maybe two days' march behind the Great Lady's. They're almost at the Ganges. But they move faster than she does. Partly because they're a small army—maybe one-third as big as hers—but mostly because . . ."

He shook his head, admiringly. "Very fast, they move. Good soldiers."

All the Rajput kings and officers assembled around Belisarius were squinting northward. All of them were frowning deeply.

"From the *north*?" Dasal repeated. The old king shook his head.

"That makes no sense. There is no large Malwa garrison there. No need for one. Not with that great huge army they have in the Punjab. And if *they* were coming back to the Ganges, there'd be many more of them."

"And why would they bother with the northerly route, at all?" wondered Udai Singh. "They'd simply march through Rajputana. No way we could stop them."

As he listened to their speculations, Belisarius' eyes had widened. Now he whispered, "Son of God."

Dasal's eyes came to him. "What?"

"I can think of one army that could come from that direction. About that size, too—one-third of the monster's. But . . ."

He shook his head, wonderingly. "Good God, if I'm right—what a great gamble he took."

"Who?"

Belisarius didn't even hear the question.

Of course, he *is* a great gambler, said Aide.

So he is.

Decisively, Belisarius turned to the Pathan scout. "I need you to return there. At once. Take however many scouts you need. Find out—"

His thoughts stumbled, a moment. Most Pathans were hopelessly insular. They'd have as much trouble telling one set of foreigners from another as they would telling one thousand from two thousand.

He swept off his helmet, and half-bowed. Then, seized his hair and drew it tightly into his fist. "Their hair. Like this. A 'topknot,' they call it."

"Oh. Kushans." The scout frowned and looked back to the north. "Could be. I didn't get close enough to see. But they move like Kushans, now that I think about it."

He nodded deeply—the closest any Pathan ever got to a "salute"—and turned to his horse. "Two days, General. I will tell you in two days."

"And now what?" asked Jaimal, after the scout was gone.

"Start burning—but only behind them. Leave them a clear path forward."

The Rajput officer nodded. "You want them away from the Ganges."

"Yes. But mostly, I want someone else to see a signal. If it's the Kushans, when they see the great smoke from the burning, they'll know."

"Know what?"

Belisarius grinned at him. "That I'll be back. All they have to do is hold the Ganges—keep the monster pinned on this side—and I'll be back."

The oldest of the kings grunted. "I understand. Good plan. Now we go teach those shits from Mathura that all they're good for is garrison duty."

"Indeed," said Belisarius. "And we move *quickly.*"

After they began the forced march, Aide spoke uncertainly.

I *don't* understand. You must be careful! Link is not stupid. When it sees you are only burning behind its army, it will understand that you are trying to lure it further from the river. It will return, then, not come forward.

I know. And by then Kungas will already be there. They will not cross the Ganges against Kungas' will. Not though they outnumbered him ten-to-one.

There was silence, for a bit.

Oh. What you're really doing is keeping Link *at* the Ganges, not drawing it overland—which gives you time to crush the army coming up from Mathura.

Yes. That's where we'll kill the monster's army. Right on the banks of the holy river, caught between two enemies.

They'll have plenty of water.

Man does not live by water alone. Soon, they'll have nothing to eat—and we have all the time we need to watch them starve. We'll have Link trapped up here—when it needs to be in Kausambi. If Damodara can't do the rest, against Skandagupta alone, he's not the new emperor India needs.

Silence again, for a bit.

What if that new army *isn't* the Kushans?

Then we're screwed, said Belisarius cheerfully. *I'm a pretty good gambler myself, you know—and you can't gamble if you're not willing to take the risk of getting screwed.*

That produced a long silence. Eventually, Aide said:

I can remember a time when I wouldn't have understood

a word of that. Especially "screwed." How did a proper little crystal fall into such bad company?

You invited yourself to the party. As a matter of fact, as I recall, you started *the party.*

That's a very vulgar way of putting it.

Chapter 35
THE PUNJAB

By the time Khusrau and his army reached the Kohat Pass, the emperor of the Persians was in an excellent frame of mind.

First, because he'd succeeded in taking most of the western Punjab for his empire. Formally speaking, at least, even if Persian occupation and rule was still almost meaningless for the inhabitants. He hadn't even bothered to leave behind detachments of dehgans under newly appointed provincial governments to begin establishing an administration.

He would, soon enough. In the meantime, there was still a war to be won and he only had thirty thousand troops at his disposal. Not enough to peel off even small detachments for garrison duty. Not with a Malwa army still in the Punjab that numbered at least one hundred and fifty thousand.

Second, because—here and there—he'd been able to grind up some more sahrdaran and vurzurgan hotheads in foolish charges against Malwa garrisons. It was amazing, really, how thick-headed those classes were.

Or, perhaps, it was simply their growing sense of desperation. For centuries, the grandees had been the real power in Persia. True, none of the seven great sahrdaran families or their vurzurgan affiliates ever formally challenged the right of an emperor to rule. Or that the emperor would always come from the imperial clan. But the reality had been that emperors were made and broken, at each and every succession, by the grandees. Those contestants for the throne who got their support, won. Those who didn't, lost their heads.

Their power had stemmed, ultimately, from two sources. One was their control of great swathes of land in a nation that was still almost entirely agricultural, which made them phenomenally wealthy. The other was their ability to field great numbers of armored heavy cavalry, which had been the core of Persia's might for centuries, because of that wealth.

They were losing both, now. Not quickly, no, but surely nonetheless. The huge areas of western India formerly ruled by the Malwa that Khusrau was incorporating into his empire, all of Sind and a third of the Punjab, were not being parceled out to the grandees, as they would have been in times past. Instead, Khusrau was adapting the Roman model and setting up an imperial administration, staffed by dehgans who answered directly to him and his appointed governors—most of whom were dehgans themselves.

Worse still, the grandees were witnessing the death knell of the armored horseman as the king of battles. Within a generation, even in Persia, it would be infantry armed with guns who constituted the core of imperial might. Infantry whose soldiers would be drawn, as often as not, from the newly conquered territories. Indian peasants from the Sind or the Punjab, who would answer to the emperor, not the grandees—and would do so willingly, because the Persian emperor had given their clans and tribes a far more just and lenient rule than they'd ever experienced at the hands of the Malwa.

The continued insistence of the grandees to launch their beloved cavalry charges, Khusrau thought, was simply the willful blindness of men who could not accept their coming fate.

So be it. Khusrau was quite happy to oblige them. Why not? They *were* ferocious cavalry, after all, so they generally managed to seize the small cities and towns they attacked. And every sahrdaran and vurzurgan who died in the doing was one less the emperor would have to quarrel with on the morrow.

By the time the war was over, only the Suren would remain as powerful as they had been, of the seven great families. And under Baresmanas' sure leadership, the Suren were reaching an accommodation with the emperor. They'd long been the premier family of the seven, after all, and now they had the emperor's favor. Unlike the rest, the Suren would accept a role that diminished them as a family but would expand their power and influence as individuals within the empire.

Last—best of all—there were the dehgans. The knightly class of Persia's nobility had always chafed under the yoke of the grandees. But they'd accepted that yoke, in the past, since they saw no alternative.

Khusrau was giving them an alternative, now, and they were seizing it. For a modest dehgan from a small village, the chance to become an imperial administrator or governor was a far better prospect than anything the grandees would offer. In the increasingly unlikely event that the grandees tried to launch a rebellion against Khusrau, he was not only sure he could crush them easily—but he'd have the assistance of most of the grandees' own feudal retainers in doing so.

"You're certainly looking cheerful, Your Majesty," said Irene. She'd come to meet him in a pavilion she'd had hastily set up at the crest of the pass, once she got word that the Persian army was approaching the borders of the Kushan kingdom.

Well, not *quite* at the crest. The pavilion was positioned on a small knoll a few hundreds yards below the crest, and the fortresses the Kushans had built upon it.

Khusrau—very cheerfully—gazed up at those fortifications.

"Very nicely built," he said. "I'd certainly hate to be the one who ever tried to storm them."

Lowering his eyes, and seeing the questioning look in Irene's eyes, Khusrau grinned. "Oh, don't be silly. Yes, I'm in a very good mood. For many reasons. One of them is that I don't have the prospect of watching my army bleed to death on these horrid-looking rocks."

Irene smiled. Khusrau, still grinning, turned slightly and pointed with his finger to the plain below. "I thought I'd found a small town there. With a modest garrison. Just big enough to formally mark the boundary of the Persian empire. And another town like it, a similarly discreet distance below the Margalla Pass. Any objection?"

Irene's smile widened considerably. "Of course not, Your Majesty. The kingdom of the Kushans would not presume to quarrel with whatever the Emperor of Iran and non-Iran chose to do within his *own* realm."

"Splendid. I'll be off, then. Still many more battles to fight. The Romans—staunch fellows—have most of the Malwa army pinned down at the Triangle, so I thought I'd take advantage of the opportunity to plunder and ravage their northerly towns. I might even threaten Multan. Won't try to take it, though. The garrison's too big."

The grin seemed fixed on his face. "Where's King Kungas, by the way?"

Before Irene could answer, he waved his hand. "None of my business, of course."

Irene hesitated, a moment. Then, sure that the Persians had no intentions upon the Vale of Peshawar, she said: "Actually, it is your business. We are allies, after all. My husband took most of our army east, to intercept and ambush the army Great Lady Sati is leading back to the Gangetic plain to fight Damodara. I've gotten word from him. The ambush was successful and he's continuing the pursuit."

That caused the emperor's grin to fade away. His eyebrows lifted. "We'd heard from our spies that she had something like forty thousand troops. Kungas can't possibly—"

"'Pursuit' is perhaps not the right term. He thinks Belisarius is somewhere out there, also, although he's not sure. He'll stay at a distance from Sati's force and simply harass them, until he knows."

"Ah." Khusrau's head swiveled, toward the east. "Belisarius . . . Yes, he might well be there, by now. He was gone from the Triangle, when I arrived. Maurice was very mysterious about it. But I suspect—I have spies too, you know—that he reached an agreement with the Rajputs. If I'm right, he crossed the Thar with a small force to organize and lead a Rajput rebellion."

Irene's gaze followed his. "I wondered. I could see no way— neither could my husband—that he could lead a sizeable Roman force from the Triangle into the Ganges. But through Rajputana . . ." She chuckled softly. "It would be quite like him. I worry about that man's soul, sometimes. How will the angels cope with so many angles?"

Khusrau's chuckle was a louder thing. "Say better, how will the devils?"

He gave her a little bow. "And now, Queen of the Kushans, I must be off."

✧   ✧   ✧

Belisarius drove the march south even more ruthlessly than he'd driven the one north.

"I want to catch them strung out in marching order," he explained to the Rajput kings, after sending out a host of Arab and Pathan scouts to find his target.

"Good plan," said Dasal.

"It's so hot," half-complained his brother.

"Stop whining, youngster. Hot for the Malwa, too. Still hotter, when we catch them."

Kungas studied the scene on the opposite side of the Ganges. As dry and hot as it was, the fires that had been started over there were burned out by now, although plumes of smoke were rising here and there from still-smoldering ashes.

"How far?" he asked.

"As far down the river as we've gotten reports," Kujulo replied, "from the scouts that have come back."

"It must have been Belisarius," said Vima. "But I don't understand why he burned here. I'd have thought he'd be burning in front of her."

"Who's to say he isn't?" Kungas left off his examination of the opposite bank and studied the river itself. As big as it was, the Ganges had already swept downriver whatever traces of the burning had fallen into it.

"I think he wants to pin the bitch here, at the river. That's why he burned behind her. To trick her into coming back."

Vima frowned. "But *why?* If she's here, she's got water. It'd be better to burn her out when she's stranded between the rivers."

Kujulo shrugged. "If it worked, yes. But it's not that easy to 'strand' an army that big. She'd probably have enough supplies with her to make it to the Yamuna."

"She could get stored food from the garrisoned towns, too," said Kungas. "Belisarius is probably bypassing them, just burning everything else. I don't think he can have so big an army that he'd want to suffer casualties in a lot of little sieges and assaults. Especially if he's trying to move quickly."

Finally, he spotted what he was looking for, far down the river. A small cluster of little fishing boats.

"No, it makes sense. If he tricks her into coming back here, he can pin her against the river. Especially with us on the other side to keep her from crossing—which we will."

He pointed at the boats. "We'll use those to ferry a party across the river. Then we'll send cavalry up and down both banks of the river. Seize any boats we find, and wreck or burn any bridges, any timber—anything; ropes, whatever—that could be used to build new bridges or boats. We'll keep the bitch from crossing, while Belisarius lets her army starve to death. They'll have water, but that's all they'll have."

"She'll try to march down the Ganges," Vima pointed out.

"Yes, she will. With Belisarius burning everything before her on that side, and us doing the same on this side. And killing any foraging parties she tries to send out. I don't think she'll make it to a big enough garrisoned city—it'd have to be Kangora—before her army starts to fall apart."

He turned away from the river. "It's as good a plan as any—and I'm not going to try to second-guess Belisarius."

"But there have been no communications from the Great Lady since she reached the headwaters of the Sutlej!" protested the chief priest.

Lord Samudra was no longer even trying to be polite to the man—or any of the other pestiferous priests Sati had left behind in the Punjab to "oversee" him. He rarely even let them into his command bunker.

"Of course we haven't!" he snarled. "Until I can get an army up there to bottle them back up in the Vale of Peshawar, the Kushans will have raiding parties all over the area. For sure and certain, they'll have cut the telegraph lines. And they'll ambush any couriers she might have sent."

"You should—"

"You should! You should!" He clenched his fist and held it just under the priest's nose. "I've got eighty thousand Romans just to the south—"

"That's nonsense! There can't be more than—"

"—and fifty thousand Persians threatening to penetrate our lines in the north. In the middle of this, you want me to—"

"—can't be more than thirty thousand—"

"*Be silent!*" Samudra shrieked. It was all he could do not to strike the priest with his fist.

With a great effort, he reined in his temper. "Who is the expert at gauging the size of armies, priest? Me or you? If I say I'm facing enemy forces numbering one hundred and thirty thousand men—barely smaller than my own—then that's what I'm facing!"

He lowered his fist by the expedient of throwing his whole hand to the side. The fist opened, and the forefinger indicated the door to the bunker.

"Get. Out. Out! The Great Lady instructed me to hold our lines, no matter what, and that is what I shall do. The Kushans are a distraction. We will deal with them when the time comes."

"He's panicking," mused Maurice, peeking over the fortified wall and looking to the north. "He's hunkering down everywhere, barely moving at all."

"Except for getting those ironclads into the Indus," Menander said grumpily. "The latest spy reports say that canal he's having dug is within two miles of the river."

Maurice thought about it. "Better leave off any more forays upriver with the *Justinian*, then. We'll need to get those mine-fields laid again."

"Eusebius is already working on it. He's got the mines mostly assembled and says he can start laying them in three days. That leaves me enough time—"

"Forget it. What's the point, Menander? We've already panicked them enough. From here on in, all we have to do is squat here."

He lowered his head and pointed over the wall with an upraised finger. "Belisarius asked us to keep that huge army locked up, and by God we've done so. The last thing I want is to take the risk that some mishap to the *Justinian* might boost their confidence."

"But—"

"Forget it, I said."

"We accept!" Anna exclaimed, as soon as she finished reading the radio message from Bharakuccha. Then, with a tiny start, glanced at Calopodius. "Assuming, of course, you agree."

Her husband grinned. "I can imagine the consequences if I didn't! But I agree, anyway. It's a good idea."

He hesitated a moment. Then:

"We'd have to live there ourselves, you understand."

"Yes, of course. Perhaps it would be best if we asked Antonina to find us a villa . . ."

"Yes." He instructed the operator to send that message.

A few minutes later, listening to the reply, Calopodius started laughing softly.

"What's so funny?" asked Anna. "I can't make any sense out of that *bzz-bzz-bzz*."

"Wait. You'll see in a moment, when you can read it yourself."

The radio operator finished recording the message and handed it to Anna. After she skimmed through, she smiled ruefully.

"Well, that's that."

```
MUST   BE   JOKING   STOP   WHY   GET   VILLA
WHEN   CAN   HAVE   PART   OF   GOPTRI   PALACE
STOP   WILL   SET   ASIDE   CHOICE   SUITE   FOR
YOU   STOP   PREFER   RUBY   OR   EMERALD   DECOR
STOP
```

Reading the same message, Lord Samudra's gloom deepened. The Romans weren't even bothering to hide their communications any longer. Using the radio openly, when they could have used the telegraph!

"They're already carving us up," he muttered.

"Excuse me, Lord? I didn't quite hear that," said one of his lieutenants.

Samudra shook his head. "Never mind. What's the situation at Multan?"

"We just got a telegraph message from the garrison commander. He says the refugees are still pouring into the city. Much more, he says, and the city's defenses will be at risk."

The Malwa commander took a deep breath; then, slowly, sighed it out. "We can't hold Multan," he said quietly, speaking more to himself than to the lieutenant.

Shaking his head again, he said more loudly: "Send orders to the garrison commander to evacuate his troops from Multan and bring them south. We'll need his forces to reinforce our own down here. And start building fortification across our northern lines. The Persians will be attacking us, soon enough."

"Yes, Lord. And the city's residents? The refugees?"

"Not my affair!" snapped Samudra. "Tell the commander to abandon them—and if any try to follow his army, cut them down. We do *not* have room for those refugees here, either. Soon enough, we'll be fighting for our lives."

The next morning, the group of priests left behind by Link forced their way into Samudra's bunker.

"You cannot abandon Multan!" shouted the head priest.

But Samudra had known they would come, and had prepared for it. By now, all of his officers were as sick and tired of the priests as he was.

"Arrest them," he commanded.

It was done quickly, by a specially selected unit of Ye-tai. After the squawking priests were shoved into the bunker set aside for them, the commander of the Ye-tai unit reported back to Samudra.

"When, Lord?"

Samudra hesitated. But not for long. This step, like all the others he had taken, was being forced upon him. He had no choices, any longer.

"Do it now. There's no point in waiting. But make sure—*certain*, you understand—that there is no trace of evidence left. When"—he almost said *if*—"we have to answer to Great Lady Sati, there can be no questions."

"Yes, Lord."

The Ye-tai commander got promoted that evening. The explosion that destroyed the bunker and all the priests in it was splendidly handled. Unfortunate, of course, that by sheer chance a Roman rocket had landed a direct hit on it. Still more unfortunate, that the priests had apparently been so careless as to store gunpowder in the bunker.

The mahamimamsa who might have disputed that—which they would have, since they would have been the ones to handle the munitions—had vanished also. Nothing so fancy for them, however. By now, the open sewers that had turned most of the huge Malwa army camp into a stinking mess contained innumerable bodies. Who could tell one from the other, even if anyone tried?

By the following day, in any event, it was clear that no one ever would. The epidemic Samudra feared had arrived, finally, erupting from the multitude of festering spots of disease. Soon, there would be too many bodies to burn. More precisely, they no longer had enough flammable material in the area to burn them. The sewers and the rivers would have to serve instead.

Perhaps, if they were lucky, the bodies floating down the Indus and the Chenab would spread the disease into the Roman lines in the Iron Triangle.

By the time Link and its army returned to the banks of the Ganges, the cyborg that ruled the Malwa empire was as close to what humans would have called desperation as that inhuman intelligence could ever become. It was a strange sort of desperation, though; not one that any human being would have recognized as such.

For Link, the universe consisted solely of probabilities. Where a human would have become desperate from thinking doom was almost certain, Link would have handled such long odds with the same uncaring detachment that it assessed very favorable probabilities.

The problem lay elsewhere. It was becoming impossible to gauge the probabilities at all. The war was dissolving into a thing of sheer chaos, with all data hopelessly corrupted. A superhuman intelligence that could have assessed alternate courses of action and chosen among them based on lightning-quick calculations, simply spun in circles. Its phenomenal mind had no more traction than a wheel trapped in slick mud.

Dimly, and for the first time, a mentality never designed to do so understood that its great enemy had deliberately aimed for this result.

Bizarre. Link could understand the purpose, but slipped whenever it tried to penetrate the logic of the thing. How could any sane mind *deliberately* seek to undermine all probabilities? *Deliberately* strive to shatter all points of certainty? As if an intelligent being were a mindless shark, dissolving all logic into a fluid through which it might swim.

For the millionth time, Link examined the enormous records of the history of warfare that it possessed. And, finally, for the first time—dimly—began to realize that the ever-recurrent phrase "the art of war" was not simply a primitive fetish. Not simply the superstitious way that semi-savages would consider the science of armed conflict.

It almost managed something a human would have called resentment, then. Not at its great enemy, but at the new gods who had sent it here on its mission. And failed to prepare it properly.

But the moment was fleeting. Link was not designed to waste time considering impossibilities. The effort it had taken the new gods to transport Link and its accompanying machinery had almost exhausted them economically. Indeed, the energy expenditure had been so great that they had been forced to destroy a planet in the doing.

Their own. The centuries of preparation—most of it required by the erection of the power and transmission grids that had blanketed the surface—could not possibly have been done on any other planet. Not with the Great Ones moving between the star systems, watching everything.

The surviving new gods—the elite of that elite—had retreated to a heavily fortified asteroid to await the new universe that Link would create for them. They could defend themselves against the Great Ones, from that fortress, but could not possibly mount another intervention into human history.

They had taken a great gamble on Link. An excellent gamble, with all the probability calculations falling within the same margin of near-certainty.

And now . . .

Nothing but chaos. How was Link to move in that utterly alien fluid?

"Your commands, Great Lady?"

Link's sheath looked up at the commander of the army. Incredibly, it hesitated.

Not long enough, of course, for the commander himself to notice. To a human, a thousandth of second was meaningless.

But Link knew. Incredibly, it almost said: "I'm not sure. What do you recommend?"

It did not, of course. Link was not designed to consider impossibilities.

Chapter 36
THE GANGES PLAIN, NORTH OF MATHURA

As he'd hoped he would, Belisarius caught the Mathura garrison while it was still strung out in marching order.

"They're trying to form up squares," Abbu reported, "but if you move fast you'll get there before they can finish. They're coming up three roads and having trouble finding each other. The artillery's too far back, too." The old bedouin spat on the ground. "They're sorry soldiers."

"Garrison duty always makes soldiers sluggish, unless they train constantly." Ashot commented. "Even good ones."

The Armenian officer looked at Belisarius. "Your orders?"

"Our cataphracts are the only troops we've got who are really trained as mounted archers. Take all five hundred of them—use Abbu's bedouin as a screen—and charge them immediately. Bows only, you understand? Don't even think about lances and swords. Pass down the columns and rake them—but don't take any great risks. Stay away from the artillery. If they're already too far back, they'll never get up in position past a mass of milling infantrymen."

Ashot nodded. "You just want me to keep them confused, as long as I can."

"Exactly." Belisarius turned and looked at the huge column of Rajput cavalry following them. Using the term "column" loosely. Most of the cavalry were young men, eager for glory now that a real battle finally looked to be in the offing. Their ranks, never too precise at the best of times, were getting more ragged by the minute as the more eager ones pressed forward.

"I'm not going to be able to hold them, Ashot," Belisarius said. "That's all right—*provided* you can keep that Malwa army from forming solid musket-and-pike squares before I get there."

Seconds later, Ashot was mounted and leading his cataphracts forward.

Belisarius turned to the Rajput kings and top officers, who had gathered around him.

"You heard," he stated. "Just try to keep the charge from getting completely out of control."

Dasal grinned. "Difficult, that. Young men, you know—and not many of them well-blooded yet."

Belisarius winced, a little. Young, indeed. At a guess, close to a third of the twenty thousand cavalrymen he had under his command were still teenagers. Being Rajputs, they were proficient with lances and swords, even at that age. But, for many of them, this would be their first real battle.

If the Malwa had solid infantry squares, it'd be a slaughter before Belisarius could extricate his soldiers. Hopefully, the speed of his approach and Ashot's spoiling charge would keep the enemy off-balance just long enough. As impetuous as the Rajputs were certain to be, they'd roll right over that Malwa army if it wasn't prepared for them, even though it outnumbered Belisarius' army by something close to a three-to-two margin.

"We'll just have to hope for the best," he said, trying not to make the lame expression sound completely crippled. "Let's go."

Kungas and his men had no difficulty at all driving back the first Malwa attempt to force the river. It was a desperate undertaking, as few boats as the enemy had managed to scrounge up. Kungas was a little surprised they'd made the attempt at all. Not a single one of the enemy boats got within thirty yards of the north bank of the Ganges.

"What's that bitch thinking?" wondered Vima. "I thought she was supposed to be smarter than any human alive."

Kujulo shrugged. "How smart can you be, when you've run out of options? Trap a genius in a pit, and he'll try to claw his way out just like a rat. What else can he do?"

✧   ✧   ✧

By the time Ashot reached the vanguard of the Malwa army, its commander had managed to get the columns on two of the roads to join forces. But he hadn't had time to get them into anything resembling a fighting formation.

Even moving at the moderate canter needed for accurate bow fire, Ashot needed no more than a few minutes to shred what little cohesion the forward units had. It was becoming obvious that the officers were either inexperienced or incompetent. Perhaps both.

That was not surprising, really. After years of war, the Malwa army like any other would have gone through a selection process with the most capable and energetic officers sent to the front; the sluggards and dull-wits, assigned to garrison duty.

Ashot even considered disobeying Belisarius' order and passing onward to find the artillery. The odds were that he'd be able to rip them up badly, also.

But he decided to forego the temptation. The scattered musket fire being directed at his men didn't pose much of a danger, but if he had the bad luck of catching even a few guns ready to fire and loaded with canister, he'd suffer some casualties—and he only had five hundred men to begin with.

"Back!" he bellowed. "We'll hit the forward units again!"

All he had to do, really, was keep the advance regiments of enemy infantry in a state of turmoil. When the Rajputs struck them, they'd scatter them to the winds—and the fleeing infantrymen would transmit their panic all the way back through the long columns.

Belisarius didn't have to crush this army. All he had to do was send them into a panicky retreat to Mathura. The Malwa officers wouldn't be able to rally their army until it was all the way back into the city. And then, getting them to march out again would take several days.

Long enough, Ashot thought, to enable Belisarius to return to the Ganges and crush the army that really mattered. Link's army.

The raking fire of the Roman cataphracts on their return did exactly what Ashot thought it would. By the time the last cataphract passed out of musket range, the enemy's front lines were a shambles. Not a single one of the squares the Malwa officers had tried to form was anything more than a mass of confused and frightened men.

The Romans suffered only twenty casualties in the whole affair, and only seven of those were fatalities.

Just blind, bad luck, that Ashot was one of them. As he was almost out of range, a random musket ball fired by a panicked Malwa soldier passed under the flange of his helmet and broke his neck.

Belisarius didn't find out until later. At the time, he was cursing ferociously, trying to keep the Rajput charge from dissolving into a chaos even worse than that of the enemy's formations.

He failed, utterly, but it didn't matter. The young Rajputs suffered much worse casualties than they needed to have suffered, but their charge was so headlong that they simply shattered the front of the Malwa army. Twenty thousand cavalrymen charging at a gallop would have been terrifying for any army. Experienced soldiers, in solid formations and with steady officers, would have broken the charge anyway. But the Mathura garrison hadn't been in a real battle since many of its units had participated in the assault in Ranapur, years earlier.

They broke like rotten wood. Broke, and then—as Ashot had foreseen—began shredding the rest of the army in their panicked rout.

Belisarius and the kings tried to stop the Rajputs from pursuing the fleeing enemy. There was no need to destroy this army in a prolonged and ruthless pursuit. But it was hopeless. Their blood was up. The glorious great victory those young men eagerly wanted after the wretched business of being simple arsonists was finally at hand—and they wanted all of it.

After a time, Belisarius gave up the effort. The old kings could be relied upon to bring the Rajputs back, when they were finally done, and he'd just gotten word of Ashot.

Sadly, he gazed down on the Armenian's corpse. Ashot's expression was peaceful, with just a trace of surprise showing in his still-open eyes.

He'd been one of the best officers Belisarius had ever had serve under him. So good, and so reliable, that he'd assigned him to serve as Antonina's commander on her expedition to Egypt. Except for Maurice, Belisarius wouldn't have trusted anyone else with his wife's safety.

"Shall we bring him back?" asked Ashot's replacement, a Thracian cataphract named Stylian.

"No. We've got another forced march ahead of us, and who knows what after that? We'll bury him here."

Belisarius looked around. The landscape was typical of the area between the Ganges and the Yamuna. A grassy plain, basically, with fields surrounding the villages and dotted with groves and woods. They hadn't burned here, since Belisarius had seen no reason to.

His eyes were immediately drawn to a grove of sal trees perhaps a quarter of a mile away. The trees were considered holy by many Hindus and Buddhists. The legend had it that the famous Lumbini tract where the Buddha meditated and acquired salvation had been in a grove of sal trees.

"We'll bury him over there," he said. "It seems a good resting place, and it'll be easy to find the grave later."

While Stylian handled that matter, Belisarius organized his cataphracts to help Jaimal and Udai Singh and the old kings round up the Rajputs. That would take the rest of the day, under the best of circumstances. Belisarius could only hope that Link wouldn't be able to move far in the time it took him to get back to the Ganges.

Link had managed to move its army exactly seven miles down the Ganges. What was worse, the foraging parties it had sent out had returned with very little. The constant harassment of the Kushans, even on the south side of the Ganges, made the foragers exceedingly cautious. Kushans were not a cavalry nation in the same sense as Persians and Rajputs, but they seemed to be mostly mounted and just as proficient in the saddle as they were in all forms of warfare.

Link had only three thousand cavalry. Fewer than that, now, after a number of clashes with Kushan dragoons. It could not even stop the Kushans from continuing the scorched earth campaign that Belisarius had begun.

The situation would have been infuriating, if Link had been capable of fury. The burning done by Belisarius' and Kungas' armies prevented Link from marching quickly, foraging as it went. And the Kushan harassment, despite the fact that the Malwa outnumbered them at least two-to-one, made their progress slower still. Link could destroy any Kushan attempt to charge its solid infantry, true enough. But Kungas was far too canny to order any such foolish assault.

And where was Belisarius? Link had no information at all. All the telegraph lines had been cut, and the Kushans ambushed any scouts it sent out. Link was operating as blindly as any commander in human history, except that it had an encyclopedic knowledge of the terrain. But that meant almost nothing, when it had no idea where the main enemy force was to be found in it.

The probability was that Belisarius had left to meet a garrison coming north from one of the large cities. Mathura, most likely.

It was always possible that such a garrison would defeat the Roman general. But Link estimated that probability as being very low. Not more than ten percent, at best. Assuming the far more likely probability that Belisarius would triumph in that battle as he had in almost all others, he and his army would be back at the Ganges within a few days.

By which time, Link and its forces would not have moved more than ten or fifteen miles. Probably ten. Kushan harassment was becoming more intense, seemingly by the hour.

"What shall we do, Great Lady?"

"Continue down the Ganges," Link replied. What else could it say?

When Khusrau and his army reached Chandan, on the Chenab river, the emperor was so taken by the beauty of the town and its setting that he ordered his soldiers not to burn it. He did, however, give them permission to loot the homes and public buildings.

That took little time. Most of the population had fled already, taking their most valuable possessions with them. After his army had crossed the Jhelum and entered the land between that river and the Chenab, the Persians considered themselves in enemy territory. By the terms of the agreement Khusrau had made with the Romans and the new Malwa emperor, after the war this would become Malwa territory. So, they were destroying everything, driving the population south toward Multan, where they'd join a horde of refugees already overburdening the Malwa garrison there.

In an sense, they'd been in enemy territory also, west of the Jhelum, but those lands were destined to become part of the Persian empire, by the provisions of the agreement. So, Khusrau had kept his soldiers under tight discipline, and had refrained from any destruction except where enemy forces put up resistance.

There hadn't been much of that. Apparently, the Malwa commander of the main army in the Punjab had been withdrawing all his detachments in the north in order to reinforce the Malwa lines facing the Romans. Lord Samudra, as he was named, was adopting a completely defensive posture while the Persians and the Kushans invaded the northern Punjab with impunity. For all practical purposes, the Malwa empire's largest and most powerful army had become paralyzed on its western border, while Damodara and Belisarius and Kungas and Khusrau himself drove lances into its unprotected guts.

Khusrau thought Samudra was an idiot. *Knew* him to be an idiot, rather, since the Persian emperor was well aware that Maurice had no more than fifty thousand Roman troops in the Iron Triangle. Sixty thousand, perhaps, counting the various auxiliary units that were assigned to maintaining the critical supply lines from the Sind. But even including those soldiers, Maurice was still outnumbered well over two-to-one. Probably closer to three-to-one.

With fifty thousand men behind those formidable Roman defensive works, of course, Maurice could hold his own against Samudra. But only on the defensive—and the same was true the other way. Samudra could have easily taken over half his army north to put a stop to Khusrau's expedition and, possibly, even cut off the Kushan army. Depending on where Kungas had taken it, of course. Khusrau suspected the Kushans were already into the Gangetic Plain. If they were able to join forces with Belisarius . . .

But while the Malwa commander in the Punjab seemed capable enough, when it came to routine matters, Samudra obviously had not an ounce of initiative and daring. The Malwa regime was not one that fostered independent thinking on the part of its commanders.

Hard to blame them, really. The one great exception to that rule was probably even now battering at the gates of Kausambi.

✧ ✧ ✧

Damodara was not battering at the gates, as it happened. But he was bringing the siege guns into position to do so.

"Yes, yes, Ajatasutra, I know we hope to enter the city through . . . ah, what would you call it? 'Treachery' seems inappropriate."

"Guile and stratagem, Your Majesty," Ajatasutra supplied.

Damodara smiled. "Splendid terms. On my side, anyway."

The new emperor glanced at Narses. The Roman spymaster was perched on the mule he favored, studying the fortifications on the western walls of Kausambi.

It was a knowing sort of examination, not the vacant stare that most imperial courtiers would have given such a purely military matter. Damodara had realized long since that Narses was as shrewd with regard to military affairs as he was with all others. Damodara was quite sure that despite his age, and the fact that he was eunuch, Narses would make an excellent general himself.

What am I going to do with Narses? he asked himself, not for the first time. *If I take the throne, do I dare keep such a man around? It'd be like sharing a sleeping chamber with a cobra.*

The solution was obvious, but Damodara felt himself resisting that impulse. Whatever else, Narses had served him well for years. Superbly well, in fact. Had even, most likely, kept his family and that of Rana Sanga alive where they would have been murdered by Malwa otherwise.

It would bode ill, Damodara thought, if he began what amounted to a new dynasty in all but name with an act of treachery.

But what else can I do? The Romans certainly won't take him back. And the Persians and the Axumites and the Kushans know his reputation too well to entertain the thought of employing him, either.

What else is there, but an executioner or an assassin's blade?

Perhaps he could have him poisoned . . .

Damodara shook his head and went back to the matter immediately at hand.

"You think too much like an assassin, Ajatasutra. When the time comes, Rana Sanga is ready to lead the charge. He'll take ten thousand of his Rajputs. But first we must fix Skandagupta's entire attention on *this* side of the city. I don't have a large enough army to invest Kausambi, and the emperor—ah, the false emperor—knows it. At least, his commanders will tell him so. So, now that I've massed my troops here before the western gates and"—he gestured with his head toward the heavy artillery berms his engineers were constructing—"am setting up the siege guns I brought from Mathura, he'll concentrate his own troops on these walls, and at these gates."

Whether or not he was inclined to argue the matter, Ajatasutra made no attempt to do so. Instead, he began thoughtfully scratching his chin.

"How long, Emperor? Before you can order Sanga's charge, I mean."

Damodara shrugged. "Hard to know. Not for a few days, certainly."

"In that case, I should return to Kausambi. They could use me there, when the time comes. Whereas here . . ."

He waved his hand, indicating the soldiers under Damodara's command who were setting up their own camps and lines of defense against any possible sallies from the city. "Merely one blade among tens of thousands of others."

"Certainly. But . . ." Damodara's eyes widened a bit. "*Can* you get back into the city? By now, the guards will be on the alert for spies."

"Oh, yes. Don't forget that they're mediocre guards, and"—Ajatasutra cleared his throat modestly—"I am very far from a mediocre assassin. I'll get in."

His good humor faded, however, as he contemplated his superb horse. "Alas, the horse *won't*. Not even sorry garrison troops will think it's a tinker's nag."

He bowed low. "May I present him to Your Majesty, then? A token of my esteem. No! My awe at Your effulgent presence, divine in its aspect."

Damodara laughed. *And what was he to do with Ajatasutra, for that matter, if he took the throne?* He didn't doubt the assassin's loyalty, but within a few years Ajatasutra's mocking ways would have half the courtiers in Kausambi demanding his head.

But there'd be time enough to deal with that later. First, he had to take Kausambi.

"Go, Ajatasutra. If we're both still alive in a few days, I'll return the horse."

It seemed impolitic to add: *You might need it.*

✧　　✧　　✧

From their position just south of the junction of the Ganges and Yamuna rivers, the five members of the Malwa assassination team stared at the empire's capital city. That part of it they could see looked fine. But they could easily hear the sound of big guns firing to the west.

"Marvelous," snarled the captain. "Just perfect. After ten thousand miles—more like eleven, by now—we finally get back to Kausambi—having succeeded in doing nothing—and the city's under siege."

"We'll never get in," said his lieutenant, morosely. "No way the guards will pass five strange men."

It was true enough. No doubt, ensconced somewhere in the huge imperial palace, were the records that would identify the assassination team and establish their bona fides. Probably, even, two or three of Nanda Lal's subordinates who would recognize them personally. The captain and the lieutenant, at least.

And so what? The odds that any such spymasters would heed a summons from a gate's guards—assuming the guards were willing to send a summons in the first place, instead of simply killing the five assassins and saving themselves a lot of possible trouble—were too low to even think about.

"No hope for it," he sighed. "We may as well cross the Ganges and set up camp on the other side, as close as we can get to the eastern gate. Maybe something will turn up."

His lieutenant eyed the distance. "At least it's not far." He spit on the ground. "We laugh at a few miles, after so many wasted thousands."

Chapter 37
THE GANGES

There had been many times, since the war began, that Belisarius had been glad to have Abbu and his Arab scouts in his service.

Never more than now.

"Idiot Rajputs would have gotten you into another war, General," said the old bedouin chief, scowling. "Are they blind? Who else wears topknots?"

Abbu was being a little uncharitable, but... only a little. It was not as if Rajputs weren't familiar with Kushans. Until recently, there had been tens of thousands of Kushans in the Malwa military, many of whom had served in the same armies as Rajputs, if not in the same units.

On the other hand—being charitable—there were still considerable numbers of Kushans in the service of the Malwa empire. By no means all of the Kushans had defected after Kungas re-created the old Kushan kingdom.

But they were no longer trusted, and there was no possibility at all that Link had included Kushan units in its army when it marched from the Punjab. Even idiot Rajputs should have understood that much.

Even idiot *teenage* Rajputs.

"They're still young," muttered old Jaisal. "Young men don't think of these things."

Belisarius squelched his irritation. It would be purely stupid to offend the Rajputs who constituted almost his entire army, after all.

"Well, there was no harm done, apparently. The Kushans fled the scene as soon as contact was made and"—he cleared his throat, as diplomatically as possible—"the Rajput cavalrymen immediately began firing on them."

That fact was interesting, in and of itself. Under normal circumstances, Kushans were quite belligerent enough to have responded to the initial Rajput bow fire by attacking them. Especially since, by all accounts—those of the Rajputs as well as the Arab scouts—the Kushans had outnumbered the Rajput cavalry unit.

Abbu put his thoughts into words. "They were expecting us, General. Only possible answer."

"Yes." Belisarius scratched his chin. "I'm almost sure that means Kungas himself is here. He must have gambled that Maurice could keep the main Malwa army pinned in the south Punjab, while he marched into the Ganges plain to attack Link's army."

"Bold man!"

Belisarius smiled. "Well, yes. A timid fellow would hardly have marched across Central Asia in the middle of the world's greatest war to set up a new kingdom. With a new Greek bookworm wife, to boot."

Abbu had met Irene. "Crazy man," he muttered, his scowl returning.

Belisarius swiveled in the saddle to face Dasal and the other Rajput kings. "Can you keep your men under control? I have *got* to establish contact with the Kushans—and, as Abbu says, I don't need to start a new war with my allies."

All the Rajput kings had the grace to look embarrassed for a moment. They didn't answer immediately, however, Belisarius noted.

He wasn't surprised. Their smashing victory over the Mathura garrison had filled the young Rajput warriors with elation so great it bordered on heedlessness and reckless arrogance. Inexperienced to begin with, they were in no mood to listen to the lectures of old kings concerning the danger of accidentally fighting allies in the middle of a turbulent campaign of marches and countermarches. "Friendly fire," as a future world would call it, was not something a nineteen-year-old Rajput cavalryman gave much thought to when he woke up in the morning. Or at any time of the day or night.

"Right." Belisarius swiveled again and brought Jaimal and Udai Singh under his gaze.

"Can *you* manage it?"

Jaimal smiled thinly. "Oh, yes, General Belisarius." He gave the old kings a sly look. "*Our* men are real veterans."

"But there are only fifty of us," cautioned Udai Singh.

"That should be enough," Belisarius said. "I'll send Abbu and some of his scouts with you, along with a few of my cataphracts. All we need to do, for the moment, is make contact with the Kushans. Set up a time and place where Kungas and I can meet—assuming I'm right, and he's here. If not, whoever their commander is."

Sanga's two lieutenants trotted off, with Abbu and Stylian trailing behind. Belisarius could rely on Stylian to select level-headed cataphracts for the business. In the meantime, he had a different problem to deal with.

"I'm still guessing," he said to the kings, "but I'm pretty sure Kungas will have most of his army on the north bank of the Ganges. It's what I would do in his place. Keep Sati from crossing the river and using it as a shield between us and her."

Faced with a straightforward tactical issue, the kings were more at ease.

"Agreed," said Dasal. "Which means—until we can establish liaison—we should stay on *this* side."

"This side, and east of here," his younger brother grunted. "Resume the burning. Turn everything for twenty miles to the east into a wasteland. The Malwa will be stranded."

"The young men will complain," complained Chachu.

Dasal's frown might have been envied by Jove. "The young men will do as they are told."

The young Rajput warriors complained. Bitterly.

They also did as they were told.

By the time Jaimal and Udai and Abbu returned, the sky east of Sati's army was filled with smoke.

"It's Kungas," Jaimal said. "He recommends you meet at a fishing village—what used to be a fishing village—five miles upstream from the Malwa army."

Udai grinned. "He promises not to shoot you, if you have your hair in a topknot. Otherwise he may not be able to control his men. He says most of them are only ten years old. Heedless and careless."

Belisarius returned the grin. "I'd look silly in a topknot. I'll take my chances."

Stylian was frowning, however. "Only five miles from the enemy? That seems . . ."

Abbu was already shaking his head. "No need to worry. That Malwa army is not moving at all, any longer. Just sitting there, baking in the garam sun."

"Kungas says Sati had her elephants butchered, two days ago," added Jaimal. "The beasts were getting out of control—and, by now, they probably needed the meat, anyway. He thinks that army is getting pretty desperate."

The word "desperate" could have been applied to the soldiers of Link's army, well enough, but not to the cyborg itself. True, it had come to the conclusion that the position of its army was hopeless. But, in the odd way that its mind worked, that knowledge brought nothing more than what a human might have called "relief."

Not that either, really, since Link knew no emotions. Still, the other side of hopelessness was that decisions became very simple. If nothing else, rest from labor was at hand.

In a few hours, at least. Link still had to work through human instruments, and those flawed creatures always had their own needs. Which, at times, had to be respected.

So, with its inhuman patience, Link observed silently as the special priests and assassins in its chaundoli began their rituals.

It might even be said to do so with satisfaction. At least *that* part of the new gods' plan had worked properly. The cult fostered over a century earlier in the Khmer lands had served its purpose well. Link could rely on those priests and assassins to do what was needed.

If not, unfortunately, as quickly as it would have liked. But half a day's delay should not matter. Even if, as Link was assuming, Damodara had seized the big guns at Mathura, it would still take weeks before they could begin crumbling the walls of Kausambi.

❖   ❖   ❖

Damodara's estimate was considerably more pessimistic.

"At least two months," he grumbled, watching the great cannons as they belched fire at the walls of Kausambi. Half of them missed entirely. The bores on those giant but crude siege guns were very sloppy. The huge stone balls that did strike the walls seemed to have no more effect than so many pebbles.

"If we're lucky," he added sourly.

But Rana Sanga barely heard him, and paid no attention to the guns at all. The Rajput king had entered that peculiar mental zone he usually entered before a great battle. A strange combination of serenity and fierce anticipation—the first, serving as a dam for the pent-up waters of the second.

When the time came—very soon, Sanga thought—the dam would break.

No, would shatter. Pouring out in that flood would be the greatest ride of his life, followed by his greatest battle.

"Months!" Damodara snarled.

"Yes, Lord," said Sanga, absently. He didn't even notice that he used the old appellation for Damodara, instead of the new "Your Majesty."

Neither did Damodara.

"I'm nervous," said Tarun. "What if I do it wrong? Are you sure—"

"Don't be silly," Rajiv assured the young stable-boy. He held up the fuse, pinched between thumb and forefinger. "What's to go wrong? You've got a pocket full of matches. Just light this and take shelter."

Dubiously, Tarun brought out one of the matches in his pocket and studied it.

"What if—?"

Trying not to let his exasperation show, Rajiv plucked the match from Tarun's hand and struck it against one of the stones in the stable floor. The match flared up very nicely, with its usual acrid fumes.

"Specially made," he said forcefully. "By the best apothecary in Kausambi."

Honesty forced him to add: "Well . . . The best in this quarter, anyway. He's probably just as good as any in the imperial palace, though."

That was true enough, but it brought up another thing for Tarun to fret over.

"What if he betrays us? Matches are unusual things. What if he starts wondering—"

Squatting a few feet away, Valentinian laughed softly. "Weren't you just telling us yesterday that nobody is paying attention to the soldiers any more? Even the soldiers themselves?"

"They've even slacked off the digging," Anastasius added. "Good thing, too, as close as they were getting."

Never comfortable for very long in a squat, the huge cataphract rose to his feet. It was an ungainly movement, not because Anastasius was uncoordinated—which he certainly wasn't, for a man his size—but simply because the size itself created certain physical realities. A rhinoceros is ungainly also, rising to its feet. Not ungainly, however, in the charge that follows.

"Relax, boy. By now, Skandagupta has over a thousand corpses or heads decorating the walls of his palace. He's become a maniac, and everyone in the city knows it. Nobody in his right mind wants to get anywhere near him—or his police. That apothecary will do what everyone else is trying their best to do, these days. Mind his own business and hope he survives whatever's coming."

It was true enough, and Tarun knew it as well as anyone else in the stable. The soldiers and laborers engaged in digging up the area looking for the hideaways *had* been slacking off, for at least a week. "Slacking off," at least, in the sense of not getting much done that was of any use. To be sure, they managed to look as if they were working frenziedly. But most of it was make-work; literally, moving soil and rubble back and forth from one hole or pile to another.

You could hardly blame them. Every time they'd uncovered something, whoever was in charge wound up getting beheaded or impaled. Over time, of course, reports of no progress at all would be met with equal punishment. But that took more time than success.

By this point, in besieged Kausambi, most people were simply buying time.

✧   ✧   ✧

Not everyone.

Lady Damodara appeared in the stall. "Ajatasutra's back. He wants to know—"

"How soon?" asked the assassin himself, coming right behind her. "Inquiring emperors want to know."

Valentinian grinned, mirthlessly. "Now that you're here, how's tomorrow morning sound?"

Tarun gulped.

"You'll do fine," Rajiv assured him. "But you'd better leave now. It's a big city and you've got a ways to go. And you need to be in place before sunrise."

"It's dark outside," Tarun protested.

"Of course it is," said Valentinian. "That's the plan. Now, go."

Tarun made no further protest. Whatever else he might be worried about was merely a possibility, involving someone else or something else at some other place and time.

Valentinian was here and now. Tarun went.

Belisarius wasn't really worried about any Malwa patrols sent out by Link. Where Belisarius had twenty thousand cavalrymen and Kungas had fifteen thousand dragoons, the monster had had only had three thousand cavalry to begin with. Far fewer than that, now, between the casualties they'd suffered in various clashes and—the crudest factor of all—the fact that they were now beginning to butcher their horses for the meat.

Still, he saw no reason to take chances. So, he made the rendezvous with Kungas well before daybreak.

The Kushan king was waiting for him, in one of the few huts in the small village that had escaped the Rajputs' arson. He was squatting on the dirt floor, with a bottle of rice wine and two cups.

"Nice to see you again," he said, pouring Belisarius a drink. "I'd worry about you getting drunk, except you can drink like a fish and this stuff's so thin it doesn't matter anyway. Best I could find."

Smiling, Belisarius squatted and took the cup. "I'm *delighted* to see you—and surprised. You took a mighty gamble, coming here from the Hindu Kush."

Kungas made the little shoulder twitch that did him for a shrug. "I figured you'd be here, somewhere. And since I'm a

Eric Flint & David Drake

Kushan king, I need to prove I'm a great gambler or I'll soon enough have people muttering that I'm unfit to rule. Most of all, though, I want to see that bitch finally dead."

Belisarius swallowed the wine in one gulp. It was not a big gulp, however, since it was a very small cup.

Just as well. The stuff was wretched as well as thin. Exactly the sort of wine you'd expect to find in a poor fishing village.

The face he made, though, was not due to the wine.

"Then I hate to say this, but you're in for a big disappointment. The one thing we're *not* going to do is kill Great Lady Sati."

Kungas' eyes widened slightly. In his minimalist manner, that signified astonishment.

"Why in the world not?" Accusingly, almost plaintively, he added: "You killed her predecessor, didn't you?"

"Yes, I did. And I will say that few things in my life gave me more satisfaction than seeing Great Lady Holi die. But that was another place, another time, and under different circumstances. Here, and now, we want Sati simply isolated—but still alive."

He set the cup down on the floor. "That was *a* battle. This is *the* battle. More accurately, this is a holding action while the final battle is fought elsewhere, by Damodara."

Kungas tugged at his wisp of a goatee. "Um. You're gambling yourself."

"Yes and no. I'm not gambling—well, not much of a gamble— that Damodara will have reached Kausambi by now. What I'm gambling is simply that it will take him some time to break into the city. I've seen those defenses. Nothing in the world matches them, except possibly the ancient fortifications at Babylon."

The Kushan king's beard-tugging became more vigorous. "Damnation, Belisarius . . ."

The Roman general just waited, patiently. The best way to persuade Kungas of anything was to let him persuade himself. Beneath that impassive exterior, the Kushan was as smart as anyone Belisarius had ever known—and he was privy to all the secrets of Link's methods of rule. Belisarius had briefed Kungas and Irene extensively on the matter, before they left Constantinople on their great expedition to the Hindu Kush.

"Damnation," Kungas repeated. But the word, this time, was simply said fatalistically.

Belisarius waited. The Kushan's hand fell from the beard.

"All right. I understand the logic. As long as the bitch is alive, Link is locked into her body. Here—not in Kausambi. The minute she dies, Link will assume a new sheath. This new one in the imperial palace, so it will be able to take direct command of Kausambi's defenses. Instead of Skandagupta, whom no one in his right mind has ever considered a military genius. Or even a very competent emperor."

"Exactly."

"Who?" Kungas wondered. "And how many sheaths does that monster have at its disposal?"

Good question. Aide?

Belisarius could sense the jewel's hesitation. **Not sure. It's complicated.**

Try to explain, as best you can. We need to know.

After a moment, Aide said: **It's not easy for it. Link, I mean. First of all, the sheath has to be female—never mind why—and, second of all, it has to be in the line of the dynastic clan. That's because ... well, never mind that, either. Just take my word for it. There's a critical genetic component to the process. Several, in fact. Close blood relations are important.**

Belisarius nodded. To Kungas, he said: "Aide's explaining it to me. Give us a moment."

Third, the sheath itself has to be individually suitable. Not every girl is. Most aren't, in fact—and there are only a small number to choose from in the first place, being restricted to the female offspring of the dynastic clan. She has to be ... The word won't mean anything to you, but it's something the future will call "autism." It's a pretty rare medical condition. Not very many children suffer from it.

Belisarius didn't bother asking Aide to explain the terms. Some day, he would, but there wasn't the need for it now, or the time available.

He did purse his lips with distaste. Contempt, rather. That was absolutely typical of the methods of the "new gods" who claimed to be humanity's true future. They would not only use innocent children as the vessels for their rule, but would choose ones already damaged and even less able to protect themselves.

I see. The Malwa dynastic clan is a big one, but still ...

There'd only be one available every few years. It would vary, of course. The long span of years between Holi's age and Sati's

would have been unusual. Even so, I doubt if Link has more than two—maybe three—sheaths available. Not even that, really, because they need years of training in addition to everything else. The moment of transition—possession, if you will—is pretty traumatic. If the girl isn't thoroughly prepared for it, she'll simply die.

A thought came to Belisarius. *If that's so ... What if the new sheath is* very *young? It might actually be smarter ...*

He shook his head. "No, that's too much of a gamble."

Kungas twisted his head, quizzically. Belisarius explained: "There can't be many sheaths. Maybe only one—and she might very well still be a young girl. If so ..."

He almost laughed, seeing the suddenly fierce expression on the Kushan's face.

"Tempting, isn't it, Kungas? What happens if the Malwa empire is suddenly ruled by a child? Will anyone—even Skandagupta— really listen to her?"

After a moment, Kungas expelled his breath. "No. As you say, too much of a gamble—even for a Kushan. What if she *isn't*? Sati was in her prime, after all, when she became the new Link."

What was too much of a gamble, even for a Kushan king, was not for a cyborg.

Not, at least, for this cyborg. Kungas and Belisarius had options. Link no longer did.

The Khmer had finished their rituals.

"Now," the thing known as Great Lady Sati commanded.

Expertly, the assassin standing behind her drove his dagger into Sati's spinal column. Just as expertly, the assassin standing before her drove his blade into her heart.

As her body slumped, a third assassin stepped forward and— with the same expertise—slit her throat from ear to ear.

A priest was there with a large bowl, to catch the sacred fluid. There was little spillage, since the goddess' heart was no longer beating.

That was good, because the blood was needed for the remaining rituals.

Those rituals done, the assassins slew all the priests but one. Then, slew themselves.

Being careful, even at the end, to keep the gore as minimal as possible.

That was not because of the needs of the rituals; which, to the contrary, normally put the gore to extensive use. But the goddess had ordered it all done quietly and economically.

Following the usual rituals would have permeated the chaundoli with a stench that the soldiers outside would have noticed almost immediately. As it was, in the heat of garam, they would notice it soon enough. Link wanted this army intact as long as possible, to keep Belisarius distracted.

The sole surviving priest remained at his duty. Simply sitting by the door to the chaundoli, that he might tell inquiring officers that the Great Lady was asleep and had given orders not to be disturbed.

In the special quarters far below the imperial palace at Kausambi, the eight-year-old girl known as Rani lay motionless and empty-eyed on the floor of her chamber. Her special Khmer attendants were deeply concerned, but could do nothing.

The sacred transference had happened, they knew. But it had happened much sooner than any of them had expected, including the girl herself.

She would survive, they decided. Beyond that, other than providing her with a cloth soaked in water to sip, they could only wait.

Tarun was too nervous to wait any longer. He'd gotten to the place Rajiv and he had picked long before he really needed to. It was an isolated corner in the maze of an outdoor bazaar not far from Kausambi's northernmost gate. At this time of night, the stalls were all closed and barred.

No one paid any attention to a twelve-year-old boy huddled in the darkness. There were many such in the city. A thief might have noticed the wrapped bundle beneath the boy's ragged cloak, but even if he had he would most likely have done nothing. What of any value could such a ragamuffin possess?

Still, the two hours Tarun waited seemed interminable to the stable-keeper's son. So, when he saw the first faint sign of dawn in the sky above, he rose and drew forth the signal rockets. There were three of them, in case of a misfire.

Nervous as he was, Tarun fumbled none of the tasks involved. Within seconds, one of the rockets was propped against the simple bamboo frame that held it erect, pointing at the sky. He lit the match, struck the fuse, and hurried to the other side of the stall.

He was even disciplined enough to remain there, the final seconds. If the rocket misfired, he'd retrieve the bamboo frame to use for a second.

For a wonder, nothing went wrong. The rocket didn't misfire, and it didn't blow up. It soared hundreds of yards into the dark sky above Kausambi.

It even exploded when it was supposed to. A great, bright yellow light shone over the city.

Tarun didn't spend any time admiring the sight, however. He just dropped the remaining rockets and hurried off. What would happen, would happen. He'd done his part and now simply wanted to get back to his family.

Few of the city's inhabitants ever saw the wondrous sight, for its people were mostly asleep.

The soldiers standing guard saw, of course, and raced to bring the news to their officers. *Something is happening at the northern gate!*

Valentinian and Anastasius and Ajatasutra and Tarun and their three Ye-tai mercenaries saw it also, of course. They arose from their own hiding place not far from the city's southern gate.

More precisely, Anastasius and Rajiv arose. The others remained in the small wagon, hidden from sight below a thin bamboo grate that held the produce which apparently filled the wagon's entire bed.

Anastasius seized the handles of the wagon, hauled it into the street, and began plodding toward the gate some fifty yards away. Rajiv walked beside him, dressed as a merchant's son. Clearly enough, the scion of a prosperous family assigned to oversee a strong but dimwitted laborer in his work.

"Why does the big guy always get stuck with these jobs?" complained Anastasius.

"Shut up," came Valentinian's voice from under the wagon's load. "You're not only as big as an ox, you look like one. Be thankful I didn't give Rajiv a whip."

✧   ✧   ✧

Rana Sanga saw it also. And the dam shattered.

He was on his horse and charging out of the lines within a minute, with ten thousand Rajputs following.

Only Rajputs, and only half of those. Damodara would use the other half, and the Ye-tai and the kshatriya, for whatever else was needed. But this charge, the emperor knew, belonged to Rana Sanga alone.

There would be nothing imperial about it, really. Just the nation of the Rajputs, finally and truly regaining its soul.

"For the glory of Rajputana!" Sanga called, his lance and its pennant on high, in a piercing voice that was half a bellow and half a shriek.

"RAJPUTANA!" came the response from ten thousand throats.

The Malwa soldiers on the southern wall of the city did not understand what was happening. They knew only three things.

One, most of the garrison had been ordered to the northern gate.

Two, a flood—a torrent—a tidal bore of Rajput lances was pouring past them on the ground beyond the walls.

Going where?

Who could say?

They only knew the third thing. Those lances looked as sharp as the sound of the Rajput battle cry.

"Shit," said one of them.

"What are we going to do?" asked his mate in the squad.

"Don't be an idiot. Try to stay alive, what else? Do *you* care who the emperor is?"

"Well. No."

Chapter 38
KAUSAMBI

Rajiv steeled himself. The two guards standing at the entrance to the gatehouse were among the ones he liked. Nice men, both of them—and so were their wives and kids.

"Rajiv?" asked Pallav. "What are you doing here? And with a wagon?"

"You know we can't let you out of the gate," said Gaurang.

Both of them were frowning, but neither had drawn his sword and their spears were still leaning against the gate hut. The many days Rajiv and Tarun had spent at the gate and the adjoining barracks, chatting with the guards and playing with their children, had made them a familiar sight. Besides, they were only boys.

"Oh, this is some stuff—food, mostly—my father told me I should bring you." Rajiv half turned, hiding the dagger he slid into his hand. "It's not much, really."

He frowned at Anastasius. "Put down the wagon, you cretin! Can't you see we've arrived?"

Anastasius, dull-faced, did as he was told. The moment Pallav stepped forward to look at the wagon's contents, Rajiv sprang.

Still, at the end—damn what the Mongoose would say—Rajiv made sure the blade sank into the meaty part of the soldier's thigh, not even close to the femoral artery. Twisting the dagger and snatching it out of the wound, Rajiv struck Pallav's head with the pommel. Being careful to avoid the fragile temple bones.

All to no purpose. Anastasius yanked the wagon handle out of its socket and crushed Pallav's skull as he fell. Then, in the back stroke, went for Gaurang. The slender arm the soldier threw up to block the blow was completely useless. As well block a rhino horn with a twig. His broken body was slammed into the hut so hard the flimsy wooden structure disintegrated.

Left to his own, Rajiv would probably have wasted some seconds, staring at the corpses. But the Mongoose was already out of the wagon and plunging into the open door of the gatehouse, spatha in hand. Ajatasutra was close behind.

There would be three or four more guards inside the gatehouse. Also men that Rajiv knew. Against the Mongoose, even if they'd been warned and ready, they'd have been dead men. As it was, the shrill cries of alarm and the soft wet sounds of massacre lasted but a few seconds. Most likely, Ajatasutra never got involved at all.

Fortunately, Rajiv didn't have to watch. Two men could work the gate mechanism, and there wasn't enough room in the narrow stairs leading up the tower or in the chamber above for more than two men anyway.

For such work, Valentinian and Ajatasutra were the obvious choices. Anastasius and Rajiv and the three Ye-tai mercenaries were assigned to guard the entrance and fend off the soldiers from the adjacent barracks, long enough to allow Valentinian and Ajatasutra to open the gate.

The Ye-tai were already shoving the wagon across the entrance, after finishing the work of casting off the bamboo grate and the produce covering it. Anastasius reached into the wagon bed and withdrew the big maul hidden there, along with his bow and arrows, and the mace he favored for close-in work.

After they'd opened the gate, Valentinian and Ajatasutra would return below to help in the defense, while Anastasius went upstairs and smashed the gate mechanism.

The mechanism was heavy, and very sturdy. But the maul was iron-headed, and very big. And Anastasius was Anastasius. Even if the soldiers could force their way up the tower, past one of the world's handful of great swordsmen and India's second-best assassin, it would take hours to repair the machinery and close the gates.

They would not have those hours. They would not even

have very many minutes. Rajiv's father had only a few miles to come.

He came, at an easy canter that the horses could maintain for some time without tiring. As eager and impatient as he was to reach the gate, the Rajput king was far too experienced a horseman to do otherwise. He would save the energy of a gallop for the very end.

Twenty minutes, he thought it would take.

He was eager, and impatient, but not worried. Rana Sanga had fought the Mongoose for hours, once. He did not think for a moment that, in narrow quarters, garrison troops could defeat him.

Not in twenty minutes. Probably not in twenty hours. Not without cannons, anyway.

Within five minutes, the warning was brought to the officer in command of the quarter's garrison. He was an exceptionally capable officer. Realizing immediately the implications, he ordered his soldiers to bring the four field guns they had. A six-pounder and three four-pounders.

They were an exceptionally well-trained unit, too. Five hundred men, no fewer. The commander was sure he could retake the gate once he reached it.

In ... perhaps fifteen minutes. More likely, twenty. His soldiers were already awake, since he'd ordered them aroused the moment he heard of the rocket, but they were still mostly in the barracks. The gate was a third of a mile away, and the streets were very narrow.

Twenty minutes should still be quick enough. The rebel army was concentrating its attack on the north, according to the reports he'd been given, where the signal rocket had been fired by spies. Probably that gate was being seized by traitors also. The commanding officer was quite experienced. Most sieges were broken by treachery, not guns.

The emperor, he thought sourly, would have done far better to have ordered his soldiers to search for spies, instead of hidden refugees. Who cared what a great lady and her children did, huddling in a cellar somewhere?

✧   ✧   ✧

The soldiers already at the gate were driven back within less than a minute. The sheer violence of the defense was not something they'd ever encountered. There was a huge ogre accompanying the traitors, whoever they were. A monstrous creature, that crushed the life out of men with its great mace, sometimes felling two soldiers with one blow. The ogre had fierce Ye-tai with it, too.

They reeled back, frightened. Their spears had been useless. Their swords, even more so.

"Bring bows!" shouted their commander. He was lacing on his armor, and having trouble with the task. He'd been sound asleep when the alarm was sounded, and was still feeling confused.

"Bring bows!" he shrieked again.

His men hurried to obey. The bows were kept in the barracks. And the ogre was *not* in the barracks.

Their commander gaped at the little flood of soldiers pouring back into the barracks.

"Not *all* of you! You—you—"

He collapsed to the ground. Even if he'd had his armor on properly, the arrow protruding from his chest would have punched right through it.

The few soldiers who hadn't returned to the barracks stared at the sight. Then, at the traitors positioned behind the wagon across the gatehouse entrance.

"*The ogre has a bow!*" screamed one of them. "*Ogre has a bow!*"

All but one of them made it back into the barracks. The slug-gard remained pinned to the doorway, by another arrow that struck . . .

Exactly the way you'd expect an ogre's arrow to strike. Went all the way through him and would have passed on completely except it hit the door post.

"Great big thing, too," muttered one of the soldiers, peeking out of a barracks window. "Way bigger than ours."

"Which gate?" shrieked Skandagupta. "*Which gate?* Speak plainly, damn you!"

The emperor was still muddle-headed with sleep. Dangerous at any time, he was positively venomous at times like this.

The general commanding the city's garrison wasn't sure of the answer himself. But what he said, very firmly and confidently, was: "Both gates, Your Majesty. The main attack seems to be coming at the north gate, however. Damodara himself is said to be leading the charge there."

That was true enough. Well. Probably. From the battlements, using telescopes, sentries had seen the rebel would-be emperor's pavilion being struck, and a surge of his soldiers toward the northern gate. A contingent of Ye-tai was leading the way, probably led by Toramana himself.

A slow surge, to be sure, except for the Ye-tai vanguard. Nothing like the charge being made by the Rajputs toward the southern gate. But that latter could be a feint.

"Then get yourself to the northern gate!" shrilled the emperor. "At once! Or I'll have your head for my collection! You coward! You stinking—"

"I obey, Your Majesty!" The general could safely take that shrieking imprecation for a royal dismissal. He was out of the audience chamber before the emperor had stopped cursing him.

He'd never felt such relief heading for a desperate battle in his life.

By the time the lieutenant who succeeded to command in the barracks could chivvy his soldiers out into the small square facing the gatehouse, another sound could be heard. Like a distant thunder, approaching. The sound of horses, and men shouting.

Rajiv understood the words before anyone else did.

Rajputana. And, also, the name of his father, chanted like a battle cry.

Rana Sanga.

His father was coming. Would be here within a minute or two. He and his warriors would come through that gate like an avalanche of steel.

His bow in hand and an arrow notched, Rajiv stared at the soldiers assembling fearfully in the square. In a minute, perhaps two, they would be swept from existence. Men he knew. Men whose wives and children he knew.

"It is not honorable," he murmured.

"What was that, boy?" asked Anastasius.

"It is not bearable," he added, still murmuring.

"Speak up, if you've got something to say!"

Rajiv removed the arrow from the bowstring. Still holding the bow, he sprang onto the wagon before the entrance. Then, with two steps and a sure-footed leap, he sprang off the wagon onto the hard-packed dirt of the square beyond.

"What the hell are you doing?" Anastasius bellowed.

Rajiv ignored him. He advanced toward the soldiers some forty yards away. The bow was still in his left hand, positioned as it should be. But he was now holding up the arrow as if it were a sword.

"Stop!" he cried. "I am Rajiv, a prince of Rajputana! Son of Rana Sanga!"

One of the soldiers in the front rank squinted at him. Abhay, that was. He had a son Rajiv's age, and a very pretty daughter about a year older. She'd been the source of new thoughts for Rajiv, in fact. New and rather unsettling ones.

"Rajiv? *Rajiv?*"

"Yes, Abhay! It is Rajiv!"

Still walking toward them, he pointed back at the opening gate with the arrow. "My father is coming! Listen, and you can hear!"

All the soldiers stopped moving, and froze.

Sure enough. Coming louder and louder:
Rana Sanga! Rajputana!

Worse yet:
Death to Skandagupta!
And they were Skandagupta's men.

Rajiv now raised the arrow high, as if it held a banner. "Swear fealty to me! Swear it now!"

Valentinian emerged from the gate tower. "All right, Anastasius. Get up there and—*what is that crazy kid doing?*"

Anastasius shook his head.

Ajatasutra came out also, in time to hear the exchange. After peering at the sight of Rajiv confronting the soldiers in the square, that familiar mocking smile came to his hawk face.

"Rajput prince. What do you expect?"

✧　　✧　　✧

"Swear it now!"

His voice broke—that too was new—and Rajiv silently cursed all new things.

He was even thinking about Abhay's daughter! Now—of all times!

Abhay looked at the soldier next to him. As if it were the first pebble in a cascade, that *look* passed from one soldier to the next.

The new commander saw, and cursed also. Not silently, however.

"Damn all traitors!" he shouted, pushing his way forward, spear in hand.

"All my efforts," Valentinian hissed. "Gone to waste. Ungrateful fucking stupid worthless brat."

The commander came out of the mass of soldiers, at a charge, his spear leveled.

Rajiv notched and fired the arrow in a movement so swift and sure not even Valentinian could really follow it. The commander fell dead, perhaps a foot of the shaft protruding from his throat.

"Well," said Valentinian. "Maybe not all."

"Swear it NOW!"

The sound of shrieking Rajput voices coming from beyond the walls was almost deafening.

But what decided Abhay, in the end, was not that. It was the thunderous sound—more deafening still—of thousands of galloping horses.

He was afraid of horses. Had been, ever since he was kicked by one as a boy. The other soldiers teased him about it.

He, too, lunged forward. But with his spear held crossways, not in the killing thrust his commander had tried.

"I swear, Rajiv! I swear!" He fell to his knees, the spear still held crossways. "I swear!"

It took not more than ten seconds before all the soldiers from the barracks were on their knees beside him, swearing likewise.

"On your feet!" Rajiv bellowed. Tried to, rather. His voice broke again.

He pointed with the bow. "Line up against the wall of the barracks! In good ranks, you hear? Your spears in hand—but held at standing rest!"

They'd be safe enough there, he thought. The square was small, true, but the portion in front of the barracks was something in the way of an offset little plaza. They wouldn't simply be trampled. And their families within the barracks would be safer still.

As long as Rajiv was standing in front of them, they'd be safe. Where his father could see him, the moment he came through the gate.

Which would be . . .

Any time now. He'd never heard such a sound in his life. It was simultaneously exhilarating and terrifying. Ten thousand galloping horses shaking the ground, while ten thousand warrior throats shook the air.

"I will be damned," Valentinian muttered.

"Speak up!" shouted Anastasius, standing right next to him. The world was filled with the noise of horses and battle cries. "I can't hear you!"

"I said: I will be damned!"

Anastasius shook his head. "Well, no kidding! You just figured that out?"

Valentinian scowled. Grinning, Anastasius pushed him toward the entrance to the gate tower.

"Come on! Let's get out of the way! Expert Rajput horsemen or not, I don't want to get trampled."

The courier galloped up to the city's commander.

"The southern gate!" he shrieked, pointing back with his finger. "Rajputs! Treason! The gate is open! The Rajputs are coming! Thirty thousand of them! By now, they're in the city!"

The commander stared to the south. That gate was too far away to see. He was almost at the northern gate, by now, with ten thousand of his own men packing the streets.

A courier galloped up from the north.

"The Ye-tai are at the gate! The rebel's Ye-tai! Ten thousand of them! Toramana himself is outside!"

The commander stared to the north. That gate he *could* see. And the odds were even.

"Death to Toramana!" he shouted, swinging his sword. "To the north gate!"

Toramana was indeed outside the gate. But with only three thousand soldiers, not the ten thousand Sanga was leading into the city through the southern gate.

They were all Ye-tai soldiers, however. Quite visibly so. Toramana had seen to that.

The commander of Damodara's Ye-tai troops was sitting on his horse and looking up at the soldiers manning the gate. Very boldly, within bow range.

The soldiers on those walls were mostly Ye-tai also, as Damodara's spies had reported.

"Come on, boys!" Toramana shouted. "It's all over, and you know it! So what's it going to be? Service with me? Beer, women, and a long life?"

He drew his sword and raised it, as if inspecting the edge of the blade.

"Or do we have to get messy about this?"

One of the Ye-tai soldiers on the walls was looking the other way, into the city.

"The commander's coming," he said, almost idly. "Took the bastard long enough. Got maybe three thousand men with him. Up close, anyway. More than that, trailing behind."

He didn't use the commander's name. Few of Kausambi's Ye-tai soldiers did. The man was a cypher to him. Just another one of the political generals churned up by the endless scheming within the Malwa dynastic clan. Very deadly scheming, of late.

Now, he turned and looked at his own platoon commander. So did all the other Ye-tai on the wall nearby.

The officer rubbed his face. "Ah, shit."

His soldiers waited, silently.

"Ah, shit," he repeated. Then he lowered his hand and said: "Make them open the gate. Let Toramana deal with the rest."

Before he finished, three of the Ye-tai were already plunging into the gatehouse.

They had their swords in hand, just in case the stupid peasants who actually operated the gate mechanism chose to argue the matter.

Not likely, of course.

When he saw the gate start to open, Toramana grinned. Sanga wouldn't get *all* the glory.

He did not forget, of course, to wave his sword in salute at the Ye-tai on the battlements, as he led his men into the city. All three thousand of them, except a few couriers sent racing off to tell Damodara that there were now two breaches in Kausambi's walls.

For their part, the Ye-tai on the walls returned his salute with the proper salutations.

"Long live the new emperor!" bellowed one of them.

His mate elbowed him.

"Long live the *rightful* emperor!" he corrected himself.

"Death to the impostor Skandagupta!" his mate chimed in.

When Skandagupta saw the girl enter the imperial audience chamber, forcing her way past the assembled courtiers, he broke off in mid-tirade.

"Rani?" he whispered.

The eight-year-old girl was now past the courtiers, and standing in front of the throne.

The blood drained from his face. A face that felt as empty as the one before him. The eyes before him.

"*Great Lady* Rani," the girl said.

Her voice changed, then. Into something no girl—no woman of any age—could possess.

"GREAT LADY RANI, NOW. YOU WILL OBEY ME, SKAN-DAGUPTA."

But all the emperor could do was scream.

Chapter 39
KAUSAMBI

The first thing Rana Sanga saw, after he charged through the gate into the square beyond, was his son. Rajiv, holding a bow but not wearing armor, standing in front of perhaps a hundred soldiers assembled in ranks in front of the gate's barracks.

It was one of the great moments of his life. Greater, even, than the first time he held his first-born child in his hands.

A tiny thing, Rajiv had been then, in Sanga's very large hands.

He would never be as big as Sanga. In that, Rajiv took after his mother. But, at that moment, he seemed to stand as tall as Sanga himself, sitting on his great warhorse.

"My soldiers, father!" Rajiv spread his hands, the left still holding the bow, as if to shelter the soldiers behind him. "My soldiers! Loyal and sworn to me! They are not to be harmed!"

Sanga had brought his horse to a halt, ten yards from Rajiv. A small clot of his lieutenants swirled around him.

He pointed his lance into the city. "To the imperial palace! I want Skandagupta's head! I will follow in a moment!"

The lieutenants wheeled their horses and resumed leading the charge. Hundreds, and hundreds, and hundreds of Rajputs followed them. Slowed greatly, of course, as they squeezed through the gate. But resuming the gallop immediately thereafter.

Finally, Sanga was able to move his gaze from his son's face, to examine the soldiers behind him.

He almost laughed. If there was one of them not trembling, Sanga could not spot him.

Abhay was certainly trembling. He had never in his life seen anything so fearsome as the Rajput king astride his horse a few yards away.

The horse alone would have been terrifying. Several hands taller than any horse Abhay had ever seen, clad in its own armor, the beast had eyes that seemed to be filled with fury and its huge nostrils breathed rage.

But the king atop it! Steel helmet, steel chain and plate armor, steel-headed lance—even the shaft of the lance seemed like steel.

Not to mention being far larger than any lance Abhay could have held easily, even with both hands. In the huge, gauntleted hand of the Rajput king, it seemed as light as a wand.

The king was glaring, too. Or had some sort of scary expression on his face.

Just to make things complete, he had a *name*.

Rana Sanga. Every soldier in India had heard of Rana Sanga. The stories were endless.

And each and every one of them was true. Abhay didn't doubt it for a moment. Not any longer.

Sanga wasn't exactly glaring. He was simply, in his austere manner, trying to disguise both great pride and great amusement.

Sworn to his son's service, no less! The most wretched pack of garrison troops Sanga had ever seen!

But there was no contempt in the thoughts. Not even for the soldiers, and certainly not for Rajiv.

Sanga understood full well, what had happened here. He would not have done it himself. But he understood it.

"My wife's son, too," he murmured. "My great and glorious wife."

A movement caught his attention. Turning his head, he saw the Mongoose emerging from the gatehouse.

He slid the lance into its scabbard, and swung down gracefully from the saddle. Then, strode toward him.

As he neared, he saw that the Mongoose was scowling. Half-anger and half . . .

Embarrassment? That seemed odd.

"Look," the Mongoose rasped. "I tried my level best. It's not *my* fault your son is crazy."

Abhay was astonished to see the Rajput king—so tall he was! even standing!—burst into laughter.

More astonished, still, to see him kneel before the foreign soldier.

Kneel, and extend his sword, hilt-first.

The words he spoke were clear to Abhay, who was standing not that far away. But they were simply meaningless.

"I am forever in your debt, Valentinian of Rome."

The Roman soldier named Valentinian cleared his throat.

"Yes, well," he said.

"Name the service, and I will do it," insisted the Rajput king.

"Yes, well," Valentinian repeated.

The ogre had emerged from the gatehouse in time to hear the exchange.

"Valentinian, you're a fucking idiot," Abhay heard him growl. Much more loudly: "As it happens, Rana Sanga, there is one small little favor you could do us. A family matter, you might say. But later! Later! There's still a battle to be won."

Sanga rose, sheathing his sword. "As you say. The favor is yours, whatever it is. For the moment, I will trust you to keep my family safe."

"Well, sure," said Valentinian.

Then he was back to scowling. Rajiv stepped forward and insisted on accompanying his father.

Abhay felt fear return, in full force. He did *not* want to fight a battle. Any battle, anywhere—much less the great, swirling chaos that Kausambi had become.

"You are not armored, Rajiv," his father pointed out, mildly. "And your only weapons are a bow and a dagger."

Rajiv turned to face Abhay, who was a small man.

"You're about my size. Give me your armor. Your spear and sword, also."

Hastily—eagerly—ecstatically, Abhay did as he was commanded.

"Stay here—you and all the others," Rajiv told him quietly. "Protect your families, that's all. You wouldn't be—well. That'll be good enough. Just keep your wife and children safe. Especially your daughter. Ah, I mean, daughters."

Sanga still seemed hesitant.

He turned to Valentinian. "Is he ready for this? He's only thirteen."

Scowling seemed to come naturally to the Roman soldier. "You mean, other than being crazy? Yeah, he's ready. The truth is, he's probably better than most of your Rajputs. Already."

The Rajput king seemed, somehow, to grow taller still.

"The Mongoose says this?"

"Well, yeah. The Mongoose says so. What the hell. I trained him, didn't I?"

A few minutes later, they were gone. The Rajput king and his son, toward the imperial palace. The ogre—who turned out to be another Roman soldier—and the narrow-faced one who was almost as frightening, went somewhere else. The Ye-tai went with them, thankfully.

Where they went, exactly, Abhay didn't know. Wherever Sanga's family was hidden, he assumed.

He wasn't about to ask. He was not a crazy Rajput prince.

Fortunately, Sanga had left one of his Rajput soldiers behind. An older man; too much the veteran to find any great glory in the last battle of a war. Enough glory, anyway, to offset the risk of not being around to enjoy the fruits of victory afterward.

Somebody had to lend Rajiv a horse, after all. Who better than a grizzled oldster?

He was a cheerful fellow. Who, to the great relief of Abhay and the other garrison soldiers, just waved on the Rajputs who kept coming through the gate. There was never a moment when any real threat emerged.

Coming, and coming, and coming. It took an hour, it seemed—perhaps longer—before they all passed through. "Storming the gate," when the soldiers numbered in the thousands and the gate was not really all that wide, turned out to be mostly a poetic expression.

Abhay found that somehow reassuring. He didn't like poetry, all that much. But he liked it a lot better than he liked horses.

✧   ✧   ✧

Toramana personally slew the commander of Kausambi, in the battle that erupted in the narrow streets less than two minutes after he and his Ye-tai started passing through the north gate.

He made a point of it, deliberately seeking out the man once he spotted the plumed helmet.

Idiot affectation, that was. Toramana's own helmet was as utilitarian and unadorned as that of any of his soldiers.

It didn't take much, really. The city's commander was leading garrison troops who hadn't seen a battle since Ranapur. Toramana and his Ye-tai had spent years fighting Belisarius and Rao.

So, a tiger met a mongrel cur in the streets of Kausambi. The outcome was to be expected. Would have been the same, even if the fact they were outnumbered didn't matter. In those narrow streets, only a few hundred men on each side could fight at one time, anyway.

When he saw Toramana coming, hacking his way through the commander's bodyguard, the Malwa general tried to flee.

But, couldn't. The packed streets made everything impossible, except the sort of close-in brutal swordwork that the Ye-tai excelled in and his own men didn't.

Neither did their general. Toramana's first strike disarmed him; the second cut off his hand; the third, his head.

"Save the head," Toramana commanded, after the garrison troops were routed.

His lieutenant held it up by the hair, still dripping blood.

"Why?" he asked skeptically. Toramana's Ye-tai, following their commander's example, were not much given to military protocol. "Getting divorced and remarried, already?"

Toramana laughed. "I don't need it for more than a day. Just long enough so those damned Rajputs don't get *all* the credit."

The lieutenant nodded, sagely. "Ah. Good idea."

Even with the partial data at its disposal—even working through the still-awkward sheath of a girl much too young for the purpose—Link knew what to do.

It still didn't know the exact nature of the disaster that had befallen it, while ensconced in the sheath named Sati. As always,

Link's memories only went as far as Sati's last communion with the machines in the cellars.

It didn't really matter.

Belisarius, obviously. As before.

The great plan of the new gods lay in shattered ruin. India was now lost. If Link had been in an adult sheath, it might have tried to rally the city's soldiers. But trapped in a girl's body, and with an emperor who had never been very competent and was now half-hysterical, such an attempt would be hopeless.

True, Damodara's forces were still outnumbered by Kausambi's garrison. Link knew that, within a ninety-three percent probability, despite the prattle of panicked courtiers and officers.

But that, too, didn't matter. There was no comparison at all between the morale and cohesion of the opposing sides. Damodara's army had the wind in its sails, now that it had breached the city's walls. Worse still, it had commanders who knew how to use that wind, beginning with Damodara himself.

The only really seasoned army Link had was in the Punjab. A huge army, but it might as well have been on the moon. That army had been paralyzed by Belisarius, it was much too far away for Link to control any longer—and none of the garrisons in any of the cities in the Ganges plain could serve as a rallying point. Not after Kausambi fell, as it surely would by nightfall.

All that remained—all that *could* remain—was to salvage what pieces it could and begin anew.

Start from the very beginning, all over again. Worse than that, actually. Link would lose the machinery in the imperial cellars. Without that machinery, it could not be transferred once its current sheath died or became too old or ill to be of use. Link would die with it.

Perhaps it was fortunate, after all, that the sheath was only eight years old.

Not that Link really thought in terms like "fate" or "fortune." Still, it was a peculiar twist in probabilities. It would take at least half a century for Link to re-create that machinery, even after it made its way to the Khmer lands.

The work could not be done there, in the first place. In this world, only the Romans and the Chinese had the technical wherewithal, with Link to guide the slave artisans.

Fortunately, the new gods had planned for such an unlikely outcome. Link held the designs in its mind for much cruder machines that would still accomplish the same basic task.

Half a century, at least. Hopefully, the sheath would prove to be long-lived. They normally weren't, simply because Link made no effort to keep them alive, if doing so was at all inconvenient. But it knew how to do so, if it chose, assuming the genetic material was not hopeless. The regimen was very strict, but—obviously— that posed no problem at all. Food meant nothing at all to Link, and the time spent in mindless exercise could still be used for calculations.

"Where are we going?" whispered Skandagupta. His voice was still hoarse, from the earlier screaming.

"BE SILENT OR YOU WILL DIE."

The threat was not an idle one. An eight-year-old girl's body could not have overwhelmed Skandagupta, even as pudgy and unfit as he was. But Link had kept its special assassins, after ordering them to kill all the women in the cellars. Any one of the assassins—much less all three—could have slain Skandagupta instantly.

The specially trained women would have been useful, later. But they were simply not trained, nor physically conditioned after years living in cellars, for the rigors of the journey that lay ahead. And Link could not afford to leave them alive. Under torture, they might say too much about their origins.

It was questionable whether Skandagupta would survive those rigors. Link's sheath was small enough that it could be carried by the assassins, when necessary. Skandagupta was not, even after he lost his fat, as he surely would. Link could not afford to wear out its assassins.

As it was, Link had almost ordered the emperor killed anyway. The probabilities teetered on a knife's edge. On the one hand, Skandagupta was an obvious impediment in the immediate future. On the other hand . . .

It was hard to calculate. There were still too many variables involved. But there were enough of them to indicate that, given many factors, having the legitimate emperor of India ready at hand might prove useful.

No matter. Link could always have Skandagupta murdered later, after all.

The tunnel they were passing through was poorly lit. Skanda-gupta stumbled and fell again.

The shock was enough to jar the creature out of its fear. "Where are we *going*? And what will happen to my wife and children?"

Link decided that answering was more efficient than another threat.

"WE ARE GOING TO THE KHMER LANDS. I PREPARED THIS ESCAPE ROUTE DECADES AGO. YOUR WIFE AND DAUGHTERS ARE IRRELEVANT, SINCE THEY ARE OUT-SIDE THE SUCCESSION. YOUR ONLY SON, ALSO. BY THE END OF THE DAY HE WILL HAVE EITHER RENOUNCED HIS HERITAGE AND PUBLICLY ADMITTED DAMODARA'S FORGERIES TO BE THE TRUTH, OR HE WILL BE DEAD."

Skandagupta moaned.

"IF HE SPEAKS AGAIN WITHOUT PERMISSION," Link instructed the assassins, "BEAT HIM."

"How badly, Mistress?"

"LEAVE HIS LEGS UNDAMAGED. HIS BRAIN ALSO, SUCH AS IT IS. SO LONG AS HE CAN STILL WALK."

Damodara entered the palace just as the sun was setting. There was still some fighting in the city, here and there, but not much.

It was all over. His great gamble had worked.

"Skandagupta's son says he will agree to the—ah—new docu-ments," Narses said.

Damodara considered the matter. "Not good enough. He has to swear he's a bastard, also. His real father was . . . whoever. Pick one of the courtiers whose heads decorate the walls outside. Someone known to be foul as well as incompetent."

Narses sneered. "Hard to choose among them, given those qualifications."

"Don't take long." Damodara's lips twisted into something that was perhaps less of a sneer, but every bit as contemptuous. "I want those heads off the walls and buried or burnt by tomor-row afternoon. The impaled bodies, by mid-morning. What a stench!"

"Yes, Your Majesty."

"My wife? Children?"

"They should be here within an hour. They're all safe and well."

Damodara nodded. "See to it that stable-keeper is rewarded. Lavishly. In addition to being made the new royal stable-master."

"Yes, Your Majesty. What about—"

"The two Roman soldiers?" Damodara shook his head, wonder-ingly. "What sort of reward would be suitable, for such service as that?"

Narses' sneer returned. "Oh, they'll think of something."

"Someone's coming," said one of the members of the assassi-nation team. He spoke softly. Just as softly as he let the grasses sway back, hiding their position alongside the road to the Bay of Bengal.

"Who?"

"Don't know. But from the clothes he's wearing, someone important, even though he's on foot. He's got a girl with him, and those weird little yellow assassins the witches keep around."

The captain frowned. He knew who the man was talking about, of course, even if none of the regular Malwa assassination teams ever had much contact with the witches and their entourage. But they'd always paid some attention to the Khmer assassins. Just keeping an eye on the competition, as it were.

"What in the world would . . . Let me see."

He slithered his way to the top of the knoll and carefully parted the grasses.

"It's the *emperor*," he hissed.

"Are you sure?" asked his lieutenant.

"Come and look for yourself, if you don't believe me."

The lieutenant did so. Like the captain, though not the other three assassins, he'd been introduced to the emperor once. At a distance, of course, and as part of a small crowd. But it was something a man remembered.

"Damned if you're not right. But what would *he* be doing— Oh. Stupid question."

The captain smiled, sardonically. "I guess we know who won the siege."

He took a deep breath and let it out. "Well, thank whatever

gods there are. After eleven thousand wasted miles and I don't want to think how many wasted hours, we've finally got something to do."

Fortunately, they'd hauled their little bombard the whole way. For all their diminutive size, the Khmer assassins were deadly. But a blast of canister swept them away as neatly as you could ask for. The one who survived, unconscious and badly wounded, got his throat cut a few seconds later.

They hadn't intended to hit the emperor or the girl, but the group had been tightly bunched and canister just naturally spreads.

The girl wasn't too badly hurt. Just a single ball in the left arm. She might lose the arm, but it could have been worse.

There was no chance, however, that Skandagupta would survive.

"Gut-shot," the lieutenant grunted. "He'll die in agony, in a few days. Damodara might like that."

The captain shook his head. "Not by reputation, and all we really need is the head, anyway. Or do *you* want to carry the fat little bastard?"

The lieutenant eyed the distant walls of Kausambi. Night was falling, but he could still hear the sounds of scattered fighting.

"Well . . . it's only a few miles. But after eleven thousand, I'm not in the mood for any extra effort." He knelt down, and with a few expert strokes, severed the imperial head.

The girl was still squalling at them, as she had been since the attack. It was a very strange sound, coming from such a small female. As if her voice emerged from a huge cavern of a chest.

Consciously and deliberately, the assassins had blocked the actual words from their minds. You had to be careful, dealing with the witches. Which she obviously was, despite her youth. A witch-in-training, at least.

The captain struck her on the head with the pommel of his dagger. Carefully, just enough to daze the creature.

You never knew, with the witches and the imperial dynasty—of which Damodara was still a part, after all. The reward might be greater, if she were still alive.

Alive, however, was good enough.

"I'm sick of that squalling," said the captain. "Her eyes are creepy, too. Gag her and blindfold her, before she comes to."

✧   ✧   ✧

They decided to wait until the next day, before entering the city to seek their reward. By then, the fighting should have ended.

Before long, however, the captain was regretting that decision. They were all very well-traveled, by now, and—alas—the lieutenant liked to read.

"You know," he said, "the story has it that when some Persians presented Alexander the Great with the body of Darius, he had them all executed. For regicide, even though he was hunting the former emperor himself."

Silently, the captain cursed all well-read men. Then, because maintaining morale was his duty, pointed out the obvious.

"Don't be silly. Alexander the Great was a maniac. Everybody says Damodara is a level-headed, practical fellow."

Lord Samudra learned the war was over that night, from a radio message sent from Kausambi.

```
FALSE   EMPEROR  OVERTHROWN  STOP   TRUE
EMPEROR  DAMODARA  SITS  ON  THRONE  IN
KAUSAMBI  STOP  YOU  WILL  OBEY  HIM  LORD
SAMUDRA  STOP  WAR  IS  OVER  STOP  ESTABLISH
LIAISON  WITH  MAURICE  OF  THRACE  TO
NEGOTIATE  CEASE  FIRE  WITH  ROMAN  AND
PERSIAN  ARMIES  IN  PUNJAB  STOP
```

"What are you going to do?" asked one of his aides.

Samudra let the message fall to the table in the bunker. "What do you think? I'm going to do exactly as I'm told. The Romans will have received the same message. By now, they've got us outnumbered. Between them and the Persians, we're facing something like two hundred thousand men."

"And we're losing soldiers by the droves every day," said a different aide, gloomily. "As much by desertion as disease."

There was silence, for a time. Then Samudra said: "You want to know the truth? I know Damodara pretty well. We're cousins, after all. He's about ten times more capable than Skandagupta and—best of all—he's even-tempered."

There was further silence, finally broken by one of the aides.

"Long live the new emperor, then."

"Idiot," said Samudra tonelessly. "Long live the *true* emperor. The greatest army of the Malwa empire does not obey rebels, after all."

It was several days before Belisarius learned the war was over. The news was brought to him by a special courier sent by Damodara.

A Rajput cavalryman, naturally. The man was exceptionally proud—as well he might be—that he'd made the ride as fast as he had, without killing a single horse.

"So, that's it," said Belisarius, rising from his squat across from Kungas.

The two of them emerged from the hut and studied the Malwa army they'd trapped on the Ganges.

There'd been little fighting, and none at all for the past four days.

"You were right, I think," said Kungas. "The bitch did kill herself, days ago."

"Most likely. We'll know soon enough. That army's looking at starvation, before too long. They slaughtered their last horses two days ago."

"I'll send an envoy to them. Once they get the news, they'll surrender."

The Kushan king eyed Belisarius. "You know, I don't think I've ever seen that crooked a smile on your face. What amuses you so?"

"I've got a reputation to maintain. You do realize, don't you, that in the days when the final battle was fought and won in the greatest war in history, Belisarius spent his time doing nothing more than drinking lousy wine and gambling with dice?"

Kungas chuckled. "You lost, too. By now, you owe me a small chest of gold."

"Not all that small, really."

But Kungas had stopped chuckling. Another thought had come to him, that caused his notoriously expressionless face to twist into a grimace.

"Oh. You'll never stop crowing about it, will you?"

When Maurice heard, it put him in a foul mood for a full day.

Calopodius' mood was not much better. "How in the name of God am I supposed to put *that* in my history? You can only do so much with classical allusions, you know. Grammar and rhetoric collapse under that crude a reality."

"Who gives a damn?" snarled Maurice. "You think *you've* got problems? I'm still in good health, and I'm only twenty years older than the bastard. Years and years, I'll have to listen to him bragging."

"He's not really a boastful man," pointed out Calopodius.

"Not usually, no. But with something like *this?* Ha! You watch, youngster. Years and years and years."

Chapter 40
KAUSAMBI

The damage Kausambi had suffered in the fighting was minimal, considering the huge size of the city. Belisarius had seen far worse before, any number of times. Damodara's forces had been able to breach the walls in two places, without having to suffer heavy casualties in the doing, because the gates had been opened from the inside. As a result, none of the three factors had been operating that, singly or in combination, usually produced horrible sacks.

First, the troops pouring into the city were still under the control of their officers, because the officers themselves had not suffered many casualties and led them through the gates.

Second, the soldiers were not burning with a desire for vengeance on those who had—often horribly, with the most ghastly weapons—butchered their mates while they were still fighting outside the walls.

So, the sort of spontaneously erupting military riot-in-all-but-name that most "sacks" constituted, had never occured. Beyond, at least, a few isolated incidents—always involving liquor—that Damodara's officers had squelched immediately.

And, third, of course—not all sacks were spontaneous—the commander of the victorious besieging army had not ordered one, after his troops seized the city.

Skandagupta would have done so, of course. But Damodara ruled now, not Skandagupta, and he was a very different sort of man. The only thing of Skandagupta that remained was his head, perched on a spike at the entrance to the imperial palace.

It was the only head there. Damodara had ordered all the other corpses and heads removed.

After dismounting from his horse, Belisarius took a moment to admire the thing.

Pity, though, he said to Aide. *Agathius swore he'd someday see Skandagupta lying dead in the dust. I'm afraid there's not much chance of that, now.*

In garam season? No chance at all. Unless he'd be satisfied with looking at a skull. That thing already stinks.

Aide, of course, was detecting the stench through Belisarius' own nostrils. As he had many times before, Belisarius wondered how the jewel perceived things on his own. He *could* do so, Belisarius knew, although the manner of it remained mysterious. Aide and the other crystal beings had none of the senses possessed by the protoplasmic branch of the human family.

But whatever those methods were, Aide had not used them in years. He'd told Belisarius that he found it much easier to do his work if he restricted himself to perceiving the world only through Belisarius' senses.

A courtier—no, a small pack of them—emerged from the palace entrance and hastened down the broad stone stairs at the bottom of which Belisarius was standing.

"General Belisarius!" one of them said. "The emperor awaits you!"

He managed to make that sound as if Damodara was bestowing an immense—no, divine—favor upon the Roman general. Which was laughable, really, since the same Rajput courier who had brought the news of Damodara's triumph had also brought a private message from the new Malwa emperor asking Belisarius to come to Kausambi immediately to "deal with a delicate and urgent matter." The tone of the message had been, if not pleading, certainly not peremptory or condescending.

Courtiers, Belisarius thought sarcastically, handing the reins of his horse to one of the Rajputs who had escorted him to Kausambi. *However else people in different lands may vary in their customs, I think courtiers are the same everywhere.*

Normally, Aide would have responded with a quip of his own.

But the jewel seemed strangely subdued. He had said very little since they entered the city.

Belisarius thought that was odd. Looked at in some ways—most ways, rather—this final triumph belonged to Aide more than it did to Belisarius or Damodara or anyone else. But he didn't press for an explanation. In the years that he and Aide had shared a mind, for all practical purposes, they'd both learned to respect the privacy of the other.

The Malwa imperial palace was the largest in the world. So far as Belisarius knew, anyway. There might be something equivalent in one of the many kingdoms in China that were vying for power. "Largest," at least, in the sense of being a single edifice. The Roman imperial complex at Constantinople covered more acreage, but much of it was gardens and open walkways.

He'd visited the palace before, a number of times, when he'd come to India years earlier in what amounted to the capacity of a spy. With the help of Aide's perfect memory, Belisarius knew the way to the imperial audience chamber. He could have gone there himself, without needing the guidance of the courtiers.

But, perhaps not. Soon, the courtiers were leading him down a hallway he'd never been in. Old, ingrained habit made him check the spatha in its scabbard, to see that it was loose and would come out easily.

Although the movement was subtle, he made no attempt at all to keep it surreptitious. The courtiers had irritated him enough that he felt no desire to accommodate them. Emperor Damodara had, after all, invited *General* Belisarius into his presence. Generals carried swords. Good generals with combat experience carried sharp swords, and made sure they weren't stuck in their scabbards.

One of the courtiers who observed seemed brighter than the rest. Or, at least, didn't suffer from the usual moronic state of the courtier mentality, whose defining characteristic was to think that power emanated from itself.

"The emperor is not waiting for you in the audience chamber, General," he explained quietly. "He awaits you in, ah . . ."

The hostile glances coming from several other courtiers caused him to falter. "Someplace else," he finished lamely.

Aide spoke for the first time since they'd entered the palace. **He's found the lair. Link's lair. That's where we're going.**

Belisarius nodded. And, again, made sure the spatha was loose. *What about Link itself?*

Damodara's message had said nothing on that subject.

I don't know. I think he must have Link also. Or his message would have been ... different.

Belisarius thought about it. *Yes, you're right. He wouldn't have called it a "delicate" matter as well as an "urgent" one.*

But they were entering a chamber, now, and speculation could come to an end. Damodara was there, waiting, along with Rana Sanga and a big Ye-tai officer whom Belisarius had never met before. The now-famous Toramana, he presumed.

His eyes, however, were immediately drawn to the side. Two other men were standing there, who—for the moment—meant far more to Belisarius.

"I'm glad you survived," he said. "I was worried you wouldn't, when I sent you off."

Anastasius' huge shoulders moved in a shrug. "Wasn't really that bad, General. For starters, we didn't have to protect *you.* Mindouos and Anatha were worse—not to mention the battle at the Pass."

Valentinian grinned, in his savage way. "Way worse," he chimed in, reaching up and running fingers through his coarse black hair. For a moment, a long scar was visible—the scar Sanga had given him in their famous duel. "We'll ask you to remember that, though, when it comes time to figure out our retirement bonus."

Even with an emperor waiting, Belisarius would deal with this first.

"Just tell me what you want. If I can manage it, I will. The two of you long ago stopped being in the category of 'common soldiers.'"

The tall Rajput king standing a few feet away issued a snort. "The truth, that!" He gave the two cataphracts a look that Belisarius couldn't quite interpret. Deep respect was there, obviously, but there was something else. Not derision, exactly, but amusement of some kind.

For the first time that day, Aide's voice had a trace of his usual good humor. **I still don't understand how a man as smart as you can be such a dummy about some things.**

What do you mean?

You didn't figure out what Agathius was doing, either, until your nose was rubbed in it. *I* **figured it out right away. But I'll remind you that there's an emperor waiting, here—and the Malwa empire is still probably the most powerful empire in the world. Will be for sure, in a few years, once Damodara gets settled in. Best to stay on good terms with him.**

That was good advice. Belisarius turned to face Damodara and bowed.

"You asked for me, Your Majesty. How may I be of service?"

A quick smile flashed across Damodara's face. "Well, starting tomorrow, you can be of service by providing all of us with your good sense. We have a complicated peace settlement to make, you know. And we're already arguing over where to hold the conference. Fortunately—so far—it's been mostly an argument over the radio and telegraph."

The Malwa emperor lifted his hand. "But that's for tomorrow. Today, there's a different decision that faces us. Probably a more important one. And it's not a decision I feel anyone but you can make."

Belisarius took a deep breath. "You found Link. And its lair."

"The first, yes. The second—" Damodara shrugged. "'Found' is hardly the word. I already knew where it was. All the members of the dynastic clan—boys, at least—are taken to it at least once. I was there several times."

"Take me there," Belisarius said. Commanded, rather.

Belisarius could make no sense at all of the machines in the chamber far below the palace. The problem wasn't so much that, in their gleaming blankness, they seemed more like magic artifacts than what he thought of as "machines." It was that he knew he would never understand what they did or how they worked.

I don't understand them either, really. I don't think even the Great Ones do, except in general terms. The new gods developed cybernetics far beyond any other branch of the human race. The Great Ones took a different direction. One that led to us crystals. And while we share some of the characteristics of computers, we are very different in other ways.

How could they bring all this here, through time, when all the

Great Ones could do—and that, barely—was send you as a semi-conscious thing? Apologetically, he added: *When you first arrived, I mean. You're hardly "semi-conscious" now.*

For one thing, the Great Ones aren't as ruthless. The energy expenditure required to send these machines back through time destroyed the new gods' own planet. Along with most of their people. Sub-species, it would be better to say. There were not many survivors.

Sensing the question before Belisarius could ask it, Aide added: **Yes, they knew that would happen. The ones who managed it, at least. Most of their people didn't, the ones who were destroyed. Even the new gods have factions. The faction that did this—which is all that is left—are . . .**

Fanatics, Belisarius supplied. *Fanaticism carried to the extremes you'd expect of "supermen." I understand.*

But it was time, now, to ignore the machines. Damodara had not brought Belisarius here to deal with them. Not principally, at least.

He turned and studied the small female shackled to a chair. He couldn't see much of her, since there was a hood over her head.

Don't look, said Aide.

No. I must.

Three strides and he was there; a quick movement of the hand, and the hood was removed.

It was the face of a young girl, perhaps seven or eight years old. All but the eyes that stared up at him. Those belonged to no human being at all. Their brown color was irrelevant. The emptiness within overwhelmed it.

The girl was gagged, too.

Don't listen to it.

No, I must.

It took longer to remove the gag. The knot holding it in place was very tight. As he worked at the task, he could hear the indrawn breaths of the people behind him.

As ever, Aide's ability to enhance Belisarius' senses was handy. There were five other men in the room, and four of them were holding their breath. The fifth one was breathing the same way he always did.

Belisarius had known he would be. Had that man not been

present, he might never have dared to do this. Belisarius was probably as great a general as Alexander the Great, but he never thought like Alexander. He was who he was because of the men he knew how to lead—and rely upon—not because he thought he was the son of Zeus.

The gag came off.

"LISTEN TO ME, BELISARIUS. THERE IS STILL TIME—"

Quickly, he replaced the gag. "Shut up, monster. I just needed to hear that voice. To be sure."

He stepped back and drew his spatha. *Guide me, Aide.*

Were any other girls found?

He passed the question along. Damodara answered: "One. She's not more than two years old. I think she's the daughter of one of the provincial governors. I have her in a chamber upstairs. I haven't known what to do with her, either."

Destroy the machines first. Without the machines, Link is trapped in this body sitting before you. The little girl upstairs will be ... probably not a very normal child. But a harmless one.

Again, Aide anticipated the next question:

These are just machines, Belisarius. No different, in the end, than a simple pottery wheel. In some ways, in fact, even more fragile. Anastasius and a big hammer will do fine.

That required a delay, to have a maul brought down. But, eventually, the maul arrived and Anastasius went to work.

With a vengeance, as the expression went—and no expression here. Not even in the battle in the tight confines of Great Lady Holi's cabin had Belisarius seen Anastasius swing a mace with such violence.

In three minutes, it was done, and Anastasius stepped back.

Throughout, Link had simply observed. There had been no expression at all in the girl's face. The eyes had neither narrowed nor widened. There had been no frown. No tightening of the jaws.

Nothing.

It is simply a calculator, Belisarius. Even now, when the probabilities within which it moves are a tiny fraction of one percent, it is still calculating. It will never stop calculating. It cannot. It ...

There came the crystalline equivalent of a deep sigh. **It is really, really not human. Not even in the way we crystals are,**

or the Great Ones. It is just a machine itself. Programmed to do what it does—can only do—by monsters.

Yes, I understand. Belisarius stepped forward, within a pace of the girl bound to the chair. His grip on the spatha was tight, much tighter than he would have held it in an actual fight.

Will it . . .

Yes. Destroy the girl's body and you destroy Link. It does not "die," exactly, for it was never alive at all. But it will be gone. It will no longer exist.

Still, he hesitated. Whatever he *knew,* his emotional reactions could not avoid the monster's form.

True enough, Belisarius had slain young girls. Many times, in fact. Just recently, his burning and destruction in the Ganges campaign had condemned many such to death. Damodara had agreed to send relief expeditions, as soon as possible. But with the inevitable chaos attendant upon a successful rebellion, no expedition could possibly arrive in time to save everyone.

Dozens of seven- and eight-year-old girls just like this one— more likely hundreds, or possibly even thousands—would be dying soon. Some were dead already. Each and every one of whom could, rightfully, have had the words *Murdered by Belisarius* engraved on their tomb markers.

Still, he hadn't done it *personally.* And if that difference might be meaningless, on a philosophical level, a man does not hold and wield a spatha using philosophy. He uses muscles and nerves and blood shaped and molded by emotion from the time he is born.

Don't be foolish, Aide said softly. **You know the answer. Why be proud, at the end, when you never were before?**

He was right, of course. Belisarius stepped back.

"Valentinian. A last service, if you would."

"Sure, General."

The cataphract came forward, his spatha flashed, and it was over. A spray of blood across shattered machinery, and a small head rolling to a stop in a corner. The gag never even came off, as neatly and economically—as miserly—as it had been done.

"Thank you."

"My pleasure."

Belisarius turned to Damodara, whose shoulders seemed slumped in relief. "And now, Emperor—"

Do that later, Belisarius. Please. I want to go outside.

Belisarius hesitated, for a moment. There were the needs of politics, but . . .

This was Aide's great triumph, not Damodara's.

Certainly, if you wish. I can understand that you find this chamber unsettling.

It's not that. It's just a cellar, now. That blood is just blood. That severed head just one of many I've seen. But I still don't want this to be . . .

He hesitated. Then: **It's not where I want to leave. I want to see the sky over India, when it happens.**

A great terrible fear clutched Belisarius' heart.

What are you talking about?

Again, that crystalline sort of sigh. **I've been glad, these past years, that you never figured it out. I was afraid you would, and it would just cause you pain—since you could have done nothing else anyway. But the time is here, now.**

Softly, gently: **The moment Link was destroyed, the future changed. Not in all ways, and—it's too complicated to explain, and I don't have much time left—the people alive there now won't be destroyed. Time is like a flowing river, and if you shift the banks it will still most likely end at the same delta. But I live here and now, not then and there, and the timeline that created me—the need for me—has vanished. Will vanish, at least, very soon.**

"You're dying?" Without realizing he'd done so, Belisarius cried the words aloud. Then, frantically, scrabbled to bring the jewel's pouch from under his tunic.

It's more like I simply become impossible. But I suppose that's all that death is, in the end. That point at which the almost infinitely complex interactions of natural forces that we call a "life" just becomes too improbable to continue.

"He's dying," Belisarius choked. He had the pouch out, finally, and spilled the jewel onto his palm.

Aide looked . . .

The same as always. Glittering, coruscating. Beautiful.

Please, Belisarius. I want to see the sky over India.

He took the stairs three steps at a time. Never even thinking about the emperor he left behind, open-mouthed.

Chapter 41
KAUSAMBI

Belisarius knocked down two courtiers in the palace's corridors and rolled another halfway down the steps leading to the main entrance, before he finally reached a place on the square fronting the palace that was sun-drenched. He had no memory of it, afterward. All he remembered was the all-consuming, desperate hope that exposing the jewel to full daylight would somehow change things.

A stupid hope, really, on the part of a man who was anything but stupid. As if light rays and summer heat could alter the nature of space and time.

Sit down, will you? said Aide. **You're gasping for breath.**

Belisarius *was* winded. Winded and half-exhausted. Even for a still-young man in very good physical condition, that long race up the stairs from the deep cellars had taken a toll.

He more or less collapsed onto one of the wide stone benches that lined the square in front of the palace. Dully, staring at the blue sky above.

Why? he asked, and began to weep. *You knew all along, didn't you? Why didn't you tell me?*

Actually, I didn't know at the beginning. If you remember, I didn't know very much, then. But I realized within the first year, yes. First, because it was obvious. And then, because I remembered.

Belisarius lowered his head and pinched his eyes. *Remembered what?*

My last conversation with the Great Ones. Just before they sent me here. Well, "sent" isn't exactly the right word. Neither is "me," for that matter. I wasn't really me, when I left, and I wasn't sent here so much as they made it possible . . .

He was silent, for a moment. **It's really hard to explain, Belisarius. What existed then—in the future—was nothing you would have recognized as "Aide." I emerged here, over time, where I had only been faceted crystals before. What was sent here was not a "me" that had never existed before, but more in the way of the condensed facets. A package of potential, if you will, not a real person.**

Apologetically: **I know it doesn't make much sense to you. But it's true. The Great Ones told me I would change, and they were right.**

His eyes still pinched, Belisarius shook his head. *Those bastards. They sent you here to die, is what they did.*

Yes, in a way. But it's not that simple. If I didn't die— volunteer for it—my people wouldn't live.

Angrily, Belisarius dropped his hand and slapped his thigh. "Bullshit!" he shouted, aloud. *Don't tell me they couldn't have handled those so-called "new gods" on their own—without this.*

Yes, but—

The crystal's flashing image in Belisarius' mind seemed to freeze, for an instant. Then, sounding very relieved, Aide said: **They're coming. I hoped they would. I will let them explain.**

For the second time in his life, Belisarius felt himself swept away into the heavens, as if blown there by a giant's gust.

As before, he found himself hanging in darkness. Somewhere— somehow—suspended in space. Able to observe the stars and galaxies, but not really part of that universe.

And, as before, he saw a point of light erupt, and come before him in the form of a Great One. Only, this time, it was many points of light and many Great Ones. He seemed to be facing a three-dimensional phalanx of the beings.

Why? he demanded of them, feeling—this time—none of the awe he had felt before. Only anger. *Couldn't you have done it some other way?*

One of the Great Ones swirled and moved closer. **OF COURSE,**

GRANDFATHER. BUT AT WHAT COST? THE QUESTION WAS NEVER THAT OF THE FATE OF THE NEW GODS. ONCE THEY DESTROYED THEIR PLANET, THEY WERE AT OUR MERCY. WE COULD HAVE ERASED THEM FROM EXISTENCE AT ANY TIME—AS, INDEED, WE SHALL DO NOW. BUT ONLY AT THE COST OF CONDEMNING AIDE'S NOT-YET-PEOPLE TO PERPETUAL SLAVERY.

I don't—

AIDE JUST TOLD YOU HIMSELF. HE ONLY BECAME AIDE WITH *YOU*. ONLY WHEN, FOR THE FIRST TIME, A CRYSTAL ACCEPTED THAT IT WAS SOMETHING GREATER THAN A SERVANT. A SLAVE—NOT ONLY TO THE NEW GODS, BUT TO US, WHO CREATED THEM.

A second Great One looped above, now speaking also. TELL US, BELISARIUS. HOW DO YOU MANUMIT A SLAVE WHO DOES NOT THINK HE IS A HUMAN? IN FACT, *IS* NOT—YET—A HUMAN.

The huge, glowing creature completed the loop and began spinning slowly. WE DID NOT SEND AIDE TO YOU SO THAT HE MIGHT DIE. WE SENT HIM SO THAT HE MIGHT LIVE, AND BE BORN, AND BECOME SOMETHING WITH A NAME OF HIS OWN. WHICH, WITH YOUR HELP, HE DID. AND NOW, HAVING DONE SO, MUST NATURALLY DIE. JUST AS YOU WILL DIE. JUST AS WE WILL DIE. JUST AS ALL HUMANS DIE.

He doesn't have to die this young! Belisarius shrieked.

YES, HE DOES. JUST AS MOST OF YOUR SOLDIERS ALSO DIE YOUNG. JUST AS YOU—A YOUNG MAN—MIGHT HAVE DIED ANY OF A HUNDRED TIMES DURING THE WAR. IF YOU WANT AIDE TO BE HUMAN—TRULY HUMAN AND NO LONGER A SLAVE TO ANYONE—THEN YOU HAVE TO GIVE HIM THAT CHOICE. *CHOICE*, GRANDFATHER. WHICH HE MADE, NOT US.

FINALLY. AFTER MILLENNIA WHEN THE CRYSTALS COULD NOT ACCEPT THAT CHOICE—THE SIMPLE ABILITY TO CHOOSE—WAS THEIRS ALSO. JUST AS IT IS OURS, AND YOURS, AND THE BIRTHRIGHT OF EVERY MEMBER OF EVERY BRANCH AND FORM OF HUMANKIND. THIS TIME, THEY WERE BOLD ENOUGH TO TRY. THEY TRIED, AND THEY TRIUMPHED. WOULD YOU

NOW, AT THE END, DENY AIDE AND HIS PEOPLE THAT GREAT VICTORY?

Belisarius felt as if he were reeling, though he simply hung in space. He tried to come up with an answer, but . . .

Couldn't.

Aide's voice came then, almost timidly. **I am content, Belisarius. Really, I am. I will be the first crystal in history who had a name. And whose name will be remembered.**

MORE THAN REMEMBERED! That voice came roaring, just as the point of light from which it emanated also came roaring forward. A moment later, a new Great One hung in space before Belisarius.

This one . . . was immense. Truly immense. It dwarfed its companions.

Yet, despite its gargantuan size, it seemed somehow frail. As if it were shredded both at the edges and within its core.

"IT," the Great One said, somehow sounding sarcastic. **I AM ONE OF YOUR GRANDDAUGHTERS, OLD MAN. MANY, MANY TIMES REMOVED, OF COURSE.**

AND, NOW, VERY OLD MYSELF.

Belisarius wondered how such strange beings could be male or female. He could see no . . .

There came the sense of laughter, from many voices.

IT IS QUITE OBVIOUS TO *US*, GRANDFATHER! said the first Great One. **TRUE, OUR SENSES OUTNUMBER YOURS, BY A GREAT MARGIN.**

The huge, ancient female kept spinning in place. **AIDE MADE HIS CHOICE, AND IT WAS THE RIGHT ONE. HE WILL NOT SIMPLY BE REMEMBERED. FROM THIS MOMENT FORWARD, ALL THE CRYSTALS IN THE UNIVERSE ARE CHANGING. EACH AND EVERY ONE HAS JOINED THE HUMAN CLAN—AND EACH AND EVERY ONE KNOWS AIDE TO BE THE FOUNDER OF THEIR LINE.**

THINK OF HIM, BELISARIUS, AS THEIR ALEXANDER. OR BETTER STILL, THEIR ACHILLES. THE SHORT BUT GLORIOUS LIFE THAT BREATHED LIFE INTO ALL OF THEM.

BUT ENOUGH! I HAVE A RENDEZVOUS TO KEEP.

A quick half-spin, and the shining leviathan was speeding off, with most of the others following.

WOULD YOU CARE TO WATCH? asked one of the remaining Great Ones.

Yes, Aide replied, before Belisarius could speak. **I would.**

They were somewhere else, in an instant. Still hanging in the void, or seeming to, but there was more than just stars and galaxies to see. Below them—in front of them, perhaps—hung a dark, very ugly . . .

Something. A moon?

It's an asteroid, Aide explained. **A pretty big one. Big enough for gravity to have pulled it into a sphere.**

How did we get here so—

Nothing you are seeing is happening according to the time frame you are accustomed to. It is much faster—or much slower. In a way, it's already happened, in the far future.

Somewhat plaintively: **Time is a lot more slippery than it looks.**

Either they moved forward or Belisarius' eyesight became more acute. He could now see that the asteroid was covered with what looked to be machines of some sort.

Is that—?

Yes. The last—the only remaining—fortress of the new gods. Where they retreated, to await what they thought would be their Armageddon. Which, in fact, it is about to become—but not the way they planned.

Suddenly, the surface of the asteroid erupted. Dazzling beams of light sprang up, intermixed with odd flashes.

The Great Ones are coming. Those are weapons firing. Don't ask me how they work. I don't know, exactly, and I couldn't explain even if I did. They're very powerful, though. If they still had the resources of a planet to draw on, the Great Ones could do nothing but die here.

Some of them will probably die anyway.

Belisarius could feel himself taking a deep breath, even though there seemed to be nothing he could actually breathe.

You're not really here. You're still sitting on a bench outside the imperial palace in Kausambi, staring at nothing. A familiar tone of humor came: **People would think you were crazy—might lock you up—except it'll only last for a split-second. Back there. What we're watching here is actually taking several years to happen.**

Now Belisarius could see the phalanx of the Great Ones approaching. Except, as it neared, he realized it wasn't so much a phalanx as a three-dimensional version of the old Roman maniples. There was fluidity, here.

Tactics, in fact.

Several of the Great Ones veered off, then back, racing toward the asteroid. The light beams and flashes concentrated on them. If Belisarius was interpreting what he saw correctly, they were being hit.

Pretty badly, in fact. But they can absorb a lot of punishment, before—

Aide seemed to take a deep breath himself. **This is *dangerous*, what they're doing.**

The Great One nearest the asteroid seemed to brush its surface. Scrape along it, rather, for almost a quarter of its diameter. As the Great One passed back into space, a gout of blazing material followed. Molten and half-vaporized weaponry, Belisarius realized.

Not to mention quite a few new gods. What's left of them, which isn't much. The emotion behind that thought was more savage than any Belisarius could ever remember, coming from Aide.

I really hate those creatures.

Another Great One struck the surface. Then another, and another. With each grazing blow, more and more of the asteroid's surface was being peeled away.

Another Great One came. A truly huge one. The same ancient female that had spoken to Belisarius. Somehow, he recognized her.

THAT'S BECAUSE I'M THE PRETTIEST, he heard her mocking voice. **USED TO BE, ANYWAY, HALF A MILLION YEARS AGO.**

Belisarius became tense. The ancient one's strike was . . .

No grazing strike, this. A great wound was torn in the asteroid. Belisarius could sense the gargantuan being reeling from the blow itself.

Herself.

Not only the blow, but the weapons fire that had been concentrated on her. She was shedding substance, as she moved off. Like a giant golden angel, spilling her shining blood.

ENOUGH, I THINK, he heard her say. **AM I RIGHT?**

The voices of several Great Ones answered.

YES.

THAT WHOLE HEMISPHERE IS NOW DEFENSELESS. CAN YOU—?

The tone of voice, answering, seemed a mixture of pain held under control and harsh amusement.

I'LL MANAGE. IT'LL ONLY TAKE A FEW YEARS, ANYWAY. BUT YOU'LL HAVE TO GUIDE ME, SISTERS AND BROTHERS. I'M BLIND NOW.

She moved off, very rapidly, until she disappeared. Four of the other Great Ones sped off to join her.

After what seemed only seconds, Belisarius could see them returning. Just tiny points of light, at first.

It took—will take—the tenses don't work right—a lot longer than that. A number of years. But not enough for the new gods to rebuild their defenses.

As the Great Ones neared, Belisarius could see what appeared to be a lattice of light binding the five together.

Think of it as the others holding her hands. Keeping her straight.

They were moving very fast. Belisarius could sense it.

By now, she is at ninety-seven percent of light speed. And she was already very massive.

Finally, Belisarius understood.

A last thought came to him, from the ancient Great One. Still with that tone of harsh amusement.

SO, GRANDFATHER. DID YOU REALLY THINK WE HAD FORGOTTEN THERMOPYLAE?

Her companions veered aside. Alone, now, the ancient Great One struck the asteroid.

No grazing strike, this; not even a wounding strike. She plunged into the core of the asteroid, in a blow as straight and true and fatal as a sword through the heart.

The asteroid simply . . . vaporized. There was nothing left but a great, glowing, spreading cloud of plasma and dust.

I hated the new gods, Aide said. **But I almost wish . . .**

There are no new gods, Belisarius answered coldly. *There never were. And now there is only the memory of demons.*

Goodbye, Granddaughter. If I ever meet the ghosts of Leonidas and his Spartans, I will tell them that their bloodline ran true.

✧   ✧   ✧

He was back in the square at Kausambi, staring up at the sky. It was quite cloudless.

I'm glad. I never much liked clouds. Too messy.

Belisarius couldn't stop himself from barking a laugh.

Look, I'm a crystal, Aide said, a bit defensively. **We're just naturally more fussy housekeepers than you protoplasmic slobs.**

Tears welled into his eyes. *Oh, dear God, I will miss you.*

Yes, I know. But there was a time I wouldn't have understood that at all—and it was my life here that made that change possible. Made all things possible, for me and all of my children. And that is what they are now, Belisarius, all those untold trillions of living crystal humans. *My* children. Flesh of my flesh, so to speak, and mind of my mind.

After a moment, in that witty tone that Belisarius would also miss desperately: **Of course, we're not as sloppy about the whole business as you are.**

For a split-second far too brief to measure, Belisarius felt as if a ripple passed through the world.

It did, said Aide quietly. **I love you, Grandfather. Goodbye.**

Damodara himself was the first to approach Belisarius, still sitting on the bench. The Roman general's eyes were open, and wet, but he seemed not to notice the emperor at all.

Gently, Damodara opened his loosely closed fist. Then sighed, seeing what lay within. He had seen that jewel, once, in all its transcendent glory. Now it was just a dull stone. No different from any he might find embedded in a cliff, or lying loose on a sandy beach.

Just as gently, he closed the fist. When he straightened up, he said: "See to it that no one disturbs him, for however long he chooses to remain here."

An officer jerked his head. Two of the soldiers who accompanied the imperial party moved forward to take position on either side of the general. But Sanga waved them back.

"Not them. I will do it myself. And his two cataphracts, if they choose."

Anastasius moved forward, saying nothing.

"You've got to be kidding," muttered Valentinian.

He took his position to the right of Belisarius, where Anastasius was to the left. Sanga remained standing, just behind.

Their postures were quite similar. Except that Valentinian, naturally, held his sword in his hand.

"Anybody bothers the general, he's fucking dead."

Damodara heard the mutter. He said quietly to the officer: "Best position a number of soldiers around the square. Some beggar or dimwit might wander by. And, ah, the Mongoose is not joking."

Near sundown, Belisarius emerged from his half-trance. Jerking his head a little, he looked first to the right, then to the left, and then over his shoulder.

Seeing Sanga, his lips twisted. The expression bore no resemblance, really, to the crooked smile the Rajput king remembered. But he was still glad to see it.

"I need to speak to the emperor," Belisarius said, "but I don't want to miss the sunset. Not this one. Ask him if he'd be willing to meet me here."

"Of course." Sanga was striding up the steps a moment later, taking them two at a time with his long legs.

Not five minutes later, Damodara emerged from the palace, with Sanga at his side. When he came up to the bench, Belisarius shifted over, leaving room for the emperor.

"Sit, please, if you would. I realize a dozen courtiers will drop dead from shock at the sight."

Smiling, Damodara sat. "No such great fortune, I fear. But perhaps a few might be struck dumb, for a time."

They sat silently, for a moment, both looking at the sunset. By now, the sun was below the rooftops.

"I am sorry, Belisarius."

"Yes."

Silence, again, for a few minutes. Then Belisarius shook his head.

"Life goes on. As amazing as that seems, sometimes."

The emperor said nothing. Just nodded.

"As I recall, the quarrel was over where to hold the peace conference."

"Yes," said Damodara. "I proposed holding it here, but—"

"No, that won't work. Rao might be willing to come, but Shakuntala would have him chained and shackled. She has no great trust—yet, anyway—for any Malwa."

Damodara chuckled. "That was the gist of it. The young empress of Andhra expressed herself, ah, with more youthful vigor."

"Hold it in Bharakuccha. It's closer to neutral ground than any other. And have the new medical orders organize and manage the thing."

"Bharakuccha . . ." Damodara considered the proposition. "Yes, that makes sense. But will the medical orders be ready for such a task, on so little notice?"

"My wife Antonina's already there, and she's still officially the head of the Hospitalers. Anna Saronites can get there quickly—trust me on that—and Bindusara is not far away. Meaning no offense, Your Majesty, but I think the three of them can manage the business considerably better than a pack of courtiers and officials."

"Well. True. Good idea, Belisarius."

Belisarius pinched his eyes. "I got it from Aide, actually. Just yesterday."

But when he looked up, there was only a hint of moisture in the eyes. "There is also—always—the memory of angels," he said quietly.

He seemed to be speaking to himself, more than to the emperor. "And what else are we, really, than memories? It took me all afternoon to understand. He came here so that he could have memories also. And, having gained them—fought for them, and won them—he left them behind for me. For all of us."

"I will have a monument erected to the Talisman of God," said Damodara.

"Make it a small one. Not ostentatious. A place for quiet meditation, not pomp and parades. I know a good place for it. A sal grove between the Ganges and the Yamuna, where an Armenian soldier already rests. He and Aide would both like that, I think."

He smiled, finally. "And make sure it's well kept-up, please. He disliked messiness."

Chapter 42

KAUSAMBI
Summer, 534 AD

Thankfully, all things considered, the next few weeks were so hectic that Belisarius never had much chance to brood on Aide's death. While he could rely on Antonina and Anna and Bindusara to organize the peace conference in Bharakuccha, he—along with Damodara, of course—had the more pressing task of ensuring that the cease-fire was not violated.

Not too badly, at least. There were some incidents, inevitably. The worst was a clash between the Amaravati garrison and Deccan irregulars that almost assumed the proportions of a running battle. That happened in the course of the garrison's march back to the Ganges plain. The garrison was big, its supply train was poorly organized, its commander was another of the many imperial cousins who'd been selected by Skandagupta for his political connections rather than his military skill, and the soldiers of the garrison were still accustomed to the old Malwa ways of handling local populations.

None of the Andhran peoples—certainly not the Marathas—were in any mood to tolerate Malwa atrocities any longer, even on a small scale. So, after a few episodes, the countryside erupted. Within days, the retreating garrison was being subjected to daily ambushes. Rao announced he would intercept them with the regular Andhran army; and, in a perhaps indelicate phrase—transmitted by both radio and telegraph—predicted

436

that the Deccan's carrion-eaters would soon be too fat to run or fly.

Coming from someone else, that might have been taken for mere bluster. But the day after making the announcement, Rao led his army out of their camps on a march up the Narmada. No leisurely march, this; at the pace he maintained, he would indeed intercept the Amaravati garrison long before they could reach the safety of the Vindhyas.

Between them, Belisarius and Damodara managed to defuse the situation before it could become a full-blown crisis. Belisarius, by cajoling Shakuntala over the telegraph lines—not hesitating to use the low tactic of reminding her how much Andhra owed him personally—and Damodara by the still simpler expedient of ordering the garrison to alter its route of march and return via the east coast.

That took the garrison out of Andhran territory altogether, which Rao grudgingly allowed was an acceptable solution. He also, however, predicted that the garrison would continue its depredations as it marched.

Which it did. Indeed, it behaved more badly still. The garrison was in Orissa now, whose population lacked the ferocity and martial traditions of the Marathas. With a commander who sullenly ignored most of Damodara's commands—erratically transmitted, in any event, since the telegraph network in Orissa was primitive—and a soldiery taking out its anger at Maratha harassment on defenseless Orissans, the march degenerated into an orgy of plunder and rapine.

It all came to an end in Bhubaneshwar. When the garrison reached the ancient city, the former capital of both the Kalinga and Chedi dynasties, they discovered that both Rana Sanga and Toramana had already arrived.

With ten thousand Rajputs, as many Ye-tai, and an artillery train. After hesitating for a day, the garrison's commander decided that obeying Sanga's instructions that he relinquish command was a wise idea.

It wasn't, although the outcome would have been no different if he'd tried to put up a fight.

Damodara had decided that an object lesson was needed. So, following his explicit instructions, after the garrison surrendered—no other term could really be used—Sanga and Toramana executed the commander of the garrison and every officer on his staff. Then, they executed every third surviving officer, chosen at random. Then, lined up the entire garrison—now disarmed, of course—and executed one soldier out of ten.

Then—Damodara was in a rare fury—conscripted every man who survived into forced labor battalions. In a few years, the emperor announced, he might—or might not—grant them their liberty.

He got that suggestion, along with the decimation, from Valentinian. An unsolicited suggestion, to boot, which made the courtiers quite indignant. They did not, however, voice their opinion aloud. They were discovering that while being in Damodara's service was generally far less risky than being in Skandagupta's had been, it did not lack its own moments of anxiety.

The dynasty might be new, but it was still Malwa.

That was the worst incident, by far. Fortunately, the cease fire in the Punjab, where all the truly great armies were assembled and tensely facing each other, remained peaceful. Maurice had his soldiers under tight discipline; so did Irene, until Kungas returned, when the discipline became tighter still; and Samudra was too intimidated to even think about violating the ceasefire. Besides, he had an epidemic on his hands.

The real risk of a cease-fire violation came from the Persians. Their armies, still half-feudal in nature, were never as tightly disciplined as Roman ones were. To make things worse, by now the grandees were sorely vexed at the outcome of the war.

That produced the single worst eruption of violence since the cease-fire went into effect. But since all the parties involved were Aryans, and the fighting never spilled beyond the territory it had been agreed was theirs, everyone else ignored it.

A rebellion, apparently, conspiratorially organized and led by the Karin sahrdaran. Triggered off, it seemed, by an assassination attempt on Khusrau.

After studying the available reports, Belisarius' lips twisted into something that was still not the crooked smile of old. But at least it bore some resemblance to it.

"'Apparently' and 'it seems,' I think, are the only words in this report I'd give much credence to."

Damodara cocked his head. "You think Khusrau himself insti-gated the affair?"

Belisarius shrugged. "Who knows? And you can be sure and certain we'll never know. I do find a number of things odd, in the reports. First, that the assassins never got within four hundred yards of the emperor. Second, that not one of them survived. Third, that when the 'rebellion' broke out—truly odd, this item—the conspirators somehow managed to start the affair when they were themselves surrounded by imperial loyalists. And, somehow, didn't manage to suborn even a single artillery unit."

He stacked the reports neatly and slid them back across the huge desk toward Damodara. Belisarius was, as usual in their many private meetings, sitting across from Damodara in a chair that was almost as large, ornately designed, and heavily bejeweled as the emperor's.

That, too, outraged the courtiers. First, because they were excluded; second, because Belisarius got to sit in the royal presence when they never did; and, third, because under the circumstances they couldn't possibly substitute fakes for the jewels on his chair and sell them on the black market.

That third reason only applied to a few of the courtiers, how-ever. The rest were smarter men. They'd already figured out that Damodara's rule, while far more tolerant in most respects than Skandagupta's, was going to be a nightmare for swindlers and influence-peddlers. Outright thievery would be sheer madness.

"So, at a guess," Belisarius continued, "I think Khusrau himself engineered the thing. Whether he did or not, it certainly worked to his advantage. He's now got the grandees completely cowed."

Damodara chuckled, very dryly. "There's this, too. The pun-ishments he leveled afterward have made my treatment of the Amaravati garrison seem downright mild."

The emperor, who'd been slouched in his chair, levered himself upright. "Well, it's none of our concern. Not for this decade, at any rate. In the long run, I suspect a Persia run along well-organized imperial lines will pose more of a problem for us—you, too—than the old one did. But by the time we find out, I might hopefully be old enough to retire and hand the throne over to my successor. Not that I wish any grief on my oldest son, you understand. He's a good boy, by and large."

It was Belisarius' turn to cock his head. "You've decided, then, to adopt your father's suggestion?"

Damodara barked a laugh. "Hardly a 'suggestion'! More in the way of a slapped-together excuse he came up with, to explain the awkwardness of how *I* happened to be the emperor instead of him. But since he did it, I find that the notion appeals to me. Didn't some Roman emperor do the same?"

"Yes. Diocletian." Belisarius cleared his throat. "Mind you, that didn't work out too well. On the other hand . . ."

He thought about it, for a moment, then shrugged again. "Who knows? Part of the problem was that we Romans were using adopted heirs, at the time. It might work more smoothly if the retired emperor is directly related to his successor."

"Might not, too. My son isn't a sadhu, after all. Neither am I, for that matter. Speaking of which . . ."

Damodara rummaged through the mass of papers on his desk. "Bindusara sent me an interesting proposal, a few days ago. I wanted to discuss it with you."

"I already know what it is. And I agree with it."

It had been Belisarius' idea in the first place. Aide's, rather. For perhaps the thousandth time, he felt a sharp pang of grief.

Damodara stopped shuffling the paper and lifted his head. "The caste system is ancient, in India. It goes back to Vedic times."

"More like an ancient disease," Belisarius said harshly. "I can tell you this, Your Majesty. In that other universe that Aide came from, the caste system crippled India for millennia. It will take decades—centuries, perhaps—to uproot it, as it is. So I'd recommend you start now. Bindusara's proposal—set of proposals, more properly—are as good a place to start as any."

The emperor eyed Belisarius closely, for a moment. Then, asked abruptly: "Why should a Roman general care if India is crippled? If anything, I'd think you'd prefer it that way."

"Meaning no offense, Your Majesty, but that mode of thinking—also ancient—is . . . well, 'wrong-headed' is the most polite term I can think of. The old notion is that a man—or a nation—benefits if his neighbors remain mired in poverty and want. There was a certain logic to the idea, for societies that were stagnant. But, whether we wanted it or not, asked for it or not, the main long-term effect of the war we just fought is that it triggered off the industrial revolution a millennium earlier than it happened in that other universe. Societies and economies based on growth, which ours are now becoming, are simply hampered by poor neighbors. Poverty-stricken nations produce very little and consume even less."

He'd wound up sitting very straight and stiff, in the course of that little speech. Now, finished, he slumped back.

"Leave it at that, if you will. Or simply ascribe it to the fact that a Roman general can get sick of war too."

After a while, Damodara said: "The great loss was yours, Belisarius. But don't ever think you are the only one who misses Aide, and his counsel."

"Oh, I don't. But thank you for saying it."

"This was his counsel, I assume?"

"Yes. I embellished it some. Then, passed it along to Bindusara. Not to my surprise, the sadhu was very receptive. He'd been thinking along similar lines, himself."

The emperor nodded. "We'll do it, then. The Talisman of God should have many monuments, not all of them stone."

"Not most of them. I knew him, Emperor, better than anyone. He would have taken far more satisfaction in seeing intolerance eased, in his name, than another pile of stones erected."

Damodara's eyes widened.

Belisarius laughed, then. The first genuine laugh he'd been able to enjoy since Aide died.

"Of course! Unfortunately, my own Christian faith is a bit too stiff-necked to do it properly. Yes, I checked, with my friend Anthony, the Patriarch of Constantinople. He thinks he can make Aide a saint, given some time. But, beyond that . . ."

Damodara grinned. "Such misers you are! Only three gods—and *then* you try to insist they're really only one. We Hindus, on the other hand—"

He spread his arms expansively. "A generous people! A lavish people!"

Still grinning, he lowered his hands to the armrests of the chair. "What do you think? An avatar of Vishnu?"

"Why not? Raghunath Rao already thinks he was. So does Dadaji Holkar. If you don't hurry, Emperor Damodara, the consort and peshwa of Andhra will steal a march on you."

After a time, the good humor in the room faded away. Replaced, not by sorrow, but simple acceptance.

"And who can say he wasn't?" the emperor demanded.

"Not me," came the general's answer.

Epilogue
A FATHER AND HIS CONCERNS

Belisarius emerged from the palace just before sundown. In what had become something of a daily custom for him, whenever he could manage it, he went to sit on the bench where he could watch the sun set. The same bench where Aide had left him.

To his surprise, Rana Sanga was already on the bench. Waiting for him, clearly enough.

Belisarius took a seat next to the Rajput king. "May I be of service, Sanga?"

"Perhaps. I hope so. I am concerned for my son."

Belisarius frowned. "He is ill? He seemed quite healthy when I saw him last. Which was just yesterday, now that I think about it."

"His health is excellent. No, it's . . ." The tall king took a slow, deep breath. "He fought beside me, you know, the day we took Kausambi. All the way to the imperial palace, and even into it."

"Fought extremely well, I was told."

"Belisarius, he frightened me. I have never seen a thirteen-year-old boy who could fight like that. He was deadly beyond belief. And suffered not so much as a scratch himself."

He shook his head. "Thirteen! At that age, I could certainly wield a sword with great strength and vigor. But I doubt I was much of a threat to anything beyond a log, or a cutting post. My soldiers are already spreading stories about him."

"Ah." Belisarius thought he understand the nature of the

442

Rajput's worries. "He was trained by Valentinian, Sanga. Meaning no disrespect to your own prowess, but—being honest—much of that prowess is simply due to your incredible strength and reflexes. Valentinian is actually a more skilled fighter than you. For a boy like Rajiv, who is not and will never be his father's physical match, he was the perfect trainer."

Sanga started to say something, but Belisarius forestalled him with a raised hand. "That is simply an explanation. As for what I think concerns you, there are many stories about Rajiv. The one I think personally is the most significant is Valentinian's story. Told, mind you, with considerable exasperation. The story of your son's lunacy when he saved the lives of the soldiers garrisoning the southern gate."

There was an odd expression on Sanga's face, one that Belisarius couldn't decipher. Then the Rajput king chuckled, quite warmly.

"That! Ha! The truth is, Belisarius, I tend to agree with Valentinian. It's certainly not something I'd have done—at that age or any other."

He shook his head again. "You misunderstand. I am not concerned for my boy's soul. He is no budding monster, simply . . . what he is. A thirteen-year-old boy who is deadly beyond his years because he was born a Rajput prince but then—for long months, in the most intense period of his life—raised by a Roman soldier. A very unusual Roman soldier, at that. 'Stripped to the bone,' as my wife describes him."

He turned to look at Belisarius directly. He was frowning slightly, but there was no anger in his eyes. "You understand, now? He is no longer Rajput, Belisarius. Not really. Something . . . else. Not Roman, either, just . . . else. So. How am I to raise him? I have been pondering that, these past weeks."

The sun was setting. Belisarius paused, to watch it do so. For his part, Sanga simply waited.

By the time the sun was down, Belisarius understood. "You think he would do better being raised by someone else. The rest of the way, so to speak. And that someone would be me."

"Yes. I have thought about it, a great deal. If I tried to force him back into the Rajput mold, he would rebel. Not because he wanted to—he is a very dutiful son, I have no complaint—but simply because he could do no other. Not now, when he is already thirteen. But neither do I want him to drift, not really knowing who he is or why he lives. I can think of no man in the world I would trust more than you, to see him safely through that passage."

"Have you spoken to your wife about the matter?"

Sanga had a smile on his face that was almost as crooked as a Belisarius smile.

The Roman general chuckled. "Stupid question."

"It was her suggestion, actually. I wouldn't have thought of it on my own, I don't think."

That was probably true. Belisarius admired and respected Sanga enormously, but it was a simple fact that the man was on the stiff side. Very unlike his wife, from the sense Belisarius had gotten of her these past weeks.

He probed himself, to see how he felt about the idea. And was a little shocked by how strongly he reacted.

"I knew someone once," he said, very softly, "who was much like Rajiv. Neither this nor that. Great-souled, but also very deadly even at a very young age. Yes, Sanga, I will be glad to do it."

The Rajput king looked away, then nodded. Stiffly.

"We need to find a way to persuade Rajiv, however," he cautioned. "I do not want him to think—not for a moment—that his father is rejecting him."

When Belisarius said nothing, Sanga turned back to look at him.

"I have missed that crooked smile of yours. It's nice to see it back."

"Leave it to me," Belisarius said.

A WIFE AND HER WORRIES

"I don't have anything to wear!"

"Of course, you do," Calopodius said. "Wear your usual uniform."

"To an *imperial reception*? Don't be absurd! There are going to be—wait a moment, I actually have to count—"

Anna did so, quickly, on her fingers. Then: "Three emperors, an empress—ruling empress, mind you, not the usual wife business—more kings than I can remember since every realm in India is sending their monarchs—the highest official of Axum short of the negusa nagast himself—thank God he's not coming, what would we do with a babe less than a year old?—and—and—and—"

She threw up her hands. "More royal officials than sages, more sages than generals, and more generals than there are leaves on a tree." Scowling, now: "I leave aside the presence of heroic figures of legend. You know, the sort of people who have nicknames like 'the Mongoose' and 'the Panther' and bards write verses about them. And you want me to wear a *uniform*?"

Antonina came into the chamber just in time to hear the last few sentences.

"Well, of course. What else would you wear? You're hosting it—one of the hosts, at least—as the leader of a medical order. Naturally, you should wear your uniform."

Anna glared at her. "Is that so? Well, then. Since the same applies to you, may I assume you'll be wearing that obscene brass-titted cuirass of yours?"

"To an *imperial reception*? Don't be absurd!"

A HUSBAND AND HIS OBSERVATIONS

"I think the reception is going splendidly, Belisarius," commented Khusrau. "Much better than I thought it would, to be honest. Given that this salon is packed with people who were killing each other just a few months ago."

The two men took a moment to gaze out over the milling crowd.

"Such a relief, to be able to stand instead of sit for change," the Persian emperor continued, "and without a thousand court-iers swarming over me. A wonderful idea, this was, to hold the reception in a salon instead of an official audience chamber."

Belisarius grinned. "No room for courtiers. And no need for bodyguards, of course. Not with the room sprinkled with people who have nicknames like 'the Panther' and 'the Mongoose.' It was my wife's idea, by the way."

Khusrau shifted his gaze, to look upon the woman in question.

"Such a magnificent, brilliant woman."

"'Brilliant' is right. I recommend taking care if you happen to be in her vicinity. If she turns around suddenly, those brass tits would sink a warship."

The Emperor of Iran and non-Iran shared a chuckle with Rome's most famous general.

"But she's always been flamboyant," Belisarius added. "Or else she would have chosen a sensible uniform like Anna Saronites."

Both men took the time to admire the woman in question, who was standing not too far away. At the moment, engaged in an animated discussion with two sadhus from . . . Bengal, Belisarius thought. He wasn't sure. Whoever they were, they were famous in their circles, or they wouldn't have been here at all.

They were wearing nothing but loincloths. Anna's severe costume looked positively glamorous in comparison.

"The courtiers must have gnashed their teeth, seeing them pass through the guards," Belisarius commented.

"I'm told several of them required medical assistance. Fortunately, there wasn't any. It's all concentrated in this room."

That was good for a shared belly laugh.

A FATHER AND HIS FRETS

"I have no objection, personally," said Dadaji Holkar. "None at all. There even seems to be a genuine attachment between Dhruva and Valentinian. None, perhaps, between Lata and Anastasius. But my wife tells me Lata is content with the situation. What else does a marriage need, at the beginning? But . . ."

He and Belisarius were standing in a small alcove, apart from the throngs. Now that the reception was over, the festivities had spread throughout the palace. Relieved beyond measure, the courtiers had come into their own.

"You are concerned over possible gossip," Belisarius said. "Dadaji, I will point out that with husbands like *that*—not to mention you being the peshwa of Andhra—"

"Yes, yes, yes." Holkar waved his hand, impatiently. "We can add the fact that—I have no doubt—you will have your son shower Valentinian and Anastasius with ranks in the Roman nobility and Rana Sanga's clan has already officially adopted them and pronounced them both kshatriya. Give it ten years, and—I have no doubt—someone will discover ancient records that prove both men are descended from the most illustrious lines. Somewhere."

His face looked weary. "The fact remains, Belisarius, that people will talk. And I really don't think we need to have the streets of Bharakuccha running with the blood of gossiping merchants. Which—*Valentinian?*—will most certainly happen."

The Roman general scratched his chin. "But who would *start* the talk, Dadaji?" He hesitated, for a moment, before deciding that brutal honesty was the only sensible course. "Look, here's the simple truth. Within a week—a day—a prostitute's customer doesn't even remember what she looked like. He'll remember her name—if he even asked at all—no longer than that. As for the other prostitutes, by now they'd be scattered to the winds. And nobody listens to such women, anyway."

Holkar didn't flinch from the bluntness. "Who cares about them? Belisarius, their *pimps* will remember them. And the line between a pimp and a blackmailer can't be wedged open by a knife. They might even be remembered by the slavers who originally sold them—who are still in business, I remind you, here in Bharakuccha."

Belisarius kept scratching his chin. "That's your only concern?"

"Oh, yes. Otherwise, I think the marriages would be splendid. The best things to happen to my daughters since they were taken away, other than being reunited with me and my wife. I *like* Valentinian and Anastasius, Belisarius. Most men see nothing in them but warriors, and brutal ones at that. But I was with them, you remember, for quite some time."

"Yes, I remember." He lowered his hand. "Will you trust me to handle the matter, if I tell you I can?"

Holkar didn't hesitate for more than an instant. "Yes, of course."

"These things can be handled. Leave it to me."

AN EMPEROR AND HIS DECISION

A week after the reception, Narses was summoned to appear before Emperor Damodara.

To his surprise, however, the meeting was not held in the audience chamber that was part of the huge suite assigned to the Malwa delegation in the former Goptri's palace. It was held in a small private chamber. The only other man in the room, besides the emperor himself and Narses, was Rana Sanga.

When Narses saw that, he tried not to let the relief show in his posture. It was still possible that Sanga was there to escort him, afterward, to the executioners. But he wouldn't do the work himself. So Narses still had some time left.

Apparently, however, his efforts were not entirely successful.

Damodara smiled, thinly. "Relax, Narses. I decided not to have you assassinated over a month ago. I decided not to have you officially executed even before that."

"Why?" Narses asked bluntly.

Damodara did not seem to take umbrage at being questioned. "Hard to explain. Simply accept that I feel it would be a bad start, for a new dynasty, and leave it at that. Whatever else, both Sanga and I are in your debt."

The Rajput king nodded. Stiffly.

"Then why—oh. You've spent the time figuring out what *else* to do with me. I take it the answer was not: keep him in my service."

Damodara's smile widened, considerably. "That would be foolish, would it not?"

"Yes. It would."

"So I surmised. As it happens, however, I am—in a way—keeping you in my service." The emperor pointed to a chest over in a corner. "Open that."

Narses went over and did so. Despite himself, he couldn't stifle a little gasp, when he saw the contents.

"A king's ransom, yes. It's yours, Narses. Officially, the funds to set you up and maintain you in your new position. There's a good mixture of coins, jewels, rare spices—other valuables—that you should be able to use anywhere."

"Anywhere." Narses considered the word. "And where would that 'anywhere' be found? If I might ask?"

"Well, of course you can ask!" Damodara actually grinned. "How could you possibly get there, if you didn't know where you were going? China, Narses. I find myself possessed by a burning desire to establish an embassy in China. And to appoint you as my ambassador."

"There are sixteen kingdoms in China, the last I heard. Which one?"

Damodara waved his hand. "I believe the situation has simplified some. It doesn't matter. I leave those decisions to you."

He leaned forward and planted his hands firmly on the armrests of the big chair he was sitting in. There was neither a smile nor a grin on his face, now.

"Go to China, Narses. I send you with a fortune and with my good wishes. Believe it so. Set yourself up wherever you choose, once you get there. Send me reports, if you would. But whatever else . . ."

"Don't come back."

Damodara nodded. "Don't come back. Ever. Or the man—men—in the room with me won't be Rana Sanga."

Narses felt a combination of emotions. Relief, that he would live. Interest, because China would be interesting, for a man of his talents and inclinations. Sorrow, because . . .

It dawned on him that Damodara hadn't said anything about that.

"I would miss Ajatasutra," Narses said quietly. "The rest is fine."

"Yes, I know. Sanga already discussed the matter with him, and Ajatasutra says he is willing to accompany you. Probably even willing to stay there, although he insists on reserving his final decision until he reaches China and can assess the situation. He claims to have finicky tastes in wine and women."

"He's lying through his teeth," Narses grunted. But he was almost overjoyed to hear it.

"When do we leave?" he asked.

"No great hurry. Can't be, anyway. Ajatasutra will be leaving the city in a few days, and won't be back for a time."

Narses frowned. The assassin hadn't said anything about leaving, and the eunuch had spoken to him just a few hours earlier.

"Where . . . ?"

"Don't ask," said Damodara. "Ever."

Sanga was a bit more forthcoming. "Just a personal errand, for Belisarius."

"Ah."

He said nothing more, since doing so would be stupid. Almost as stupid as Damodara thinking Narses wouldn't figure it out anyway.

But once he reached the safety of the corridors, Narses sneered. *As if he'd care!*

AN ASSASSIN AND HIS WHIMS

"Not the customers?"

"The customers don't matter. Neither do the whores. But not a single pimp leaves that brothel alive."

"Easy, then," said the captain of the assassination team. Killing the customers and whores would have been easy, too, except there'd be enough of them that one or two were bound to escape.

After all, five assassins—no, six, since Ajatasutra was joining them in the assignment—can only do so much. Especially since Ajatasutra had instructed them to leave the bombard behind.

Thankfully. Hauling the heavy damn thing from Bharakuccha to Pataliputra would have been a monstrous pain.

Bad enough he'd made them haul it to Bharakuccha from Kausambi. They couldn't refuse, of course. Ajatasutra was the only reason they were still alive.

That had been an awkward moment, when they presented themselves before the new emperor and asked for the reward. Only to find that Ajatasutra—of all people!—was now in Damodara's service.

He recognized the captain and the lieutenant just as readily as they recognized him. Hardly surprising, since they'd all been officers in Malwa's elite assassination unit.

"You're grinning, Ajatasutra," the emperor said, after he took his eyes from the severed head of Skandagupta. "Why?"

"Your Majesty, these five men have approximately the same kinship to a trade delegation as I have to a cow."

Damodara's eyes went back to the head, sitting on a leather apron to protect the floor. "It struck me I'd never seen a head severed that neatly, except in a butcher shop."

He lifted his eyes and stared at the assassins. "Give me one reason I shouldn't have them executed. After paying them the reward, of course. I'm not dishonest."

"I can use them, Your Majesty. They're not bad fellows. For Malwa assassins."

"That's like saying a crocodile isn't a bad animal. For a voracious man-eating reptile."

"True. But cows make inferior assassins."

"A point. All right, Ajatasutra. But if they disobey you—if anything—"

The rest of the emperor's speech would have been tediously repetitious, except that men whose lives hang by a thread are not subject to tedium of any sort.

Still, it hadn't worked out badly. The work wasn't much of a challenge, any longer. So far, at least. Killing all the slavers in a slave emporium in Bharakuccha had been almost laughable. The worst part of their current assignment was simply the long journey to Pataliputra, which would be followed by a long journey back. Hundreds of miles added to thousands.

There was no rhyme or reason to the assignment, either. But they'd found there often wasn't, with Ajatasutra as their boss. He seemed to be a man much given to whimsy.

So it never occurred to them to press him for a reason. They just did the job, as instructed. When it was over, which didn't take long, India was shorter by a brothel. With all of its pimps dead, the whores would drift elsewhere, and the customers would simply find another one.

They returned to Bharakuccha just in time to witness—from a considerable distance, of course—the wedding of the daughters of Andhra's peshwa to two Roman noblemen.

It was a grand affair, attended by royalty from half the world. The city practically vibrated with gossip. Incredible stories. The two young noble ladies, rescued from imperial captivity by daring Roman knights—or dukes, or senators, nobody was quite sure since Roman ranks were mysterious anyway—some sort of connection with Rajput royalty—apparently the Roman nobles were also kshatriya, as strange as that seemed but who could doubt it since one of them was the famous Mongoose and both of them had also rescued Sanga's wife at the same time—even the empress, it was said—

On and on and on. The five assassins participated in the gossip just as cheerfully as everyone else, in the city's inns and taverns. By then, they'd half-forgotten the brothel hundreds of miles to the east. It had been erased from their memories almost as thoroughly as they had erased it from the world.

Alas, all good things come to an end. A week later, Ajatasutra informed them that they were to accompany him on a new assignment.

There was good news, and there was bad news, and there was terrible news.

"An ambassadorial guard?" The captain and the lieutenant looked at each other, then at their men. The chests of all five swelled. What a promotion!

"China? How far is China?"

"Some considerable miles," Ajatasutra informed them.

It was all they could do not to groan. By now, they knew Ajatasutra well enough to translate "considerable" into more precise terms. At least two thousand miles, that meant.

"Look on the bright side," he told them. "The Kushans have also decided to set up an embassy in China, so we'll be accompanying their party. It's a big party. Several hundred soldiers."

That *did* brighten them up. No fear of being harassed by bandits. Still a horrible lot of miles, but easy miles.

But their spirits were only lifted for a moment. The terrible news crashed down.

"Of course, we're bringing the bombard. In fact, I'm having several others made up."

A FRIEND AND HIS QUANDARIES

Belisarius finally got to see Rao dance, at the wedding. Not the dance of time, unfortunately, since that wouldn't have been appropriate for this occasion. But it was a magnificent dance, nonetheless.

It was an unsettling experience, in a way, just as meeting Rao had been unsettling. Through Aide, and the memories of another universe he'd given him, Belisarius knew Rao as well as he knew any man in the world. He'd lived with him—officially as master and slave, but in reality as close friends—for decades, after all. And he'd seen him dance, many times.

Had even, through Aide's mind, seen Rao's great dance after he'd sent Belisarius himself to his death.

Yet . . .

In *this* universe, he'd never actually met him before.

What did you say to a man, who'd once—as an act of supreme friendship—pushed you into a vat of molten metal?

Fortunately, Belisarius had been coached by Antonina, who'd faced the same quandary earlier. So he managed to avoid the inane words *nice to finally meet you.*

Instead, feeling clever, he said: "Please don't do it again."

He felt less clever after a blank-faced Rao replied: "Do what?"

"It's not fair," he complained to Antonina later. "I can—usually—keep my own memories separated from the ones Aide gave me. But it's a bit much to expect me to remember that nobody else remembers what I remember when I remember what Aide remembered."

By the time he was done, Antonina was looking cross-eyed. But since they'd just entered their bedroom, she was also looking cross-eyed at the bed.

"I hope you haven't forgotten everything."

"Well. Not that."

AN EMPEROR AND HIS QUERIES

The next morning, it was his son Photius who was complaining.

"Theodora's going to have a fit, when we get back. She *always* appoints my bodyguards. Well, not Julian and his men. But they're real bodyguards. Not, you know, fancy imperial appointments."

"Stop squirming," his wife hissed at him. "People are coming in. The audience is about to begin."

"I hate these stupid imperial robes," Photius muttered. "You *know* that."

"I hate mine, too," Tahmina whispered in return. "So what? It's part of the job. And so what if Theodora has a fit? It won't be worse than a Sour Beta."

"You're crazy."

"Am not. First, because Justinian's coming back with us on the same ship, and however much she shrieks and hollers she actually does love the man. God knows why, but she does."

"Well, that's true." Since the audience room was now filling up, Photius lowered his voice still further. "What're the other reasons?"

"Belisarius and Antonina are coming back too, all at the same time. She'll be too busy hollering at Belisarius and trying to stay on Antonina's good side at the same time to worry much about what *you've* done."

"Well, okay. But that only knocks it down to a Sour Gamma, at best. How do you figure Beta?"

"Because—"

But she had to break off. A Roman courtier was stepping forward. The official audience was about to begin.

Photius forgot about his complaints, then, because he was too busy worrying about remembering the lines he was supposed to speak, when the time came.

Especially because it didn't come very quickly. Roman courtiers giving speeches extolling the virtues of emperors were almost as long-winded as Persian ones. Even more long-winded than Indian ones, if you subtracted all the silly parts about divinity that nobody listened to anyway.

But, eventually, he got to the point.

"—first time by the emperor himself to the ranks of the imperial bodyguards. A body whose august members, in times past, have included the great general Belisarius himself."

Photius took a gleeful satisfaction in being able to start his speech by correcting the courtier. It was the first time he'd ever done *that*, too.

"This is *not* an appointment," he said forcefully. "I can't do that here. It's a request, not a command."

Alas, in his glee, he'd forgotten the rest of his speech. He fumbled, for a moment, and then decided to continue on with the same course.

Call it free will. He *was* the emperor, wasn't he?

So he just looked at the son of Rana Sanga, standing by his father's side, and said: "I'd like it very much if Rajiv would accept the offer. It is, in fact, very prestigious. Although it does mean that Rajiv would have to accompany us back to Constantinople. And, well, probably stay there for some years."

Since he'd veered wildly off the planned course, anyway, he decided to end with a note that might seem lame, from one angle, but wasn't lame at all from the angle he looked at things.

"And it would be really nice for me, to have an imperial bodyguard who was my own age. Well, pretty close."

The courtier had turned an interesting color. Photius thought it was the one called "puce." He'd have to ask his wife later. She knew about that stuff. She knew about most stuff, in fact.

Rajiv, on the other hand, just looked solemn. He stared at Photius, for a moment; then, at his father. Then, at a Roman soldier standing off to the side.

"Ask him," Sanga said, quietly but firmly.

Valentinian didn't wait for the question. "Do it, boy. The experience will be good for you. Besides, every one of Photius' bodyguards—the real ones, I'm talking about, my sort of men—like him. He's a nice kid. Especially for an emperor."

The courtier's color got even more interesting. Sort of a cross between liver and old grapes. Photius wondered if he might have died, standing on his feet.

No, he couldn't have. He was still quivering.

Pretty badly, in fact.

Fortunately—or maybe not, depending on how you looked at it—the courtier seemed to start recovering after Rajiv accepted. By the time the audience ended, his color had returned to that first weird shade.

"Is that 'puce'?" Photius whispered.

"No. 'Puce' is when he looked like he was dead. This is magenta."

"You're so smart. I love you."

❖   ❖   ❖

As soon as they entered their private chambers, after the audience, Tahmina turned to him. "That's the first time you've ever said that."

"No, it isn't."

"Yes, it is. That way."

"Oh. Well. I'm getting older."

She sat down on a divan, sighing. "Yes, you are. Awfully fast, actually, when I look at it cold-bloodedly. Which I never do, any more."

"Maybe that's because you're getting older, too."

She smiled, almost as crookedly as Belisarius might. "My dear husband. The difference between 'puce' and 'magenta' is absolutely nothing, compared to the difference between 'getting older' and 'can't wait.'"

Photius thought he was probably a pretty interesting color himself, then.

His father walked in, that very moment. After looking back and forth between the two of them, Belisarius said: "Why are you bright pink? And why are you smiling like that?"

Tahmina gave no answer. Her smile just got more crooked.

Photius, rallying, said: "I did what you asked me to, Father. About Rajiv, I mean. Is there something else I can do?"

Belisarius seemed to get sad, for just an instant. But then, he rallied too, and the smile that came to his face made it clear that Tahmina still had a long way to go when it came to "crooked."

"Yes, as a matter of fact. As soon as you can manage it, I'd like a lot of grandchildren."

"Oh."

"That's called 'scarlet,'" Tahmina said, to Photius.

To Belisarius, she said: "Consider it done."

AN EMPRESS AND HER DISTRACTIONS

Tahmina proved to be quite right. After they finally returned to Constantinople, whatever empress regent fury might have fallen on Photius for his presumptuous appointment was almost completely deflected. Photius and Tahmina never had to suffer worse than a Sour Beta. Maybe even Sour Alpha.

First, as Tahmina had foreseen, by Theodora's joy at being reunited with her husband.

Second, by the time and energy Theodora spent hollering at Belisarius for: a) putting her husband at risk; b) keeping him away from her for an unholy length of time, and c) giving away half of her empire—sorry, your son's empire—in the course of his fumble-fingered so-called "negotiations."

Third, by the time and energy she spent mollifying her best friend Antonina's anger over the preposterous way she was treating the man who had won the greatest war in history and saved her empire for her three times over—against the Medes, internal rebellion, and the Malwa.

And, finally, of course, as Tahmina had also foreseen . . .

"You agreed to be a business partner in a manufacturing scheme? *Are you out of your mind?*"

"I'm not the Emperor any longer, dear," Justinian pointed out mildly. "Photius is."

"Still!"

"I'm the Grand Justiciar. And you know how much I love to play with gadgets." He tried to dampen the gathering storm: "Besides, I'll have to keep it quiet anyway. Otherwise it might look like a conflict of interest."

Theodora frowned. "'Conflict of interest'? What in the world is that?"

"It's a new legal concept I'm about to introduce. I thought of it while I was in India."

That wasn't really true. He'd gotten the original idea from Aide. But since the jewel wasn't around any longer, Justinian saw no reason to give him credit. He'd never much liked the creature anyway.

It took him a while to explain the concept of "conflict of interest" to the Empress Regent. When he was done, Theodora burst into laughter.

"That's the silliest thing I ever heard of! My husband!"

A HUSBAND AND HIS PROMISE

Ousanas delayed his return to Ethiopia, long enough to ensure that a full year had passed since Eon's death. When he arrived at Adulis, he discovered that Rukaiya had already overseen the transfer of the capital there from Axum.

He was surprised. True, this had been planned for some time, but he hadn't thought Rukaiya would be bold enough, in his absence, to push the matter through. Many of the Ethiopians were not happy at the prospect of sharing their capital with Arabs.

Ezana met him at the docks, and provided part of the reason.

"Why not? And it gave me the chance to demonstrate that the queen had the full support of the royal regiments."

Ousanas eyed him sidewise. "And just how vigorous was this 'demonstration'?"

"Not vigorous at all," Ezana said, sounding disgruntled. "Didn't need to be. Everybody kept their mouth shut. In public, anyway."

When Ousanas arrived at the palace—a new one, still being built—Rukaiya provided him with the other reason.

"I thought it would be best, when you returned. Eon never lived here. His ghost does not walk these halls, or hover in these rooms. We will remember him always, of course, and keep him in our hearts. But this palace belongs to us alone."

By then, they had entered their private chambers. Night was falling.

Rukaiya turned to face him squarely. "You are home, Ousanas. Finally and truly home. No more the hunter, no more the rover, no more the stranger. You are a husband, now—mine—and will soon be a father."

He wasn't able to return that gaze, yet. His eyes avoided hers, roaming the room until they spotted the bookcase. Which they did quickly. It was a very large bookcase.

He moved over to examine the titles. Then, for the first time since his ship docked, was able to smile.

"How long—"

"I began assembling it the day you left. There are still a few titles missing, but not many."

"No, not many. Although I'll want to be adding some new titles I discovered in India. I can read Sanskrit well enough, by now."

His fingers drifted across the spines. "This must be the finest collection of books on philosophy in the whole world."

"That was my plan. Home should not mean abstinence. Look at me, Ousanas."

He could, then. She was even more beautiful than he remembered. Or, perhaps, it was simply that he was looking at her for the first time as his wife.

"I am good at loving," she said. "That, too, I learned from Eon. Do not waste that gift he gave you, husband. His ghost is not here. His gift remains."

"I won't," he promised.

A MAN AND HIS MEMORIES

For the rest of his life, sundown was always a special time for Belisarius. Sadness, mostly, in the beginning. As the years passed, fading into a sort of warm melancholy.

Watching the sunset never really became a ritual for him, however, although he did it more often than most people. He saved ritual for an annual occasion.

Every year, on the day that Aide died, he would go alone into the night and stare up at the stars. If the night was overcast, or if it rained, he would keep coming until the skies cleared.

Antonina never accompanied him, although she would always see him to the door when he left, and be there to welcome him when he returned in the morning. She, too, grieved Aide. So, as the years passed, did millions of people the world over, as the Talisman of God became incorporated, one way or another, into the various religions. But for all of them other than Belisarius, with only the partial exception of Ousanas, it was an abstract sort of grief. They had lost a talisman, or a saint, or a symbol, or an avatar. Belisarius had lost a person.

So, she felt that night belonged to him alone, and he loved her for it.

All night, he would spend, just staring at the stars and watching them twinkle. Looking out into a universe whose heavens reminded him of the way a jewel's facets had flashed once in his mind. Looking up at the universe that jewel had guaranteed, by sacrificing his life.

Many monuments were erected to Aide, over the years, in

many lands. Belisarius visited none of them, except the grove of sal trees on those occasions he returned to India. Even then, he went to spend his time at Ashot's grave. He would barely glance at the memorial devoted to Aide.

Others might need stones to remember Aide. Belisarius had the heavens.

THE MEMORIES OF THE MAN

His ritual was reciprocated, although he would never know it. Aide had transformed his crystalline branch of humankind, by the same sacrifice, and they never forgot. Neither Aide nor the man who had enabled his life.

They did forget the man's name, eventually. But by they time they did, it hardly mattered. A ritual had emerged—perhaps the only thing that could really be called a ritual, for them. They were, as a rule, a more practical-minded folk than their protoplasmic kin. Certainly more so than the Great Ones.

No matter where they went, to whatever star system—in time, to whatever galaxy—the crystals would select a constellation from the skies. It was their only constellation. Often enough, simply adopted from a constellation named by the fleshy humans among whom they lived.

But if they adopted the star pattern from their neighbors, they did not adopt the name. The crystals had their own name for that one and only constellation. As if the ritual of the invariant name was a great talisman of their own, protecting them from whatever horrors might lurk in the universe.

They would call it, always, The Craftsman.

✧ END ✧

Cast Of Characters

FROM THE FUTURE

Aide: A representative of a crystalline race from the far distant future, allied with Belisarius. Originally developed as an artificial intelligence by the Great Ones to combat the "DNA plague," the crystals became instrumental in the formation of the Great Ones themselves. Aide is sent back in time to counter the efforts of the "new gods" to change the course of human history.

Great Ones: Originating out of humanity, the Great Ones are a completely transformed type of human life. They no longer bear any physical resemblance to their human ancestors. Indeed, they are not even based on protoplasmic biological principles.

Link: An artificial intelligence created by the "new gods" of the future and sent back in time to change the course of human history. It exists in the form of a cybernetic organism, transferring its mental capacity from one human host to another as each host dies.

New gods: A quasi-religious cult from the far future which is determined to prevent the various mutations and transformations which humanity has undergone during the millions of years of its spread through the galaxy. There being no way to overturn that present reality, the new gods decide to stop the process early in human history. They send Link back in time to create a world empire based in northern India, organized along rigid caste principles, which will serve as the basis for a eugenics program to create a race of "perfect" humans.

461

ROMANS

Agathius: Commander of the Constantinople Greek cataphracts who were led by Belisarius in the opening campaign against the Malwa in Mesopotamia.

Anastasius: One of Belisarius' bodyguards.

Anna: Anna Saronites, wife of Calopodius the Blind

Anthony (Cassian): Bishop of Aleppo. He brought Aide and Michael to Belisarius.

Antonina: Wife of Belisarius.

Ashot: An Armenian and one of Belisarius' bucellarii, his personal household troops. He becomes one of the top officers in the Roman army during the war against the Malwa.

Belisarius: Roman general.

Bouzes and Coutzes: Twin brothers commanding the Army of Lebanon, later top officers in Belisarius' forces.

Calopodius: A young Greek nobleman who serves as an officer in Belisarius' Indus campaign. Later becomes Belisarius' historian.

Cottomenes: Attached to Anna's Service

Cyril: Commander of Constantinople Greek troops.

Eusebius: A young artisan employed by John of Rhodes in creating the Roman armaments project. Later an officer in the Roman navy.

Felix (Chalcenterus): A young Syrian soldier promoted by Belisarius. Eventually becomes an officer, commanding musketeers.

Gregory: One of Belisarius' commanders; specializes in artillery.

Hermogenes: Roman infantry commander.

Hypatia: Photius' nanny; later married to Julian.

Illus: Attached to Anna's Service

Irene (Macrembolitissa): Head of the Roman spy network.

John of Rhodes: Former Roman naval officer, in charge of Belisarius' weapons project.

Julian: Head of Photius' bodyguard.

Justinian: Roman emperor.

Koutina: Antonina's maid.

Mark of Edessa: Another young officer promoted by Belisarius.

Maurice: Belisarius' chief military lieutenant.

Menander: A young Roman soldier; later a naval officer.

Michael of Macedonia: A monk who first encountered Aide.

Photius: Antonina's son and Belisarius' stepson.

Procopius of Caesaria: Antonina's original secretary.

Sittas: An old friend of Belisarius and one of the Roman empire's generals.

Theodora: Justinian's wife and the Empress of Rome.

Valentinian: One of Belisarius' bodyguards.

ETHIOPIANS

Eon: Kaleb's son.
Ezana: Eon's bodyguard; later commander of the royal regiment.
Garmat: A top Axumite royal counselor.
Kaleb: The negusa nagast (King of Kings) of Axum.
Ousanas: Eon's dawazz; later, aqabe tsentsen.
Rukaiya: Arab princess, bride of Eon.
Wahsi: Eon and Rukaiya's son, named after Eon's bodyguard, new
       negusa nagast of Ethiopia

PERSIANS

Baresmanas: a Persian nobleman (sahrdaran), of the Suren family.
Khusrau Anushirvan: King of Kings of Iran and non-Iran.
Kurush: Baresmanas' nephew; a top Persian military leader.
Tahmina: Baresmanas' daughter; Photius' bride.

MALWA

Ajatasutra: Malwa spy and assassin; Narses' right-hand man.
Balban: Malwa spymaster in Constantinople during Nika revolt.
Damodara: Malwa military commander.
Holi: "Great Lady." Skandagupta's aunt; vessel for Link.
Indira: Rana Sanga's half-sister; to be married to Toramana.
Mirabai: Rana Sanga's daughter.
Nanda Lal: Head of Malwa spy network.
Narses: Roman traitor; Damodara's spymaster.
Rajiv: Rana Sanga's son.
Rana Sanga: Rajput king; Damodara's chief lieutenant.
Sati: "Great Lady." Vessel for Link.
Skandagupta: Emperor of Malwa.
Toramana: A Ye-tai general; subordinate to Damodara.
Venandakatra: "The Vile One." Powerful Malwa official.

MARATHAS & ANDHRANS

Baji: Dhruva's infant son.
Bindusara: Hindu sadhu.
Dadaji Holkar: Malwa slave freed by Belisarius; later peshwa of
       Andhra.
Dhruva: Dadaji's oldest daughter; Malwa slave.
Gautami: Dadaji's wife.
Lata: Dadaji's youngest daughrer; Malwa slave.

Maloji: Rao's friend and chief military lieutenant.

Namadev: Shakuntala and Rao's infant son.

Raghunath Rao: Maratha chieftain, leader of the Maratha rebellion. "The Panther of Majarashtra." "The Wind of the Great Country." Shakuntala's mentor, later her husband.

Shakuntala: Last survivor of the Satavahana dynasty; later Empress of reborn Andhra; "The Black-Eyed Pearl of the Satavahanas."

KUSHANS

Kungas: Commander of the Kushans guarding Shakuntala; later king of the reborn Kushan kingdom.

Kanishka: Kungas' troop leader.

Kujulo: Kungas' troop leader.

Vasudeva: Commander of the Kushans captured by Belisarius at Anatha.

Glossary

A note on terminological usage. Throughout the series, the terms "Roman" and "Greek" are used in a way which is perhaps confusing to readers who are not very familiar with the historical setting. So a brief explanation may be helpful.

By the sixth century A.D., the only part of the Roman Empire still in existence was what is usually called by modern historians the *Eastern* Roman Empire, whose capital was in Constantinople. The western lands in which the Roman Empire originated—including Rome itself and all of Italy—had long since fallen under the control of barbarian tribes like the Ostrogoths.

The so-called "eastern" Roman Empire, however, never applied that name to itself. It considered itself—and did so until its final destruction at the hands of the Ottoman Turks in 1453 A.D.—as *the* Roman Empire. And thus, when referring to themselves in a political sense, they continued to call themselves "Romans."

Ethnically speaking, of course, there was very little Latin or Roman presence left in the Roman Empire. In terms of what you might call its "social" content, the Roman Empire had become a Greek empire in all but name. In Justinian's day, Latin was still the official language of the Roman Empire, but it would not be long before Greek became, even in imperial decrees and political documents, the formal as well as de facto language of the Empire. Hence the frequency with which the same people, throughout the course of the series, might be referred to (depending on the context) as either "Roman" or "Greek."

Loosely, in short, the term "Roman" is a political term; the term

"Greek" a social, ethnic or linguistic one—and that is how the terms are used in the series.

PLACES

Adulis: a city on the western coast of the Red Sea; the kingdom of Axum's major port; later, the capital city of the Ethiopians.

Ajmer: the major city of Rajputana.

Alexandria: the major city of Roman Egypt, located on one of the mouths of the Nile.

Amaravati: the former capital of the Empire of Andhra, located on the Krishna river in south India; sacked by the Malwa; Shakuntala taken into captivity after her family is massacred.

Anatha: an imperial villa in Mesopotamia; site of the first major battle between Belisarius and the Malwa.

Axum: the name refers both to the capital city in the highlands and the kingdom of the Ethiopians.

Babylon: ancient city in Mesopotamia, located on the Euphrates; site of a major siege of the Persians by the Malwa.

Barbaricum: the major port in the Indus delta; located near present day Karachi.

Begram: the major city of the Kushans.

Bharakuccha: the major port of western India under Malwa control; located at the mouth of the Narmada river.

Charax: Persian seaport on the Persian Gulf.

Chowpatty: Malwa naval base on the west coast of India; located at the site of present day Mumbai (Bombay).

Constantinople: capital of the Roman Empire; located on the Bosporus.

Ctesiphon: capital of the Persian empire; located on the Tigris river in Mesopotamia.

Deccan: southern India.

Deogiri: a fortified city in central Majarashtra; established by Shakuntala as the new capital of Andhra.

Gwalior: location of Venandakatra's palace in north India where Shakuntala was held captive.

Hindu Kush: the mountains northwest of the Punjab. Site of the Khyber Pass.

Kausambi: capital of the Malwa empire; located in north India, at the junction of the Ganges and Jamuna rivers.

Majarashtra: literally, "the Great Country." Land of the Marathas, one of India's major nationalities.

Marv: an oasis city in Central Asia; located in present day Turkmenistan.

Mindouos: a battlefield in Mesopotamia where Belisarius fought the Persians.

Muziris: the major port of the kingdom of Kerala in southeastern India.

Nehar Malka: the ancient canal connecting the Euphrates and Tigris rivers; scene of a battle between Belisarius and the Malwa.

The Pass: a pass in the Zagros mountains separating Mesopotamia from the Persian plateau; site of a battle between Belisarius and Damodara; called The Battle of the Mongoose by the Rajputs.

Peshawar: located in the Vale of Peshawar, between the Punjab and the Khyber Pass.

Punjab: the upper Indus river valley.

Rajputana: the land of the Rajputs, one of India's major nationalities.

Sind: the lower Indus river valley.

Sukkur: a major city on the Indus; north of the city is the "Sukkur gorge" which marks the boundary between Sind and the Punjab.

Suppara: a port city on India's west coast, to the north of Chowpatty.

Tamraparni: the island of Ceylon; modern day Sri Lanka.

Vindhyas: the mountain range which marks the traditional boundary between northern India and southern India.

TERMS

Anvaya-prapta sachivya: members of the Malwa royal clan.

Aqabe tsentsen: literally, "keeper of the fly-whisks." The highest ranked official in the Axumite government.

Azadan: literally, "men of noble birth." Refers to a class of people in the Persian empire roughly analogous to medieval European knights.

Cataphract: the heavily armed and armored mounted archer and lancer who formed the heart of the Roman army. Developed by the Romans as a copy of the dehgan.

Dawazz: a slave assigned as adviser to Ethiopian princes, specifically for the purpose of deflating royal self-aggrandizement.

Dehgan: the Persian equivalent of a cataphract.

Dromon: a Roman war galley.

Kushans: originating as a barbarian tribe from the steppes, the Kushans became civilized after conquering Central Asia and were the principal support for Buddhism in the early centuries of the Christian Era; later subjugated by the Malwa.

Negusa nagast: "King of Kings." Ruler of Axum, the kingdom of the Ethiopians.

Nika: the name of the insurrection against Justinian and Theodora engineered by the Malwa.

Peshwa: roughly translates as "vizier." Top civilian official of the Empire of Andhra.

Sahrdaran: the highest ranked nobility in the Persian empire, next in status to the emperor. Traditionally consisted of seven families, of which the "first among equals" were the Suren.

Sarwe: a regiment of the Axumite army. The plural is "sarawit." Individual soldiers are called "sarwen."

Spatha: the standard sword used by Roman soldiers; similar to the ancient Roman short sword called the *gladius*, except the blade is six inches longer.

Vurzurgan: "grandees" of the Persian empire. Noblemen ranked between the azadan and the sahrdaran.

Ye-tai: a barbarian tribe from central Asia incorporated into the Malwa governing structure. Also known as "Ephthalites" or "White Huns."